Debra Webb  estselling author of m... ...novels, including those in reader-fav... series Faces of Evil, the Colby Agency and Shades of Death. With more than four million books sold in numerous languages and countries, Debra has a love of storytelling that goes back to her childhood on a farm in Alabama. Visit Debra at debrawebb.com

Janie Crouch writes passionate romantic suspense for readers who still believe in heroes. After a lifetime on the East Coast—and a six-year stint in Germany—this *USA Today* bestselling author has settled into her dream home in the Front Range of the Colorado Rockies. She loves engaging in all sorts of adventures (Triathlons! Two-hundred-mile relay races! Mountain treks!), travelling and surviving life with four kids. You can find out more about her at janiecrouch.com

Also by Debra Webb

Lookout Mountain Mysteries
A Place to Hide
Whispering Winds Widows
Peril in Piney Woods

A Winchester, Tennessee Thriller
In Self Defense
The Dark Woods
The Stranger Next Door
The Safest Lies
Witness Protection Widow

Also by Janie Crouch

San Antonio Security
Texas Bodyguard: Luke

The Risk Series: A Bree and Tanner Thriller
Security Risk
Constant Risk
Risk Everything

Omega Sector: Under Siege
Daddy Defender
Protector's Instinct
Cease Fire

Discover more at millsandboon.co.uk

ALIBI FOR MURDER

DEBRA WEBB

PROTECTIVE ASSIGNMENT

JANIE CROUCH

MILLS & BOON

All rights reserved including the right of reproduction in whole or in part in any form. This edition is published by arrangement with Harlequin Enterprises ULC.

This is a work of fiction. Names, characters, places, locations and incidents are purely fictional and bear no relationship to any real life individuals, living or dead, or to any actual places, business establishments, locations, events or incidents. Any resemblance is entirely coincidental.

Without limiting the author's and publisher's exclusive rights, any unauthorised use of this publication to train generative artificial intelligence (AI) technologies is expressly prohibited. HarperCollins also exercise their rights under Article 4(3) of the Digital Single Market Directive 2019/790 and expressly reserve this publication from the text and data mining exception.

® and ™ are trademarks owned and used by the trademark owner and/or its licensee. Trademarks marked with ® are registered with the United Kingdom Patent Office and/or the Office for Harmonisation in the Internal Market and in other countries.

First Published in Great Britain 2025
by Mills & Boon, an imprint of HarperCollins*Publishers* Ltd
1 London Bridge Street, London, SE1 9GF

www.harpercollins.co.uk

HarperCollins*Publishers*
Macken House, 39/40 Mayor Street Upper,
Dublin 1, D01 C9W8, Ireland

Alibi for Murder © 2025 Debra Webb
Protective Assignment © 2025 Janie Crouch

ISBN: 978-0-263-39723-9

0825

This book contains FSC™ certified paper and other controlled sources to ensure responsible forest management.

For more information visit: www.harpercollins.co.uk/green

Printed and Bound in the UK using 100% Renewable Electricity at
CPI Group (UK) Ltd, Croydon, CR0 4YY

ALIBI FOR MURDER

DEBRA WEBB

Chapter One

Woodstock, Illinois
Friday, June 6
Foster Residence
Ridgeland Avenue, 5:30 p.m.

"I hope you'll complete the survey when you receive it. We at GenCorp are always here for you, twenty-four seven."

Allie Foster ended her final call for the day—for the next ten days, actually—and removed the wireless headset. She exhaled a big breath, stood from her desk and stretched. There was something about Fridays, even when you didn't have plans for the weekend or her first vacation in years happening.

Fridays marked a milestone of completing a week's work, of having two days off ahead. Well, ten in this case. It was a good feeling.

Or it would be if she had plans of any kind. Sadly she did not.

"Woo-hoo," she grumbled as she placed the headset on her desk. She shut off the desk lamp and walked out of her office. She was taking a vacation and going *nowhere*.

How exciting was that?

She would do yard work and maybe finally paint her bedroom. A really old-fashioned getaway from work. Wasn't she the globetrotter?

Admittedly, Allie had always been a little on the old-fashioned side. Came from being raised by much older parents, she supposed. Technically, they were her grandparents. Her parents had died in a car accident when she was a toddler. She had only the faintest memories of them.

Frankly, she wasn't entirely certain she remembered them at all, she decided as she slowly descended the stairs. The framed photos of her family, her parents when she was little and her grandparents as well as her over the years, lined the wall along the stairs. There was a strong likelihood that the stories she'd heard growing up and these photographs along with the many family albums carefully curated by her grandmother were the actual memories she recalled.

Allie banished the idea and focused on mentally shrugging off the workweek and the stress that often went with providing patient services. Answering calls all day might not sound like a tough job, but these were questions from patients who were, for the most part, terminally ill. Either they or a family member had questions about their medications or their appointments or simply what they should do next. GenCorp was a huge medical operation. The services provided extended across the country and involved cutting edge, sometimes experimental, pharmaceuticals, procedures and end-of-life patient care.

There were always questions and emotions and financial issues. And although, as a nurse, Allie's job was to answer questions regarding the medical side of things, that didn't prevent frustrated patients and family members from spilling conversations over into the other difficult parts of terminal illnesses. Life during those times was complicated and painful.

What she needed now was to relax with her evening glass of wine and chocolate bar.

"Better than sex."

Probably not true, but it had been so long since she'd had sex, she wasn't entirely sure. But to believe this was the case made the idea of no prospects far more palatable and much less depressing.

No one's fault but your own, Al.

Relationships didn't generally come knocking on the door. One had to actually put in some effort to acquire one.

Not going there.

Out of habit, she walked around the first floor and checked the windows and doors. Woodstock's crime rate was fairly typical for a town of its size. Not a big town, more on the small side. Still, decades ago her grandparents had a security system installed. It wasn't the best, but it remained serviceable. Although it was no longer monitored, it made a long, loud noise when breached. Since Allie took over the house five years ago, she hadn't bothered changing it. She wasn't really paranoid about crime or the possibility of intruders. She preferred to consider herself careful.

Or maybe she was paranoid since she hadn't changed the fact that there were three—count them, three—deadbolts on the front door. As a teenager, she'd always wondered why there were three on the front door and none on the back. And she had always intended to add one to the back but never bothered.

Which, all things considered, likely made her every bit as paranoid as she'd been certain her grandparents were.

Satisfied that the house was secure, she wandered into the kitchen. One cupboard was dedicated to her favorite bottles of red. The drawer beneath the counter in that same spot held her chocolate stash. She was a simple girl. Many years from now, hopefully, when she was found dead and no doubt alone in the house, no one would think less of her for having plenty of wine and chocolate on hand.

Maybe she was also slightly paranoid about running out of either.

Laughing at herself, she removed the cork from the bottle. Any burglar would no doubt be disappointed if he broke into her home. Wine and chocolate—well, and her computer—were the only valuables in the house. There was no stash of cash or collection of coins. No jewelry, unless you counted the costume stuff her grandmother had adored. No weapons except the BB rifle her grandfather had used for scaring off pesky squirrels and birds from his garden out back. Not that he ever hit one or even tried. It was all about the noise of hitting something nearby, he had explained. It worked every time, he'd insisted.

Allie retreated to the living room with her glass of wine and the chocolate bar. The old box-style television still stood in the corner of the room. It was the perfect size for her aquarium. As she passed, she checked the auto feeder to ensure it held an adequate amount.

"Hello, Nemo and friends." She tapped the glass and smiled as they darted around.

She frowned at the collection of dust on the dinosaur of a television. This was something else she needed to do on her vacation. Dust, not replace the set. She hadn't watched it in years, even before it died. The news was far too depressing, and the entertainment industry had stopped making decent movies ages ago.

She picked up her book from the side table and opened it to the next chapter. Books never let her down.

Who needed television when they had books?

The buzz of the doorbell made her jump. For a moment, she felt confident she must have imagined it. She had no deliveries scheduled. No one ever came to her door, not even the neighbors' children selling cookies or doing other fundraising activities. Her house sat back farther from the street than any of the others, and her grandparents had never cut a single tree from their property, so it was difficult to see—and, once you did, the house was a little spooky to kids. One would think this would be the hotspot at Halloween, and she always prepared, but no one ever came.

The buzzing sound came again, and there was no denying it.

Someone was at her door.

Allie placed her glass and her book on the side table and stood. She wandered first to the front living room window and peeked out. A four-door sedan was parked in the drive. Dark in color, blue or black. No markings that suggested it was some sort of salesperson or business vehicle.

Since she couldn't see who had stepped up onto her

porch from this window, she moved to the entry hall and had a look through the security viewer on the front door. One man, one woman. Both wore business suits. Both displayed serious facial expressions. Not the typical-looking salespeople. More like police officers or investigators of some sort.

Could be trouble in the neighborhood. A missing child.

Allie took a breath. She really disliked unannounced visits, but she certainly did not want to hinder the search for a criminal or a missing person. "Can I help you?" she asked through the door. Sounded better than "Are you lost?" as an opening.

The man withdrew a small leather case from an interior jacket pocket and opened it for Allie to see through the viewer. The credentials inside identified him as FBI Special Agent Elon Fraser. The photo matched his face, though he'd put on a few pounds since it was taken.

Why on earth would the FBI be calling on her?

"Would you state your business, please?" A reasonable request, in her opinion.

The female spoke up this time while simultaneously flashing her own credentials in front of the viewer. "We are here to speak with Allison Foster," Special Agent Uma Potter explained with visible impatience.

Allie unlocked the door—all three deadbolts. The deadbolts, she remembered now, were her grandfather's idea. He was always certain someone intended to break in and steal his stamp collection or his humidor with his imported cigars. Allie's grandmother would roll her eyes every time he mentioned the idea. Like she had any room to judge. The memories made her smile in spite of the strangers standing on the other side of the door.

She opened the door and surveyed the two once more. "I'm Allison Foster."

Agent Potter gave her a steady perusal as well. "May we come in?"

"Of course." Allie stepped back and opened the door wider. The agents crossed the threshold and waited while she closed and resecured it.

"What are you here to talk about?" Allie looked from one to the other. She had thought Fraser was lead—he was older and had knocked on the door—but maybe she'd been wrong.

"This may take some time," Potter suggested.

Allie nodded. "Follow me." She led the way to the living room, cringed at the sight of her half-finished glass of wine and chocolate bar on the table next to her favorite chair. "Have a seat." She gestured to the sofa.

Fraser waited for his colleague and then Allie to sit before doing the same.

"Ms. Foster," Fraser began, "do you live here alone?"

Not exactly the sort of question a woman who actually did live alone liked to answer when asked by a stranger, but the man was FBI.

"Yes."

"Are there any weapons in the house?" he asked.

"Only my grandfather's BB rifle."

"Your grandmother left you this place?" This from Potter.

Allie nodded slowly. "She did." A frown worked its way across her forehead. "What's this about?" Why would the FBI want to know how she'd come into possession of her property?

Was someone trying to steal her property? She'd heard

of this on one of the podcasts she occasionally tuned into. The house was the one thing of real value she owned. Worry needled her.

Potter pulled out her cell phone and tapped the screen. "You're thirty-two years old. Born to Alice and Jerry Foster, who died in an automobile accident when you were four." She glanced up at Allie when she said this as if to gage her reaction.

"That's correct."

"Your mother's parents, Virginia and Gordon Holt, raised you. You graduated high school right here in Woodstock and went on to the nursing program at McHenry."

Now Allie was just annoyed. She leaned forward and held up her hands in a stop-sign fashion. "I'm not answering any more questions until you tell me what this is about."

Technically, they weren't even questions, just recitations of the facts about her life to which she automatically agreed. People did that far too often. Gave away too much information about themselves without even realizing they were confirming details that might haunt them later. Like for someone who might be trying to steal her home.

Stop, Al.

"You're employed by GenCorp," Fraser went on, taking the lead now that Allie had shown her irritation at Potter. "You started with them from their inception, ten years ago."

"Again," Allie said, "I will know what this is about before we continue the conversation."

"Ms. Foster," Potter resumed, "there was an incident

at the hospital where you worked which precipitated your leaving the hands-on side of the nursing field and moving to what you do now."

The memory of a patient dying in her arms caused Allie to flinch. She was not going back there. She stood. "I think we're done here."

There was absolutely no reason to talk about that tragedy. Allie had been investigated by the hospital, the nursing board and the local police. She had been cleared of wrongdoing. It was the doctor in charge of the case who'd made the mistake; Allie had only tried to save the poor woman, and sadly, all her efforts had failed.

"Please—" Fraser eased forward a bit but didn't trouble himself to stand "—bear with us, Ms. Foster."

With visible reluctance, Allie settled into her chair once more. Barely resisted the urge to gulp down the rest of the wine in her glass. Not exactly the sort of move to make with two federal agents staring her down and going over her life history.

"One week ago," Fraser explained, "there was an incident at the hospital where you once worked. A patient was murdered in his room."

Allie drew back, sank deeper into her chair. "I'm sorry to hear that." She allowed a beat to pass. "But what does that have to do with me?"

"Did you see anything about it on the news?" Potter asked.

Finally, a question to actually answer. "I'm afraid not. I never watch the news." She shrugged. "I see the occasional headline pop up when I'm at the computer checking my email, but I rarely follow the link or read whatever commentary accompanies it. I have a weather radio that keeps me informed of the weather, but that's about it really."

The two agents exchanged a glance.

"Can you tell us where you were on Friday, one week ago, from about five in the evening until midnight?"

Allie felt taken aback at the question. "Seriously?"

The way the two looked at her confirmed they were indeed serious.

She shrugged. "Okay. Let me confirm with my phone." She pulled up her calendar app. "I never do anything unless my phone tells me to." She laughed, or attempted to laugh, but the sound came out a little brittle. The agents watching her said nothing. "Okay, here we go. That would have been May 30, and I worked from eight until five, then I had dinner and a shower and started a new book."

When the agents continued staring at her without uttering a word, she looked from one to the other. "*The Great Gatsby*. I've read it like five times, but I sometimes read it again when I haven't decided on anything new."

"We've looked into your lifestyle," Fraser said.

A painful laugh burst out of her before Allie could stop it. Were they joking? "My lifestyle?"

"You don't leave the house often," he explained. "You order most everything online and have it shipped or delivered."

This time, Allie's laugh was more sarcastic. "Since the pandemic, lots of people use online ordering and home delivery. And when you work from home, you don't go out as often." What was the big deal with her shopping habits? Many, after being shut in all that time, just kept living that way. So what?

"Can you tell me the last time you left the house?" Potter inquired.

Allie drew in a deep breath and worked hard to tamp down the irritation that continued to rise. "I don't know. Maybe last month? I think my semiannual dental cleaning was last month. Maybe the fifth. I could check my calendar if you need an exact date."

"With Dr. Rice right here in Woodstock," Potter said.

Okay. Allie braced herself. It was one thing for these two to know her background, but to have been looking into her schedule and her comings and goings? Something was very wrong here.

Before she could say as much, Fraser spoke again. "Ms. Foster, we're here because the victim was part of an ongoing case the Bureau is deeply involved in."

Allie shook her head. "I don't see how my having worked an entire decade ago at the hospital involved has anything to do with your current case."

Again, the two exchanged one of those suspicious glances.

"Just get to the point please." Her frustration refused to stay hidden any longer. She'd had more than enough of this game.

Potter tapped the screen of her cell again, then stood and moved to where Allie sat. "This might give you some clarification."

The screen was open to a video. A woman with brown hair dressed in scrubs paused at room 251. Allie frowned. The woman started into the room but paused long enough to glance first one way and then the other along the corridor, giving the camera a full-on shot of her face.

Allie's attention zoomed in on the image. She studied the face.

Hers.

The woman going into the room was *her*.

Shock funneled inside her. She stared up at Potter. "Why would you have this video? It has to be from at least ten years ago." Allie stared at the frozen image. Her dark brown hair was in a ponytail, the way she'd always worn it—still did. In the video, she wore the required blue scrubs.

"This video," Potter explained, "is from one week ago. That room is where the patient was murdered."

"No. No. No." Allie heart started to pound. She snatched the phone from the agent's hand and watched the video again. "That's me rightly enough. But that could not have been a week ago." She paused the video and tried to zoom in much closer on her face, but it was too blurry to determine if the couple of crow's feet she had developed recently were absent—which, to her way of thinking, would be proof of when this video was actually taken.

She shook her head, passed the phone back to its owner. "I have no idea why you or anyone else would believe that video is only one week old. I haven't been in that hospital since—"

"Your grandmother died at the beginning of the pandemic," Fraser offered.

Allie blinked, a new level of uncertainty settling in. "That's correct." She watched as Potter resumed her seat next to her colleague. "If you know this, then why are you suggesting that video is only a week old?"

"Because it is," Potter stated with complete certainty.

"Every second of security footage from that hospital has been scrutinized repeatedly. The clip you watched is the one that occurred outside the victim's room just before he was murdered last Friday. There's another that shows you coming into the hospital that day, but nothing showing you leave."

This was wrong. Allie shook her head, her nerves jangling. "What you're suggesting is impossible."

Fraser moved his head slowly side to side. "I wish it were."

No. Absolutely this had to be some sort of mistake. "But you know I haven't been in that hospital for years. You said so yourself." Worry started to climb up Allie's spine. They were serious. *This* was serious.

"The victim was Thomas Madison."

Allie rolled the name around in her head. "I don't know any Thomas Madison."

This was completely insane. She focused on slowing her breathing. The way her heart thundered she was headed for a panic attack. She did not want to go there in front of these two.

"You may have seen him before." Fraser turned his cell screen toward her. The image displayed there was of a man who appeared to be in his late sixties to early seventies. Gray thinning hair. Light colored eyes. Saggy jowls.

"He doesn't look familiar."

"He worked with your father…before his untimely death."

Allie hesitated. "My father was a research technician at Ledwell…"

At the time—nearly thirty years ago—Ledwell had

been the leading-edge AI research facility. Still was. Her father hadn't been a doctor or a scientist, just a tech, but he had been very good at his work. Her grandparents had told Allie stories about how good he was. Most of those in charge at Ledwell had believed him to be far better than any of their academically trained scientists.

"Did you know," Fraser said, "there was an investigation into your parents' accident?"

The transition into her parents' deaths unsettled her further. "I can't say that I knew it growing up, but, looking back, I'm sure that would have been the case. Aren't all accidents, particularly those involving deaths, investigated?"

"Usually, yes," Fraser admitted. "But there was more to your parents' accident. There was some question about whether it was actually an accident."

The wallop that slammed into her chest was Allie's own heart. She gasped, pressed her hand to her chest and fought to calm herself. "I was not aware of this, no. Do you have any evidence of what you're telling me?"

"A couple of reports. The investigation was standard protocol," Fraser said, "in light of certain anomalies related to the way the accident happened. And no, I don't have all the details, but suffice it to say there were questions. None of which were answered, in my opinion. No matter, the case was closed, and that was the end of it."

Allie got up. She had to move. She started to pace. Didn't care what her guests thought. Why wouldn't her grandparents have told her this?

These two couldn't answer that question any more than she could. What she needed just now was to focus on this moment—this bizarre meeting.

"What does my parents' accident have to do with this Mr. Madison and his murder?"

"We don't know," Potter admitted. "That's what we'd like to find out. Which is why we're here."

Allie paused and aimed a what-the-heck expression at her. "How would I know? I was four years old when they died."

"Right," Potter agreed. "We're hoping your grandparents left notes, letters or some sort of information about the investigation back then that will give us some insight. Apparently the local law enforcement office suffered a fire in the storage area where old case files were kept, so there's nothing on the investigation."

Allie digested this information. "If my grandparents kept anything related to the accident, I am unaware of it." They never talked about the accident. Much was said about her parents, of course. In part to ensure Allie knew how much they had loved her and also to help her remember them. But not much was said about that awful day other than exactly that—what an awful day it was.

"We assumed as much," Fraser said. "We hoped you might allow us to have a look around the house—unless of course you've purged any and all old papers and files."

"No. I would never do that. This was their home. Their papers and other things are right where they left them." It was a big old rambling house. No need to purge. Not that she would have anyway.

"Then you won't mind if we look for anything useful on finding the truth about what happened to your parents?" This from Potter.

Yes was on the tip of Allie's tongue, but then logic kicked in.

"You came here to question me about a murder." She looked to Fraser. "You have a video—or two—that seem to show me entering the hospital and then the room of the victim on the day of the murder and, I'm assuming, around the time of his death. But then you segued into my parents' accident."

"Because we feel the two are related," Fraser insisted.

"Twenty-eight years apart," she countered.

"Yes," Fraser insisted.

"So you're looking for any thoughts, notes, letters et cetera my grandparents may have kept related to the accident. You're not here to find evidence that would somehow prove your theory about me going into that hospital room and murdering a patient." This was not a question. She already knew the answer.

"Oh," Fraser said with a no-way expression and a wave of his upright palms, "no, we're certainly not looking to railroad anyone. We're here to find the truth."

"So your search warrant will be very specific about what you're looking for," Allie suggested.

"If one is required," Fraser said. "I don't see any need to make it that sort of formal search. Agent Potter and I could just have a quick, casual look around as long as you're agreeable."

Allie almost laughed out loud. These two clearly thought she was a naïve shut-in. Obviously, they also thought she was a murderer.

Bottom line, she had no idea whatsoever if her parents' accident was anything other than an accident. She also had no clue as to whether their accident was related to this murder at the hospital. And she certainly did not know the victim.

But what she did know was that she wasn't a fool.

Allie paused in her pacing. "Well, thank you for stopping by and giving me so much to consider." She gestured toward the entry hall. "But I believe we're quite finished here."

"You're refusing to cooperate with our investigation," Potter suggested.

Allie smiled at the less-than-subtle pressure technique. "No. I'm just choosing to take advantage of my legal right to say no, not without a warrant. Now, if you'll excuse me, I have a glass of wine and a chocolate bar to finish."

With another of those shared looks, the two federal agents rose from the sofa and walked to the front door. Once they were gone, Allie secured all three deadbolts then went to a window to watch them drive away.

She wondered how long it would be before they were back with a warrant and a team of fellow agents to search the house.

She couldn't think of a reason why she should be worried—there had to be some kind of mistake. But the fact that they had the video showing her in the hospital, supposedly one week ago, entering the room of a man who was murdered, was startling enough to take a moment to think this situation through. As much as she would love to believe it was just some sort of mistake—a woman who looked like her—this was not the case.

This was something very, very wrong.

She had no family attorney. The one who had settled the estate after her grandmother passed away had since passed away himself. She had no friends who were in the legal profession.

In truth, she had lost touch with anyone she had considered a friend years ago. Not due to any falling outs or disagreements. Just because she wasn't much of a socializer, and it was simply easier to focus on work and taking care of her grandmother, and then the pandemic came along.

Life changed.

She leaned against the locked door and racked her brain for anyone who might be able to advise her. Someone she could trust.

Wait. A smile tugged at her lips.

Steve Durham.

He'd joined the police department in Chicago when he graduated high school. She remembered him well. He was a year older, but she'd had a serious crush on him. Not long before her grandmother died, she and Allie had bumped into Steve's grandmother at an appointment at the medical center. The two had discussed being widows and having grandchildren. Allie remembered Mrs. Durham talking about how Steve had left the police department after only a year, deciding instead to go to university. Then he'd gone on to law school. He'd been hired right away by some fancy, as she called it, private investigations agency in Chicago. What was the name of it?

Oh yeah. *The Colby Agency.*

Chapter Two

Chicago, Illinois
Colby Agency, 6:30 p.m.

"I realize it's late," Victoria Colby-Camp, the head of the agency said. "But—" she gazed at her most trusted associates around the long conference table "—we have to make a decision before any of us go home for the weekend."

Steve Durham smiled. Victoria was never one to mince words. Nor was her granddaughter, Jamie. She'd come on board just six months ago, and already she was doing a stellar job. Jamie was so much like her grandmother. It was clear to Steve and everyone at the agency how very proud Victoria was to have Jamie at her side.

Tonight's after-hours meeting was about the two open investigator slots. The agency's clientele list continued to grow, and actually they needed to add at least five. But it was difficult to find the caliber of investigator this agency employed. The Colby's longstanding reputation was one of the reasons Steve had decided to become a part of the agency.

Lucky for him he had started right out of law school.

Victoria had personally sought him out and offered him a position. She'd explained that one of his professors at Northwestern had called to say Victoria needed to have a look at Steve. He'd been damned surprised and extremely humbled by the recommendation. According to Victoria, his background in law enforcement made him uniquely qualified as an attorney, in her opinion.

Steve was grateful. He had five years at this agency so far and hoped for many, many more. It was an honor, really, to work with Victoria.

He scanned the faces around him. Working with people like Ian Michaels, Nicole Reed Michaels, Simon Ruhl and Victoria's son, Jim, was an opportunity he'd never expected. He glanced at the young woman seated next to Victoria. Jamie held her own with the very finest the agency had to offer. She had proven very quickly that she deserved to be the leader of the agency—in training of course. She represented the next generation of this agency and represented it well. And then there was Lucas Camp—Victoria's husband—who was a legend in his own right. Just knowing him was a privilege.

Steve genuinely appreciated that his work here was not confined to the typical corporate or financial legal business of being an attorney. He was more like one of the investigators, but his job was to advise and steer any investigator who might find themselves in a tight situation, legally speaking, out of trouble. It was the perfect combination of practicing law and putting it into action in the field.

"I'm in agreement," Ian Michaels spoke up. "Jamie and I have interviewed both candidates, and we're more than pleased with what we've seen."

"The two are a perfect fit," Jamie agreed with a nod of her blond head. She smiled. "I wish we could find two or three others so qualified."

Good news for the two candidates, for sure. Those gathered around the table weren't impressed by anything less than outstanding performances.

Jim Colby spoke up next. "On separate occasions, I was accompanied in the field for a day, first with Chance Rader and then with Billie Jagger. I was also impressed with their bearing and communication skills. I say let's do it."

There was a whole barrage of other requirements for agency investigators that included self-defense skills and the use of weapons. Every investigator was as fully trained as any police officer on the street. From time to time, a case required those skills, and the Colby Agency never let down a client.

All looked to Steve then. "I have thoroughly reviewed the backgrounds of both candidates, and I'm fully satisfied we should move forward with offers of employment."

"Very well." Victoria smiled. "Jamie, if you will relay the good news so that our new investigators don't have to spend their weekends in suspense."

Jamie stood. "I'll make those calls now."

Victoria rose from the head of the table. "And I will get home to the celebration dinner Lucas is preparing."

Victoria and Lucas were celebrating the birth of another grandchild. Lucas's son, Slade, and his wife, Maggie, had just brought home a new baby. This was number three for the couple and a bit of a surprise since their others were fourteen and twelve. Life had a way of tossing out those little surprises. Fortunately, in this case, all were pleased.

By the time Steve closed up his office and headed for the elevators in the lobby, everyone else was gone. They all had families waiting at home. Busy weekends ahead, no doubt.

He tapped the call button and waited for a car to return from the lobby.

Behind him the agency phone started to ring. He glanced at his watch. Half past seven. Since the office was closed, the call would go to the answering service, where it would be appropriately routed.

Indeed, the ringing stopped, so he stayed put at the elevator doors, waiting. When the ringing began once more, he couldn't ignore it. He crossed to the receptionist's desk and picked up the handset.

"The Colby Agency."

The silence on the other end suggested the caller had either given up and disconnected or that the call had gone directly to the answering service after that second ring.

Oh well, he had tried.

"Hello."

He'd had the handset headed toward its cradle and scarcely heard the faint word. "This is the Colby Agency." He rested the handset against his ear once more.

"I know it's late." The voice was a woman's. She released a breath. "I really thought you'd be closed, and I'd be able to leave a message."

His initial thought was to ask if she preferred that he direct her call to voicemail. Some matters were of such a private nature that a client might wish to say them to the voicemail rather than to a person, a stranger, first.

Before he could suggest as much, she spoke again. "I'm glad you're not." There was a hesitation, then, "I think I might be in trouble."

Her confidence was building, and his curiosity was doing the same. "Would you like to make an appointment to come into the office?"

"Well, I'm... I'm actually looking for Steve Durham. Can I leave a message for him?"

Interesting. "No need. You've got him. This is Steve."

The woman lapsed into silence once more.

"How can I help?" he prodded. The elevator chimed, and the doors slid open. Since he was on the office phone, he couldn't go for it. He'd call another when this conversation was finished. There was no reason to rush. Unlike his colleagues, he had no one waiting at home.

"You might not remember me," she said, the hesitation back. "My name is Allie Foster."

Recognition flared instantly. A smile spread across his face. "Allie, yes, I remember you. Of course I do. If not for your brilliant mind, I might never have managed pre-cal." Wow. Talk about a blast from the past.

The damned class had given him nightmares. At the time, he'd told himself it didn't matter because he wasn't going to college anyway, but his mother had insisted he take all the right classes in case he changed his mind later.

His mother was a very smart lady.

"Yes. That was a tough semester, but you got the swing of it by second semester."

The smile in her voice told him she had relaxed a bit. "Are you in Chicago now?" How long had it been? Sixteen years? Fifteen for sure.

"No. I'm... I'm still in Woodstock living in my grandparents' house." A strained laugh followed. "I'm sorry to call so late, but I'm not sure this can wait."

"I understand." He checked his watch. "I could be there in just over an hour. Why don't I drive out? If you haven't had dinner already, I could pick up takeout and we'll catch up. Figure out the situation."

The whole idea came out in such a rush, he felt walloped by the force of it. But, for some strange reason, he sensed it was the right thing to do. Maybe it was the hint of desperation in her tone or just the fact that she reminded him of the good old days. Whatever the case, he wanted to help. Her return to silence suggested he'd maybe pushed a little with the idea.

"Or we could wait for you to come to the office on Monday. I'm good with either plan, Allie."

"I'm not sure waiting is a good idea. If you could come now...that would be great." She exhaled a big breath. "But that's so much trouble. Are you sure you don't mind?"

"I do not mind at all. In fact, I insist." His lips twitched with another memory. Her grandfather showing him how to change a tire. Steve had borrowed his father's little project car—a two-seat convertible—without permission that hot summer day to impress a girl who wasn't impressed with him at all. Never was. He'd gotten a flat right in front of the Foster home. Allie had watched the tire-changing session from the window and then the porch, but she'd been too shy to come out and say hello. The next year, his pre-cal teacher suggested Allie as a tutor. It had taken some time, but she had eventually learned to relax in his presence.

"Good," she said with relief. "Great, I mean. Do you remember the address?"

"I do. You up for Chinese, or would you prefer Mexican?"

"You choose."

"Chinese it is. See you in an hour or so."

"Okay. Thanks, Steve. Really, thank you so much."

"No thanks necessary. I owe you, Allie Foster."

He placed the handset back in its cradle and called another elevator car. This late the traffic wouldn't be so bad.

There was a great Chinese place on the way.

He smiled. *Allie Foster*. How many times had he thought of her over the years? Several. Why had he never called or dropped by to see her? Asked her to dinner? He should have kept up with her. She was a really nice person.

This was the perfect opportunity for him to make it up to her for all the times she or her family had helped him out.

Foster Residence
Ridgeland Avenue, 8:50 p.m.

STEVE SENT ALLIE a text to let her know he'd arrived at her street. As he navigated his SUV into the driveway, she switched on the exterior lights. The porch and yard area close to the house brightened as if the sun had suddenly risen and shone only on that spot. The over-the-top exterior lighting reminded him of something else about Allie's family. His mother had insisted that after the accident—meaning the car crash that took the life of the Holts' daughter and son-in-law, Allie's parents—the family hadn't been the same. It was as if they had feared that something would happen to their granddaughter—their only surviving family member. They'd hovered over her, keeping extra close tabs on her every move.

Maybe that was part of the reason she'd been so painfully shy. She was the quietest kid he'd known.

But then she was the only one he'd known who had lost both parents before she was old enough to go to school.

It was a tough break.

She was also brilliant and pretty and very sweet.

But that was a long time ago, he reminded himself. Things and people changed. She might not be that same wallflower anymore.

He shut off the engine, grabbed the bags of food from the passenger seat and climbed out. He would know soon enough. By the time he was on the porch, the door opened—but not before he heard at least three locks disengaging.

Maybe she had her reasons. Either way, no judgment.

"You're here."

The genuine surprise in her voice and her expression made him wonder if she'd been let down a lot by friends who promised to drop by or do her some favor.

"Food, too." He held up the bags. The smell of lo mein and fried rice had haunted him all the way here.

She ushered him inside and to the dining room, which was actually a part of the kitchen. A typical L-shape allowed the smaller part, the dining room, to flow directly into the living room. It was one of those houses with a larger second floor. The best he recalled there was nothing on the first floor beyond the main living space. All the bedrooms were up one floor. No basement, if he remembered correctly. He glanced around. Definitely not much had changed about the place.

"This is like déjà vu," he said as he settled the bags on the table.

She laughed a soft sound. "I really haven't upgraded anything, just replaced whatever gave out. Decor isn't my thing."

He nodded his approval. "I like it. Your grandmother had great taste."

Allie glanced around. "She wasn't like the other grandmothers, that's for sure."

The very sixties-seventies vibe was evidence of that statement. In his opinion, the couple had been the coolest grandparents ever. Steve had always seen Virginia Holt and her husband, Gordon, as old hippies who probably smoked pot in the basement and were saving the wild parties for when Allie would eventually be away at college.

Except, according to Steve's mother, Allie never went away to college. She'd stayed right here in Woodstock. In this very house. Allie hadn't changed much, either. Still had that long brown hair trapped in a ponytail. He vividly remembered how her brown eyes lit up when she laughed. He would wager she had no idea how gorgeous she was. With her tee that sported flowers and I'd Rather Be in the Garden along with well-worn jeans, she looked eighteen instead of thirty-two. Her grandmother had dressed the same way and always looked far younger than the other grandmothers, even with her long gray hair that she'd always worn in a braid.

"Wine or beer?" Allie asked. "I usually drink wine, but I had beer delivered after we talked."

Home delivery almost any time of the day or night was an amazing thing. "I'm good with whichever is handy."

Once they were settled with plates filled and drinks handy, Steve suggested, "Why don't you start at the beginning and tell me what's going on."

After her call, there hadn't been an opportunity for him to do any sort of research or to call anyone from the agency who could do a bit for him this evening. Ultimately, he'd decided to wait and hear what she had to say first.

Walking into the situation cold wasn't a big deal, he'd known her most of his life.

He watched her face as she spoke, going over the visit from the two federal agents. Allie really looked so much like the young girl he'd known in high school with her fresh, makeup-free face and ponytail. Unlike him, she didn't seem to have aged at all. Her voice still had that lyrical rhythm to it. He liked the sound of it. And when she got going with a story, her face came to life, emotions on full display. Her memory appeared to be outstanding as well. Her account of the conversation held with the agents was very detailed.

"I did a little looking into the murder," she said as she poked at her rice, the momentum of her retelling slowing down. "Thomas Madison was a big deal—a partner at Ledwell. You probably don't remember, but that's where my father worked when he died."

"Ledwell." Steve nodded. "I'm familiar with the company. Fortune 500. Hot investment even all these years later. They've held their own in a very competitive marketplace."

"I found that surprising as well. Usually someone else comes along who is a little better, but no one has been able to get ahead of Ledwell in the AI race. This murder has sent shockwaves through the industry and Wall Street, which I suspect is part of why the FBI is involved. Fraser and Potter said Madison was part of an ongoing case, so my guess is their case had something to do with the research currently being conducted at Ledwell or something from recent years."

Steve chewed thoughtfully for a moment. "Ledwell is the one that won that huge government AI contract just last year."

"You're right, and I'm sure you've heard about the various issues coming to light. There's a lot of controversy in the AI arena right now. According to Google, Ledwell is pushing back on any new restrictive legislation. They've basically had free reign until recently, and they're not taking the changes well."

Steve reached for his cell, tapped the notes icon and started a list. "We'll put AI R&D at the top of our list of motives for the situation—not necessarily for the man's murder but for whatever is happening behind the scenes right now that may have impacted in some way the event or events that culminated in his death."

Allie set her fork down, and her shoulders sagged with the way she let go a weary breath. "I'm so glad I found you and that you came."

He grinned. "Of course. It's what friends do."

Maybe friends was a stretch considering the time gap, but she no doubt understood his intent.

They ate in silence for a while. Steve watched her. She ate with considerably more enthusiasm now that her trouble was on the table. It wasn't every day someone was visited by the FBI and accused of the murder of a man she didn't know in a place where she hadn't been in years. She had every right to be upset and defensive. He appreciated that she had enough faith in him to sound reasonably relaxed and open in spite of the concerns likely reeling in her mind.

Steve pushed his plate aside and settled his forearms on the table. She did the same, her gaze on his, searching. The pulse at the base of her throat fluttered again. She was visibly braced for his conclusions.

"I don't practice criminal law or really any other at this time," he explained. "I primarily counsel and advise the agency on operational matters. I can represent you if that's what you want."

"Yes!" Her relief was palpable. "Please. Thank God."

He smiled. "Our first step is to learn what the FBI believes and what the two agents working the case wish to prove with their visit to you. Are you their only suspect? Is closing the case quickly more important than digging around for other possibilities? I want to meet with Agents Fraser and Potter and get a feel for where they are with all this. Once we discover what precisely they want from you and what they hope to gain by pushing for the search of your property, we'll have a better handle on just how bad the situation is for you."

Her shoulders sagged again. "The woman in the video is me. I'm reasonably confident it is," she admitted. "But I was not there last week or any other day in the past five years."

"Videos can be doctored—made to show what the editor wants others to see."

She nodded. "I'm aware, and I considered that might be the case."

"There's also the possibility the video is from when you worked at the hospital. The room number may have been altered for the purpose of making it fit the narrative they wanted to present. The big question in my mind is why are they so convinced it's real? The Bureau has the ability to determine if the video has been altered. I'm guessing that not showing that card gives them leverage—something to use to get what they want."

"It must have been altered. There's just no other explanation." She bit her lip as if considering whether to say the rest of what was on her mind.

"Do you have other thoughts about how that happened?"

She shook her head no. "I was thinking that it might be a good idea to go through the house. Maybe see if I can find anything at all related to Ledwell or this Thomas Madison. But I was worried it would make me look guilty if they showed up with a warrant and I'm in the middle of tearing the place apart."

"It's your home," he pointed out. "You can search it any way at any time you choose."

She looked away a moment, the heavier worries seeming to catch up with her once more. "I don't understand why this is happening." She set her gaze on his. "I've lived right here my whole life. I don't know this victim. I don't see how someone could have picked me out and decided I would be the person they used to get away with murder."

"Obviously it's someone who needs an alibi and is aware that you worked at the hospital before and that there was a connection—your father's employment with Ledwell. If he or she is involved with AI, chances are we're looking at someone with above average intelligence. Perhaps even a fixer or…" He shrugged, almost hated to bring this up. "Or maybe an assassin whose skill set includes cleaning up after him or herself. You would be part of that clean up."

"My God, I hadn't even considered anything along those lines."

"I hope that's not the case," he offered, "but we need to consider all possibilities."

"I was four years old when my parents died," she said, frustrated. "I barely remember them. Why would I go after someone all these years later who may or may not have been a part of whatever was being investigated after the accident? I had no idea there was an investigation beyond the usual kind related to automobile accidents. My grandparents never told me." She turned up her hands. "I am utterly in the dark about all this."

"It's possible they didn't know," he ventured, though he thought that was unlikely. "Do you know if there was a settlement related to the accident? Was anyone else involved?"

"No. It was a single-car accident chalked up to a mechanical failure. At least, that's what I was told."

He studied her a long moment. "Why did you leave the hospital—when you were a nurse there?"

She exhaled a weary breath. "I loved helping people. It felt good and important—like what I was meant to do. Sadly, there are those in the field who don't always do good or even close to good. I saw that firsthand right from the beginning." She shook her head. "Long story short, when someone died, I couldn't pretend I didn't know why it happened. When I went to the administrator about it, I was made to look like the bad guy. At that point, I had two options. Get fired or quit. I chose the latter and decided to find a different way to help."

"You're saying someone in the hospital's administration gave you an ultimatum." Not good for the current situation. It could be seen as motive.

"Not in a straightforward way, but basically that was what the situation boiled down to."

"But you never pursued legal action? Never went back and raised hell? Nothing like that?"

She shook her head. "Nope. Just did what I wanted to do in a different way."

He supposed that was what he was doing, practicing law in a different way than the typical attorney. Nothing wrong with achieving your goal using a different path.

"It's late," he said, considering that at minimum it was an hour's drive home. "I should get going. But I'll be back in the morning, and we'll nail down more of our strategy, and who knows?" He smiled. "Maybe we'll do a little digging around here if you're up for it."

"I am definitely up for whatever you think we should do." She drew in a big breath. "Thank you so much for coming all this way. We should probably discuss what your fees are."

The look of hope and gratitude on her face was more than enough payment. Part of what had made him want to go into the legal field was to be able to help those who were being unjustly persecuted.

This was a perfect example—at least based on what he had heard and seen so far.

"You don't need to worry about any fees."

Before she could argue, he insisted on helping to clean up, and then she walked him to the door. Even with the strange story of her being suspected of murder, he had to admit he had enjoyed seeing her again.

The doorbell abruptly buzzed.

Startled, Allie looked from the door to him. Shook her head. "No clue."

He checked the viewfinder and discovered two suits and a row of personnel dressed in CSI garb lined up on her porch. He didn't have to wonder who the suits were. Federal agents.

"They're back." He turned to Allie. "And they obviously have a warrant. Don't answer any questions. In fact, don't say a word. Let me handle this."

She nodded her understanding.

Since it had only been a few hours since the agents questioned Allie, it seemed out of the ordinary that the pair was back so soon with a warrant. Warrants generally took time. Whenever an investigation was being pushed fast and hard, there was either an imminent danger of some sort or someone powerful who wanted this done ASAP pushing for a rapid turnaround.

He opened the door to the two agents and their party. Steve didn't have enough information to hazard a guess one way or the other, but what he understood without doubt was the situation was not in Allie's best interest.

This was a clear and present threat to her.

Chapter Three

Saturday, June 7
Foster Residence
Ridgeland Avenue, 5:00 a.m.

Allie watched as the group of agents filed out of her house for the last time.

Outrage did not begin to describe how this felt. These people had combed through her house, through all her things, literally all night. She had been forced to stay outside. Steve had tried to talk her into going to a hotel, but she'd refused, so she'd ended up in his SUV for the duration.

As her attorney, he had been allowed to stay and to watch the proceedings inside the house. He'd come outside to check on her more times than she could remember. Actually, she remembered every single one. His blond hair was darker now, more a light brown. And his eyes were the most calming shade of blue.

Stop, Al. He was here to help with legal issues not fulfill her fantasies.

She straightened in the passenger seat, now that it appeared to be over, finally. Maybe she could put this behind her and life would go back to normal.

She blinked. Had her life ever been normal?

Allie pushed the thought away. She wasn't going there right now.

Steve stood on the sidewalk and watched the crew load up and drive away before returning to where she waited. She reached for the door handle. All she wanted to do was get in her bed and sleep…put this nightmare out of her head. Maybe check her email. Social media wasn't her thing. She was probably the only person her age on the planet who had no social media account.

He opened the driver's side door and slid behind the steering wheel. "You up for Red's?"

A frown furrowed across her brow. How could he sound so chipper? Then again, he wasn't the one whose life was suddenly upside-down. Besides, he likely experienced situations like this in his work. It was probably par for the course on any given day at the agency. While her life was a continual routine of bed at ten, up at six, work and then repeat. There was something to be said for routine…but mostly her life was dull.

Allie took a breath. Red's was a local diner that opened at five every morning for breakfast. The good, old-fashioned kind of food like her grandmother used to prepare. As if that wasn't incentive enough, when was the last time a handsome man had invited her anywhere?

Her stomach rumbled, but she shook her head. "I'm really not hungry. I'd like to go inside and—"

"Let's have breakfast first." He started the engine and turned the vehicle around.

She plowed her fingers through her hair, imagining

how utterly awful she looked. The ponytail had to go hours ago. "It must be bad if you don't want me to go in there before having sustenance."

"They put things back where they found them, just not quite as neatly."

She groaned. "Yay. I might as well do a little late spring cleaning." That would make her vacation even better. How much more exciting could her life get? *Woo-hoo!*

Considering she was under suspicion for murder, maybe that might not be a good question to ask herself. In this case, excitement was a little overrated.

He drove to Red's, which was only minutes from her house. She ordered delivery from them a few times each month. It was her grandparents' favorite dining spot. Maybe because Red Shepherd, the owner, was an aging hippie just as they had been. Allie couldn't help smiling. She missed them so much.

She covertly glanced at the driver. Her grandmother had always said Steve was a good boy. Like his father, she'd said. Allie had seen photos of her mother as a teenager with Steve's father. Her grandmother had given the impression that she'd wished those two had ended up together.

Steve glanced at her. "You must be thinking about the past." He guided the SUV into a parking slot. "The present certainly wouldn't prompt a smile like that one."

She touched her lips. Hadn't realized she'd been smiling. "I was thinking about my mother."

He smiled back at her. "You look like her. Exactly like her."

"Everyone always says that." And the family photo albums confirmed it.

He hopped out of the vehicle and hurried around to her door before she could rally the energy to open it.

"Not that I really remember her," he said as she emerged. "But my mom has lots of photos of family gatherings that included your parents."

"I've seen a few in my grandmother's albums." Allie smiled. She and her grandparents hadn't gone to very many gatherings with neighbors after her parents were gone. Things had changed after that.

The bell over the door jingled as they opened it and walked inside.

"Looks like we're the first customers today," Steve noted.

The smell of bacon drifting from the kitchen had Allie's stomach rumbling again. "I think I changed my mind. I'm starving."

He grinned. "Good. We need to load up on carbs and sugar and then deal with this thing."

There was something to be said for his strategy. Allie just wasn't exactly sure what it was quite yet. She was, however, immensely grateful to have someone to help her navigate this nightmare.

They took a booth near the back since the diner would likely fill quickly on a Saturday morning. A waitress materialized, carafe of fresh coffee in hand. She filled the waiting mugs and took their order.

When she disappeared back into the kitchen, Allie said, "Tell me about your work at the Colby Agency." It would be nice to think about something else for a little while.

He nodded. "The Colby Agency is the best in the business. Truly the best. Victoria is an incredible force, as is the entire staff. It's a privilege to be a part of the team. I'm happy there."

"Do you investigate cases?" She pressed a hand to her chest. "Like this mess I find myself in?"

"Actually—" he took a sip of coffee then set his mug aside "—I don't do the investigating, but I get involved when there are potential issues that fall into the legal category. I do a lot of advising on cases with the investigators. My time with Chicago PD helped with that aspect of my work. It's one of the reasons Victoria was interested in interviewing me when I finished law school."

Allie studied him for a moment. "I always got the impression that college was not your thing. I mean, you never talked about it. What made you change your mind and go to college and then to law school? That's a serious commitment for someone who wasn't big on the idea of university life."

He laughed. "I think my experience is a little like your own. I very much enjoyed my work on the force, but I felt there was more I could do from this perspective, so I changed gears."

The waitress arrived with their orders, and they dug in. Apparently, Allie really had been starving. She'd barely eaten last night. The food he'd brought had been great, but her appetite had been absent. The whole situation with the murder and those FBI agents had been overwhelming.

It still was, but her body was adjusting to this new stressor.

After the need for food had been satisfied for the most part, she lifted her gaze to his. "Tell me about what happened inside my house. You spoke to Fraser and Potter, I assume."

He nodded and set his fork aside. "Both are convinced the woman in the video is you."

Her hopes sank.

"That said," he went on, "both are fully aware the video could have been created from one taken when you were employed at the hospital. They aren't convinced that you are the person who murdered Mr. Madison, but the only evidence they have points to you. For the most part, I believe they feel whatever happened is somehow connected to you, and this is the leverage they have, so they're using it."

Allie shook her head. "Why would I kill a man I don't even know?"

"Exactly. They're aware."

"Did they go into the case that involved Madison—the one they were working prior to his death?"

"They did not, but it is related to Ledwell. I was able to get that out of Fraser. This has something to do with the company, and your father's connection—however old—to that company lends credence to your possible involvement. Which is why they wanted to see whatever was in the house and on your computer."

Allie's heart sank, joining the hopes that had fallen around her feet. "They took my computer."

He nodded. "And your laptop and cell phone and tablet."

The thought shook her. How would she do anything without one or the other of those devices? Her whole life was electronic.

She sagged deeper in the booth.

"They will return all your belongings," he promised. "The only question is when. For now, we will get you another phone and a laptop if you need one for work."

She shrugged. "I'm on vacation until a week from Monday. I can live without my laptop. But not my phone."

He grinned. "Who could?"

"Well, well, if it ain't my favorite goddaughter."

The boom of Red Shepherd's voice turned every head in the diner, and the place had pretty much filled up at this point. Allie wasn't so much concerned about anyone recognizing her. She rarely left the house. Anyone who had known her growing up wouldn't remember her now. Likely wouldn't even recognize her.

Along with social media, she hadn't bothered to cultivate friends. Her life was all about work. But there were other people—ones who had known her parents and grandparents—who still remembered her. There were a few at work she considered friends, sort of. She knew their online work profiles, their voices.

But that didn't really fit the definition of a friend.

Allie worked up a smile. She wasn't actually Red's goddaughter, but he had claimed the title when she was a kid. "Great to see you, Red."

He slid into the booth next to her. He studied Steve a moment. "You're Martha's boy, aren't you?"

"Yes, sir."

Red looked from one to the other. "Good to see folks from the old neighborhood still coming around."

Allie decided to take a chance. She was here. She might as well. "Red, do you remember much about my father?"

He made a puffing sound. "Are you kidding? Course I do. He stole the heart of the prettiest girl in Woodstock." He grinned. "Lots of guys around here never forgave him."

Allie laughed. "I wish I remembered more."

Red nodded, his face somber. "What happened was a terrible thing."

"Do you remember anything about his work at Ledwell?" Steve asked.

Red studied him for a long moment before answering. Allie's nerves went on edge.

"His work was not something he talked about. It wasn't allowed. No one talked about what went on in that place. Still don't. But, to answer your question in a roundabout way, there was a problem at Ledwell back then," he said with a covert glance around their booth. "There was tension. Your grandparents," Red went on, his gaze shifting to Allie, "were concerned about what he was getting into. He wouldn't talk about it, but they suspected it was bad business."

"Do you believe my father was involved in some illegal activity?" Allie's grandmother had certainly never said anything of the sort.

"No." Red swung his head in a firm negative. "It was something bad though. Your mother wanted him to leave the company, but he was afraid he'd be blackballed and wouldn't be able to get another job, so he stuck it out."

"The Holts never mentioned anything specific," Steve nudged the older man, "as to what the issue was?"

Red gave another shake of his head. "No, but we all knew there was funny business at that company. Getting into all kinds of research that was going to come back to haunt anyone involved, I suspect. All our concerns got played off, and we were called paranoid and what-have-you, but we were right. It's all coming out now." He leaned forward. "All that AI business is going to be the end of us, you mark my word."

There were those with that opinion, for sure. Allie wasn't sure where she stood on the matter.

"Do you think my parents were afraid?" All these years, she had believed it was a simple car crash that took their lives. Bad luck. Wrong place, wrong time. But maybe that wasn't true.

"I know your grandparents were." He nodded, his face grave. "And after the accident, Virginia and Gordon went to the police, to the FBI—to anyone who might listen. But no one would. They were labeled crazy... overwrought with grief. Didn't matter. They knew that accident was no accident. We all knew it."

For a moment, Allie couldn't speak. There had been questions. She always sensed that, even as a child. But no one had ever uttered those words out loud.

No accident?

"Do you have any evidence?" Steve pressed. "Did the Holts ever talk about any real evidence?"

To Allie's knowledge, they certainly never had, but she kept quiet...mostly because she wasn't sure what to say.

Red smirked. "What do you think?"

Allie held up her hands. "I don't understand why I have no memory of this...this nightmare you're describing."

Red smiled sadly. "I'm sorry. I get carried away when I allow myself to think about it. The reason you don't remember, I guess, is because a year after the accident your grandmother put her foot down and called it enough. She and Gordon were fighting a losing battle, and they knew it. Nothing they had done had gotten the investigation beyond some BS mechanical malfunction conclusion. Virginia decided there was nothing she could do about what happened to her precious daughter and her husband, but she could be a part of what became of you. *You* were more important. They decided they would put the past behind them and focus on taking care of you. On giving you the best life possible."

Allie didn't doubt this for one second. Her grandparents had always been overprotective and had over planned everything for her. They offered to send her to the best college, but she turned down all options except the one that kept her close to home. After all they'd done for her, she couldn't bring herself to abandon them. Maybe deep down she had always known something wasn't right with what happened to her parents.

All this time, that vague notion had simmered inside her...and now it was out. She didn't know exactly how to feel.

"I think," Allie began, "what you're telling me is someone murdered my parents, in all likelihood, because of something my father knew or did in his work. My grandparents let it go in an effort to protect me."

Red held her gaze for a long moment. "That's exactly what I'm telling you."

She wanted to jump up and demand to know where the cameras were and what reality television show had decided to make her the subject of its newest episode. But she understood that wasn't the case. Her emotions were spinning. One moment she was angry, the next terrified and then...just numb. But...this was real. All these years, the things she had believed about her family were stories made to keep her safe...to keep her happy and not digging around.

Yet now...somehow...something had gone wrong. A glitch in the stream of life had occurred, and now she was being drawn back into this no matter that she had no idea what this was.

Red shook his head again. "I've said too much."

"No." She managed an appreciative smile for him. "It's way past time I learned the truth. You did the right thing."

"But your grandparents worked so hard to protect you, and I just undid two-and-a-half decades of their efforts." The emotion shining in his eyes warned that he was dead serious.

Allie wasn't exactly sure what to say to make him feel better.

"Unfortunately, Mr. Shepherd," Steve said, letting her off the hook, "someone else has already opened that door, and now we need all the help we can get to figure out who and why. What you've done is give us a starting place for finding answers."

The older man's relief was so visibly overwhelming Allie thought he might actually cry.

"I'll give you something else," he said with another of those covert glances around. "Find Jesus. He can give you way more information."

"Jesus?" Steve and Allie said in unison with equal surprise.

"Jesus Rivero." Red winked. "He was a hotshot reporter back then. Almost got himself killed a dozen times trying to get the story, and he always did...until that accident. Talk to Jesus—if you can find him. He'll know how to help."

Steve tried to pay the tab, but Red insisted it was on the house. Allie gave him a hug.

All they had to do now was find Jesus.

Chapter Four

Wonder Lake, Illinois
Rivero Residence
Lake Shore Drive, 8:00 a.m.

Steve parked in the small driveway. Allie surveyed the street. She'd never had reason to be in the area. The properties here were miles beyond her price range. Surprisingly, the house that was their destination sat practically in the street, as did most along this stretch of the neighborhood. It was also much smaller than she had expected for such a pricy area. In all probability, the reason was because the houses on this private lake did their showing off out back, not in front. Though she couldn't recall ever having been here, she had seen the property online. She'd looked it up on the way here. This side of the house was for access from the street, while the other side was the one with the view and the jagged and plummeting landscape down to the water.

 A white, vintage Land Rover Defender sat as close to the house as was possible without the rear bumper contacting the stone and wood facade. She hoped the vehicle being there meant the owner was home. Although, considering the dust and tree sap clinging to the surface, it may have been sitting exactly where it was for a good long while. Maybe he had another vehicle and a garage somewhere she couldn't see.

On the drive over, she had used Steve's phone to do some research on Jesus Rivero. Thirty years ago, he had been the hottest reporter in the Chicago market. He'd even been slated for his own primetime show, but then something happened and he just dropped off the face of the earth.

Red had passed along that part, but he hadn't known where Rivero had disappeared to. There was nothing on the net about his whereabouts either. Recently, the former bigtime reporter had been spotted in the Chicago area, but he hadn't moved back to his penthouse apartment there. Instead, he'd sold it for one dollar to the family who had been leasing it for all those years. According to the online county records, and Allie had checked several counties surrounding Chicago, he'd bought this house on Wonder Lake around that same time, just three months ago.

The man, various articles had purported, was a recluse, given that he was rarely seen in public. Allie couldn't ignore the fact that, in that regard, their lives were a little alike. Though she had never considered herself an actual recluse. Not in the truest definition of the word anyway. But maybe that was what she was. She didn't socialize with friends. Didn't do social media. Had no dating prospects. Rarely left the house since the pandemic. Maybe her friends from her childhood and school, as well as those from her time working at the hospital, all thought she had dropped off the face of the earth too.

During those years she'd taken care of her grandmother, there had been no time to worry about anything else other than work. It was an around-the-clock gig. Not for one second did she regret the choice. Even after her grandmother died, the pandemic had made it far too easy to stick with the status quo. Stay home and shop via delivery services.

Something similar may have happened to Rivero. Maybe his disappearance was no mystery at all, just a tragic life event.

"Shall we go to the door?"

Allie jerked at the sound of Steve's voice. "Sorry, I was lost in…the past again."

"You need sleep. When we're done here, I should take you home and let you get some sleep."

Did that mean he was leaving? The idea sent fear spiraling through her.

Rather than express that fear, she nodded as she reached for the door handle. "I really appreciate you taking so much time with me. I can't believe it's evolved into such a nightmare. I'm sure you have to get back to Chicago."

She didn't even want to imagine what he thought of her. Poor, pathetic Allie. Giving herself a mental kick, she put aside the idea. There was no time for self-pity right now. She was in trouble, and she needed his help—whatever his motive for going above and beyond.

"I do need to make a quick run to the city," he agreed, "to grab a few things, but I'll be back. This is far from over, Allie. I'm not leaving until this is done—at least, not as long as you want me here."

Her spirits lifted as high as possible, bearing in mind she really was exhausted. "Thank you. I'm not sure I know the right words to adequately express how grateful I am." She opened the door and climbed out before embarrassing herself by going further overboard with the relief and appreciation.

He joined her in front of the SUV, and they walked side by side to the door of the house. Steve rang the bell. No answer. Two more rings were required before there was a response. Allie's pulse had pounded harder with each passing second. At this rate, she was going to hyperventilate before they even spoke to the man.

"If you have a package," the muffled voice echoed over the speaker next to the doorbell, "just leave it at the door."

Steve glanced at Allie. "Mr. Rivero, this is Steve Durham of the Colby Agency in Chicago. I need a moment of your time, sir."

"Who is *she*?" the voice demanded.

Allie had just noticed the camera tucked into the soffit over their heads. Well, of course he had cameras. She had considered adding a few herself but never got around to it. Maybe she should.

"Allie Foster," she answered. "You may have known my father, Jerry Foster. He was a technician at Ledwell before being killed in a car crash."

The silence went on and on. Her stomach twisted into knots. Was his hesitation because he did know her father? Or because she had mentioned Ledwell?

"You were working on a big story related to Ledwell," Steve said, obviously hoping to prompt a response other than silence. "We just want to ask you a few questions about what happened back then."

"I can't help you," the disembodied voice muttered.

Desperation rose sharply in Allie. Red was convinced

this man knew something, which meant Allie needed to talk to him. "Thomas Madison is dead. Murdered. They think I killed him, and I don't even know him. I believe his murder is somehow related to what happened to my parents. Please, Mr. Rivero, I really need your help."

"What you need," the man inside the house snapped, "is to go home and forget anything you think you know because I promise you, you don't know *anything*. You don't want to know anything. Not if you want to stay alive."

Allie's jaw dropped. Was this guy for real? "I can't fight an enemy I don't recognize," she argued. The idea might be a bit over the top, but that was exactly how she felt just now. "At least help me determine what I'm up against here."

"That's all we're asking for," Steve tossed in, "just a few minutes of your time."

"You're up against a brick wall," the voice said. "I can't help you."

"You mean," Allie countered, furious now, "you won't help me."

The distinct click of the man inside turning off the intercom link confirmed her conclusion.

"I guess he doesn't want to talk," Steve suggested.

"Maybe Red was wrong about him."

They walked back to the SUV and drove away from the disappointment. Allie abruptly felt lost and utterly out of energy. How had this happened? It made no sense whatsoever. If her grandparents had known there was some big, dangerous mystery, why hadn't they warned her?

She had to assume they either hadn't known or expected that as long as she knew nothing about it, the trouble would never come to her.

If that was the case, they had been wrong. She refused to believe they would purposely have left her open to trouble.

"We can always try again," Steve offered. "We'll do as much research as we can without his help, and then we'll hit him up again. Meanwhile, I have some sources I can reach out to."

Allie couldn't remember when she'd felt so frustrated. Didn't reporters like talking about their work? It was possible Rivero was just a burned-out old man who didn't want to admit that he had no stories left in him. Or that the one he'd been pursuing before his disappearance had turned out to be nothing of relevance.

Bottom line, there was pretty much nothing she could do about Jesus Rivero's decision. But there was something that would not wait any longer.

"I need a phone."

"That's our next stop," Steve assured her. "We have to get you connected to the world again."

She wasn't so sure she'd ever really been connected. Maybe that was her mistake. How did a person provide an alibi for murder or any other crime without a witness—someone who could vouch for them. Allie had no one. No friends—at least none with which she communicated, outside the few at work who only knew her voice. Her alibi was that she had been at home. Alone. Since she rarely left the house, her neighbors certainly couldn't provide an alibi.

In the eyes of the two FBI agents, that was no alibi at all. An evening with F. Scott Fitzgerald didn't count.

Foster Residence
Ridgeland Avenue, 11:30 a.m.

NOT ONLY DID Allie buy a new phone, but she also splurged on a new laptop as well. The one the FBI agents had taken was four years old already. It was time. Besides, who knew when she would get her devices back.

At her front door, since Steve still had the key, he unlocked and opened the door. She held her breath, dreading what she would find inside. He'd warned her that things were a bit disorganized.

She set down her bag of new goodies and wandered through the downstairs rooms. Not so bad, she decided. Nothing a little straightening wouldn't take care of.

"Did they take anything with them—besides my devices?" She turned to the man following along behind her. "I saw some of the agents carrying boxes."

"They took a number of files from your office and a few photo albums. Not that much really. What any investigator leaves a scene with is always telling. They obviously didn't find the stash of goods or files they had hoped to discover. For now, we can consider that good news."

Allie surveyed the entry hall then glanced up the stairs. "I keep trying to wrap my head around what's happening, and it's just not working. It feels like a bad dream. Like I should wake up any time now, and it will all be over."

"Completely understandable." He nodded. "I'm heading to my place for clothes and a few other things I need. I'll be back in a couple hours. Get some sleep. We'll start breaking this down when I return."

"Thanks. I really appreciate this, Steve."

He gave her a quick hug. "This will be just a bad memory before you know it."

She had her doubts, but she could hope. The surge of warmth she felt with his arms around her was certainly something she would not soon forget.

Foolish, Al. You definitely need a life.

When he'd gone, she secured the three deadbolts and climbed the stairs to see the damage there. Her office was on the second floor, so she would charge her new phone and laptop and get them activated as well. The sooner she could do something constructive, the better.

He had suggested she sleep, but Allie wasn't sure she would be doing that again anytime soon.

At least not until she understood what was happening here.

She stood at the door to her grandparents' room and felt sick at how the agents had pilfered through their things. But it wasn't until she reached her parents' bedroom that she wanted to throw something. They had taken the room apart, one piece at a time. The furnishings and the things in those furnishings hadn't been touched since the car crash. But those damned federal agents had come into the house and gone through their belongings with no care for their sentimental value to Allie. The items in this room were all she had left of her parents.

Once she'd calmed down and set her new devices to charge, she headed for the shower. Losing herself in a long hot shower would be a relief right now.

Her mind wouldn't slow down even with the hot water sluicing over her skin. She tried to relax, to find that Zen place that would allow her to think clearly and focus on the details of what was happening. So she closed her eyes and thought of the man who'd spent the last several hours with her.

She hadn't seen him in what? Fifteen years? He was still just as handsome as she remembered. Maybe more so. And smart. Really smart and kind. Back in high school, he was one of the nice guys while others his age had been busy showing off. Not Steve.

A bit of time was required and a whole lot of hot water, but the effort to focus on anything but the FBI and their murder accusations eventually started to work. Her shoulders and neck and then the rest of her stopped fighting the need to relax.

When she turned off the water and stepped out into the cool air, she felt much better. She brushed her teeth, dressed in her favorite sweats and climbed into her bed. She hadn't meant to sleep, only to relax, but suddenly she just couldn't keep her eyes open any longer.

Thoughts of that hug she and Steve had shared followed her into sleep.

A SOUND POKED at Allie. She told her eyes to open, but they refused. She was so tired. She needed to sleep just a little while longer.

Then the sound crept deeper into her consciousness.

A buzzing...like the doorbell.

Why would anyone be at her door? She never had visitors. Only deliveries.

But the buzz came again, and her eyes fluttered open this time.

Someone was at her door. She sat up. Her head felt fuzzy, and she had to think a moment before she could find her way back to the here and now.

Murder.

The video of her going into a patient's room.

Steve Durham. The Colby Agency.

The FBI was investigating her.

For an instant, she wanted to drop back onto the pillows and close her eyes tightly to block this crazy reality. Instead, she climbed out of the bed and stumbled out of her room and along the hall. Steve was probably back. She finger combed her hair on the way down the stairs. With a puff of breath into her hand, she tried to gage if it was fit for exposure to anyone beyond herself. Vaguely she remembered adding toothpaste to her toothbrush last night.

Another insistent buzz. She was almost at the door.

She reached for the first of the deadbolts but stopped herself. She needed to be sure who was on the other side, especially now.

Going on tiptoe, she checked the viewfinder in the door and smiled. Steve stood on her porch, a leather overnight bag in one hand and a briefcase in the other.

What time was it?

As she unlocked the door, she checked the grandfather clock just behind her. Three thirty. She'd slept better than two hours, closer to three.

She opened the door and smiled, hoping she didn't look a hot mess but fairly confident she did. "You're back."

"I am and I have some news."

As soon as he was across the threshold, she closed and locked the door. "Potter and Fraser made a mistake, and it's not me they're looking for?" she asked hopefully.

"Not quite that, but additional information that can

help us with finding our way out of this mess perhaps just a little more quickly."

"I'll take any kind of break at this point."

Amazing what a difference twenty-four hours can make. A mere twenty-four hours ago, she had been working her final shift before vacation and had no idea trouble was headed her way. Blissful ignorance. She should have appreciated it more.

"Did you manage to get some sleep?" He dropped his bag onto the bench next to the door but hung on to the briefcase.

"Oddly enough, I did."

"You up for coffee or tea?"

Coffee sounded amazing as a matter of fact. "I can put on a pot while you tell me what you discovered." She led the way to the kitchen.

Once she had filled the reservoir and added grounds to the filter, he kicked off his update. "Your father was one of six staff members closely involved in the SILO project."

Allie set the machine to brew. "Never heard of it." Surely if the project had been significant, she would have heard something about it in all these years. Artificial intelligence, or AI, was certainly in the news frequently enough. Even more so lately.

"You wouldn't have," he explained. "The project carried the highest security clearance requirement the US government uses."

Well, okay then. "Tell me about the project."

She leaned against the counter, the smell of coffee filling the room. Inside, she dared to smile. He had this way of making her feel totally comfortable—as if it hadn't been a decade and a half since they'd seen each other. As if they had been friends all this time.

"Special Intelligence Learning Operative," he explained. "They were working on the creation of AI operatives who could go under deep cover and learn everything there was to know about the enemy. Ones that could anticipate the movements of the enemy based on their knowledge of said enemy. All without risking human life."

Okay, they had just entered the twilight zone.

"Robots who look and behave like humans well enough to infiltrate the enemy?" Maybe not a total surprise. She supposed that particular goal had been an ongoing effort since the inception of AI.

"Yes," he confirmed. "Except this project hoped to take it further than ever before—for the timeframe we're talking about. That said, the really important part as far as you're concerned is the fact this project was primarily funded by the CIA and the military. Not your usual government scientific research."

This gave Allie pause. "So, we're talking about spooks and secret agents."

"In all likelihood, yes. My contact confirmed there were some issues related to where this project was headed, and it was eventually disbanded—or so that was the claim."

Nothing he'd told her sounded particularly troubling. Government projects were started and then stopped all the time. Issues cropped up, et cetera. "What makes the cessation of the project different than any of the others we hear about all the time?"

There were plenty of examples of hidden research

that came out years or decades later. In some ways, she understood that the technology race had to be secretive. There were far too many in the world who would use it for all the wrong reasons.

"No idea about what makes this one different—as of yet," he admitted. "But what we do know is that five of the six employees closely involved in the project died suddenly and tragically within just a few weeks or months of the shutdown."

A shock wave shuddered through Allie. "Then my parents' accident was likely no accident." On some level, she didn't want to know this...she wanted to let the past be just what it was...the *past*. She wanted to go on with her life believing the loss was merely another of life's tragedies, and her grandparents had picked up the slack.

Except it was too late for that. She'd already heard the words.

"I don't see how we can continue to call it an accident," Steve agreed. "But there's still a lot to discover before we can confirm a conclusion along those lines."

"Who was the lone survivor?" She already knew the answer, but she needed him to confirm her suspicion.

"Thomas Madison."

The corroboration quaked through her. She busied her hands with pouring the coffee. She didn't use cream, and based on breakfast this morning, Steve didn't either.

"Why was Madison allowed to live until just recently?" She passed a mug of steaming brew to him. "Seems like a loose thread to me."

"That's the part that doesn't fit neatly into what I'm hearing about this project so far. I have people digging. For now, that's the best we can do."

She cradled her mug of coffee and wondered what the hell any of this meant. "Potter and Fraser may not want to wait about making an arrest." The truth was, she could be sitting in a jail cell by dark or by morning. There was just no way to know which way this was going to go.

"Fraser has requested a meeting at ten on Monday morning." Steve shrugged. "If an arrest was imminent, I'm not sure there would be a reason for the meeting."

She wanted to feel relieved, but then again, all the delay suggested was that their people would spend all weekend going through the things they had taken and trying to find something relevant to the murder so that they could charge her.

Allie exiled the negative thought and sipped her coffee. Better to be optimistic and to see this upcoming meeting as a good thing.

"Until then," Steve said, "we'll search this house again just to be sure they didn't miss anything, and we're going to visit Mr. Rivero again. Maybe two or three times until he will talk to us or files a complaint with local law enforcement."

That all sounded like a good plan. She set her mug aside. But there might be one glitch. She should have broached the subject already, but things had been a little out of control until now.

"I know you said I shouldn't worry about fees, but we really need to talk about your retainer." She had some money saved. She had her grandparents' insurance funds as well. Whatever the Colby Agency fee, she should be able to handle it. But if she couldn't that was a whole other nightmare.

He looked her straight in the eye and said, "There will be no retainer or fee of any sort."

"Wait." She frowned, shook her head. "No. You're here representing me and a lot more. You need to be paid your usual fee. I'm sure your agency will expect me to be treated like any other client." No way was she having him do this for free.

"No." He shook his head. "I'm doing this for a friend. I've already taken some of my vacation time so I can be right here working on your case for as long as it takes. And no worries. I'll still have all the support I need just one phone call away. Although we'll be spending most of our time here or in the field in pursuit of information, I reserved myself a room at the Baymont."

"No." Him getting a room at a hotel was ridiculous. "Look, there's plenty of space right here. If you insist on this no fee thing, the least I can do is put you up and feed you."

He laughed. "That would be the most efficient choice—if you're sure."

"I am positive."

"Then I'm staying here."

Allie relaxed then. She had faith in Steve. He'd proven he could handle those agents, and he had all sorts of resources if even half of what she'd read about the Colby Agency was true.

In all honesty, she still felt unsettled by the idea of not being a paying client of the agency. But that was his choice, and she had to get right with it. Because the one thing she understood with complete certainty was that this man was likely the only way she was getting out of this nightmare free of a murder charge.

Chapter Five

Foster Residence
Ridgeland Avenue, 5:30 p.m.

Over the course of the past two hours, they had searched the house again. Allie had taken the bedrooms; Steve focused on the common areas. She had picked through every single article of clothing…every little thing.

She supposed this was why by the time she reached her parents' room, which she saved for last, Steve had finished with the rest of the house.

"You searched your office as well?" Standing in the doorway, he surveyed the room that had belonged to Jerry and Alice Foster.

"I did." He'd suggested a thorough search of her office when they first started. Even though she had been the one to set up all the furniture and the other odds and ends of her workspace, she'd done so while her grandparents were still alive. One or the other could have hidden something there later. In some distant part of her brain, she'd considered as much before Steve mentioned the possibility, but she hadn't really wanted to believe either of her grandparents would have hidden anything from her. The very idea was ludicrous.

This whole situation was ludicrous. She eyed the man standing in that doorway...except for him. He was the one thing keeping her grounded amid this ever-escalating madness.

Pushing aside the worrisome thoughts, she considered that whatever she had believed about the past and her grandparents, here she was in a total state of uncertainty about both. Clearly many things had been hidden from her.

Whatever else she believed at this point, Allie was completely certain her grandparents only did whatever they did to protect her. Red had said as much, but she hadn't really needed his confirmation. Her grandparents had loved her. She had absolutely no question about that.

"Let's go at this room," Steve suggested, surveying the twelve-by-about-fourteen space that had been her parents' bedroom, "from a different angle."

Allie was ready for just about anything as long as it helped solve this mystery. "Tell me what you mean."

"Let's consider that your parents hid something specific for reasons other than what Red suggested—that they were protecting you."

She made a face. "I'm confused. I thought we were looking for anything they'd hidden for whatever reason."

He shrugged. "We've been looking for anything hidden, yes. But what if this was some sort of insurance for them? At the time it was hidden, they may not have realized that you might be in danger as well. Any move or decision a person makes is always motivated by some necessity. Each move or decision is different based on the immediacy and/or the necessity involved."

Allie thought maybe she got it now, though she wasn't entirely sure. "You're saying that they may have hidden something differently if it was related to a more immediate need the two of them had versus some future need I might have."

He smiled. "Precisely."

Made sense.

They started with the ceiling. There were no ventilation registers in the ceiling, and only one light fixture which was actually a ceiling fan. Steve rounded up a ladder and checked the tops of the blades to ensure nothing was tucked there. He examined the main part of the fixture as well. Nothing but dust.

While he examined the curtains and blinds on the windows, Allie studied the walls. She looked behind framed items hanging there. She scrutinized every single crack in the plaster for possible openings. She removed the covers from electrical outlets, including the light switch, to ensure nothing was hidden in those either.

Piece by piece, they moved the furniture away from the wall and inspected the backside, the underside—including those of the drawers. It wasn't until they pulled the bed from the wall that they found a possible *former* hiding place.

"This—" Steve pointed to a spot in the wood on the back of the headboard "—is a place that was once covered. Maybe by a label of some sort or by something taped there."

The spot wasn't very large. About the size of a postcard. She traced it, felt a sticky residue. She nodded. "It may have been nothing more than a manufacturer's label. But there was something stuck there."

He pointed to an actual label on the opposite side. "This is larger. Why have two labels on the same piece of furniture when the others by the same manufacturer and in the same set we've already examined do not?"

He was right. The bedroom suite's matching dresser and side tables only had one label each, always posted on the back of the item.

"Whatever was hidden here is gone now." It felt very much like they were grasping at straws. Playing a guessing game. What if? Maybe this...

He smiled, though the expression looked as weary as she felt. "We are reaching. And it's frustrating. But we're trying, and until one of my resources comes through, it's the best we can do."

"Beats sitting around waiting for the other shoe to drop." Allie would openly admit that she was one of those people who needed to be focused on something most all the time.

"Always," he agreed.

Then they checked the floor. Each board of the hardwood was touched and examined for looseness and the possibility of being removed, along with the floor registers and the duct work leading up to those registers. Still nothing.

They had moved everything. Looked in, on and under everything.

Allie lay on her back on the floor. There was nowhere else to look.

Her gaze shifted from the bedroom door to the closet door. They had examined by hand each of the doors, smoothing their palms over the surfaces. The closet door was different from the main one leading into the bedroom. Not original, she decided. The door that led in and out of the room was like all the rest in the house. Paneled insets with wood stiles and rails. The usual type found in homes of this age and style. The closet door was similar in that it looked the same, but it wasn't. Allie rolled onto her hands and knees and made her way to it. The inset panels weren't really panels with stiles and rails. Each side of the door was molded to resemble a paneled door to create a "fake" paneled door.

Had the original door been replaced because it was damaged?

Steve crouched next to her. "This door is different. Newer."

She sighed. "Still no place to hide anything as far as I can tell."

"Except—" his gaze narrowed "—some newer doors, like this one, are called hollow core. They're mostly hollow on the inside with just a little wood here and there for holding the whole thing together." He ran his fingers along the edge, between the floor and the bottom of the door. Then he stood, went for the ladder they'd been using and stationed it next to the door. He climbed up and inspected the top.

"Anything?"

The smile that spread across his face answered the question. "There's wood, maybe an inch or so thick, typically across the top and bottom for stability. But a section has been removed here." He tapped the top. "Very carefully removed."

"Do you see anything in there?" Her pulse started to beat faster. It was about time they got a break.

Using the forefingers of both hands, he probed the space, eventually pulling out a plastic bag that had been taped inside. "Not your typical hiding place," he noted, "but certainly effective."

Apparently nothing about her parents had been typical.

He stepped down from the ladder and passed her the plastic slide bag. Allie settled on the bed and opened it. A white envelope folded over photographs was all that it contained.

Heart racing at the possibilities, she shuffled through the photographs. There were three couples total, all three in one photo, one or two in each of the others. Her parents and two other couples she didn't recognize. The photos appeared to have been taken during outings or get-togethers of some sort. Their clothing was casual… smiles on their faces.

"Let me see that again." Steve pointed to one of the photos she held.

She passed it to him. It was a photograph of a couple she didn't recognize. She stared at the remaining three. Why would these be hidden so carefully? What was the relevance of the photos? Location? The people? There were no objects in the setting that appeared wrong or out of place. Were they playing some private couples' sex game they feared these photos would point to? Allie didn't see how. They all looked completely innocent to her.

"This—" Steve tapped the man in the photo "—guy looks familiar."

Allie leaned closer and studied the face. "Wait. You're right. I think maybe…"

She got to her feet. "I need my laptop."

Steve was right behind her as she hurried to her office. She opened her laptop and pulled up the most recent file she'd sent to her email. She'd saved what she was able to find on Thomas Madison there.

The row of images were from Madison's career at Ledwell over the years. She pointed to the oldest photo, where he appeared the youngest. "That's him."

The man in the photos—in two of the photos found in her parents' hidden place—was a younger Thomas Madison.

Her gaze settled on Steve's. "He and my parents were friends."

Steve pointed to the photo. "Is the woman his wife? A girlfriend?"

"His wife died three years ago." She selected another photo in the file. The woman pictured there certainly looked very much like the one in the photo. Older, of course. "It could be her."

"What have you found about her?" He shifted his attention to her laptop.

"Her name was Jane. Maiden name Talbert. Died three years ago." She shrugged. "That's it."

Another dead end.

"Do a search on Talbert. See if she has any surviving family."

A few clicks of the keys and lines of search results spilled onto the screen. "Here we go." Allie selected the one for Jane Talbert in Woodstock, which helped to narrow the results significantly considering the size of her little town.

Steve leaned toward the screen, a hand braced on her desk, while he read over her shoulder. She wished she could claim not to be affected by his nearness—this certainly wasn't the time—but she was undeniably affected. Warmth spread through her body. He made her feel… safe…alive.

"Father is deceased," he said, his jaw so close to her cheek. "No mention of her mother."

Allie forced herself to focus on the screen. She opened another tab and tapped on the obituary for Jane Talbert Madison listed on the new webpage. "No children. The obit mentions no surviving family at all other than her husband, Thomas Madison." Allie frowned. "But her mother's name isn't mentioned. Just the names of her father and siblings, who died before her. I suppose it could have been an oversight."

"Let's have a look at any property owned by Jane or her father," Steve suggested.

Allie opened another tab and went to the official county property search site. A few taps of the keys later and she had just one listing on screen. The property was different from the one listed as Thomas Madison's home. A look into transfers and Allie figured out it was the property owned by the wife's father that she had inherited more than thirty years ago. Again, no mention of her mother.

"She inherited this property about five years before my parents died," Allie noticed, saying as much out loud.

"Which means your parents may have visited the Madisons there. You may have as well."

"Only one way to find out." Allie closed her laptop. "Let's have a look."

"You'd make a great investigator," Steve said as he followed her out of her office.

Allie laughed. "I may have been guided toward where I needed to look by someone with considerable experience."

He chuckled. "We all start somewhere."

She couldn't help thinking again how lucky she was to have him helping her out with this total mystery that had descended upon her life.

She just hoped that, however this ended, it wouldn't be the conclusion of this rekindled friendship.

If she was really lucky it would be just the beginning.

She almost laughed out loud. *Wishful thinking, Al.*

Talbert/Madison Residence
Justen Road
McHenry, Illinois, 7:00 p.m.

THE PROPERTY WAS around half an hour away from Allie's home.

But it was not what she had expected at all. The twenty acres had been listed on the county map, but the house was totally different from what she'd envisioned. It was a massive barn that had been renovated into a home. Those sorts of renovations had become popular in recent years, but it seemed unexpected three decades back. Maybe the Madisons had been ahead of their time where home design was concerned. Or perhaps Mr. Talbert had done the renovations before giving it to his daughter.

As they parked, Allie noted a good many other details. The place was a little rundown. Slightly overgrown. It looked as if no one had been here in years. Made sense, she supposed, since Madison's wife had been dead for three years. Maybe he hadn't found the time or the desire to see after the property. They had moved to their most recent residence twenty-nine years ago.

Steve parked. "You want to get out? We still have some daylight left."

Allie nodded. They were here. Might as well have a look around.

She almost smiled at the idea. Though she rarely left the house, he somehow managed to have her ready for all sorts of adventures. Just went to show that you could do whatever necessary when thrust into a situation like this one.

Maybe all she'd needed this whole time to come out of her protective shell was someone to be adventurous with. Or perhaps the more likely scenario was that deep down she wanted to impress him. She did not want this man to see her as a shut-in or a recluse...or a nobody.

What better way to prove the rumors untrue than to be adventurous?

The woods were thick all around the yard that had been carved from it. The house sat smack in the middle of that clearing, lending even more privacy to the structure since only the driveway made any sort of path through the thick circle of trees. Based on the aerial view she'd seen on the county listing, more woods and some pastureland rolled out behind the yard and the house.

They emerged from the SUV and walked to the front door. Sunlight filtered through the massive windows along the side of the house as they passed, allowing her to see inside. There was furniture. Did that mean someone lived here? Maybe. A ring of the doorbell and a knock on the door garnered no response. A repeat of both resulted in the same.

A cautious walk around back found more needed maintenance for the home and landscape and no sign of human habitation. How strange that the house had been seemingly abandoned with all its contents. Didn't people usually take their things or sell them when moving?

Allie studied the outside of the house. She suddenly felt jittery, and she had no idea why...until she discovered the large pavilion—a gazebo-like structure detached from the back of the house and almost hidden in the trees. The fading sunlight trickled through the vines and shady branches that grew over it. Something about the way the faint light dappled through and formed shapes tugged at her memory.

"I know this place."

The words she whispered were so soft she doubted Steve had heard her, but she was lost in a memory she couldn't quite capture. Some elusive slip of something she recognized but couldn't grab on to.

Allie walked around, studying the wood structure with all its vines and overgrown shrubs. The wood was failing in places, screaming for attention.

"You believe you've been here before?" Steve appeared next to her.

"I don't know...but it feels like I have." She turned to him. "You know that feeling of having been somewhere, but you can't quite place it? Maybe I saw it in photos. If my parents had been here, then there were likely photos. My grandmother said my mother loved taking photos."

"Then let's take our time." He assessed the yard that

spilled beyond the trees to a fenced pasture. "We'll walk the grounds and then come back to the house and have a look through any window we can reach."

She was moving before he finished speaking, her mind searching for a place to land. A place that some part of her recognized.

At one time, the property had been beautifully landscaped. The long-neglected shrubs were not the sort to be found growing wild. Many boasted scattered blooms that spoke of their beauty. Others were just beginning to bud. Stacks of stones and boulders guided them into other little venues designed for outdoor use. Tables and benches dotted the landscape, most badly in need of maintenance.

In the center of it all was a massive swimming pool that sat half full of dark green water. The pool had an hourglass shape. Allie could imagine that at one time it had been gorgeous. A path that meandered from the pool toward the woods circled a large three-tiered fountain. Around the base of the fountain were rose bushes. Some struggled to bloom, but most were overgrown with weeds, the leaves speckled with holes from whatever insect had decided to feed on them. So sad.

She wandered back to the house. The windows on the first floor didn't prompt any additional feelings of recognition. But she peered at length through each one nonetheless. It was almost dark by the time she felt she had seen anything potentially relevant to the fleeting memory that tugged at her.

"You need to see anything else?" Steve's patience seemed endless.

Her own patience had run out, but she took one last

lingering look around. "I think I've seen all I need to. Whatever I feel like I remember, I can't quite capture it."

"You want to grab dinner at a drive-through on the way back to your house?"

She paused at the front of his SUV. "Works for me."

She hadn't placed a delivery order for groceries in a while. The offerings in her fridge and pantry were likely sparse.

IT WAS DARK when they reached Woodstock. She insisted that Steve choose the fast food. Burgers and fries were his choice, and she was so thankful. She could use all those carbs right now. She wouldn't have selected a burger joint for fear of insulting his culinary senses. He looked so fit. She suspected he ate only the healthiest items on a menu. It was good to know he was an occasional let's-eat-the-greasy-stuff guy.

It was also nice to know he wasn't totally perfect. No matter that he seemed completely perfect to her.

"What does your girlfriend think of you staying with an old friend for a few days?" She suspected he wasn't married since there was no ring or mention of a wife, but surely there was someone.

If she hadn't been completely exhausted and floating in anticipation from the scent of those fries wafting from the bag on the console between them, she might have done a better job of filtering herself.

Too late to regret the question now.

He glanced at her. "I do not have a girlfriend or a wife." He exhaled an audible breath as if saying so saddened him somehow. "I've been so focused on the agency for the past few years there really hasn't been a lot of time for a social life."

"A totally overused excuse," she told him straight up, feeling bolder now, maybe because she was almost home and he was...*single*. "Try again."

He glanced at her, grinned. "I've dated. Just haven't found the right one."

"Is that because you're too picky?" This was also a seriously overused excuse.

He laughed then. "Maybe. How about you? Are you too picky or just too busy?"

No one to blame but herself for creating the corner into which he'd just backed her. "I'm not sure I've even considered a social life. Not since college anyway." She shrugged, thinking back to the last time she actually thought about dating. "I had lunch with someone a couple of times before I left the hospital. Not really anything since. I guess I'm just a loner." She laughed. "Wow. That's pretty sad. Almost ten years with no tangible social life."

"We're busy," he repeated as he navigated into her driveway. "You had your grandmother to take care of. I was finishing law school."

"That's such a lie," she suggested with a soft laugh. "Personally, I think it's easier to believe I'm too busy than to put myself out there and risk... I don't know. Rejection? Dissatisfaction? Total emotional gutting?"

He shot her a look. "You may have a point." He parked and shut off the engine. "You're what? Thirty-two? I'm thirty-three. Going forward, we should make ourselves a priority. I'm game if you are."

"All right, Dr. Phil. I can do that."

They both had a good laugh at that one. Laughter was good. She, for one, had needed a decent laugh.

Steve unlocked the door and went inside first to ensure there was nothing amiss. Allie kind of enjoyed the chivalry. It was a pleasant change from doing everything herself. He was a nice guy. Even nicer now, she decided.

Again, she considered how fortunate she was that they had reconnected, in spite of the reason.

While he unbagged their dinner, she went to the bookcase where her grandmother had kept all the family photo albums. That memory she couldn't quite grab from the gray matter deep in her head had nudged her all the way home.

She sat down on the floor and picked up first one and then the next album, flipping through the pages looking for something she couldn't name.

Then she paused, her fingers on the edge of a page she'd been ready to turn. "Found it!"

Steve joined her on the floor. She moved the album to where he could see the photos as well. There were several pages of two of the couples, the Madisons and her parents, all photographed at the Madison/Talbert property.

"Wow," she said, "it was really beautiful back then. I knew I'd seen it somewhere."

"But why hide the photos we found in that closet door and not these?" Steve studied the photos. "It had to be about the third couple—the mystery couple—or surely these photos would have been hidden as well."

He was right. That third couple was the only different aspect in the photos. Made sense.

Allie turned to him. "We need to figure out who the

third couple is, and maybe we'll learn some part of the story."

"You took the words right out of my mouth."

She stared at his lips, thought of how he would taste.

"But first—" he hitched his head toward the dining room "—we need to eat those cold burgers and fries."

"Oh." She grimaced at herself for staring at his lips. "Sorry about that. I got completely caught up in figuring out where I'd seen the place before and lost all track of time."

He stood and offered his hand to assist her in getting up. "The wine will help the fries go down easier."

Allie grabbed his hand and pulled herself up. She glanced at the table. He'd found her stash and opened a new bottle of red. The flush of embarrassment crept over her cheeks.

"You know I really don't drink that much. I just believe in having plenty on hand in case of an emergency."

"It's always best to be prepared." He grinned at her. "I have my own stash exactly like that at home."

Her heart took an extra beat. Preparation was important. She'd always believed so. She really liked that he did too.

But after years of self-imposed seclusion, she wasn't sure it was possible to be adequately prepared for this man.

Panic nudged at her...all the other thoughts she wanted to ignore closing in.

Or being suspected of murder.

Chapter Six

Sunday, June 8
Foster Residence
Ridgeland Avenue
Woodstock, 8:00 a.m.

Allie finished off her toast. It wasn't such a great breakfast, but when she had suggested it based on the offerings available, Steve claimed cheese toast was one of his favorites. The toast and coffee had done the trick for her. She wasn't a huge breakfast fan anyway. Her typical days consisted of brunch and dinner. As for the menu, like this morning, it was generally driven by whatever was in the house. Or something she had delivered if she was feeling the urge.

She really needed to get better organized. Her grandmother had always taken care of running the kitchen. Until she was no longer physically able to do so, she had insisted that it was her domain. Allie could be in charge of all the rest, but she was to leave the kitchen to her grandmother. It was great until her grandmother could no longer handle the job. Then Allie had just felt guilty for being inept at kitchen duties. Her culinary skills still left much to be desired.

During her grandmother's illness, Allie had tried to

carry on with the usual menu items. Her grandmother had many cookbooks with dog-eared pages. But once she was gone, sandwiches and microwave meals became the norm.

Maybe Steve was right. Allie should focus a little more on herself.

Working at home made the concept more difficult, in her opinion. It was far easier to pull on a pair of sweats and tuck her hair into a ponytail and not care. Who would see her? No one. And the whole cooking for one was not as simple or as stress-free as it sounded.

Steve glanced at his cell, answered an incoming call and wandered out of the kitchen. Allie cleared away the paper plates—another bad habit of hers—and wiped off the table.

Who wanted to wash dishes for one? There was a dishwasher, but it would take days to load it with enough items to feel it wasn't wasteful to turn it on.

Just another excuse.

She had to admit it had been nice to fall asleep last night knowing someone else was in the house. Even nicer to wake up and share coffee and toast with a really smart, handsome man who…

Okay, slow down, Al.

She shook off the random thoughts and rinsed their coffee mugs, then placed them on the drainer.

Steve came back to the door, his call obviously completed. "That was my mother. She insists we come to dinner. You okay with that?"

For one moment, fear paralyzed her. What would she wear? What would Mrs. Durham think of her now? Would she believe Allie capable of murder? The story hadn't been in the news yet as far as she knew, which surprised her, but still people talked in small towns. His mother lived here. She would no doubt hear all the rumors and gossip.

Allie faked a smile and nodded with pretend enthusiasm. "Sure."

"We'll take the photo of the mystery couple," he suggested, completely undaunted by the idea. "Mom or Dad might know who they are."

"Good idea." He'd sent a copy to one of his colleagues. Hopefully between that person and the Durhams they would learn the identity of the mystery couple. The fact that the photos with that couple were hidden seemed to imply some sort of secret.

But who knew if it was related to anything. It could be a waste of time.

Allie breathed a little easier about having dinner with Steve's family. All she had to do was focus on the issue at hand. Everything else would work out.

"You ready?" he asked when she lingered at the sink.

She pushed aside the worries and shifted her attention to where it belonged. "Absolutely."

They were taking another field trip—this one to Thomas Madison's most recent home. Maybe they would notice something the federal agents had not. Like some clue that pointed to the truth.

Probably wishful thinking.

Madison Residence
Hamilton Road
Woodstock, 9:30 a.m.

THE MADISON HOME was neglected like the Madison/Talbert property. Not quite as overgrown but utterly rundown with lots of deferred maintenance.

The place was well off the beaten path. The home stood a good distance back from the road, at least a mile, amid eighty acres of wooded land, according to the county property records. Obviously it was an expansive property. The nearest house on either side of the road was quite a distance away, but there was one directly across the road from the long driveway.

Also like the other property, the house was an older one. Not a refurbished barn this time but one of those boxy modern styles with too many angles and lots of windows so popular in the 70s and 80s. Since it sat where the property sloped downward on one side, there appeared to be a walk-out basement level.

It was unusually warm today. Allie was grateful for the shade of the generous number of trees around the house. She and Steve climbed the steps to the front stoop, which was too narrow to officially be called a porch, and rang the bell. The light above the door was on as if waiting for the owner to return. She put her hands on either side of her eyes and peered through the glass sidelight next to the double set of doors.

A foyer led directly into a large, open-concept room with a soaring ceiling. Wood beams, wood floors. Exactly what one would expect in a home of this style and era. It was furnished the same way, with some modern-looking pieces.

No one came to the door since the owner was lying on a stainless-steel slab at the morgue. He had no family to take over the property, much less to claim him or to see to his final arrangements.

Infinitely sad.

Allie suddenly realized she was in that same boat. No

next of kin. No close friends. All her work associates were nothing more than voices on radio waves bouncing off cell towers.

She drew back mentally, banished the sad thought. Not exactly reaffirming.

Steve walked down the steps and started around the corner of the house, and Allie followed. In addition to the garage that was part of the house structure, there was a detached garage. Beyond that was what might be a barn. Not big and tall like the older ones, but something more modern and space conscious with a lower roof line.

The two of them peered through each first-floor window just as they had at the other house. The more they looked, the more obvious it was that the house had been thoroughly searched. Drawers either weren't quite closed all the way or sat askew. Items atop those same pieces of furniture sat in no particular arrangement. Pillows and cushions on the sofa and chairs were not fully tucked into place. All appeared *out* of place. As she had thought, on the one end where the ground sloped, there was a lower level that opened to the outside with windows and French doors. The shades or blinds were drawn tight over those windows as well as the doors.

There was nothing about the property that felt familiar to Allie. Nothing at all.

"I don't recall any of the photos having been taken here," Steve mentioned.

"I was just thinking the same thing. Most were in public places, at our house or at the house on Justen. This is such a large property I'm surprised they didn't do hikes or picnics or something here." She supposed they could have and for whatever reason hadn't taken photos that day. It was a very attractive property, discounting the needed maintenance, particularly if one was a nature lover.

"Let's check out the detached garage and barn."

Allie followed him, still wondering why no photos had been taken here. It really was the perfect setting. They had moved here an entire year before her parents died, so it wasn't because it had been unavailable to them at the time.

The detached garage was unlocked. Although they had no official business here and certainly no legal right, Allie needed to look. Before she could say as much, Steve opened the door and they went inside. The electricity was still on, so the flip of a switch provided the necessary light to survey the interior. Inside were the tools found in most home workshops. Those for making repairs around the house as well as a few for vehicle maintenance. Nothing that personalized the space. No photos or calendars or brand memorabilia hanging on the walls.

The low roof-line barn was their next destination. Inside were stalls for horses but no indication horses had ever been there. The floors were clean. No leftover animal droppings or deteriorating straw or hay. No gear for riding horses in the tack room. The barn looked as if it had never been used for any purpose.

From there, they returned to the house.

"I guess we've seen all there is to see," Steve commented, "unless we opt to do a little breaking and entering. Bearing in mind the Bureau and the police have both likely searched the place already, I don't see any reason to cross that line. Yet, anyway."

Allie glanced around. "I'm with you on that one. I suppose we could have a look under some of these flowerpots. They don't appear to have been disturbed recently, and there's a lot of them." She smiled with a memory. "My grandmother used to hide a house key under one. Sometimes when we played games, she would hide clues under the flowerpots."

This was probably a task that really would prove a waste of time, but why not give it a shot?

Steve considered her at length, his expression serious. "I really do like the way you think, ma'am. Your grandmother too."

She laughed. "You can let me know if you still believe that when we're done and all the spiders who probably call those pots home have shown their displeasure."

The clay and ceramic pots were in various sizes and styles as well as colors. The plants in each were long dead. Allie resisted the urge to dump the contents just in case something was buried in all that potting soil.

Just because the FBI and cops had been here already didn't mean they wouldn't be coming back. No one would be happy with the news that Allie and Steve had been on the property having a look. Disturbing anything at all that would be easily noticed wouldn't be smart. They hadn't broken into anything—technically. But they were trespassing, and the foray into the garage was not exactly a legal move. Maybe not the barn either, no matter that it was fully open with only stall gates on one side.

She kind of liked that Steve wasn't afraid to stretch the boundaries. Another indication that he wasn't so perfect or so uptight.

The fact was she liked everything about him.

The distinct sound of an engine and then a car door slamming had them both lowering the pots they held.

The next sound they heard was someone shouting, "Hello." Female.

"Stay here." Steve walked around the end of the house toward the voice.

Allie wasn't inclined to follow orders at the moment, so she did the same, ensuring that he was well ahead of her and didn't notice.

A woman stood next to a white sedan. She held a shotgun braced against one shoulder, but the barrel was extended toward the ground. "This is private property," she stated, looking directly at Steve.

"Yes, ma'am." Steve came to a stop at the front corner of the house. His arms hung loosely at his sides. His hands visibly open. "My name is Steve Durham. I work for a private investigations firm, the Colby Agency, and I'm following up on Mr. Thomas Madison's death."

This was true. Mostly.

The woman leaned to one side and peered past him. "Is this your colleague?"

Allie came to stand beside him. "My name is Allie Foster. Mr. Madison was a friend of my family. I'm the one who hired Mr. Durham."

The woman was older than she had looked from a distance. Closer to seventy than sixty. She was trim and well dressed. Her light-colored hair was actually a very flattering shade of gray. And she appeared quite fearless.

"The FBI and the police have been here already," she said. "I can't imagine what you hope to find."

"We have a photo," Steve said, "if you wouldn't mind taking a look. It's a couple who associated with the Madisons, and we're attempting to identify them. We believe knowing who they are might be very helpful to our investigation."

She hitched her head for them to come to her, but she didn't put down the shotgun. "I'll have a look."

Steve went first. Allie stayed close behind him.

"Do you live nearby?" Allie wondered how this woman had known they were here.

"I live across the road. I saw you turn into the driveway. My husband and I always kept a watch on the place for Thomas. He traveled a lot with his work."

"You've been neighbors a long while," Steve suggested.

"We were here when he and Jane bought the place."

"You knew Jane well?" Allie hoped for more information on the other property.

"Well enough," the woman said without further explanation. She reached for the photo Steve held. She studied it for several seconds, then shook her head. "I don't recall ever seeing them." She handed the photo back to him. "Why do you want to find them? The photo is obviously quite old."

Allie took another photo from her purse and handed it to the woman. This one was of her parents. "What about this couple?"

The woman stared at the photo for a while, her face blank. Then she shook her head. "Never seen them before either." She passed the photo back to Allie. "Again, why are you trying to find people in old photographs?"

"We have reason to believe they may have information," Steve said. "It's important that we find them."

"I have no idea who they are. Now, obviously you've had your look around, so you need to go. I don't want to have to call the police and report the suspicious activity."

She kept her gaze on Steve. Wouldn't look at Allie. The idea that this woman way lying about not knowing the people pictured in those photos had a stranglehold on Allie.

"Alice and Jerry Foster," she said to the woman, ignoring her edict and waving the photo again. "They were my parents."

The woman blinked, then reluctantly dragged her gaze back to Allie. "I'm sorry for your loss, but I never saw them before."

"Did Thomas live here alone?" Steve asked, drawing them past the awkward moment.

"After his wife... Jane died," the nosy neighbor confirmed, "he almost never came home anymore."

Allie fired another question at her. "Did he sometimes stay at the McHenry property Jane's father gave them?"

The neighbor stared long and hard at Allie then. "I have no idea. I don't know anything about that property."

"Like this one," Steve said, "it looks abandoned. Overgrown. Didn't Thomas have someone to take care of the place?"

"There was a man who did the lawn mowing and things like that," she said, "but I haven't seen him in a while."

"Do you know his name?" Allie asked.

The woman shook her head. "I never spoke to him myself. Just saw his truck coming and going."

"When was the last time you saw him here?" Steve prodded.

She shrugged. "Maybe a month ago."

"There was no business info on his truck?" he asked.

Good question.

"Nothing. Just a plain white truck pulling a black trailer with a riding lawnmower parked on it."

"I have a business card I'd like to give you." When she didn't argue, he reached for his wallet and removed one. "I hope you'll call me if you think of anything else that might be useful in our search for the truth."

She accepted the card but frowned at the question. "What truth?"

"The truth about who murdered Mr. Madison," Steve explained. "I'm sure you and your husband will feel safer when that person is identified and brought to justice."

Another series of slow blinks. "Yes, of course."

"Do you know what happened to Jane's mother?" Allie asked. "Her father passed away, but there was no mention of her mother."

The neighbor looked startled at the question. "Luellyn. Luellyn Talbert. She and her husband were estranged, but I don't think they ever officially divorced. She had nothing to do with the family."

"Is she still alive?" Allie wasn't sure yet why it mattered, but she needed to check off that box.

"As far as I know. The last time Thomas mentioned her, he said she was a resident at Our Home, an assisted-living facility on the other side of town. She's been there a good many years. Maybe seven or eight." She frowned. "Why would you want to know about Jane's mother?"

"We want to know about anyone who may have any insights into Madison's final weeks of life." Allie felt confident the woman understood this but wanted to ask just to get a response. "Or who might be able to identify the couple in the photograph I showed you."

The neighbor nodded, the vaguest of movements.

"Thank you, Mrs...?" Steve shook his head. "I'm sorry, I didn't catch your name."

"Gayle Fischer. My husband Frank and I live across the road."

"Thank you for speaking with us, Mrs. Fischer," Steve went on. "We're doing all we can to figure this out."

"Isn't that the job of the police or these FBI people who've been coming around?" She looked suspect of Steve and Allie's motive for being on the property.

"I'm sure both the police and the FBI appreciate any help they can get."

She made a maybe-so face. "I'll talk to my husband. See if he has anything to pass along."

"Thank you," Steve said.

Fischer, still holding on to her shotgun, loaded back into her car. Before turning the vehicle around, she took a last, long look at Allie.

When the neighbor had driven away, Allie turned to Steve. "She knows me or my parents. Her reaction to their photo was different from her reaction to the mystery couple."

"I noticed."

"Should we drive over and talk to her husband?" Allie's pulse had started to race. These were people who may have known her parents. There were so many things she wanted to ask. So much she apparently needed to know.

"Not just now. We should go see Mrs. Talbert. If the FBI hasn't interviewed her yet, we have a far better chance at learning anything she may know."

Something else Allie liked about this man. He was really intuitive and could see the bigger picture.

He was exactly what she had needed to get through this.

Chapter Seven

Our Home
Route 14
Woodstock, 11:30 a.m.

The assisted-living facility looked nothing like Allie expected. As lovely as the wood and stone facade was, the landscaping along with the nature setting was what set it apart from the average property of its kind. The building sat back in a vast estate well off the road. Water features and living sculptures dominated the entrance. The cobblestone parking area gave the feel of a European resort.

Completely unexpected.

The lobby was a flurry of activity. With it being Sunday, there were lots of visitors. Again, the medicinal smell she'd expected was pleasantly absent.

Steve provided their names at the reception desk, and they were given visitor badges and directions to Mrs. Talbert's room. They had no idea about her physical or mental condition, but the fact that she was in assisted living versus a more comprehensive care facility offered hope that she might be able to answer questions.

When they reached her room, which was in the Caribbean wing, Steve pressed the doorbell. Since the resident they had come to see was ninety-three, they waited patiently for an answer rather than tapping the doorbell again after only a few moments.

Extra patience, Allie reminded herself, was sometimes necessary to reach a goal.

Steve checked his cell. Allie glanced around the corridor, appreciating the wall of windows opposite the long line of doors. Lots of sunshine and more of that purposefully manicured landscaping for the residents.

The shuffling sound on the other side of the door drew Allie's attention back there and suggested the lady had arrived at last. A rattling sound and then the click of a lock preceded the opening of the door. Allie drew in a deep breath and braced for whatever she might learn next.

Luellyn Talbert was not tall like her daughter, though part of the reason might be age. Her hair was white and woven into a loose bun. But it was her vibrant green eyes that reminded Allie of Jane Talbert Madison. Their eyes were exactly the same.

"Mrs. Talbert," Steve said with a charming smile, "it's very nice to meet you." He offered his hand. "I'm Steve Durham, and this is my friend, Allie Foster."

He'd changed his opening to something less official this time. Good strategy.

Luellyn placed her thin hand in his and gave it a shake. "Nice to meet you as well." She looked to Allie. Her gaze narrowed. "You look so familiar. Do I know you, dear?"

Hope budded in Allie's chest. "I believe you knew my mother, Alice Foster."

Mrs. Talbert's mouth opened in surprise. "Why, yes. Alice was Jane's friend. You look exactly like her."

"Thank you." She liked when people told her this.

"May we come in and visit with you?" Steve asked.

"I don't see why not." She turned and shuffled deeper into her room. "Come along and find a seat."

Steve waited for Allie to go first. The room was far more like the main living area of a small apartment. There was a tiny kitchen and dining nook as well as a generously sized living space. A small hall to the far left led to additional doors, likely the more private spaces, while the window-filled wall directly across the main living space looked out over the large well-appointed courtyard that separated the various resident wings. Allie doubted that all the little apartments had such a view. French doors provided access to that area.

Luellyn settled into what was obviously her preferred chair. Allie chose the twin chair. The two were separated by a table. Steve made himself comfortable on the sofa.

"If you've come to ask me about Thomas," the elderly woman said, "you've come to the wrong place. Thomas and I didn't get along. He didn't like me, and the feeling was mutual." She lifted one frail shoulder in a shrug. "Perhaps in the beginning we were fine. It's just hard to remember any good times since they were so very long ago."

"Actually—" Allie reached into her purse "—I was hoping you could tell me who these people are." She first passed along the photo of all three couples. "My parents and the Madisons I recognize, of course. It's the other couple I don't know."

Luellyn took her eyeglasses from the table next to her and propped them into place. After a time, she nodded, her attention fixed on the photograph. "This was taken at the house my husband gave Jane as a wedding present." She looked to Allie. "Jane held the most wonderful social gatherings there—the home was certainly well suited for such things. The floor plan was perfect for having a big family too. We all fell in love with the possibilities it offered. But they didn't live there very long. Not after what happened."

Allie and Steve exchanged a look.

"Would you share with us what happened?" Steve asked.

Mrs. Talbert blinked. She looked to Allie as if she had asked the question or maybe because she felt more comfortable addressing her since her mother had been Jane's friend. "Little Tommy died there."

"Tommy?" Allie held her breath. She'd found no mention of a Tommy in any of her research. Since Steve hadn't mentioned anyone by that name, he likely hadn't either.

"My grandson. Jane's only child." Mrs. Talbert smiled sadly. "He was only three years old. Such a precious, sweet little child. He was the spitting image of his father, other than his eyes. He had my daughter's vibrant green eyes. Jane and Thomas were so proud of him. In those days, Thomas would have died happy for no other reason than the blessing of that child." She looked away a moment. "But he didn't die. Our sweet Tommy did."

Suddenly the numerous framed photos around the room of a little boy came into vivid focus. Photos Allie had skimmed minutes ago without really registering. The child had big green eyes like his mother and thick black hair like his father. Now, Allie also noticed a young Jane and Thomas in one of the photos. Allie had been so focused on the woman, Luellyn, she'd paid scarcely any attention to the rest.

Allie waited for Mrs. Talbert to go on, while part of her already regretted having asked the question.

"It was the swimming pool. He sneaked out. Made his way to the pool...fell in and..." She exhaled a weary breath. "Jane tried to save him, but it was too late. As if that misery was not enough to bear, she had just found out she was pregnant with their second child, but the trauma caused a miscarriage. Jane was never the same afterward. Nothing I could do. God knows I tried. Nothing her father or Thomas could do. A few months later, Thomas moved them to a different home and then everything changed. He became secretive. Jane said he was rarely home. Always at work. Her father and I had to have an appointment to see Jane. Thomas didn't want us just showing up. It was very strange."

"What a terrible time that must have been," Allie said, though the word *terrible* didn't even begin to describe how devastating it must have been.

Mrs. Talbert nodded, the move barely visible. "When I refused to go along with his rules, Thomas cast me out. Said I could no longer see Jane, and when I refused to obey his edict, he took out a restraining order. Claimed all sorts of lies about my behavior. It was a nightmare."

Allie couldn't even imagine.

"What about your husband?" Steve asked. "Did he receive the same treatment?"

"He did and..." She inhaled a deep breath as if to fortify herself. "...that was the end of us. He blamed me for the loss of our daughter, and maybe he was right."

Allie would never understand that sort of behavior toward a good parent, and what this woman was describing was a caring mother desperate to help her daughter. Allie would give most anything to have had her parents growing up, which raised another question. "Why didn't Jane stop him?"

The flash of hurt in the older woman's eyes shamed Allie. "I'm sorry. I shouldn't have asked."

Luellyn waved a hand. "No. It's all right. That was a long time ago, and although I will never stop feeling the loss, I have learned to live with it. What choice did I have?" She appeared to think a moment about what she wanted to say next. "But to answer your question, for a while Jane and I had secret rendezvous." A slight smile returned to her lips. "We talked and cried together. It was sad that we had to hide this from Thomas, but it was the only way it seemed. The year after…we, she and I, had a little birthday celebration for Tommy."

She fell silent for a moment, the memory obviously difficult. "The last time I saw her was right after that celebration. She told me not to worry anymore, that Thomas had come up with a plan that would make everything all right. I tried to question her about it, but she said she couldn't talk about the details." She drifted into silence again for a beat, then two. "I never saw her again after that day. I tried going to their house when Thomas was at work, but no one answered the door. I called, but the phone number was changed to an unlisted one."

"Was Jane also having secret meetings with her father?" Steve asked.

"She would never say, and my husband, of course, wouldn't tell me anything. But after she went into seclusion, he came to see me and said he was worried about whatever Thomas was doing, so I'm thinking that perhaps he found a way to see her at least once more. Then, the next thing I knew, he'd had a heart attack and was gone."

"You suffered such losses during that time," Allie offered. "It must have been difficult for you."

"No one knows what it's like to lose a living child unless they've experienced it."

"Do you believe Thomas was somehow working all that time to turn your daughter against you and her father? Perhaps it finally kicked in." Steve glanced at Allie as he asked this.

"The way I feel about Thomas Madison," Mrs. Talbert said with a sharp point to her tone, "I would love to say yes, but I believe there was some other reason. I think he was doing something to keep Jane happy and that he felt we wouldn't understand. I know he loved my daughter. But he eventually isolated her completely." She gestured to Allie. "Your mother was Jane's best friend. Not long after Jane shut me out completely, your parents were shut out as well. Alice came to talk to me about how sad it made her. She too mentioned being concerned that Thomas was…" She pinched her lips together as if to think a moment. "The term she used was 'out of control.' She promised to keep me posted about Jane, but less than a month later, she and Jerry had that horrible, horrible accident."

The idea that Thomas Madison may have had something to do with the accident caused an uncomfortable twinge to creep up Allie's spine.

When the silence dragged on a bit too long, Allie said, "Thank God for my grandparents. They took very good care of me."

She wanted to ask what efforts Mrs. Talbert had made for the next twenty years to try and reach her daughter, but it felt wrong to keep picking at that painful wound.

"You never said—" Allie nodded to the photograph Luellyn still held "—if you recognized the third couple."

"Aw, yes." Mrs. Talbert nodded, attempted a smile, then adjusted her glasses and focused on the photo once more. "Hmm. They do look vaguely familiar." She cocked her head, first one way and then the other. "Wait, I know. They were at Jane's Christmas party the same year this photo was taken." She looked to Allie. "A couple of years before your parents had their accident, I believe. Before my grandson died."

"Do you recall their names?"

Luellyn pursed her lips. "She was Lucille, and I believe her husband was Dennis." She shook her head. "But for the life of me I can't recall the last name. The only reason I remember her first name is the red hair. I thought of Lucille Ball when she was introduced to me. You can't really see her eyes in this photo, but she had the same bright blue eyes too."

Allie had thought the same thing when she first saw the photo. She'd certainly watched plenty of old Lucy episodes with her grandmother.

"Were they close with Jane and Thomas the way Allie's parents were?" Steve asked.

"They were new in town when I met them," Luellyn said. "I think the husband had just been hired by Ledwell."

"Do you recall if Lucille came to Jane's funeral?" Allie wasn't sure if the question would be uncomfortable for Luellyn, but it would certainly clarify whether the mystery couple had still been around as recently as three years ago. And it allowed her to ask if Luellyn had been at the funeral without actually asking. Surely Thomas Madison wouldn't have kept her from her own daughter's funeral.

"She was not. All the friends Jane made during her marriage were noticeably absent. It was a very small gathering. Not becoming of my precious daughter, I'll certainly say that. She would have invited everyone."

"Thomas must have spoken to you at some point during the service." Allie hoped this was the case. The idea of him ignoring her would only add to the horror that had been their shared history.

"He allowed me to sit in the front pew with him. He even hugged me when the service ended, but he said virtually nothing to me. He was anxious to get away, it seemed. Perhaps he had someone new already."

Painful. It happened that way sometimes. But there was nothing in the research Allie had done to suggest he'd had someone in his life even just before his death, three years after his wife's.

"Do you remember," Allie ventured, "Jane mentioning anything regarding my parents and the work at Ledwell? Or maybe some other problem with them?"

"Jane adored your mother," Luellyn said without hesitation. "The two did everything together. Tommy was just a year younger than you."

Allie hadn't considered that she and this Tommy were likely close in age. Maybe he was the reason she remembered the house with the pavilion and pool. Maybe they had played there together.

How sad it was that their families had been riddled with tragedy.

"I was there once when you and your mother visited. You and Tommy were going round and round outside, the sun trickling over your big smiles. It was such a nice day."

Allie felt her chest constrict. "Did my mother seem happy?" She put her fingers to her lips. She hadn't meant to ask the question. What difference did it make really? And yet, even after all these years, it was...still important to Allie. She felt confident her grandmother would have told her if her mother hadn't been happy, but having an objective observation would be useful.

Luellyn smiled at Allie. "How could she not be? She had a beautiful daughter. Her husband was the kindest man you would ever meet. Even Thomas often said that Jerry was far too kind for his own good. But to answer your question, yes, your mother seemed very happy. As did you. If there were any sort of problems, she gave no indication whatsoever."

Allie was profoundly relieved. "Thank you."

Luellyn's face fell as if she'd just remembered something that pained her. "I remember Thomas making some statement...later." She shrugged. "No wait, I'm wrong. This was perhaps a year after that day when you and Tommy were playing. Maybe days after the accident that took your parents' lives. Yes, that's right, just before what would have been Tommy's fourth birthday. Christmas was only a few weeks away."

"My fifth birthday was in the January after the accident," Allie said, hoping to help prompt her memory. "I don't even remember Thanksgiving since the accident had just happened. But I do remember that it was the worst Christmas and birthday of my life."

"Thanksgiving." Luellyn held up a finger as if to emphasize the point. "Yes. Jane and I got together that last time. This was when she mentioned Thomas having a plan. She also said something like Thomas thought Jerry had grown too much of a conscience. I didn't understand what she meant and said as much. But she ignored the comment and moved on. Her brain worked that way after Tommy's death. Skipped around and sometimes obsessed over seemingly unimportant things."

"Seems an odd statement to make." Steve pointed out exactly what Allie was thinking.

"It does." Luellyn nodded. "I have no idea what he meant, but I heard through the grapevine that Ledwell was having growing pains. Serious growing pains. With the nature of the work they did, back in those days, one can only imagine the sorts of things you had to be willing to overlook."

She had Allie's curiosity cued up now. "You mean like ethical challenges?"

Those appeared to be the biggest stumbling blocks today in the warp-speed research and development of AI. Many wanted to take a step back, to slow down the forward momentum until better ground rules could be established. Some wanted it stopped altogether.

"I suppose so," Luellyn agreed. "Without a conscience for our guide, what might we humans be capable of under certain circumstances?"

A bell chimed somewhere in the apartment.

"That's my cue," Luellyn said. "We have a special lunch on Sundays for anyone who no longer has family to visit—or just for anyone who wishes to attend." She stood. "I hope you'll forgive me, but I never miss our special lunches."

Steve and Allie stood as well. "Of course," he said. "We appreciate the time you've shared with us already."

"It was so very nice to meet the two of you." She looked from Steve to Allie. "I hope you find the answers you seek and that you'll share anything you find about my Jane with me."

"You have my word, Mrs. Talbert," Steve assured her.

Allie and Steve walked to the main restaurant with Luellyn and watched as she joined her friends. Allie admired that, despite all the sadness in her life, the woman had managed to find a way to go on.

"I sure hope I'm partying and socializing when I'm ninety-three," Steve said.

"She certainly sets a high bar," Allie agreed.

Allie suddenly wondered why she had allowed so much time to pass without jumpstarting her life beyond work.

Fear, she decided. Fear of the unknown. Fear of the uncertainty. Keeping her routine was far easier than putting herself out there and wondering what would work and what wouldn't.

She furtively watched Steve as they made their way back to his SUV. Somehow this man had her thinking a whole lot more about what she should be doing for herself. Thus, the sudden interest in the future.

How ironic. After all this time of hiding and pretending not to notice the world going on without her, she unexpectedly realized she was missing so much.

Just in time to be framed for murder.

Steve braked at the end of the long drive before turning onto the highway. He shot her a sideways glance. "You worried about what Madison said about your father?"

Allie pushed the other concern away and nodded. "The timing is tough to ignore." She bit her lip. "Do you think my father was against something Ledwell was doing? Maybe strongly enough to make himself a target? The same as the others involved with the SILO project?"

"If the crash was no accident," Steve began as he pulled out onto the highway, "then there had to be an impetus—something that motivated the step. When you consider the work Ledwell was doing—is still doing—it makes a great deal of sense that there would be issues from time to time. Those issues couldn't be allowed to become a real problem, if you know what I mean. No backing down. Not when you were racing against competitors to achieve something so big—something no one else has."

"Like the first robot to look human," she offered. "To act human?" The various companies involved would insist those sorts of things were not the primary goal and had only recently become actual priorities. But what if that was a lie? In Allie's opinion, based on her limited knowledge, it probably was.

"Something like that, yes. At this point, I think it's safe to assume that if your parents' car crash was not an accident then it had something to do with the work at Ledwell—with SILO. That can only mean the company was doing something not acceptable for the time. Whether it was illegal or not, it may have been something your father wasn't willing to turn a blind eye to.

And it was likely something the company wanted to keep secret."

"We need to find Lucille and Dennis." Allie needed someone who could tell them what had been going on at Ledwell twenty-eight years ago and why her father had to be silenced.

Was that also what had gotten Thomas Madison murdered? Had the burden of all those secrets suddenly grown too much for his conscience after all these years?

Chapter Eight

*Durham Residence
Club Road, 7:00 p.m.*

Steve would be the first to say that his family had never been the country club type, no matter what their address said about them. Martha, his mother, appreciated a nice home in a nice neighborhood that came with a good school district—no question about that. Quentin, his father, had gladly worked extra hard to see that his wife had the dream house she so wanted as they started their family.

The tri-level brick was far larger than they needed now that they were nearing retirement age, but they both loved the neighborhood so much neither would budge on downsizing. His mom insisted they were waiting on a smaller home in the same neighborhood to become available. Steve didn't see that happening anytime soon. It was that sort of neighborhood: people came and they put down permanent roots.

In the end, the decision to stay put turned out to be the right one when his older by two years sister, Amanda, ended up getting divorced and moving into the lower level with her two kids.

His mom could not be happier. The kids were in serious heaven because Nana and Papa rarely said no to any request.

For their special guest this evening, Steve's father had set up a buffet on the kitchen island. Everyone grabbed a plate, took a stroll around the island and filled it as they went. Then it was on to the dining room, where wine, water and lemonade for the boys waited.

When Steve had been a kid, both sets of grandparents were still alive, and his parents had believed in having a table large enough for the whole family to be together, thus the table for twelve.

Amanda and her kids sat on one side, Steve and Allie on the other with his parents at the ends. A family gathering was a nice change of pace. He hoped the camaraderie would help Allie relax a little after the intense forty-eight hours she'd endured. Either way, the food smelled great, and Steve felt confident Allie was as hungry as he was. He was glad for once his sister and her kids appeared focused on eating rather than arguing about who got to pick the after-dinner movie. With boys, one eight and one ten, getting through a meal without a battle was sometimes difficult, especially in the summer when there was no homework or time at school to have worn them out.

"Your mother and I were friends when we were kids," Quentin said to Allie.

She smiled. "Be careful, Mr. Durham, or I'll be asking you questions about her all night."

"Call me Quentin, please. As for questions, ask anything you'd like."

Allie nodded. "Quentin."

Steve cut into his steak, grateful that Allie appeared comfortable with his family. Family was important to him. He couldn't imagine being totally alone. That had to be difficult for her sometimes. As sure of that as he was, he hadn't missed how strong and seemingly resilient she was. He liked that about her.

Frankly, he liked a lot of things about her.

"Well," his mother spoke up, "I can tell you that Alice was a very nice woman who never met a stranger. When Quentin and I first married, I was a stranger to the neighborhood. I knew no one. Your mother went out of her way to be kind to me. Your grandmother too. Another lovely lady. And you should call me Martha." She flashed that signature smile of hers—the one that said everything was okay as long as you were here with her.

Steve was fairly certain he lacked any measure of objectivity, but his mother's smile was the kind that really could heal those wounds that couldn't be seen.

"Martha," Allie said. "Thank you. Do you recall much about my parents during the time just before the accident?"

Steve had known that question would be coming. "We spoke with someone," he explained before one or the other of his parents could respond, "who suggested there might have been issues with Allie's father and his work at Ledwell."

Quentin made a harrumphing sound. "Anyone involved with Ledwell generally had issues, particularly during that timeframe."

"How so?" Allie lowered her fork rather than taking the bite of salad there. She leaned slightly forward...intent on whatever words he planned to convey.

Quentin shared a glance with Martha. This look was also something Steve knew well. Did they say what was on their minds, or did they let it go? That brief, silent exchange was the pause they used to measure the worth of one decision over the other. The couple had been together so long they had this ability to communicate without words.

Steve couldn't help wondering if it was even possible to develop that kind of relationship these days. How amazing it must be to have that level of closeness.

"I don't mean to spoil this lovely dinner," Allie said when no one spoke, her cheeks flushing. "It's just important. Really important. At least to me."

"Of course it is." Martha reached out and gave Allie's hand a kind pat.

"There were rumors," Quentin said finally. "Rumors of bad things happening at Ledwell. The sort of things you might see in a science-fiction movie."

"Or a horror film," Martha put in. She shook her head. "There were protests outside the facility. People were spreading all sorts of frightening stories. It really was a scary time. That year—when your parents' accident happened—was particularly tumultuous. A number of employees had freak accidents—at home, not at work. One woman suffered a lethal electrical shock from her coffeemaker. Another man had an accident while fishing. They say he fell out of his boat and wasn't able to climb back in—yet he was a seasoned fisherman who always used a boat."

"And others," Quentin pointed out. "Obviously we can't say how your father felt about any of this or where he stood with the company. We can only say how concerned many in the community were about the company in general."

"It was an uncertain time," Martha agreed. "Ledwell employees and their families felt isolated—your mother told me this. They were looked upon as being culpable because of their employment. Alice said she couldn't go to the market without feeling as though everyone was staring at her with suspicion. Judging her for the company's perceived wrongs. It was a truly difficult period."

"Did you speak at length with her," Allie probed, "about her concerns? Did she say anything that may have led you to believe she was afraid?"

Martha stared at her plate for a moment. Steve hadn't considered how difficult this might be for his parents, his mother in particular. He was aware his parents had known Allie's parents…but maybe there was more they'd never said out loud before.

"The last time I spoke with her—" Martha lifted her gaze to Allie's "—Alice mentioned that she was very worried about her husband. She wouldn't say why, but I could tell she was, as you say, afraid."

"After the accident," Quentin picked up from there, "no one would talk about it. No one. Those of us not involved with Ledwell had no idea there was anything to talk about other than the tragedy of it and all the rumors buzzing around. Even twenty odd years later, we still don't for that matter. But when Steve told us you had concerns, Martha and I started to think back. There was something wrong about the whole situation related to that accident and the others that happened, but there's not a single comment, rumor, certainly not a headline I can put my finger on to explain the feeling. It was just a sudden series of blunt traumas that left a gaping hole in the community, and then it was as if it never happened. As if none of it ever occurred. In time, people stopped talking about it."

The way Allie's eyes shone now, Steve worried she was on the verge of tears.

"Did the two of you," Steve asked his father, "have a chance to talk about the Madison child and what happened to him?"

Bringing up yet another tragic accident at the dinner table felt necessarily improper under the circumstances. Steve couldn't get past the fact that after leaving Mrs. Talbert, they'd found nothing online about the child's death. No obit. No headline. Not one mention. It was beyond strange. It was almost as if any record of the child and his death had been scrubbed from the internet. If Steve wasn't fully aware that it was possible to do exactly that, he would think the notion was a little on the unreasonable side.

But it was possible. It had been done more times than the average person realized. There were services available for the right price to make just about anything go away.

"We weren't really acquainted with the Madisons," Steve's father said. "We knew Alice and Jerry primarily because she and I grew up in the same school district. Our parents were friends. But Alice did talk to Martha a few days after it happened." He turned to his wife. "I remember you were quite upset about the conversation."

Martha nodded. "Alice told me about it. She and I were both flabbergasted that there was nothing in the paper after...what happened. Nothing at all. We discussed the idea that perhaps the Madisons had managed to keep it quiet to avoid all the painful drama. But I don't think Alice believed that. I know I didn't. I firmly believed that it was Ledwell's doing. It felt like they wanted to avoid any and all bad press no matter the circumstances. I didn't see her again for months." She frowned. "Maybe closer to a year. I remember it was only a few weeks before their accident. She seemed distracted and worried. *Unsettled.* I wish I had tried harder to find out what was going on."

Allie smiled, her lips trembling with the effort. "You couldn't have known. No one could have."

"Looking back, Allie," Quentin said, "I believe there was more to your parents' accident, and I am equally certain there was something the Madisons wanted to keep hidden about their own tragedy. The old saying hindsight is twenty-twenty is sadly true. We can see so much now that we didn't then. In part because we didn't realize we needed to look. Basically, we ended up chalking it all up to gossip and fear of the unknown. I mean, let's face it, even now the AI stuff is a little unsettling."

Martha nodded. "All that aside, there was something odd about some of the things that went on with Ledwell back then. Looking at each piece or incident individually—as we did when it was happening—it didn't feel so pressing, so overwhelming. But when you consider it all as a whole, it's entirely overwhelming."

"There's no question in my mind," Quentin went on, "that those same sorts of things are still happening. They're just better at hiding their secret activity these days. It's funny. With social media, the average person's whole life is out there for all to see. But those with the power can hide just about anything."

Steve knew all too well how true that statement was.

"I can't help wondering," Allie said, "if what happened back then is the reason Mr. Madison was…" She looked toward the kids. "Why he went away so mysteriously."

Steve noted that his sister was scrolling on her phone with one hand and lifting her fork with the other. As a single parent of two kids, she rarely got a moment to herself to do as she pleased. She took her moments where she could find them. He stifled a grin at the boys, who stared wide eyed at Allie, mouths slightly open.

"Don't worry," Amanda said as she glanced up at Steve, "they're really into mysteries right now. The scarier the better."

The boys, Clint and Carson, immediately launched into tales of their favorite true-crime episodes.

By the time dinner was over, Steve wondered if his sister was raising future investigators or serial killers.

While everyone else drank more wine and had cake, the future crime fighters retired to the den downstairs to catch up on whatever was streaming. Amanda insisted on cleaning up, and Steve and his father pitched in. His mom had family photo albums to show off to Allie.

When the cleanup was nearly done, his dad hitched his head toward the door. "Go on. Make sure your mom is not boring her to death."

Steve tossed the dry towel onto the counter. "You know Mom is never boring."

"You haven't lived with her as an adult," Amanda challenged from the refrigerator, where she was storing leftovers.

Steve laughed. "You talked me into it. I'll go check on them."

He found his mom and Allie on the sofa in the living room. The fact that they were laughing suggested there was no boredom with which to be concerned.

Allie held up a handful of photos. "Your mom gave me most of the photos she had that included my parents. One even has me in it."

Steve sat down beside her. "I didn't realize there were so many," he said to his mother.

"Neither did I. Oh." Martha raised a hand as if to rally their attention. "I think the mystery couple is Lucille and Dennis Reger or Regers. I'm not sure about the last name. I ran into Lucille, the redhead, in the market. She was with Alice. She seemed very nice."

"That could really help." He smiled. "Thanks, Mom."

"I could ask around," she offered. "I still have a good many friends from back then. A few who even still work for Ledwell. Someone else might recall some relevant fact about the couple."

An alarm triggered in Steve. "As much as we appreciate the offer, I'd feel more comfortable if you waited a bit on any actions like that. We don't want to stir up any undue attention to what Allie and I are doing. We've already hit a number of roadblocks."

Her mouth formed an O, and she pressed her hand to her chest. "Oh my. I never considered this was more of an undercover investigation. You're right." She pinched her thumb and forefinger together and slid it across her closed lips. "I won't say a word to anyone."

"Thank you so much for the thought," Allie spoke up. "You've already been so helpful. Really. I cannot tell you how much it means to me to hear these details about my parents. My grandparents found it difficult to talk about that time, and I never wanted to press."

Martha smiled sadly. "I understand. I assure you, Allie, if we think of anything at all that might help, we'll call Steve and let him know."

Steve was surprised at just how quickly his mom and Allie had bonded. He was also surprised at how very much he'd missed family gatherings like this one. He had to make more of an effort to be here for these times. He watched his mother's vibrant expression as she spoke. No one was promised tomorrow. Something else he should be keeping in mind—especially when involved with a case like Allie's.

AN HOUR LATER, there was a round of hugs at the door in another Durham family tradition. Nobody left the house without a big hug and an *I love you*. Amanda hugged him harder than usual. While her cheek was pressed to his, she whispered, "She's a keeper. Don't let this one slip away, bro."

He smiled as he drew away. "I'll keep that in mind, sis."

She punched his shoulder. "Good. Be smarter than me."

As a kid, he would have tossed back that he already was, but as an adult he recognized how intelligent his big sister was and what a tough lesson she had learned about trust. Cheating spouses sucked.

Outside, the night had grown sultry. The June temps were record-breaking this year.

"Your family," Allie said as she settled into the passenger seat, "is really amazing. I love your mom."

"I think she's very fond of you as well." He closed Allie's door and walked around to slide behind the steering wheel. "I'm glad we were able to get together."

"I didn't realize how much I missed family dinners." She stared out the window as she said this.

"I had the same thought." The difference was, he still had that option. He wanted to say more, but he wasn't sure any words he drummed up would fill that void.

Instead, he drove through the darkness, his mind rushing forward to find a way to put the information they had gathered into perspective. He really enjoyed his work, but this was the first time it felt personal. Others had told him how difficult it was when a case crossed that line. Now he understood. It was a physical pain.

Allie relaxed deeper into her seat. "Thank you."

He glanced at her, grateful for the reprieve from his thoughts. "For?"

"For coming to my rescue." She turned to him as he slowed for a red light. "I know that sounds a little dramatic, but you could have said no. You could have put me off on another investigator."

"No way. This is what you do for friends."

"Well, again, thank you for remembering me and being my friend."

He almost told her how easy she made the effort, but he decided maybe that might be a little more forward than she would find comfortable.

"Home sweet home," she said as he pulled into her driveway.

He wondered if she actually saw it as home sweet home or home lonely home. The thought of her here alone so much of the time bothered him. A lot.

Allie wondered what Steve was thinking as they climbed out of his SUV and walked toward her porch. He and his family had been so kind to her tonight. And more helpful than she'd anticipated.

The photos Martha had given her were priceless.

Steve unlocked the door and insisted on going in first. She locked it once more while he wandered through the first floor. Flipping a couple of switches, she turned off some of the exterior lights. She liked leaving them on for when she was out and would be returning home in the dark. But once she was here, she toned it down.

Until now, she hadn't really understood why her grandparents were so fixated on security. She so wished they had shared their concerns with her. On one level, she understood why they hadn't. They had wanted to protect her, and, honestly, she would likely have started looking into all these odd circumstances if they had. She supposed she should be glad they hadn't told her.

Putting the worries aside for now, she needed to find her phone charger. With all the calls and research she'd been doing, she had almost drained the battery.

If she remembered correctly, she'd left it in the bag from the store. Upstairs. In her room. Or maybe in her office. She headed that way, turning on the hall light as she reached the top of the stairs. In her bedroom, she grabbed the bag. "And there it is." She snagged the charger and headed back out of her room.

She'd almost made it to the stairs when she stalled. Her gaze had stumbled over something. She backed up a couple of steps. The door to her parents' bedroom was open. Hadn't she closed it? She usually left it closed. It was just a habit of hers. Same one her grandmother had. Leave a room, flip off the lights and close the door.

Moving in a sort of slow motion, she turned and took the two steps to the door. Her fingers slid over the wall next to the frame, turning on the light.

The room looked as if a small tornado had gone through it. She blinked twice, told herself she wasn't seeing clearly. Still the same. Her parents' room had been ransacked. Clothes and other personal items littered the floor. Drawers had been dragged out of their slots and left upside down on the floor. The closet looked as if someone had tossed a hand grenade inside.

Someone has been in the house.

She turned all the way around in the room. Maybe they still were.

But the door had been locked.

"Steve!" She backed out of the room as she shouted. She looked right then left along the hall to ensure no one was coming out of another room.

The intruder could still be here.

"Steve!"

He was bounding up the stairs before his name stopped echoing in the air.

He looked from her to the open door and back. "What happened?"

"Someone's been here."

He crossed to the door and had a look inside. "Downstairs is clear. Let's have a closer look up here."

They walked from room to room, checked the usual places. Under beds, in closets, behind doors. There was no one hiding anywhere they looked.

"They're gone now," Allie acknowledged, "but someone was definitely here."

"No question. We can call the police and report the intrusion if you'd like."

She shook her head. "No. If we do, we'll just be alerting the FBI, and they'll likely show up again. At the moment, I just want to know how he or she got in the house."

"Should be easy enough to determine," Steve suggested. "Let's check the doors and windows more closely."

They returned to the first floor. The front door had still been locked when they arrived. It was doubtful anyone had entered the house from there in light of the three deadbolts, but Steve had a look anyway. No indication the locks had been tampered with.

"No scratches," he confirmed, "or other marks to indicate the locks were tampered with."

Moving on to the kitchen, they found the back door shut but unlocked. There was no deadbolt like on the front. Allie watched as Steve knelt and examined the lock.

"Oh yeah. Someone used a flat tip screwdriver or something like that to jimmy the lock. You need a new one installed on this door." He stood. "You need a deadbolt as well. Makes their work more difficult. We can call someone tomorrow."

"Okay." She chewed at her lip. "I guess my grandparents never thought about it either. Seems strange in retrospect."

All this time, she'd felt so secure with her triple deadbolts on the front door. She should have had this door secured properly ages ago.

"You never had any reason to worry about it."

She nodded. Sounded better than just not thinking at all. "I suppose we can rule out the FBI. They've already been here. And they had a warrant, so breaking and entering wasn't necessary."

Steve chuckled. "No. This, I'm guessing, is either someone looking for something the FBI missed or someone who wants you to be afraid." He settled his gaze on hers. "Either way, we need to secure this door until we can get a new, proper lock."

"I have something I think we can use for that." She rounded up the longest screws she could find and the battery-operated drill driver she'd bought herself when she added shelves to her office.

"That will definitely work as long as you don't mind my marring the wood." Steve accepted the items.

"Mar away. I can repair that with a little wood filler and paint."

"As you wish." He prepared to secure the door.

"I think I'll clean up the mess upstairs and call it a night."

He frowned. "It's been a strange day. You handling all this okay?"

"Sure." She backed toward the door. "Thanks again for everything. Really. You've done so much."

He smiled, making her heart react. "No problem. Goodnight."

"G'night."

What she didn't tell him was that she was totally exhausted with all of it. She had realized she didn't know very much about her parents and the final year of their lives. But now she was certain she had no idea what really happened to them either. What little she did know from that time didn't feel like the truth anymore. But she was certain her grandparents would never have lied to her.

They couldn't have known. She refused to even entertain the idea.

Allie wasn't sure what she actually knew at this point. But she intended to find out.

Upstairs, she started with the closet. Rehanging clothes and tidying shoes and scarves. Her mother's two favorite handbags went back on their hooks. Every single item made Allie miss these people she'd scarcely known so much more. She missed her grandparents too.

It wasn't easy being alone. Funny, she hadn't really noticed so much until now.

This time with Steve and tonight's dinner with his family had been a stark reminder of what she was missing.

By the time her parents' belongings were put away, she was dragging. Steve paused at the door. Evidently he'd finished up downstairs. At one point, she'd felt certain she heard him talking. He'd likely had calls to make.

"Need any help?"

"It's done." She surveyed the room. She'd put the framed photographs back where they belonged as well as the little trinkets her mother had cherished. Sadly, she only knew these things because her grandmother had told her.

"Did you notice anything missing?"

She shook her head. "Nothing. Whatever the intruder was looking for, it obviously wasn't here."

As she walked toward the door, she noticed something

on the floor just under the edge of the bed. She leaned down and picked it up. It was another photo of the mystery couple. What in the world was it doing on the floor? She turned it over, and their names were written there.

Lucille and Dennis Reger.

Mrs. Talbert and Steve's mother had been right.

Allie studied the photograph. "I don't think I've ever seen this one." She passed it to Steve. "My grandmother was very meticulous with photos. She kept them all in albums or frames. None were ever loose like this."

As Steve examined the photograph, a thought occurred to Allie. "Maybe," she suggested, "the intruder didn't break in to take anything. Maybe to leave something."

"A clue he thought you might need."

Allie nodded slowly, her attention fixed on the couple in the photograph. "Maybe he thinks we need a little help."

"Or he's playing with us," Steve countered.

The kind of playing, Allie realized, that got people killed.

Chapter Nine

Monday, June 9
Chicago
Colby Agency, 8:00 a.m.

The elevator doors opened, and Allie stepped into the lobby of the Colby Agency.

This was exactly what she had expected based on all she'd read about the venerable Victoria Colby-Camp. The agency—the woman, really—was legendary. Whether you were in Chicago or Paris, those in the know recognized the Colby name.

The lobby was large and decorated in a sophisticated yet comfortable style. A glass desk that actually looked like a work of art stood in front of an enormous glass wall that showed off the breathtaking view of the city beyond it. Also behind the desk was a woman, who Allie decided must be a receptionist.

"Good morning, Ms. Foster." The woman, who was around Allie's age, smiled then looked to the man right behind her. "Mr. Durham, Victoria and Jamie are waiting for you."

"Thank you, Madeline."

Steve pressed a hand to the small of Allie's back and gently guided her toward a long, wide corridor. Still gawking in an attempt to take it all in, she wondered how different these offices were from the original ones. According to her research on the Colby Agency, the original offices had been blown up by a longtime enemy. The family had withstood far more than their share of personal attacks and tragedy. But they were survivors with a truly incredible history.

Allie could not believe she was here. She only wished she didn't feel so underdressed. The black slacks were the closest thing to dressy she owned. The white button-down with the big collar was from forever ago. She'd spotted it online and had to have it. She'd worn it one other time besides today. The biggest change to her usual look was that she'd left her hair down.

She never did that.

She glanced at the man next to her. It was mostly because of him. He looked great. It was impossible not to feel lacking in style around him. His navy slacks and the lighter blue button-down looked amazing just because he was wearing them.

Good grief, she was besotted with the man. Which was only going to make it harder to say goodbye when this was over.

Dismissing the thoughts, she focused on this place and how lucky she was to be here. The agency hired only the very best and had a reputation for being the most discreet in the industry. She was so grateful to have this team on her side. She was reasonably certain she had told Steve this countless times already.

She sent him a sideways look. "This place is amazing."

He smiled. "It is. More than you know."

No doubt, she mused.

The desk in Victoria's private lobby was empty.

"Rhea, Victoria's personal assistant, is off today," he explained as he walked straight through to Victoria's door. He opened it and waited for Allie to go in first.

Always the gentleman. As old-fashioned as it sounded, she liked that too.

Holding her breath, Allie stepped into the head of the agency's private domain.

Victoria met them in the middle of the room. Allie had seen images of her online, but she wasn't fully prepared for just how awe-inspiring it was to be in the woman's presence. There was a sense of sophistication and wisdom that made Allie want to curtsy as if standing before a queen.

She definitely wouldn't say that out loud.

"Allie." Victoria extended her hand. "It's a pleasure to meet you. I've heard so much about you already."

Allie glanced at Steve as she took the other woman's hand. "The pleasure is mine, ma'am." She bit back all the new gushing compliments that came immediately to mind.

"Please, call me Victoria." She gestured to a young woman seated at the small conference table on the far side of the office. "This is my granddaughter, Jamie."

Jamie extended her hand across the table as Allie approached. "It's such a pleasure to meet you, Allie."

"The pleasure is all mine, I assure you." Allie couldn't help smiling as she shook the other woman's hand. She wore her blond hair down around her shoulders, and her blue eyes literally sparkled when she smiled. The gray sheath she wore looked as if she'd just stepped off a fashion show runway.

"Let's sit," Victoria urged, taking her seat at the head of the table. "The others will be with us soon. I'm aware you have another appointment, so we'll make this quick."

With those FBI agents. Allie wished she could forget about that meeting, but unfortunately it was impossible.

They all settled into upholstered chairs around the table just as three other members of the Colby team entered the office.

Steve made the introductions. "This is Nicole Reed Michaels and Simon Ruhl—he worked at the Bureau in a former life. He may be able to provide some insight into their agenda in your case."

"A very long time ago," Simon pointed out.

Allie smiled at the two. "Thank you for all you're doing to sort this mess."

"And this," Steve said, gesturing to the final arrival taking a seat, "is Jackson Brennan. He is a former bounty hunter and very, very good at tracking the missing and solving cold cases."

"Thank you," Allie said. "I am truly lost in all this."

Jackson gave her a nod. The man was tall, young. Midthirties maybe. If she were a bad guy and this man was tracking her, she would be very afraid.

"You needn't worry," Victoria assured Allie, drawing her attention to the head of the table. "We will get to the bottom of things as quickly as possible."

"We've tracked down the mystery couple," Jamie said. "They moved from Woodstock to Yuma, Arizona, twenty-six years ago. They declined to be interviewed by phone or in person. We have a local contact who showed up unannounced and made an attempt, but Mrs. Reger shut it down."

Allie's heart sank a little. She was really hoping the couple would be willing to answer questions. The husband having been employed at Ledwell and the two being friends with her parents had given Allie such hope they would know something helpful for moving forward.

"We've also looked," Nicole spoke next, "into the death of the Madison child, Tommy. There was no autopsy conducted—at least not in the state of Illinois—and the single document related to the child's death that we did discover indicated his remains had been cremated. This document was from a funeral home in Woodstock. The Wembley." She looked to Allie then. "But the part I found strange was that there was nothing else. No further indication that he died or that he was even born. No birth certificate. No medical records that we've been able to locate. We've been searching every available database for the past twenty-four hours, and there is simply nothing."

"Are you suggesting," Steve spoke up, "that the child was perhaps not the Madisons' biological child? Maybe there was an adoption they kept secret for whatever reason."

"That's possible, of course," Nicole agreed. "But what I've found is that, for all intents and purposes, this child did not exist. Not on paper."

"How is that possible? There were photos of him," Allie spoke up, "at the grandmother's house. Basically everyone we've spoken with who knew the family recalled the child."

"Private adoption," Steve suggested. "Illegal adoption."

"We ran his description," Jackson said, "through more

databases to see if a child matching that description was reported missing during the target timeframe. Not a single name popped up. Then we searched for infants and toddlers in that category. The few we found who fit the search criteria were part of cases that were all solved favorably."

"It's possible," Nicole explained, "this is why there was no coverage of his death. If the child had been stolen, the last thing the Madisons would have wanted to do was have photos of him in the news."

Allie's heart had started to pound at this new scenario. "What I'm getting from this is that my parents may have somehow figured out the child was stolen, and they were killed to prevent them telling others what they had discovered."

"It's certainly a theory that merits consideration," Victoria agreed. "There are documented cases of personnel having bizarre accidents and people protesting the work being done at Ledwell, which we, as you know, believe to be the primary scenario related to the possibility of how the accident happened. I fear we'll have to dig much deeper to find anything one way or the other. The person or persons behind all this have been very careful in covering their tracks."

"But there were no investigations," Allie said. "At least, none that were conducted officially. How can we prove these allegations or suspicions if we can't get anyone to talk?"

"None we've found so far," Victoria reminded her. "But, in my experience, if you poke at a bear you'll get a reaction. Maybe not the first time, but he won't ignore you for long."

Allie smiled. She really liked this lady and the way she thought.

"I've reviewed the accident report from the night your parents died," Simon spoke up. "Mechanical failure is the only cause listed—which you already knew. The deputy who was first on the scene and who investigated the accident is retired now." To Steve, he said, "I've forwarded his contact information to you. Unfortunately, the mechanic mentioned as having conducted the actual examination of the vehicle has since died."

"The reporter," Nicole said, "Rivero, may be an important link in this chain of information. If you can get him to talk—" this she directed to Steve "—he could provide useful details."

Steve nodded. "We'll get him to talk."

Allie was still reeling with all she'd heard when it was time to go. As she and Steve rode the elevator down to the main lobby, she tried to remember if she'd thanked everyone. They were all working so hard—even using their weekends—to help her find the truth.

Without the truth...she could end up being charged with a murder she didn't commit.

Federal Bureau of Investigations
Roosevelt Road, 10:00 a.m.

ALLIE FELT COLD. Her nerves were fluttering. Palms sweating.

She wanted to scream that she had no idea what any of this was about, but that was no longer true. She understood that it was about the past, and somehow her parents were involved. Allie also got that there were things—

secret things—that were being kept from her to cover up for other secret things...none of which were good.

Steve had said that powerful people sometimes went to great lengths to conceal their tracks. Allie understood this. She might be a bit of a recluse, but she didn't live under a rock. Still, his telling her was valid. Most people—even those aware that things like this happened—didn't really recognize just how deep, just how bad these cover-ups could be. Most people were like her, she supposed. She walked through life believing others were good until something happened to change her mind.

Evidently that wasn't true in some cases.

Driving up to the FBI's complex felt like arriving at a prison. A three-building complex of concrete, steel and glass stationed on twelve acres with mazes for parking lots and other things—little box-shaped metal things—she couldn't identify.

Inside was a whole other story. The lobby was certainly not one found in any prison with its endless glass and marble panels for walls all showcased by granite flooring and meticulously placed plants and stylish seating areas. The ceiling soared two stories with all that glass allowing sunlight to fill the space. They might have been in a luxury resort hotel on a tropical island somewhere.

Special Agent Fraser met them in that grand lobby.

"Thank you for coming." He looked to Allie as he spoke.

Like she had a choice.

"We'll be going up a few floors, where we'll catch up with Agent Potter in a private conference room."

"Lead the way," Steve said, cutting straight to the chase. No smile. No handshake. Not even a hello.

Allie reminded herself to breathe as they rode the elevator upward. Fraser said nothing. Steve said nothing. Allie was ready to erupt with tension. But then Steve glanced at her, smiled, and she felt better. Calmer.

Funny how that worked.

The elevator stopped, and they prepared to exit. Fraser started forward then abruptly paused and indicated that Allie should precede him. She did so and waited for the two to join her in the corridor. Other staff members hurried along to meetings, speaking quietly to colleagues going in the same direction or to someone via a cell phone.

They all appeared focused on their own agenda, intent on some destination, and not a single one paid the slightest attention to her and the two men accompanying her.

The conference room was small but private. Agent Potter was already seated at the oval table. A large binder sat in front of her. Next to the binder was a medium-sized box, flaps closed, concealing whatever was inside.

The fluttering nerves were back.

Potter gestured to the remaining chairs around the table. "Find a seat and we'll get started."

Steve pulled out a chair for her, and Allie lowered into it. She focused on slowing her respiration. Reminded herself that she had a secret weapon—the Colby Agency. And Steve. She watched as he settled into his chair. She relaxed. He had her back.

"I'd like to start this meeting," Potter said, "by passing along that we have confirmed the video provided by hospital security was edited."

Allie barely resisted the urge to do a fist pump and squeal.

"That's not to say," Fraser added with a look directly at Allie, "that we're convinced you had nothing to do with or have no knowledge of the events leading to Thomas Madison's death. But we are aware of this aspect and wanted to let you know."

Her glee vanished. "I'm sorry. I don't see how you can still believe I'm involved. I didn't even know the man."

"I'm assuming," Steve said, "you're looking into who had access to surveillance systems at the hospital."

"Of course," Fraser confirmed.

Potter opened her binder and turned it toward Allie and Steve. "In your parents' room—in the home where you live—we discovered these."

The first plastic sheet protector held a blank page with two photos mounted on it. One photo was of Thomas Madison coming out of a local market. The next was of a vehicle—presumably his—turning into his driveway. Based on his age in the one at the market, the photos were recent.

"I've never seen these photos before." Allie shook her head. What the heck was this? "You couldn't have found these photos in the house. They don't belong to me, and no one else lives there."

"These photos are recent," Fraser pointed out. "Just days before he was hospitalized and murdered. And they were found in your home."

Potter turned the page. More photos of a similar nature. Allie shook her head again. "I can't help you with this." She turned her palms up and gestured to the binder. "I don't know anything about these."

Clearly they were photos taken by someone following Madison around, but that person wasn't her. Until Friday night, she'd had no clue who he was or that he even existed, for that matter.

"But these photos were also in your home," Potter repeated. "You surely saw them. They weren't hidden in some out-of-the-way place. They were in the drawer next to the bed."

Allie tried to think when she'd been in that room last, much less prowled around in the drawers. The door stayed closed, and she went in there once in a great while to dust and vacuum, but she never searched or even touched anything beyond moving a framed photo to dust or something like that.

"I'm telling you," she insisted, "I have not seen these photos before."

Her mind went immediately to the photo she'd found in her parents' room today. She'd never seen that one before either. Maybe the person who'd been in her house yesterday had been in there before. She decided not to mention as much. If Steve wanted the agents to know, he would tell them the story.

Potter flipped over to another page. "What about these?"

The photos were of her parents and the Madisons. With the mystery couple captured on the edge of one of three snapshots. Allie wondered how much the FBI knew about the couple. The Colby Agency had located the couple, but they refused to talk. The two were a dead end so far.

"I recognize my parents and the Madisons—only because of what has happened since Friday night."

"This is the Regers." Potter tapped the image of the mystery couple. "They were assets of the Bureau working at Ledwell at the time your father was employed there."

Allie and Steve shared a look. No wonder the couple refused to speak with anyone from the Colby Agency.

Steve turned up his hands. "Ms. Foster has already explained that she has no knowledge of these photos or how they came to be in her home. I suggest we move on."

Potter turned to the next page. This one showed a series of photos of a vehicle Allie didn't recognize parked in front of her house. The photos appeared to have been taken at different times, maybe on different days. She couldn't be certain, but the vehicle was parked at slightly different locations. The shade from a nearby tree hit the vehicle at barely perceptible variances in each photo.

She looked to Potter. "Someone has been watching my house?"

Potter nodded. "Thomas Madison."

Allie shook her head. This made no sense. "He never came to the door. If that's him, I had no idea he was there." She looked Potter straight in the eyes. "Why would he be watching my house?"

"We have no idea," Fraser admitted. "We hoped you might be able to tell us."

Allie held up a hand. "This man was part of an investigation you were conducting prior to his death." She looked from one to the other. "You mentioned this in our first meeting. Why didn't you tell me he had been watching my house? And how did you get these photos?"

"We're asking the questions here, Ms. Foster," Potter pointed out.

"We can't help you solve your case. We have no reason to believe any part of it is connected to Ms. Foster, and she had no prior knowledge of the details you've revealed." Steve gestured to the binder. "My guess is someone is playing you. Trying to derail your investigation. For all we know, Thomas Madison was losing his grip on reality before he died. Whatever the case, I believe it's pretty clear that Ms. Foster is not involved. You're far too focused on a woman who has no idea who Thomas Madison was rather than the identity and motive of the person who wanted to take his life."

Potter and Fraser exchanged a look.

"There's one more thing," Fraser said.

Allie couldn't wait to hear this one.

"Thomas Madison," he went on, "was murdered with an injection of phenobarbital into his IV fluids."

A large enough dosage was one way to put someone down, certainly. It didn't take a medical professional to understand how that sort of thing worked.

"You're a nurse," Potter pointed out. "You would know the drug to use and how to inject it."

"So would anyone else who bothered to google it," Allie countered. Now she was just angry. This was enough.

"Funny that you mention googling," Potter said. "We found several searches on your laptop about the best ways to cause sudden death."

Allie's jaw dropped. That was impossible. "I didn't do any such searches," she argued. Her skin flushed, and a combination of fear and outrage roared through her.

Steve turned to her. "We're done here, I think."

Allie was more than happy to hear that.

"You're going to have to do better than this," he

warned the agents, "if you plan to keep dragging my client through these emotional minefields."

He stood. Allie did the same.

Potter pushed the box toward them. "Your laptop and other devices."

Steve took the box. "Good day, agents."

As they moved toward the door, Fraser spoke up. "Be careful where you step in this minefield, Ms. Foster."

Maybe she was a fool, but Allie turned back to hear what he had to say.

"We still haven't figured out all the players, much less who the true bad guys are."

She gave a dry laugh. "Maybe because you're looking in the wrong place."

Allie walked out. She had nothing else to say. But she couldn't help wondering if the agents were the bad guys because they damned sure seemed intent on framing her.

The one thing she was certain of in all this was her innocence.

She just hoped Steve and the Colby Agency could help her prove it.

Chapter Ten

Wonder Lake
Rivero Residence
Lake Shore Drive, Noon

Steve knocked on the door after two attempts to rally the resident with the doorbell.

Rivero knew they were here, and they knew he was in there. He had the cameras, and his vintage SUV was parked near the door like before. It was backed up to the house as if the owner wanted to ensure a swift and unencumbered getaway.

"He's not going to answer." Allie's shoulders sagged.

The meeting at the Colby Agency had buoyed her hopes, and then Potter and Fraser had sunk them with their ridiculous accusations.

"He will answer as long as he's still breathing," Steve argued. He fisted his hand and rapped again, hard enough to rattle the door on its hinges. "Because we're not leaving—" he stared directly at the camera "—until he does."

"If you keep pounding on my door," Rivero said, his voice sounding scratchy over the speaker, "I'm calling the police."

Steve pulled out his cell phone and stared up at the camera. "I'll do you one better. I'll call FBI agents Potter and Fraser and tell them you're ready to talk about all the secrets you uncovered at Ledwell. Particularly those about the child, Tommy, and his parents' strange behavior after his alleged death."

Thankfully, Allie concealed the surprise she might be feeling at his statement. His goal was not to make her think he knew something he hadn't shared with her. His intent was to get the guy to come to the door. It was a strategy he hoped to hell would work. They badly needed a break—sooner rather than later.

The release of locks clicked in the silence that followed.

Steve resisted the urge to grin. *Gotcha.*

The door opened and Rivero stood there, a couple of feet back from the actual opening, as if he feared catching something or being yanked out of the house by the collar of his hoodie. For such a former hotshot, his look had gone to hell. Sweatpants and a hoodie. Unshaven and his gray peppered hair badly in need of combing.

He exhaled a big breath. "Come in. Let's get this over with."

Steve flashed Allie a knowing look. She walked in, and he followed.

Rivero locked the door behind them. Like Allie, he had multiple deadbolts.

Then he led them deeper into the house, to a large main living area that looked out over the lake through a wall of glass. Not a bad view.

The former star reporter gestured to the sofa and then took a seat in what appeared to be his preferred chair.

The leather recliner showed the wear of its preference, whereas the matching sofa looked new.

"What do you want to know?" He looked from Steve to Allie. "I can't promise I'll answer every question you ask, but I'll give you what I can."

When Allie started to speak, Rivero held up both hands stop-sign fashion. "Be aware that I'm only doing this because Fraser and Potter are closing in on a court order that I may not be able to ignore. I'd love to get a step ahead of them."

Good to know the two agents were rattling his cage as well.

"What do you know about the accident that killed my parents?" Allie started with the issue closest to her heart.

Steve wasn't surprised that was her first question. This thing that had begun haunting her less than seventy-two hours ago had reopened that old wound, relentlessly tearing at it.

Rivero considered her question for a time before responding. To make something up? To figure out the best lie? Who knew.

Now that Steve was this close, he noted that beneath the I-don't-care attire and lack of grooming the man didn't look so different from the way he had more than two decades ago. He'd allowed his hair to gray, but he still looked fairly lean for an older man. Judging by the equipment on the other end of the room, he stayed fit. Weights and a stair climber as well as the latest in bike machines. The eyeglasses were new. Or maybe he'd worn contacts back when his face was all over the news channels. If not for the downgrade in his appearance, he might still look the part.

"Your father," he began, "was young, not so highly educated and a bit naïve when he started with Ledwell."

Allie shifted in her seat. No doubt feeling the sting of his blunt words about her father's education level.

"You mean he wasn't Ivy League educated like the scientists at Ledwell," Steve corrected.

"Of course that's what I mean. The place was full of pompous geniuses." He looked to Allie then. "Don't get me wrong, your father was a brilliant man. He had the kind of brilliance an expensive university couldn't give. That's why Ledwell wanted him."

She visibly relaxed. Steve wanted to keep her that way. This was tough enough without added nonsense.

"There were rumors of trouble," Allie said. "I found a few news reports, headlines in papers online but nothing deep or revealing. Nothing that ever prompted people, much less the authorities, to sit up and take notice."

"That's because Ledwell owned everyone back then. The press, the powers that be, they all said what Ledwell wanted them to say. When I tried to find a damned outlet that would publish my story or let me tell it in an interview, no one would touch me. I ended up blackballed." He looked away a moment, stared out that enormous glass wall. "I had to get away. I disappeared for a while. Wrote the book." He shrugged. "Who knows, maybe one day it will be published."

"What was *your* story?" Allie prodded, shifting gears like a reporter herself.

Steve kept quiet. Let her do the asking. Reporters liked when a story was personal. This was as personal as it got for Allie. The connection would be stronger with her.

He looked from Allie to Steve and back. "I need to know that you aren't wearing a wire of any sort."

Frankly, Steve was surprised he hadn't attempted to strip search them when they first entered his home. Maybe age had slowed him in that respect as well.

Rivero got up and picked up a device from the table next to his chair. "If you're carrying anything electronic, this will pick it up."

Steve stood and removed his cell phone from his pocket and placed it on the coffee table. He stepped away from the sofa, held up both arms. "That's all I have."

Rivero moved the device over his body from the tips of his fingers to the ends of his toes. Careful not to miss an inch. When he was finished, he nodded and turned toward Allie.

She opened her purse and took out her cell then placed it on the coffee table next to Steve's. Rivero checked her purse then scanned her body as he had Steve's. When the man nodded, Allie sat down. She tucked her cell back into her purse.

Steve settled onto the sofa once more.

"I heard rumors that Ledwell was going beyond the established limits in their AI research and development. No surprise really. They were all doing it to some degree, but something about the way Ledwell operated gave me pause. Made me want to find the dirt. Eventually I found myself a whistle-blower. A janitor, Harvey Culver, who worked the evening shift." He fell silent for a moment. "This was a year or so before your father's death. This janitor was keeping an eye out for me. Reporting back what he saw. I bought him a camera he could easily conceal to snap pics of whatever he thought might be of interest to me."

Again, he paused and stared out that massive window wall for a time. "This went on for a while. It wasn't like he could bring me something after every shift. It was only on those rare occasions when no one noticed him around and allowed an opening for him to see something or hear something. The wait was difficult but necessary."

"Did you eventually learn the details that would give you the story you were after?"

He looked annoyed at Allie's question, but it was a perfectly logical one.

"You don't look for something that will give you the story you're after, Ms. Foster. The story draws you to it, and you look for the evidence that will confirm what the story is telling you. A true reporter doesn't create a story. He reveals the truth of the story that seduces him—lures him in."

Steve got it, but he didn't see the need to be so dramatic. "Which was?" he prompted.

"That Ledwell was way ahead of everyone else. Twenty-nine years ago, they already had robots that looked and behaved so much like a human it was nearly impossible to decipher between them."

Allie looked to Steve. He wasn't completely surprised, but she appeared to be.

"It was a race," Steve suggested. "What made this so newsworthy?"

"They were using human…" He hesitated. "Human parts in their development. Granted these were humans who had left their bodies to Ledwell for R&D, or so that was the claim. But their work was outside the parameters of what was considered ethical at the time. The laws…" He shrugged. "Were reasonably straightforward in those days. Not like now, where there's so much ambiguity. To tell the truth, I can only imagine what they're doing now." He looked directly at Steve then. "Whatever you imagine, multiply that times about a thousand. We should all be scared."

"How did my father play into your investigation? Was it because he was part of SILO?"

Like Steve, Allie recognized that was where this was going. She had hoped this man could shed some light on at least some of the unknowns.

Rivero stared at her for a long moment before responding. "We don't say SILO out loud. We don't text about it. We don't talk about it period. It was the CIA's baby, and that will get you taken out quicker than a dose of cyanide."

"We'll take that as a yes," Steve fired back.

Rivero held up his hands. "To answer the first part of your question, when the janitor died suddenly—"

"How did he die?" Steve interrupted.

"An accident, what else?" Rivero shook his head and considered his inspiring view yet again. "The official conclusion was that his truck fell off the jack onto him while he was working under it."

Allie winced. Steve sent her a reassuring look.

"I watched your parents for weeks to find the right opportunity to connect with your father." He took another of those long pauses. "There was a carnival in Woodstock. Your parents took you. I followed them, and while your mother rode with you on the carousel, I approached. A crowd of fathers and grandfathers were gathered in a cluster to try getting photographs of their offspring aboard the wooden horses. I pretended to be one of them. I got as close to your father as possible and told him who I was. In those days, I always wore disguises when out in public. It was the only way for me to have a moment of peace."

"Comes with the territory," Steve pointed out. From the videos he'd watched of Rivero's heyday, he had loved every minute of it.

"Why my father?" Allie asked, the ache of the question in her voice. "Why not someone else?"

"Harvey had given me the names of those who knew the most and who I might be able to trust. I certainly didn't want to approach anyone who would out me. Otherwise, I might have ended up under a car like poor Harvey."

"Or dead on the side of the road with your wife."

Allie's words hit their mark. Rivero grimaced.

"The truth was," Rivero went on, "Jerry was looking for a way out. He'd been contemplating just leaving town. Taking his family and disappearing. But your mother wouldn't hear of it." His gaze settled on Allie once more. "Your mother didn't want to leave her parents, and they refused to move."

Allie's expression warned that his words stabbed deep. Steve knew she had loved her grandparents. The idea that a single decision on their part caused this had to be immensely painful.

While she struggled for what to say next, Steve asked, "What about the Regers? Dennis and Lucille? Were you watching them as well?"

"The redhead." Rivero nodded. "Those two were a

bit on the strange side. The husband, Dennis, was from Germany. He spoke with a heavy accent. He'd met Lucille in New York when he moved to the US. He'd decided to take a short vacation there before continuing on to Woodstock to join Ledwell. They had recruited him from a competing firm in Berlin."

Steve understood now. Lucille was likely the FBI connection. Apparently, the Bureau had been watching Ledwell even then.

"I'm sure your friends at the Bureau told you they were assets," Rivero said, echoing Steve's thought. "It was actually Lucille who was the agent. Dennis was the target she turned once he was in position at Ledwell."

"If the FBI had some idea what Ledwell was doing all those years ago," Allie spoke up, "why did they allow them to continue with research and development that was not allowed at the time?"

Rivero laughed. "Well, Ms. Foster, if you haven't learned this yet, let me bring you up to speed. The government works in mysterious ways. They were willing to keep an eye on Ledwell in hopes of making sure the government benefited. Besides, the CIA gets what the CIA wants. The trouble was, Ledwell was aware. They were very careful about what they allowed to be disseminated to the government. They used Dennis Reger to pass along what they wanted the Bureau to know. This, of course, was the CIA's idea. The two agencies do not play well together. If Potter and Fraser tell you differently about any of this, it's only because they're ignorant of the actual facts or they're in denial. At this point, I'm stunned the feds even still fish around Ledwell. They're clearly getting what they want, or this would have ended years ago."

"Did you warn my father that what he was doing by helping you might be dangerous?"

Steve understood she felt her family had been betrayed by this man, and they likely had been. But he doubted that her father had not been aware of the risk, perhaps not to his family but certainly to himself.

"He was well aware," Rivero insisted. "We all were. He saw things that troubled him, and he couldn't live with the idea of keeping those secrets. When two of his colleagues on the team died under suspicious circumstances, he was ready to do something."

"Do you have proof of what he and the janitor saw happening?" Steve wasn't sure it was even relevant at this point, but there was no statute of limitations on murder.

"I had what I needed to do my story." Rivero didn't actually answer the question. "I had photos and copies of documents."

"Had?" Steve nudged for clarification.

"My office was robbed. My home. My car. They found and destroyed everything." He tapped his temple. "Except what I have right here. They couldn't take that because I vanished before they got the opportunity."

Steve shared a look with Allie. This was the reason the much-touted story never surfaced. It was why he'd never gone to anyone who might be able to stop what was being done at Ledwell. Because he had no proof of what he believed—beyond what was in his head.

"Do you believe they killed my parents?"

"Of course they did. Just like they killed four other

members of his team as well as Harvey and no doubt anyone else who got in their way."

"Do you have proof of any sort?" she demanded.

He shook his head. "Jerry was bringing me proof that night. He and your mother were taking you and leaving right after he met with me. Your grandparents had figured out something was very wrong and urged them to go. That night, he would give me what I needed, and then the three of you would disappear. But he never came. Hours later, I followed every route between his home and where we were to meet until I found the car in the ditch, almost hidden from view."

The pain that captured Allie's face then made Steve's chest tighten.

"There was nothing I could do for them. They were dead. But—" he took a big breath "—I searched the car, and whoever killed them had obviously already taken the files because I found nothing." He stood, walked to the fireplace and wiggled a stone free. He removed something from the space behind it and brought it to Allie. "This was clutched in your mother's hand." Then he plopped back into his chair as if he'd dealt his final hand and was waiting for her to top it or to fold.

The delicate silver chain wasn't large enough for a necklace. A bracelet, Steve decided. Tiny silver blocks hung on the thin line of silver.

"This was my baby bracelet." Allie's eyes filled with wonder. "My grandmother said my parents put it in the time capsule they made when I was born."

Rivero must have had the same thought as Steve because they both asked at the same time, "What time capsule?"

"The day I was brought home from the hospital," she explained, seemingly unaware of their tension, "my parents added this bracelet and both my and my mother's hospital bracelets to the time capsule they had prepared. They buried it in the backyard."

Rivero turned to Steve. "If they took this out of the time capsule because the mother wanted to take it with them when they left—" the man had to take a moment to get his emotions under control before he could go on "—maybe the only thing they planned to give me was the location of the time capsule." He stood, started to pace. "It makes total sense. That way they wouldn't be caught transporting the only evidence that existed outside the walls of Ledwell. Oh my God, all this time. Why didn't I think of that? The bracelet meant nothing to me." He turned to Allie, his entire being on alert. "We have to find that time capsule. *Now.*"

Foster Residence
Ridgeland Avenue, 2:30 p.m.

ALLIE WASN'T SURE they had fully convinced Mr. Rivero they would keep him apprised of what they discovered. He'd called every twenty minutes for the past hour and a half. He wanted to come but hadn't been able to bring himself to leave the house. Allie had read about and watched movies and documentaries about people who couldn't leave their homes, but she'd never seen it firsthand.

"I'm sorry." She wiped the sweat from her forehead with the back of her hand. "I really thought it was in the butterfly garden." She remembered seeing photos her grandmother had taken of the big day. Allie looked around. "It was right here." She surveyed the various flowers and shrubs that attracted butterflies, all surrounded by a cute little picket fence.

"We should have a look at those photos if you know where they are."

"Good idea." One she should have thought of nearly two hours ago.

She hurried into the house and to the bookshelves where all those photo albums were stored. It took a minute, but she found the one that held the photos from that year—the year she was born. Her grandmother had been very careful to ensure all her albums matched and all were dated with a gold metallic marker. It was an obsession of hers, she'd said.

Allie flipped through the pages, found the right one and grinned. The butterfly garden had been a lot smaller then. She carefully removed the photo that provided the best overall shot of her father digging the hole.

She hurried back outside to where Steve waited, sleeves rolled up to his elbows and the shovel in hand. Like her, he'd started to sweat quickly in the afternoon sun.

"This is it."

He wiped his hand on his thigh and accepted the photo. After studying it at length, he turned around slowly, surveying the garden enclosed with that white picket fence. At least it had started out white. It had faded and chipped in places. Something else Allie needed to take care of.

He pointed to one of the lilac bushes. "I think it might be under part of that bush."

Allie bit her lip. The lilacs had been her grandmother's favorite. "Be really careful. I'd hate to kill the bush."

He pointed his shovel toward it. "There are times when sacrifices must be made."

She laughed, mostly because she was emotionally drained and physically spent. The small silver bracelet felt cool in her hand, but she couldn't bear to let go of it. Her mother had been holding it when she died. And this was for her parents. "Just do it."

It didn't take a lot of imagination to conjure up images of her parents rushing out here in the darkness of night to dig up the time capsule they had planted four years prior. She could see her father doing what he had to do once it was out of the ground, stuffing evidence inside while her mother picked through the mementos that had been hidden there. Allie could see her holding the delicate silver chain—the very one she now held. Tears burned her eyes, and she forced away the images.

Get this done, Al.

To his credit, Steve took his time and used extra care when digging around the base of the bush. At last the blade of the shovel slid into the ground, and there was a distinct metal-on-metal sound.

Steve smiled, crouched down and started to dig with his gloved hands.

Allie held her breath, afraid to hope but unable to stop herself.

The dirty object he withdrew didn't look like the one in the photos. A frown worried her brow. Wait…

He wiped the dirt away, and there it was…the stainless-steel cylinder-type canister she'd seen in the photos.

Maybe she would finally have the evidence she needed to uncover the truth.

Chapter Eleven

3:50 p.m.

After Steve had covered all the holes made to protect the lilac bush, they brought the canister inside. Despite her earlier insistence about the bush being her grandmother's favorite, Allie really hadn't wanted to take the time to cover the holes, but Steve pointed out that the agents could show up at any moment. It was best not to leave anything too obvious for them to find. They couldn't ask about something they didn't know.

And she and Steve weren't sharing this find with anyone—at least not until they had time to evaluate what they actually had.

Now, after waiting patiently for longer than she wanted, Allie's heart was about to burst from her chest. Steve struggled to get the canister open. Her father had closed it tightly, and it had been in the ground for more than three decades. A serious round of elbow grease and some extra time was required, but he finally loosened the top. Then, without so much as a peek inside, he handed it to Allie.

She nodded and gave the twist-off top a final turn. Holding her breath, she turned it up to pour the contents onto the table.

Nothing came out.

Allie shook it harder. Still nothing. Panic building, she looked inside. Oh, okay, there were papers stuffed inside.

The evidence Rivero had been looking for?

Allie unfurled the paper…not evidence. A newspaper from the day she was born. She set it aside and turned up the capsule once more. This time several items tumbled out. A baby rattle. She touched it, smoothed her fingertips over the pink flowers painted on it. Then there was a shoe, her first presumably. She tucked a finger inside, found nothing. A silver spoon. And photos. Several of Allie and her parents along with a couple of her with her grandparents.

Disappointment bled through her. "Looks like it's a bust."

"Maybe." Steve had opened the newspaper and was perusing the pages. He smiled. "Copy this down."

Anticipation zinged Allie again. She pulled out her cell, which promptly rang again with a call from Rivero. She tapped the decline button and opened her notes app. "Ready."

"L…o…o…k. Look," he murmured.

"Yep." Allie's finger was poised for the next letter.

"H…r…w…s…e…h…e…e…"

"Where or here…he or she," Allie said as she put the letters in order to spell out whatever words best fit.

"Here's more," Steve said. "R…i…b…u…d…e." He flipped through the pages. "That's all the circled letters I see."

Allie couldn't help grinning at the idea that her mother or her father had thought to send a message this way. "Where she…where he's… Does the *s* have an apostrophe with it?"

"Damn." Steve turned back to the necessary page.

His gaze bumped into hers. "It does. The final word is *buried*. Where he's buried."

"The child?" Allie nerves were jumping now. "Where the little boy's remains are buried."

Steve skimmed the pages once more. "That has to be it." He folded the newspaper carefully and put it aside. "So where is Tommy Madison buried or were his ashes spread somewhere—assuming he actually was cremated?"

Her cell started to ring again. This time, she answered. "There was no evidence in the time capsule." She waited until Rivero finished spewing expletives. "Do you know the location of the little boy's final resting place?"

Rivero did not know where the child was buried, but he did know the name of the man who had worked at Wembley Funeral Services at the time of his death—a man who liked his Jack, as in Jack Daniel's, when he could afford it. Allie ended the call with another promise that she would keep him up to speed on their movements.

"He gave me a name and an address." Allie gathered the precious items from the time capsule and placed them back inside. "We should go there."

Steve grabbed his keys. Allie decided she wasn't leaving the time capsule here for someone to break in and steal. At this point, she didn't trust anything or anyone... except this man.

Griggs Residence
Shady Acres Mobile Home Park
Barrington Road, Wauconda, Illinois, 5:00 p.m.

ALLIE LEANED FORWARD as Steve drove slowly through the mobile home park. They had found a liquor store on the way and bought the gift they hoped would get the man talking. Mitchell Griggs, former funeral home attendant, lived in a rental about twenty-five miles from Woodstock.

Only he didn't use the name Griggs. He went by Mitch Butler, his mother's maiden name, according to Rivero. He'd left Wembley Funeral Services only a few weeks after Tommy Madison died. No one had heard from him for a while, then he'd shown up at another funeral home, this one in Chicago, but he'd used the Butler name. He'd been using it since.

There were many reasons why a person would want to disappear and to change his identity. Allie got it. Sometimes she thought about doing exactly that. But she only needed the answer to one question from Mitchell Griggs, aka Mitch Butler.

What really happened with the little boy?

Maybe two questions.

Why all the secrecy?

Steve parked. "You want me to do this one alone?" He glanced around. "This place looks a little sketchy."

"No way." She reached for the door and grabbed the bottle of Jack with her other hand. "I'm going with you."

They exited the SUV and climbed the steps to the small deck. The numerous shade trees made the hour seem later than it was. The place was low rent for sure, but it was all the dark corners and narrow alleys between the rows of homes with their overflowing trash cans that gave it that truly sketchy feel.

Allie had just raised her fist to knock on the door when it opened outward. She stepped back, bumping into Steve in the process.

The man, short, thin, sixtyish, eyed her up and down then glanced at Steve. He had the tiniest eyes. Beady eyes and thin hair that had once been black but was mostly gray now. "Whatever you're selling, I ain't buying. If you're from the police or any other law enforcement organization, come back with a warrant."

"None of the above." Allie extended the bottle like a peace offering. "I'm Allie Foster, and this is my friend, Steve Durham. We're here to ask you about a little boy who died twenty-eight years ago. Tommy Madison."

The man grabbed the bottle from her at the same instant his openly suspect expression closed like a slammed door. "I don't know what you're talking about. I never heard of any kid by that name."

"You worked at the Wembley Funeral Home," Steve countered, "where his body was prepared."

The other man shook his head. "You got the wrong guy." He started to close the door.

Allie stepped into its path, blocking it with her shoulder. "We know you did, Mr. Griggs. We're not here to cause trouble. We just want to ask you a couple of questions."

His eyes narrowed to an even beadier size. "Now why in the world would I answer any of your questions?"

"My father was Jerry Foster. He worked for Ledwell back then. I think they killed him and my mother in a car accident. I just haven't been able to prove it."

He barked a laugh. "I really can't help you now. I want no part of that kind of crap."

This time, Steve reached above Allie's head and caught the door when Griggs would have tried to pull it past Allie. "Where was the child buried?"

Griggs blinked. "Who said he was buried?"

"The dead are usually buried," Steve argued.

Griggs heaved a put-upon breath. "I know I'll regret

this." He looked at the bottle he held. "The kid was cremated."

"Now that wasn't so difficult, was it? Look, you don't have to invite us in." Steve hitched his head toward Allie. "But you do need to answer her questions."

Allie bit her lips together to prevent smiling. She really liked this guy.

"You're certain you didn't hear anything about where he would be buried? If—" Allie amended "—he was going to be buried?"

Griggs leaned against the doorframe. "I was curious, so I hung around that evening. I heard the father say something about taking him home to bury him."

"But you're certain they cremated him," Allie pressed. "It's important, Mr. Griggs."

"I put him in the furnace myself," he said with a covert look side to side. "That was my job at the time—when there was a call for it. Cremation wasn't as popular then as it is now. Especially when it involved kids."

Allie could certainly understand why. It would be a difficult decision. "Why did you leave Wembley a few weeks later?"

He shrugged again. "I changed jobs a lot back then. Why not? They all paid the same. I could walk down the block and get another job doing something completely different, and I'd still get paid minimum wage."

Valid point.

"According to Wembley," Steve spoke up, "you were discovered in a compromising position with one of the female—"

"That was a lie." Griggs pointed his finger at him. "They made that crap up because they wanted to scare me. They knew what I'd seen, and they wanted to make sure I stayed quiet." He sneered. "Don't pretend to know me or understand what I've been through in my life. I know what I saw."

"What did you see, Mr. Griggs?" Allie asked. "I think it may have been related to what got my parents killed."

He studied Allie for a long moment before deciding to respond. "Why does it matter? Really? Finding the truth won't bring your folks back. It won't make you feel any better about them being dead. So what's the point? I mean, these dudes are too big to bring down. If that's your goal, that will never happen. Digging around in this will get you the same place it got your folks—dead."

"You leave that part up to me, Mr. Griggs," Steve pressed. "We won't use your name. We just need to know what you know about the little boy. Then we'll leave you alone."

"Fair enough." He shifted his attention back to Allie. "But don't make me regret trusting you. If some form of the po-po shows up here after you leave, I'm gonna—"

"They won't," Steve inserted, his words a little on the lethal side.

"The parents brought the kid in. They were both distraught, you know. Tore all to pieces, like you'd expect. They waited while I did what had to be done. But—" he cast another of those furtive looks first right then left "—before I took him back, the mother leaned down and kissed him. Not unusual." He shrugged. "But she whispered something to him. Not I love you or something you'd expect."

"What did she say?" Allie asked when his dramatic pause went on a beat too long.

"She said, 'Daddy will bring you back.' It freaked me out a little, I have to tell you."

A chill raced over Allie's skin. "Did you see or hear anything else?"

He nodded. "When I prepared him for the crematorium, I noticed something weird. Trust me, I've seen some weird stuff in my time—working with the dead, I mean. But this was really creepy considering that one of the parents would have had to do it."

"What exactly did you notice?" Steve prompted. "If you could be as precise as possible."

"His eyes were missing." He patted one eyelid. "You know, the whole eyeball."

Allie's heart stumbled then started to race. "You're certain?"

He nodded. "Oh yeah. I checked. I'm sorry, but that is just bizarre. Who takes their own kid's eyes? I mentioned it to the manager later, and he told me never to talk about it again. It was a matter of discretion. He said I'd be fired if I ever mentioned it to a soul. So I didn't ask anything else, but I did talk about it with a couple of guys at the pub. I was a little drunk. I guess it got back to the wrong person. The next thing I knew, I was being followed."

"You're sure someone was following you?" Steve countered.

Allie could understand why Steve would be skeptical. The guy gave off a less-than-reliable vibe. Still, what he'd said so far made her feel ill.

"Definitely. I've been the target of drug dealers, loan sharks, pissed-off broads, I know when I'm being followed. It didn't take me long to figure out who it was. Especially after that sleazebag reporter, Rivero, tracked me down. I knew it was Ledwell. Damn it. I knew it, and I got the hell out. I had heard what those bastards did to people who saw things and dared to talk."

For a moment, Allie couldn't find her voice. Of course the idea had been in the back of her mind that Ledwell had been taking care of anyone who might dare tell his secrets. Rivero had confirmed as much…but this was the sort of affirmation that made her worry about what she might find at the end of all this.

Didn't matter. She was on a mission to find the truth about her parents' accident and to prove she did not murder anyone. "Did you happen to overhear the Madisons mention what they planned to do with his ashes?" She really needed to know where he was interred.

You planning to dig him up?

Allie banished the voice. If that was what it took to find answers then…yes. Maybe.

Griggs drew in another of those big, exaggerated breaths. "The wife mentioned she wanted him with her roses. Whatever that means."

Allie's breath stalled in her lungs. She knew exactly what that meant.

Talbert/Madison Residence
Justen Road
McHenry, Illinois, 7:00 p.m.

THIS HAD BEEN Jane and Thomas Madison's home at the time of their son's death. Mrs. Talbert, Jane's mother, had explained as much. This was the place where they entertained their friends and probably business associates as well. It was the place where their son died. *This* was the place where Jane had grown her roses.

The backyard was shrouded in shadows now. They had very little daylight left, but they had to try.

Steve had brought the shovel from her house. He had started to dig amid the overgrown rose bushes. Allie held a flashlight to aid their ability to see between the overrun shrubs. When he'd loosened most of the ground around the fountain and the rose bushes were out of the way, she got down on her knees and picked through the loosened clumps. They didn't have any gloves—they'd forgotten them—but she didn't care. She needed to find an urn or box. Something!

Steve knelt beside her and dug in as well. The more she plowed her fingers through the dirt and found nothing, the tighter desperation banded around her chest. There had to be something here. There just had to be. Tears burned in her eyes. This could not be another dead end.

But there was nothing. Not unless they had buried the child's remains far deeper.

"We can try again tomorrow," Steve promised as he dusted off his hands.

Allie dusted off her hands as best she could. "You're right. It's too dark…we're not prepared. Tomorrow will be better."

She was exhausted, and she was certain he was as well. It had been a very long day, and it wasn't as if they hadn't made some new discoveries.

Baby steps.

Like those of a little boy who was buried around here somewhere. Maybe with evidence that would prove Ledwell had reason to want her parents, a janitor and God knows who else dead.

On the way back to the SUV, she called Rivero and gave him the bad news. He didn't take it well. The man was such a jerk.

Back at his SUV, Steve loaded the shovel, and Allie watched the last of the light sink into the treetops. She wished she could remember the times she had been here...the things that happened... Had she played with that little boy more than once? Had she overheard hushed conversations that might help her now?

"Hey." Steve came to her at the passenger-side door and gave her a hug. "We'll get there." He drew back and smiled down at her. "Don't worry."

"Thanks." She dredged up a smile. "I needed a hug."

"I thought you might. What do you say we go home and crack open a bottle from your stash?"

"I say that sounds amazing."

As did a long hot bath and maybe a nice salad.

And some time just to be.

Thankfully, Steve had a package of wet wipes in his SUV, and they were able to reasonably clean their hands. Her whole body pulsated with something...an urgency she couldn't label. Maybe what she needed was to feel something more...a connection to another human—like this man.

Don't get ahead of yourself, Al. This is work for him.

Besides, now wasn't the time. She needed to focus.

The drive back to her house felt as if it were taking forever. "We should just grab something at a drive-through," she suggested. There was nothing at home. She really did have to do a better job of keeping her pantry and fridge stocked. She was kind of pathetic at the job.

She thought of the baby bracelet. Why the hell had

Rivero kept it all this time? And why didn't he talk to her the first time they went to his house? The whole idea infuriated her now that she thought about it. Particularly after he'd basically hung up on her when she told him they hadn't found anything beneath the roses at the former Madison home yet. He'd been furious they had dared to leave rather than continue to dig. *Jerk*.

Like Griggs said, Rivero was mostly a sleazeball.

"We can do that. Just name your preference."

"I'm easy," she assured him. "Just pull in at the next place we pass."

Blue lights suddenly throbbed in the side mirror. Allie twisted around in her seat. A police cruiser, lights blaring, nosed up behind them and sounded off a quick burst of its siren.

"What the hell?" Allie turned to Steve. "Were you speeding?"

"I was not." Steve slowed and eased to the side of the highway. "I guess we'll find out what I was doing."

Allie could not remember the last time she had been pulled over by the police. But then she didn't do a lot of driving, so that wasn't making a point at all.

Steve powered his window down and placed his hands on the steering wheel.

The officer took his time getting out and then approaching their vehicle.

Allie just wanted to go home. She felt more tired than she had in her entire life.

A flashlight pierced the interior of the SUV. She squinted to block the blare.

"License and registration," the officer demanded.

Steve reached for his wallet, removed his driver's license and handed it to the officer. "Is it okay if I reach into the glovebox and get the registration?"

The officer studied his license and then shone the flashlight directly in Steve's face. "That won't be necessary, sir. I need you to step out of the vehicle."

Allie's pulse reacted. Was this normal procedure?

"I will step out of the vehicle when you tell me the reason you pulled me over and why you need me to get out."

"Sir, there's an APB out for your arrest, and I'm going to need you to come with me. You can call your attorney once we're at the station. But I would prefer that we not have any trouble here on the street."

Steve held up his hands. "I'm certain there's been a mistake, but I'm happy to cooperate. If you'll allow me, I'd like to make a call and confirm that the APB is actually for me. I believe I'm well within my rights to request confirmation."

"If you'll step out of the vehicle, sir," the officer repeated, "you can make the call from my patrol car."

"I'll make it now," Steve countered. "We'll go from there. I'm an attorney. I know my rights."

"I'll stand by." The officer didn't move or take his flashlight's beam off the two of them.

Steve picked up his cell from the console and made the call.

Allie's frustration and anger mounted with every second that passed. This was ridiculous. How the hell could there be an APB out on Steve?

"Thanks." Steve ended the call. "Looks like I'm taking a ride to the city jail."

"This is insane," Allie argued. "You haven't done anything."

"Don't worry," he assured her. "My team is on it. You can follow us there. This shouldn't take long to clear up, but I need you to follow us there and stay within view of the officer manning the lobby at the jail."

"You should go home, ma'am," the officer spoke up. "This may take some time." He opened the driver-side door.

"Follow us," Steve repeated. "I want you nearby."

"I will."

Allie watched in horror as Steve was handcuffed then escorted to the cruiser and placed in the backseat. What the hell was going on here?

She climbed across the console, settled behind the steering wheel and adjusted the seat. When the police cruiser pulled away from the curb, she did the same. She followed the vehicle through the dark streets. This was so wrong. She shivered. But what could she do? How did she prove it was a mistake?

Maybe she should call Rivero. He might have a contact with the police from back when he was such a big news star. There likely weren't very many people in this little town that he didn't know.

But that had been a long time ago.

Then again, the Ledwell group didn't just know people. They appeared to own people. How did you stop a machine like that?

Not alone, for sure.

Steve had called his people. The Colby Agency would know what to do. If anyone could stop them, it was the Colby Agency.

Chapter Twelve

Woodstock Police Department
Lake Avenue, 10:30 p.m.

Allie sat in the lobby, frustration roaring inside her. What the hell were these people doing? She glared across the room at the desk sergeant. She wanted to rant at the woman. But it wasn't her fault.

The molded plastic seats were incredibly uncomfortable. Allie shifted to another position. The tile floor and walls were basically the same color, a sort of off-white. The place reminded her of what she imagined a morgue would look like.

The officer who had pulled them over had taken Steve beyond those double doors that required being buzzed in to pass through. She was left to sit here and wait. Her mind kept whirling with the bits and pieces that had come out today. Not that any of it added up to a firm answer, but it was starting to come together toward one. Rivero kept sending her text messages asking what was happening. She'd given him the short version of events, and he'd only responded with Oh.

Yeah, she mused, *oh*. He hadn't mentioned knowing

anyone who could help, so her decision not to call him had been the right one.

She got up and started to pace. She could not sit still a moment longer. The desk sergeant watched her for a moment then returned to whatever she was doing on the computer. Allie figured the people who sat behind that desk saw plenty during a shift. She wasn't about to give anyone a show. Her goal was to walk off some of the building agitation.

The walls suddenly felt as if they were closing in on Allie, and she couldn't breathe. She walked to the desk and fixed a smile on her lips. "I'm going out to the car for a while," she said to the woman beyond the glass. "I'll be back in a few minutes."

The woman nodded but said nothing. It wasn't her job to keep up with Allie or to provide information to Steve about her whereabouts. Why had she even walked over and said anything?

Whatever.

Allie crossed the sterile lobby and pushed through the exit door into the muggy night air. She drew in a deep breath and glanced around. The parking lot was quiet. A few other cars but no sign of people. She walked to Steve's SUV, unlocked it and climbed inside. She pressed the lock button immediately. She surveyed the parking lot again to make sure she was alone. Another hard shiver passed through her.

Maybe being outside wasn't smart, but she couldn't be in there anymore.

She needed to do something.

Her phone buzzed with another text from Rivero. She rolled her eyes and returned a message of Still waiting.

She tossed her phone onto the console and stared at the bracelet the man had kept all this time. She fingered the tiny silver blocks engraved with the letters of her name. Her mother had been holding this bracelet. Had she thought it would be a good-luck charm? Or just a way to cling to her love for Allie while they did what they had to do in hopes of escaping?

What had her father known that put them in such danger? What if the newspaper had been a ruse, and she and Steve had missed something in the time capsule? Her brain felt under pressure from all sides. She couldn't get a deep enough breath. Allie shook her head. She had to do something, or she was going to have a full-blown panic attack. Taking care, she placed the bracelet in the cupholder on the console, then she reached into the rear floorboard and grabbed the time capsule. She opened it up and removed the contents, placing each item on the passenger seat.

She flipped on the overhead lights and started with the newspaper. Maybe the circled letters were the ruse. After all, they were a little obvious. Even the message, now that she thought about it, was in-your-face recognizable. Her father was too smart for that. Allie smiled. If she had learned nothing else, she had discovered how very smart her father was and how loving her mother was.

Taking her time, she reviewed each headline, each ad for local shops and businesses. The classifieds received a thorough read. How many spies had used classifieds? Her father would have considered that as well.

Thankfully, the paper didn't consist of that many pages, so her work wasn't too terribly time consuming. Nothing jumped out at her. She moved on to the photos. She shuffled through them one at a time, taking in every detail of the image. Most of them were taken in the backyard at home. Nothing new or notable in any of those either. Then she picked up the shoe. She smiled. It was so tiny. She wondered if she'd actually worn it at all since the time capsule was buried the day she was born. Maybe from the hospital. On the other hand, it had been dug up later when evidence was supposed to be added. But her parents wouldn't have had adding sentimental items on their minds at that time.

Nothing in or on the shoe. No writing. Nothing. The spoon was just a spoon. Stainless, not real silver. No brand engraved on the handle. Lastly, she reached for the rattle. It wasn't one of the fancy silver ones. Just plastic. Yellow with pink and blue flowers.

She looked it over carefully, gave it a good shake. The rattle didn't sound the way she'd expected. She frowned. More a plunk effect than a clatter. She traced the seam where the baby toy was put together, and her finger stopped then went back over the right side of the seam. There was a tiny piece missing on the little lip on the one side that closed over the other. In that area, the two sides felt as if they weren't pushed together all the way. She studied it more closely. The sides appeared to have been pulled apart and then shoved back together. Her gaze traveled down the length of the now vintage toy to the part she held in her palm. The stem or handle had been broken and maybe glued back together.

As if someone had broken the handle while prying apart the two sides of the round end that held whatever was supposed to make the rattling sound.

Allie hesitated for only a second, then she started to

tug, using her fingernails, which were dirty from digging, to pry at the narrow little gap in the seam. She couldn't get it. Damn it. She needed a screwdriver or… maybe a key.

She dug in her purse until she found her house key. After placing the rattle on the console, she held it in place with the fingers of one hand and jabbed and pried at the seam with the key in her other hand.

It took a bit, and she cracked the bigger part of the rattle to get the job done, but it opened. Rather than small beads or something on that order to clatter around inside, there was a small, slim, silver object. She picked it up, her eyes communicating what she saw to her brain but her gray matter rejecting the idea.

Thumb drive…flash drive…whatever one chose to call it. It appeared to have a small cap. She tugged it free, and sure enough, there was the USB port plug.

"No way," she murmured.

Instinctively, she reached up and turned off the light, anticipation soaring through her.

Then she sat, unable to move or really think, for a moment.

This couldn't be…

Her parents had died twenty-eight years ago. About three years before flash drives were available on the market for everyday consumers…but they had existed. She knew this from some movie she had watched, and she'd been certain they'd made a mistake, but she googled it, and sure enough, the writers had been correct.

Still…she should check again. She looked at the name on the tiny little device.

Allie grabbed her phone and searched flash drives and

the name. She remembered correctly. They did exist—this brand in particular—well before they were widely available on the market.

Okay. Her disbelief drained away. This could be loaded with evidence. From her father. About Ledwell and SILO.

What the heck was she thinking? Of course it was. It was in the time capsule that *they* had buried, and it was inside her baby rattle. What else would it be? Anticipation seared through her veins. Her right leg started to pop up and down.

She glanced at the police department building. There was no way to know how much longer Steve would be. Her house was like two miles from here. All she had to do was rush home, get her laptop and come right back. No biggie. Ten minutes tops.

Heart pounding, she hit the start button on the SUV and drove out of the parking lot. She drove slowly, maybe too slowly. So possibly the trip would take fifteen minutes. She couldn't remember the last time she'd driven anywhere, so slow was likely the best option. Even at her turtle-like speed, it took her a whole fourteen minutes to make the short trip.

She turned into her driveway. The house was so damned dark. If she'd had any idea they would be gone so long she would have left the outside lights on. She shuddered as she parked. She could do this.

She could.

Just because someone had killed her parents and several other Ledwell-associated people didn't mean she was in that same sort of danger.

The storage device clutched in her right hand seemed to grow warmer as if warning her to think again.

Don't be naïve, Al.

Before getting out, she sent a text to Rivero and told him that she may have found something and had come back to her house for her laptop. She left it at that. No need to give him any other specifics. Then she sent a text to Steve's phone. It had most likely been confiscated, but he needed to know where she was just in case he came out in the next ten minutes before she was back in the parking lot.

She surveyed the darkness outside the vehicle. She had lived in this house her entire life. Played in every corner of this yard. At one time, she had known all her neighbors. Granted, this was an old neighborhood, so the houses were farther apart than in newer communities, and there were trees—lots of trees. Lots of hiding places.

She banished the notion. She knew every tree. This was home. Not some wilderness she'd never explored.

Deep breath. She opened the door and climbed out. She touched the door handle and locked the SUV. Continually scanning the darkness for movement, she tucked her cell into one back pocket and the fob into the other. Clutching her house key and with the flash drive in her front pocket, she hurried to the door. She unlocked each of the deadbolts with the key. Every click making her look around to ensure no one had appeared out of the shadows. The back door was still an issue, but Steve had screwed it shut from the inside, so that wouldn't be easily used by an intruder. This door had been locked, so it wasn't likely anyone had gotten in again. She relaxed a little.

Of course, there were plenty of windows to be broken and climbed through.

She shook off the thought.

"Focus," she muttered.

The door opened into the little entry hall, and she flipped on a light switch. She breathed easier then. No one jumped out at her. No sound of running footsteps. It was all quiet. Since Steve had arrived, she'd been forgetting to set the security system, not that it would have alerted anyone, but it did make enough noise to probably deter a would-be intruder. She would be sure to set it when she left this time.

"Okay." She closed and locked the door, all three deadbolts, then put the key in her front pocket. Moving quickly, she went from room to room, turning on lights, to ensure all was clear before heading upstairs.

Once in the second-story hallway, she checked the rooms up there too. When all appeared clear, she hurried to her office and reached for her laptop.

She froze, the laptop in her hand.

Why drive back to the station to have a look? Why not look right now? Assuming the contents weren't password blocked or somehow encrypted, she could see what she had in like ten seconds.

She really should get back.

But what if this was the information they had been looking for that would lead them to the truth?

Her need to know won the battle.

She slid into her chair and opened the laptop. It took a moment to get the flash drive into the proper port. Even more time was required for it to launch and load.

"Come on," she muttered, her nerves jumping.

Then it started.

Holding her breath, she watched as folders loaded onto

the screen. None were labeled beyond the basic numbers 1, 2, et cetera.

She clicked on the first folder and, sluggishly, it opened. Dozens of documents populated the screen. She clicked on the first one, and it opened. The title on the page was Test Subject One. The accompanying image had her jaw dropping.

The detailed description of the head…the shoulders and torso…arms…legs…was that of a man except it wasn't…human.

But it looked human.

She read through the notes quickly. Daily reports…monthly progress.

Heart pounding, she closed that one and opened the next. Another of the same, only this one was a woman.

"Holy…"

Glass shattering downstairs made her jump.

Allie stilled. Listened.

There was a sound…

She strained to hear…too terrified to move. There was a crackling noise.

What the hell?

More shattering glass.

She yanked the flash drive from the port and started to shove it into her pocket but decided to put it in her bra. Moving soundlessly, she eased to the door. No one in the upstairs hall. She crept along toward the staircase, listening and watching.

What was that smell? Gasoline.

She paused at the top of the stairs.

The distinct sound of a whoosh filled the air.

Fear rammed into her chest.

Fire.

She had to get out of here. Couldn't go downstairs… whoever had started the fire was down there somewhere…maybe waiting outside the door.

Slowly, she backed away from the staircase. She could go out a window.

But she was on the second floor.

Allie hesitated, then she smiled. Didn't matter. Her grandparents had put in an emergency ladder. Her grandmother said Allie's father had insisted.

"Thank you, Daddy," she murmured as she rushed to her grandparents' room. There were three windows… which one was it?

All the windows had blinds and curtains.

She went to the middle one. Not that one. Not the one on the left.

At the final window, the ladder was attached to the wall behind a small table her grandmother had used to camouflage it.

Allie unlocked the window and pushed upward on the sash. It didn't budge. Fear throttled through her veins. She pushed again, using every ounce of strength she possessed. It didn't give.

The odor of smoke grew thicker.

Her lungs seemed to seize in anticipation of filling with the deadly carbon and airborne particles. She had to hurry.

Think, Al.

What had she heard her grandmother say about old windows being stuck? Sometimes the paint made them stick… She needed something to slide between the sash and the frame that held it in place.

Heart pounding, she rushed to the table on her grandfather's side of the bed, dragged open the drawer and picked through the items there. He'd always collected and carried pocketknives. She grabbed the largest one in the drawer and rushed back to the window. It took her a moment to figure out how to open it. Once she did, she stuck the blade between the sash and its frame and started to wiggle it and then to slide it up and down. She did one side before moving on to the other. By the time she'd finished, the smoke was thick in the air. Her body resisted the impulse to breathe.

She had to get out of here.

Dropping the knife, she got a grip on the sash with both hands and tugged. She groaned with the effort of lifting it, desperation rushing through her body.

The sash gave way, sliding upward a few inches.

Allie cried out with relief. She placed her hands beneath the lower part of the sash this time and pulled upward again and, thank God, up it went.

Her knees went weak with relief.

It took a few seconds to get the screen out of the way. She allowed it to fall to the ground outside. It was pitch dark in the backyard. She wished she'd turned on some exterior lights when she arrived and started turning on lights in the house.

She released the ladder and pushed it over the ledge and out the window.

Now all she had to do was climb down. She stuck her upper body out the window and stared toward the ground. It was quite a ways to fall.

"You can do this."

She could. She really could.

She drew her upper body back inside, next one leg went out the window, then the other. The position she'd chosen left her sitting on the window ledge with her legs hanging out. With a deep breath, she rolled onto her stomach and eased her lower body out farther.

Now her legs dangled in the air. The window casing cut into her abdomen.

She focused on finding the ladder with her feet. First one foot hooked on to a rung and then the other. Her heart in her throat, she tested her weight. No snap and break, no sudden drop. Okay. She started down. One rung at a time. Right. Left. Repeat.

When her feet were on the ground, she wilted against the side of the house.

She was down without breaking anything.

The fire blazed in the first floor windows.

Fear snaked around her throat.

The house would soon be fully engulfed.

The photo albums. Her family's things! Her entire history. Allie slapped her hands over her mouth to hold back the scream that burgeoned there.

But she couldn't scream. Whoever had set the fire could still be out there watching to make sure she went up in flames with the house.

She needed to call 911.

She reached into her pocket for her phone.

Not there.

Had she left it on her desk? In the SUV? Had it fallen on the floor in her grandparents' room or on the ground outside?

A loud sound in the front part of the house or on the porch shattered the air. Had a room caved in?

She had to get out of here. Find help. Get back to Steve.

After a quick glance side to side, she rushed into the wooded area between her house and the one next door. She ran through the trees, stumbled over things she couldn't identify in the dark. She ran until she reached the clearing that was the yard of the next house. It was dark. The occupants were either in bed or away.

Gasping for air and moving slowly, she made her way to the street. Fear pulsed in her veins. If she could make it across to the yellow house, she would knock on the door. The Simpsons lived there. They were friends of her grandparents. Their car was in the driveway.

She checked both ways then started across.

Just as she reached the halfway mark, a car barreled around the curve on her left.

She froze for an instant then turned and rushed back to her side of the street in hopes of reaching the cover of the trees before she was spotted.

The car skidded to a stop.

Not a car she realized. An SUV. Oh God.

She was about to dive into the woods when, "Hey, get in before they find you!"

Rivero.

A dozen questions shot through her head, but there was no time to analyze the situation. She could stay and hope to find a way out of here, or she could go with him.

She turned back to the street. The vehicle was his vintage Land Rover.

He could take her to Steve. Okay. She ran toward the vehicle, the door opened and she climbed inside. "They set my house on fire."

"Buckle up." He stamped on the gas, and the vehicle rocketed forward.

When they passed her house it was fully involved.

"Damn," he muttered.

"Everything is gone," she murmured. Her entire history was gone. Her family's history.

"At least you're alive." Rivero glanced in her direction.

She nodded, her body starting to shake from the receding adrenaline.

"You came for your laptop. Did you get a look at whatever you found?"

She nodded again, watching in the side mirror as her house disappeared in the distance as they drove away.

"I wish you hadn't looked." His words were spoken so quietly she almost didn't hear him.

"Why?" Her voice sounded weak and somehow frail.

Everything was gone…her heart hurt.

He glanced at her again, his expression grim in the dim light from the dash. "Because you can't unsee it."

Chapter Thirteen

Tuesday, June 10
Woodstock Police Department
Lake Avenue, 12:05 a.m.

"I assure you, Mr. Durham," Special Agent Potter insisted, "this was a mistake. I checked in with my point of contact regarding your and Ms. Foster's activities, and he took me completely out of context."

"Trespassing," Steve said, rolling down his sleeves as they walked out of the building. "Vandalism."

"Well, you and Ms. Foster were digging on private property," she argued.

Alfred Mannington held up a hand. "I believe we've cleared this up, Agent Potter. I see no reason to continue with this discussion. Mr. Durham has been through enough tonight."

Mannington was the agency's top attorney. Steve hated to drag him down here at this hour, but he'd needed help in a hurry. Help with serious connections. Mannington was close friends with the governor as well as several other state representatives. Woodstock's chief of police was only too happy to put in an appearance to handle the situation.

Potter acknowledged Mannington's suggestion with a nod. "Very well. Good night, gentlemen."

Steve waited until she had climbed into her vehicle and driven away before turning to Mannington. "Can you give me a ride to the Foster home? When they returned my personal items, I had a text from Allie—about an hour and twenty minutes ago—saying she was running to her house for her laptop." He scanned the parking lot. "But she's not back, and that worries me."

"Sure thing."

As they strode to Mannington's sedan, Steve considered that as tired as Allie had been she might have fallen asleep at her desk or on the sofa. But he wasn't banking on anything that simple. She should be back by now. At the very least, she should be answering her phone, and she was not. He'd called twice.

Worry and outright fear had his pulse shifting into overdrive. He had promised her everything would be okay. She was safe with him.

He'd let her down.

Steve gave his colleague the directions as they drove. He could use a decent cup of coffee. The stuff back at the police station had been in the pot far too long. He'd drunk two bottles of water trying to get rid of the bitter taste. But coffee would have to wait. He had to find Allie and make sure she was safe first.

The instant they turned onto Allie's block, he spotted the emergency vehicles, lights blazing in the darkness. Neighbors had come out onto the sidewalks.

Fear grabbed him by the throat. "Oh hell." He leaned forward in an attempt to see more clearly.

Mannington slowed for the officer standing in the middle of the street blocking traffic.

The uniform came around to the driver-side window. "I'm afraid you can't—"

"That's my house," Steve interrupted him with the necessary lie to cut to the chase. "I have to get over there."

The officer stepped back and waved them through.

"This does not look good," Mannington pointed out.

"Park here." Steve was already opening the door when the car eased to the curb. He jumped out and rushed across the street.

More uniforms tried to stop him. He gave the same story, which got him directed to the man in charge.

"Can you tell me if anyone was home this evening?" the fire marshal asked.

Steve was grateful the man didn't ask for identification. His driver's license showed his address in Chicago. "My girlfriend was here." He spotted his SUV then. It was parked to the side and didn't appear to have been damaged. He would have felt better if it hadn't been here. "She drove my SUV here around ten thirty or so."

Despite the fear funneling inside him just now, somehow calling Allie his girlfriend felt right. At the same time, he was terrified she was hurt...or worse.

"Where were you?"

Steve pushed aside the distracting thoughts. He had expected the question. "I was at the police department. We've been looking into an old case." He put a hand against his chest. "I work for the Colby Agency in Chicago. I'm helping my girlfriend with the case. Anyway, I was speaking with Special Agent Potter from the FBI and Chief of Police Williams this evening. She needed to get home and…" He gestured to his SUV. "I need to know that she's okay."

What he needed was to get closer…to scream her name. To find her!

The fire marshal nodded. "Would this investigation trigger something like this?" He indicated the burned-out house with his notepad.

Steve fought for patience. If he expected to be allowed anywhere near the house, he had to play the damned game. "Unfortunately, that's a strong possibility." The house—it was a total loss as was everything inside. The reality crashed into him again that Allie could have been in there. "I have to go in there. I have to make sure she's not in there."

The urgency was a palpable force inside him. He started for the house, but the fire marshal grabbed him by the arm and pulled him back.

"I'm afraid no one can go in there right now, sir. I don't mean to be insensitive, but if she was in there, it's too late to help her now."

Mannington was suddenly next to him. "We should let them do their jobs, Steve."

Steve wanted to punch them both and make a mad run for the house.

Two firefighters suddenly appeared. Steve's determination withered a little as he braced for bad news. How the hell had he allowed this to happen? He should never have let her out of his sight. This was on him. Damn it.

This was his mistake. He should have asked for more help from the agency.

"Sir," one of the firefighters said to the marshal, "there's an emergency ladder around back coming down from one of the upstairs windows. Looks like whoever was in there released the ladder and either got out or tried to."

Hope flared in Steve's chest. He should have known better than to give up on Allie. She was a survivor. She wouldn't go down so easily.

"Have you searched the yard? The property goes into the woods. She could be out there injured," Steve demanded, hope daring to expand once more.

"We have, sir," the same firefighter said. "We've done all we can until things cool down a little." He held up a clear plastic evidence bag. "We found this on the ground near the ladder."

Allie's cell phone was in the bag. She had come down that ladder in a hurry, which would explain how she'd lost her phone and hadn't taken the time to look for it.

She'd feared someone who wanted to hurt her was close.

Steve reached for the bag. "May I see it?"

The fire marshal shook his head. "Afraid not, sir. This is evidence. We have every reason to believe this was arson."

"Please," Steve urged, "can you just show me the final text messages and phone calls?"

Mannington stepped into the conversation then. "This is a matter of life and death, Marshal. Time is of the essence. We need whatever we can find to point us in the right direction. Allie Foster is—" he gestured to the house "—as you can see, in danger."

The marshal passed the bag to Steve. To the two firefighters, he said, "You two are my witnesses if there's any trouble about this decision."

Yes sirs echoed from the pair.

The last call, besides the missed ones from him, was before they were pulled over and he ended up being hauled away in a police cruiser. The final text was one she'd sent to Steve, but the one before it was to Rivero, telling him she suspected she'd found something, and she was going to her house to have a look at it.

Fury chased away the cold uncertainty in Steve's gut. He passed the phone back to the marshal. "Thank you. Is there anything else I can do here to help?"

"I need your name and contact info," the marshal said. "Then it would be best if you got out of our way like your friend suggested."

Steve pointed to his SUV. "Can I take my vehicle?" He had no idea where the fob would be. He glanced at the house. Probably fried inside.

"Afraid not, sir. Anything close to the house has to be considered evidence in cases like this one."

Steve nodded. "Thanks anyway."

He and Mannington walked back to his car. "I think I know where she is," Steve told him. "The last text she sent to anyone besides me was to someone we've been interviewing."

Mannington looked at him over the top of the sedan. "I can call for a car. Take me to a diner or someplace I can hang out, and you can use my car. Find her. Do whatever you have to."

"Thanks, man, I appreciate it."

Mannington pointed a finger at him. "Do not wreck my car."

Steve smiled. "I won't get a scratch on it."

He drove Mannington to Red's. It was closed, but a quick call to Red had him waiting at the door to open up and keep Steve's colleague company.

Steve headed for Rivero's place. If the man tried to pretend he had no idea where Allie might be, Steve intended to beat the daylights out of him.

Chapter Fourteen

Madison Residence
Hamilton Road
Woodstock, 12:30 a.m.

Allie had a bad feeling something was going on with Rivero.

First, she had been stunned that he'd left his house to come to hers. Her impression was that he never left the house. Granted, maybe he was like her in that he preferred to stay home but wasn't a true recluse or agoraphobic.

The fact that he'd driven fast but competently and continued to speak fairly reasonably had assuaged her concerns. Still, she'd wanted to text or call Steve, but she'd lost her phone, and Rivero insisted he'd forgotten his in his haste to get to her house. The driving around in all sorts of directions for half an hour or so had seemed reasonable to ensure they weren't followed.

All that aside, it was when their frantic journey ended on the road to Thomas Madison's house that alarm bells were triggered.

"Why are we here?"

He pulled deep into the driveway, past the house and

right up to the detached garage as if he'd been here before. She imagined he had. He'd been following this story for thirty years. Why wouldn't he have tracked down the Madisons and tried speaking with one or both.

"This is where it all came apart." He shut off the engine and turned to her.

The interior lights of his vehicle dimmed until they went completely dark. An exterior light on the detached garage provided some illumination—enough for her to see his face. He appeared calm now.

"I don't know what you mean." She worked on achieving her own state of calm. He didn't appear to have any sort of weapon. He hadn't threatened her. No reason to be concerned. She hoped.

He reached for his door handle. "Come on. We'll go inside, and I'll explain."

She climbed out and followed him toward the back of the house. "Do you think they had anyone watching my house who might have seen you pick me up? Should we be worried about our safety?"

At the back door, he hesitated. Swatted at the bugs swarming around the light next to it. "We're safe. I'm guessing whoever they hired to set your house on fire split as soon as the flames were going well enough to be confident the job was done."

"The job," she repeated, then swallowed with effort. "You mean eliminating me?"

He made a sound that wasn't quite a laugh, more a grunt. "What else? These guys are ruthless. I thought you got that part already."

"I suppose it's my eternal assumption that people are good that makes me seem naïve."

He shot her a look before opening the door. "Time to leave the gullibility behind. There's no room for ignorant bliss in this situation."

She supposed he was right about that. There was no more deniability. Ledwell did bad things, and people, including her parents, had been murdered to protect their secrets.

Allie had lost everything.

Ledwell had taken it all from her.

They entered the house through a mudroom. Rivero flipped on lights as if he came here all the time. In the kitchen, he did the same, turning on the overhead light, which was one switch in a panel of six.

How had he known exactly which one to flip?

Tension worked its way through her, but she asked no questions. No need to give him a heads-up that she was suspicious again. If she was lucky, since the power was still on, maybe there was a landline in the house. She'd gotten rid of the landline at her house long ago, but some people preferred to keep them even with cell phones.

He turned to her. She jumped, just a little. She prayed he didn't notice.

The smile that appeared when she jumped was the oddest expression.

Oh yes, he had noticed.

"Let me show you around. There's something I think you should see."

She nodded. Summoned a smile. "Sure." Damn. That was not what he would expect her to say. She was in the home of Thomas Madison—her father's former friend and colleague. "I hope you found something that will help me prove Ledwell murdered my parents."

He glanced back at her as he strode toward the staircase. "Oh, I think you'll find this most interesting, and it will confirm everything you already think you know."

She followed him to the stairs. Rather than go up the staircase, which went both ways, he headed down.

The way the house was designed, there was a lower level that opened to the outside on the far end of the house. People often built houses with exterior access to a basement level when on a hillside. She and Steve had seen this when they were here before, but the window and door coverings had prevented them from seeing inside.

The lower level was pretty much what Allie had expected. A large den with a kitchenette and dining area. Wood floor, area rug, white walls. Well-used sectional and a television. An open door led to a bedroom. Allie could see one corner of the bed beyond the doorway. Another door on the opposite wall was different. More like a vault door with a keypad.

"You see," he said, sounding proud of himself, "this is what's going to blow you away."

Anticipation and a twinge of fear pricked her. She glanced around. No sign of a phone. Damn it. If she just ran, she might be able to outmaneuver him but maybe not. At least, right now, he had no idea she was suspicious. "What exactly are you about to show me?"

"You think that flash drive you found is interesting. Wait until you see this."

Did Thomas Madison have files locked away down here?

Wait. "You know what's on the flash drive?" She felt like biting her tongue after having asked the question, but this was growing more bizarre by the moment. Under the circumstances, it was a fair question.

He turned his hands up and gave a look that said *duh*. "I knew what they were doing. I just couldn't prove it."

She nodded slowly, her head trying to wrap around what he was actually saying. "You're here, in this house, and it seems like you've been here before. Had you and Thomas Madison become friends?"

He made a face. "I wouldn't say we were friends." He shrugged, glanced at the door. "I have a friend who works at the hospital who let me know he was not doing so well. He'd been in the hospital two other times over the past several months. His deteriorating condition was what brought me back to Woodstock."

Allie's heart rate started to climb. She wished she had found some way to get in touch with Steve. This was bad. She no longer had any doubts. This was really bad. Rivero was not trying to help them, and it didn't matter if he believed she was suspicious. This was not going to end well.

"The last time he was in the hospital, before his demise—" he shrugged "—about six weeks ago, I paid him a visit after he got home. The home health nurse was out smoking a cigarette, and I sneaked in. She never even knew I was here. I just hid and waited until she left. I'd parked my Rover at a house down the road. It's for sale, you know."

"I saw the sign," Allie said, going along. Her best chance of surviving this was to keep him believing she wasn't on to him until she could figure out a way to escape.

"I made my way through the woods and just waited for the right opportunity." He shrugged again. "What else do I have but time?"

He walked to the French doors and opened the blinds

there. That was when she spotted his cell phone in the hip pocket of his jeans. Either that or he was carrying some other thin rectangular object the right size.

If she'd had any doubts, she now knew the bastard had lied to her. She wasn't surprised, just disappointed in herself for trusting him in the first place.

"We had quite the time catching up." He laughed, the sound just shy of evil. "His physical condition didn't allow him to force me out of his house or stop me from doing whatever I wanted. Tying him to the bed was easy enough. Of course, I had to do so carefully otherwise the nurse would have noticed any bruising."

"Smart," she said when he didn't immediately continue.

"He told me that it wasn't Ledwell who put out the hit on your father."

Allie drew back as if he'd slugged her. "But it's the only thing that makes sense. You said Ledwell was responsible for their deaths and numerous others."

"They are responsible. Just not directly. The CIA has always been at the top of everything they do."

"So it's the CIA." She held up her hands to put an end to this. She'd had enough. Whatever was about to happen, she just couldn't do this anymore. "Okay, Mr. Rivero. I really need to call my friend Steve. He'll be worried, and I'm really tired."

He pursed his lips and did some head shaking of his own. "Unfortunately, it's too late to turn back now."

"What does that mean, Mr. Rivero?" Fear started to ramp up inside her, but she refused to back down now. She had known it would go this way if she gave him any trouble. It was now or later. It wasn't like she could walk this back. "Are you threatening me? I thought we were on the same side."

He moved toward the door that looked like one on a vault or large safe. "I've always been on my own side. There were times, I suppose, it seemed we were on the same one, but your definition and mine are clearly different."

"I'm done here." She could go across the street to that neighbor's house, the one who showed up when she and Steve were here before.

Rather than wait for his reaction, she walked away. She had reached the stairs when he stopped her with, "But then you won't see the proof you need to reveal who killed your parents. I can give you that."

Did she walk away and risk never knowing? She had the flash drive…but was it enough?

"Fine." She turned around. "But don't expect me to go into wherever that leads." She nodded to the door in front of him.

He laughed. "Don't worry. You don't have to go in."

No matter what he said, she opted to stay near the staircase. If she got uneasy again, she was out of here unless he physically stopped her. Frankly, at this point, she couldn't be sure what he intended. One moment she was convinced he planned to harm her, and the next she wasn't so sure.

He pulled the keypad free of the door, swinging it to one side. Then he reached into his pocket and retrieved something. A key, she realized, as he inserted it then gave it a twist, reached for the handle and opened it. The big, no question about it now, vault door opened.

"He wouldn't give me the code," he explained. "But

I knew there would be a key somewhere. It took some time, but I found it."

"And what is it you believe I need to see?" She folded her arms over her middle in an effort to conceal the shaking that had started. She would not be afraid, she repeated silently.

"The most explosive secrets that Ledwell has are right here. A maze of files, including videos, and the perfect example of what they were and are still doing in the sublevels of that high security lab."

"If you had access to this," she said, her anger rising again, "why the hell didn't you tell me. I wouldn't have been running around all over the place trying to find evidence." Another realization had her drawing back. Wait just one damned minute. "Why would you need the evidence my father had if you had access to this?"

"But you would've missed all the fun. And there is the small matter of tying up loose ends." He gestured to the room. "Have a look."

Ensuring that she stayed beyond arm's reach from him, she moved closer until she could see inside the room.

Bookshelves covered two walls, each lined with binders. Rows of filing cabinets stood against the other two walls. In the center of the room was a round table with four chairs.

A man suddenly appeared in the doorway, stepping from one side of the door as if he'd been hiding or cowering there.

"May I come out now?"

Allie stumbled back. The man inclined his head and stared at her. "Who is this?"

He was medium height and build. He had black hair and vibrant...*green* eyes.

The photos she had seen of Tommy Madison filled her head.

"Tommy?" The name slipped from her lips before she could catch it.

He frowned, stared at her. "Do I know you?"

"You don't know her," Rivero spoke up. "She's your target for today."

Allie's attention swung to him. "What did you say?"

Rivero smiled. "Don't mind me, I was just leaving. It was nice to have known you, Allie Foster. Thank you for finding that evidence and bringing it right to me. One less bit of housekeeping."

"What the hell are you doing?" she demanded.

Rivero paused in his obvious exit. He turned back to her. "I'm doing what I've waited twenty-eight years to do, leaving with all the loose ends accounted for so that I may live the rest of my life in peace."

Allie shook her head. "I don't understand."

He exhaled a put-upon breath. "If you must know, here you go. I was Ledwell's watchdog, so to speak. My career was on a downward spiral." He shrugged. "It happens. One day you're at the top, and the next someone younger and more handsome takes your spot. At any rate, I was in a bit of a pinch money wise, and I approached Ledwell with a proposition. I would keep the trouble from their door for the right price. They knew I was like a magnet to people who wanted to tell their stories."

Allie's chest constricted. "You lured in would-be whistle-blowers with your reputation for exposing the dirty laundry of big tech and politicians."

He smiled. "Smart girl. It was the easiest money I'd ever made. Every single one swallowed the bait. Except your father screwed me. He was supposed to have the evidence with him, not your mother. I never liked being responsible for the deaths of innocents."

She rushed toward him. He reared back in mock fear, laughing in her face.

"You killed them."

"Your father killed himself by betraying his employer. Killed his wife too. And he left me hanging. I had to disappear to prevent the same fate."

Fury twisted her lips. "Why did you bother coming back after all these years? Why didn't you just stay gone?"

"Well, you know what Dorothy said: There's no place like home. But I knew I could never come back...unless I found a way to make it right. What better way than to put it all on a dead man's shoulders? I only had to wait for him to die—well, I may have hastened it along. He was dying anyway. When the dust settles, I'll be able to get any price I want for my book, and no one, no one, will be able to touch me."

"I don't believe you." She had to keep him talking until she figured out some sort of new plan. "How could you have learned what was happening and then pulled all this off?

"I still have a few of my old contacts. I learned of a certain someone's failing health, and a plan came to me. I could kill two birds with one stone, as they say. With your grandparents long gone and you so lonely, all cooped up in that old house, I estimated you were ripe for the picking." He grinned. "I love it when I'm right." He glanced over her shoulder. "Well, it's past time I left. You two enjoy yourselves."

He turned and walked out the French doors.

Allie started after him. She wanted to tear into him. He slammed the door in her face and locked it. She reached to unlock it, but it was the type of lock that required a key. And he had that key.

"Damn it!"

She ran for the staircase.

"Where are you going?"

She dared to pause and look back. "I'm sorry, Tommy, but I have to leave." No matter that she would love to know how he was here...she had to get word to Steve. Rivero could not slip away again.

"Apologies," this man—Tommy—said, "but you cannot leave. I can't allow it. You are the target."

Allie started to ask what that meant, but she actually knew. No need to try buying time. So she rushed up the stairs instead.

The sound of his footfalls behind her echoed in her ears.

Rivero Residence
Lake Shore Drive, Wonder Lake, 2:00 a.m.

ALLIE WASN'T HERE.

Steve felt way beyond desperate. He had to find her.

Mannington had made another call to the chief of police, and every available uniform on the city's payroll was helping with the search. An APB had been issued for Rivero and his SUV.

Steve had even called Agent Potter for help. She and Fraser had shown up ASAP. He supposed he should appreciate the effort, but to his way of thinking, Allie wouldn't be missing if not for Potter's little game.

With the house fire and Allie missing, the chief had declared exigent circumstances and Rivero's home had been searched.

The bastard had all sorts of evidence related to Ledwell. He'd had it for years it seemed. Insurance? Blackmail? Whatever his game, it was not about getting evidence for his long overdue story or the book he claimed to have written. This was about something else entirely.

Two detectives had been sent to the home of Edgar Ledwell, the man who'd started the company. Several officers were posted outside the lab. Another pair of detectives had gone to the home of Ledwell's son, second in command at the renowned company. So far, no sign of Rivero, his vehicle or Allie.

"I think it's safe to say," Fraser spoke up, "that Rivero is on Ledwell's payroll."

Steve resisted the first response that came to mind. *You think?* Instead, he grunted an agreement. Right now, he cared about just one thing: finding Allie safe.

He swiped his forearm across his face to clear away the sweat. Fatigue tugged at him. He smelled of smoke and sweat from Allie's home. Fraser got a call and moved away. Steve watched as he motioned for Potter. The police were still searching the property.

Rivero had no other properties—at least none listed in his name.

Where the hell would he take her? And why? She had nothing in the way of concrete evidence unless what she'd found in that time capsule was significant.

Maybe that was the problem. Rivero might not want her to have it, particularly if he was working for Ledwell.

Steve swore again. He had to find that lowlife bastard.

In his pocket, his cell vibrated. He hoped to hell this was something, anything to help. The number wasn't one he recognized. No matter, he hit accept. Allie could be using someone else's phone. "Durham," he said in greeting.

"Mr. Durham, this is Gayle Fischer."

Madison's neighbor on Hamilton Road. The nosy one. Why would she be calling at this hour? Hope rushed into his throat. "How can I help you, Mrs. Fischer?"

"Well, I don't know if this is anything, but just before 1:00 a.m. a vehicle went into Thomas's driveway. I might not have noticed it, but I was outside on the porch because I couldn't sleep. Insomnia is my companion all too often lately."

"Can you describe the vehicle?" Steve wasn't waiting, he walked to the car, scanning those around him to ensure no one noticed. He climbed behind the steering wheel and started the engine. He cringed at the sound, but no one paid the slightest attention.

"It was some sort of SUV. One of those foreign jobs. White, I think. I woke up my husband, and he said it had been there before, but sometimes he gets things wrong, so I watched."

Steve resisted gunning the engine. Instead, he rolled slowly and quietly away from the other vehicles gathered around Rivero's house. "Can you tell me if the vehicle is still there?"

"It left just a few minutes ago, and that's why I'm calling you."

He drove, moving faster as he put distance between him and the cluster of official vehicles. "Were you able to see who was in the vehicle?" If she'd seen Allie, that would explain her calling him instead of the police. Hope dared to swell in his chest.

"No. Unfortunately not. But after the SUV left, I walked over there to see if anything had been disturbed. Lights were on, so I approached with caution. I saw the woman who was with you the other day. She and a man were in the kitchen. It looked to me like they were just talking, but when she moved toward the door, he blocked her path. I don't know what's going on, but I think she might be in trouble."

"I'm on my way," Steve assured her.

"I'll stay where I can see them through the windows, but I don't think I should go inside," she said. "I don't want to have to shoot anybody, and I never could tolerate a man pushing a woman around."

As much as he wanted Allie protected, he said, "You shouldn't go inside, Mrs. Fischer. Stay back from sight. I'll be there in a few minutes. Call me back if anything changes."

"I will."

The call ended, and Steve pressed the accelerator even harder.

The faster he could get there, the sooner Allie would be safe. A part of him wanted to inform Potter and Fraser and the police, but he didn't have a handle on the situation. The last thing he wanted was for a show of force to put this guy into desperation mode. Better to go in quietly and assess what needed to happen.

Steve didn't stop for red lights. He just kept going.

He had to get there.

Now.

Chapter Fifteen

Madison Residence
Hamilton Road
Woodstock, 2:27 a.m.

"Why am I a target?" Allie struggled to maintain her composure. Strangely, it seemed staying calm made a difference.

"The answer is one I can't provide," Tommy said.

He sounded human. Maybe he was. She had no idea who that scumbag Rivero had been keeping locked downstairs. By his own admission, he came into this house after Thomas Madison's health became so bad he couldn't care for himself or defend himself. He'd been here often enough to know all the secrets of the home and its owner.

"What did that man who was here before, Rivero, do to your father?"

His brow lined in thought. "My father's time here was finished. I was supposed to go before him, but he grew too ill to perform the necessary dismantling. Mr. Rivero explained that he would be supervising my continued existence."

Allie tried to remember if Rivero had hit her on the

head or drugged her somehow. This couldn't be happening.

She kept recalling the man who'd done the Madison child's cremation saying that his eyes were missing, and now...

Allie looked directly into this man's eyes—the ones that looked exactly like that little boy's. But that was impossible. This person was...too human to be a robot?

"Is Rivero the one who made me a target?"

"Yes. He has that authority now."

Allie stared at the back door he had effectively blocked by standing in front of it.

"I need to go home, Tommy. Can you please just let me go home? Someone burned down my house, and I need to see if I can salvage anything."

She told herself she could talk her way out of this. This man—person, whatever he was—was about her same age, and if he had lived with the Madisons all this time, he surely understood how relationships worked. Could he experience emotions? Determine right from wrong?

Good grief, she should have done more research on the subject. She really had no idea how far the technology had advanced, much less how it worked.

"You cannot go home, Allie. You are the target, so your existence must be terminated. I'm sure you understand the decision is out of my hands."

Somehow she had to get past his sweet, boyish looks and the charm he emanated and understand that apparently he was a cold-blooded killer. She had to be prepared to defend herself.

With what? She surveyed the kitchen for a knife... anything.

Dear God...would a knife even work? Was it possible to stop him?

"I understand you're disturbed by this news. I suggest we make this as quick and painless as possible. There are a number of options. We can discuss them if you would like, or I can choose and surprise you."

Her heart quickened, started to pound. This was like a nightmare come to life. She wanted desperately to believe this was not actually happening...but it was. She was right here looking her would-be executioner in the eye.

He smiled suddenly. "I'm aware that you're thinking there has to be a way out of this. Anyone would think the same, but please be advised that I am faster than you. Much stronger than you and far more capable at the art of strategy."

She was screwed.

There was maybe a dozen feet between them. She stood just inside the wide cased opening that led from the living room into the kitchen area. He stood directly in front of the back door, blocking her escape. She'd made a run for it, dashing up the stairs and toward the back door, which generally didn't have as complicated a locking system as front doors.

He'd easily overtaken her, but instead of grabbing her, he'd rushed ahead of her and placed himself in her path.

Did that mean he liked to play with his targets?

"Have you had other targets before?"

He blinked, considered her question. "Yes, but only electronic ones. My father and I played games together. Sometimes I even allowed him to win."

Electronic games. Allie nodded. "So you haven't ever terminated a living being?"

"No. You are the first living being, as you say, I've encountered other than my parents and Mr. Rivero."

The pieces started to come together in her head. His parents had been devastated when their child died. The mother had said his father would bring him back. She made that promise because his father worked at a cutting-edge lab that was already building robots who looked human and behaved like humans.

What parent wouldn't do whatever necessary to have their child back?

But this was not a child…this was a grown man. Was this man/machine capable of growing, or had they built a new model as needed and transferred the necessary data?

Oh God, she felt ill.

Steadying herself, she tried another approach. "Tommy, I think there are rules about robots hurting humans. Did anyone talk to you about those rules? Mr. Rivero is a bad man, and what he has asked you to do is illegal and immoral."

"All targets are evil," he argued. "You are a target, and therefore you are evil. You must be eliminated."

"The targets you and your father eliminated were in games, not in real life."

"Mr. Rivero said the games have invaded real life now. We can no longer trust what we once thought was the difference between this life and those in games."

Well shoot. That scenario pretty much eliminated any hope of swaying him with reason. Okay. He talked about strategy. Well she had one. And only one, as far as she could see. "Your mother would not want you to do this. She was friends with my mother. You and I played together when we were children…at the other house—the one with the pool."

He gave her a knowing look. "Targets often make up stories to mislead."

Oh crap. "What about photo albums? Your mother kept photos. Where are they? I'll show you that I'm telling the truth."

Please, please let the woman have kept photos from before…before this Tommy.

"Turn around," he instructed, "walk into the living room and to your right. You will see a bookcase that contains our family albums."

If she turned her back, would he rush up behind her and strangle her or break her neck?

This is the only option, Al.

She took a breath and turned around, following his instructions exactly. Three rows of shelves were lined with photo albums. She searched for the ones from twenty-eight to thirty years ago.

"Here we go." She removed two then carried them to the coffee table. She sat in a chair that faced the sofa in hopes he would decide to sit there. No such luck. He crouched beside her.

It took only a moment to find the photos she needed of their parents together. She pointed to her parents. "That's my mother and father. Your mother, Jane, and my mother, Alice, were best friends. Your father, Thomas, worked at Ledwell with my father, Jerry."

He studied the photos. "Where are the ones of you and I?"

Allie reminded herself to breathe. "Well let's see if your mother kept any of those photos in here." She turned a page, then another. Fear crept up her spine when there were no photos of them. Still, she kept turning pages.

"This is the house—" she pointed to a photo of the house where the Madisons lived before "—where the pool is."

He nodded. "I know about the pool." He looked directly at her then. "I drowned there."

She nodded. "You did." She turned another page. There was a whole page of photos with Tommy in them and two included her. Her relief was so profound she barely kept her wits about her. "See." Her voice squeaked a little. "I told you we played together when we were little."

He leaned closer and studied the photos. "You are correct." He studied her face. "Our families were friends. We were friends."

She summoned a smile. "We were."

He turned back to the photos in the album. "I was very sad when my mother died."

"Me too. My mother and father both died not long after these photos were taken."

"What happened to them?"

"They died in a car accident."

He considered her words. "Who took responsibility for you?"

"My grandparents, my mother's parents." Another thought occurred to her. "You have a grandmother. Did you know that?"

"I do not."

"Yes. You do." Allie flipped back several pages, the idea or maybe her desperation gaining momentum. "This is your grandmother." She pointed to a photo of Mrs. Talbert and Jane.

"She died when I was a child."

"No," Allie argued. "I saw her two days ago. She is alive, and she misses you very much."

"My father would not lie to me." Anger flashed in his eyes, echoed in his voice.

Maybe this particular part of her strategy hadn't been such a good one. "I think he may have been afraid she might accidentally tell someone about you, so he had to keep you a secret from her and her a secret from you."

"Take me to see." He stood. "I will pause your termination until you do this for me."

Allie nodded. "We'll need a car."

"There is a car in the garage."

"All right." She closed the photo album. "But we have to wait until morning. She lives in a building where there are certain visiting hours. We can't go in the middle of the night like this."

Headlights swept across the front window.

Tommy moved to the window and stared out. "Someone is here."

Allie wished she knew what the best course of action was.

She should run while he was distracted. It could be Rivero coming back.

"A man is coming this way." Tommy turned around. "We should go downstairs."

Shouting outside drew Allie's attention beyond Tommy and to the window. Banging on the front door came next.

"Allie! Are you in there?"

Steve. She started for the door.

A strong hand clamped on her arm. "We cannot allow him inside."

Allie winced at his tightening grip. "This man is my friend. His name is Steve, and he isn't here to cause trouble. He wants to help."

"How can I be certain?"

"Why would I lie to you?"

"You are a target. Targets often lie."

"I told you Rivero is the one who lied," she reminded him.

"Allie! Are you in there?"

"Please," she urged. "Steve and I will see that you get to your grandmother, but you have to trust me. Please."

He released her.

Allie walked to the door and unlocked it.

Steve stared at her. "You okay?"

She nodded.

"Thank God."

She moistened her lips, struggled with whether she should tell him to run or...didn't matter, he wouldn't. "I think you should come in."

"Where's Rivero?" he asked as he stepped inside.

That was the moment Steve's gaze landed on the other person in the room.

Allie saw the recognition flare in his eyes. "Hello." He extended his hand. "I'm Steve. Durham. Steve Durham."

Tommy looked at his hand a moment then grasped it with his own. "Tommy. Madison. Tommy Madison."

Steve glanced at Allie. She explained, "Rivero introduced me to Tommy, and then he left."

Steve nodded. "I see."

"You're taking me to my grandmother," Tommy explained. "I have paused my termination of the target until I determine the accuracy of her statement."

"Rivero told him I'm today's target." Allie winced. "Like in a video game."

Steve looked to Tommy. "Then I guess we should get going."

"I explained," Allie said, to maintain some sense of continuity, "that it might be difficult to get in to see her before daylight."

"I can arrange an afterhours visit." Steve smiled at Tommy. "I'll make a call en route."

Tommy looked to her. "I am trusting you, Allie. We are friends."

She nodded. "We are."

They walked out of the house. Allie inhaled her first deep breath since Rivero turned on her and started spilling all the ugly details of his heinous betrayal of so many people.

On some level, she felt vindicated that she now knew her parents had been murdered by someone associated with Ledwell. And yet, her heart wanted to break with a new kind of grief.

Her parents had been murdered—stolen from her when she needed them most.

"You've ruined everything!"

Allie froze.

Rivero.

The gun he held was aimed at Allie. But he'd left. Had he been watching?

Steve stepped in front of her and warned, "Every law enforcement agent in the county is looking for you, Rivero."

Rivero shook his head. "Doesn't matter now. I had barely driven away when the call came. Ledwell has thrown me under the bus. Used me to do their bidding, and now they're refusing to protect me." He looked beyond Steve's shoulder, straight at Allie. "All because of you." His gaze slid back to Steve. "And the Colby Agency."

Despite the fear shrouding her, Allie understood one thing with complete certainty. Tommy was listening to this exchange, and he would analyze the words and come to conclusions. Whatever else happened, she needed to try and make sure he came to the right ones.

"If you hadn't set up the murder of my parents," she railed at Rivero, "and all those other people, you wouldn't be in this situation. You are the one who told them who to go after time and time again."

"I did what they paid me to do," he growled, aiming at her head now. "Those people loved making all the money Ledwell paid them but didn't have the courage to recognize the significance of what the company was doing."

"Is that why you killed Thomas Madison and tried to pin it on me? To take out two problems with one swipe."

"That wasn't my call," he argued, "but it was the right one."

"But the person who ordered his termination only did so because you told them his health condition was a security risk," Allie argued, guessing basically.

"He had been a security risk for a long time, and the powers that be just didn't want to see it. I made sure they had to see what was right in front of them. He should have been eliminated when his wife died. He was basically worthless after that." He waved the gun at them. "Now, go back inside. We're not doing this out here."

Allie and Steve started walking in reverse, toward the house. Neither wanted to turn their back on this wacko.

Tommy followed their example.

Once they were inside, Rivero ordered, "On the floor, face down. All of you."

Steve shook his head. "You're wasting time. If you want any reasonable possibility of getting away before you're caught, you should have been gone long before now."

"On the floor," Rivero shouted.

"It is true?" Tommy stepped forward. "Did you see that my father was terminated?"

"On the floor, Tommy," Rivero said. "I'm in charge now. You must do as I say."

"Answer the question." Tommy took another step toward Rivero.

Rivero swung his weapon toward Tommy.

Steve made a move. Rushed him. The two struggled.

The weapon discharged.

Allie grabbed the nearest object, a small sculpture on the table by the front window. She raised it to slam into Rivero.

The two men suddenly rolled to the right, and Steve had him pinned to the floor. The weapon had flown out of his hand. She tossed the statue aside, and it landed with a thump.

Before she could locate the weapon, Tommy had picked it up. He stared at the gun, then at Allie.

"You should let me hold the gun." Her heart thundered.

He stared at it a moment longer, then handed it to her. Her knees wobbled with relief.

Steve shouted over his shoulder, "I need something to restrain him."

"A moment please," Tommy said before rushing toward the kitchen.

"Grab my phone from my back pocket," Steve said, "and call 911."

"Gladly." Allie plucked his phone from his pocket and made the call.

Tommy returned with a dog leash. He thrust it at Steve. "We had a dog once."

"Thanks." Steve took the leash and secured the man.

Rather than rant and curse, Rivero said nothing. He was done, and he knew it.

Allie wasn't done by a long shot. She intended to see that Ledwell was brought to justice for every life they had damaged or taken.

The determination she felt was bone deep...soul deep.

Foster Residence
Ridgeland Avenue
Woodstock, 1:30 p.m.

ONCE RIVERO WAS booked and both Steve and Allie had given their statements, they took Tommy to see his grandmother. Mrs. Talbert had been thrilled and humbled to meet him. She was a little confused about how he was here, but it would take time for the full ramifications of what had happened to sink in. The Colby Agency had called in a specialist from another AI research and development lab to determine how best to help Tommy. That expert would determine how to move forward with ensuring Tommy was properly cared for.

According to Fraser and Potter, Ledwell's son had spilled his guts. And, ironically, the CIA was claiming no knowledge or involvement whatsoever in the mess that was Ledwell Labs.

When there was nothing more they could do, Steve had driven to Allie's ruined home. They sat in the driveway staring at the damaged structure. She doubted there was much inside that could be salvaged. More than anything else, she regretted the loss of all those family photos. Thankfully, she had the few photos that had been in the time capsule. Her baby bracelet, shoe and spoon.

"You're going to be okay."

She turned to the man behind the steering wheel of the borrowed car. "You think so?"

He smiled wearily. "I know so."

They were both utterly exhausted. "Thank you. I'm glad you have so much faith in me."

"You're smart. You're determined." He leaned into the headrest. "And I plan on being around to see that you have everything you need to be okay."

A smile slid across her lips. "I like that plan."

He leaned toward her. "Good." Then he kissed her, one of those slow, sweet kisses.

When they drew apart just far enough to get their breath, Allie realized she desperately needed a shower and to brush her teeth. She must look a fright. And she was starving.

"I am starving," she confessed. The shower and all else could wait.

"We should drive over to Red's and order everything on the breakfast menu."

"At this hour, we might have to settle for lunch."

Steve smiled. "I think he'll make an exception for the two of us after what we've been through."

"Sounds great."

As he drove away from the place that would never again be her home, he said, "You need a place to stay until you decide what's next."

She sighed. God, she hadn't even thought of that. "I do."

"I know this great place in the city where there's an extra room."

She turned to him. "Are you serious?"

He glanced at her. "I am completely serious. That's what friends do."

"I guess it's a good thing we're friends."

He reached out and took her hand in his and rested it on the console. "We are friends, and I want very much to explore the possibility of more."

She squeezed his hand. "I'm all in for further exploration."

Maybe she'd ignored her social life all this time because somewhere deep down she had known the right one was coming.

Allie couldn't wait to see what happened next.

* * * * *

PROTECTIVE ASSIGNMENT

JANIE CROUCH

This book is dedicated to the gals like me
who have been reading Mills & Boon's great books since
we were teens stuffing as many into our bag as
we could check out from the library.

Chapter One

Cade Thatcher drummed his fingers on the steering wheel and sighed as he made the turn off the main highway and onto the long, winding mountain road that would lead him to the Warrior Peak Sanctuary.

Was this really a good idea? It wasn't as though he had much of a choice. Right now, it was the only option he had if he didn't want to sit around home feeling like he was losing his mind for the next few months as he finished his recovery.

And seeing his brother would be a good thing, right?

When Carter suggested he come up and visit for a while, he had been reluctant, but he hadn't had any better options come along lately, so he'd decided to accept the offer. It would be a change, being with his actual brother instead of the brothers-in-arms he had worked with in the military, but he needed to get used to his new life, his new body and his new existence after his injuries.

A shock of pain raced down his arm and he winced, releasing his suddenly tight grip on the steering wheel. He needed to remember to stay loose and relaxed. Any sudden tension in his neck and shoulders still caused some discomfort, sometimes even stealing his breath. It had been getting better the last few weeks, but there were still moments where it really stung. His doctors were just impressed that he had managed to recover as well as he had, but he was still frustrated at the pain that seemed to get the better of him now and then.

When he'd first woken up in that hospital bed, the doctors hadn't been enthusiastic about his chances of ever making a full recovery. He could still remember, all too vividly, the look on that one doctor's face when she had told him how bad things were. His shoulder, broken in several places from taking a bullet, damage to his lower back and basically his entire body from shrapnel, then head damage to top it all off. He hadn't been able to move, let alone think straight. His whole body swollen and in constant pain, as he tried to wrap his head around what had happened. And even that was hard with the huge gaps of missing time and memories he had tried to recall. He'd always known working in the military was risky, but this? This was the kind of thing he hadn't been ready for at all. It was downright terrifying.

They hadn't been sure if he was going to be able to use that arm again or even walk when it was all said and done, but he had defied the odds. Not a chance in hell he was going to sit around the rest of his life. Even if he couldn't fight or be with his brothers-in-arms again, he could still do something. Still be useful in some capacity, help make a difference in some way. He'd thrown himself into physical therapy, trying to get control of his shattered bones and aching muscles once more. He wasn't going to let his life fall away from him just because of one injury.

And now he was back on his feet. Only literally, of

course, because he felt like the rest of his world had collapsed around him. He had wanted to be a soldier for as long as he could remember. From the day he graduated high school, he had focused all his time and energy on what he could achieve and on building the strong bonds he had with the other guys in his unit. But now?

Now he was floundering with no clear direction, not knowing what came next. Unable to do the one thing he'd always wanted and been good at had left a huge void he didn't know how to fill. Now that he was close to fully recovered, he had to figure out what his life looked like on the other side of healing.

The drive up to the lodge was quiet and scenic and empty; no other cars passed and not even a building lined the side of the road. Just forest for as far as the eye could see. In fact, there wouldn't have been anything to break up the monotony at all, if it hadn't been for her.

Cade furrowed his brow when he spotted her on the side of the road. What was she doing out here in the middle of nowhere? A woman, wearing a long dress that covered almost every inch of her body, with her thumb held out like she was hitchhiking. She couldn't have had much luck out there, given how few cars there were on the road. She had an old-school military backpack, stuffed to the brim, slung over one shoulder, and as Cade drew closer, he could see it had seen some serious action.

He slowed his truck down and pulled over to the side as he reached her.

"Hey," he called to her, rolling the passenger window down. "You okay? You lost?"

"I'm not lost," she replied, a little curtly. "I need a lift."

"Your car broken down or something?" he replied,

glancing around to see if there was another vehicle he hadn't spotted. She shook her head.

"I'm heading north," she explained. "You going that way?"

"I am, but just as far as the Warrior Peak Sanctuary," he replied. "That enough for you?"

She hesitated for a moment, eyes darting around, but then nodded. "That works."

"Come on in," he told her, reaching over to open the passenger-side door. She readjusted the backpack over her shoulder and hurried to the door, slipping into the seat next to him. Outside, the sky had started to darken and rain began to pour, one of those North Carolina cloudbursts that seemed to come out of nowhere.

"Looks like I timed that well," he remarked, and she gave him a tight smile, holding her pack tight on her lap, like she was trying to use it as a shield to protect herself. Cade quickly glanced in the rearview mirror, then over his shoulder before he pulled the truck back on to the road, and continued up the mountain toward the lodge.

"You hitchhiked the whole way up here?" he asked, trying to fill the strained silence between them.

She nodded again.

"If you need to charge your phone—" he began, but she cut him off before he could go any further.

"I don't have a phone," she replied, shaking her head.

He noticed that she was shivering slightly. The dress she wore obviously hadn't provided much coverage from the elements, and he thought about offering her his jacket, but he doubted she would take it. He reached over to adjust the heat settings instead and noticed her tense and shift closer to the door, like she was ready to bolt at a moment's notice. She also looked disheveled and tired, as if she'd been out in the wilderness for a while. Was she in some kind of trouble? A young woman on the side of the road like that, hitchhiking—it didn't seem like a good situation.

"I can call someone for you, if you want," he offered, and she jumped slightly at the sudden sound of his voice before shaking her head again, her eyes fixed on the window.

"It's fine," she replied, and he turned his attention back to the road, his mind racing as he tried to make sense of the situation.

"I'm Cade, by the way. Cade Thatcher," he told her, hoping to put her at ease, and maybe get some information out of her in the process.

She paused for a moment like she wasn't certain she wanted to tell him her name. "River," she replied finally, nodding in greeting.

River. Interesting name.

"Where you from, River?" he asked, trying to keep the conversation going.

"Florida."

"You're a long way from home," he remarked. "What brings you north?"

"Just needed a change," she replied, looking down to the bag on her lap again. He frowned. Was it him or was she seriously wary of making small talk? Almost like she was afraid she'd let something slip if she had a conversation with him.

Cade couldn't stop his mind from running through possible scenarios. What was she doing in the woods by herself? Was she getting out of a bad situation? On the run from someone? Judging by her simple, understated look—longer hair, her plain homemade dress, no makeup, no piercings or jewelry—maybe she had been in some kind of cult.

Or maybe he had been watching too much TV these last several months. He hadn't had a whole lot else to do since his discharge from the military aside from concentrating on his therapy. He kept his eyes on the road, and figured he should let her catch her breath before he started interrogating her. It really wasn't his business, but he couldn't help being curious. It wasn't far to the lodge, and maybe he could get a little more out of her then. If she was willing to share.

Finally, the road led them past the Warrior Peak Sanctuary sign to a big, sprawling complex that hung on to the top of the mountain for dear life, surrounded by trees and with a view down over the forest below. Cade climbed out of the truck, grabbed an umbrella from under the seat and went around to open her door. But before he could, it swung open and nearly hit him in the face as she hurried to get out. He shot out his hand to grab it before it could make contact.

"You should go inside and warm up," he suggested as she hooked the backpack over her shoulders again and tried to contain a shiver. He opened up the umbrella and held it out to her.

She hesitantly reached out to take it from him and eyed him skeptically, as if trying to decide if she should trust him.

"There'll be plenty of people in the lodge who'll be heading north soon enough that you could ask for a ride. You can't stand out here in this rain—you'll get soaked to the bone, probably end up sick too," he pointed out as he stepped around her to get his bag out of the back.

He hadn't packed a whole lot, just a large duffel and his backpack; his brother had told him he wouldn't need it. Anything he was missing he could get there at the lodge or he could make a run into the small town below.

He held up his old military backpack and grinned at her. "Look, we match."

For the first time since he'd laid eyes on her, a smile spread over her face. Cade was momentarily stunned.

With a smile on her face, she looked like a whole different person. Those huge blue eyes lit up, and dimples appeared on her cheeks; even though she looked as though she had been living in the woods for the past few years, she was seriously beautiful.

Cade stared at her for a long moment before he pulled himself together again. He was curious to find out more about her, and he hoped he could convince her to stick around for at least a night before she took off to wherever she was headed. Shaking his head to clear it, he reached for the umbrella and held it over the two of them as they walked toward the entrance.

She hung back behind him as he made his way to the huge wooden doors of the lodge, and he chanced a glance over his shoulder at her. There was a flash of fear in her eyes, and his heart twisted seeing her like that. He might not have known what she was running from, but at least he could try to get her to stay the night out of the weather where she could rest and take some time to settle down, right?

"Come on in," he told her. "There's a cafeteria in there,

and there's probably a spare room you can use to sleep for the night."

She frowned. She still didn't look convinced, but out here, in the middle of nowhere, what choice did she have?

"It's freezing out here," he reminded her. "And you saw those roads—nobody else is going to be coming up here tonight. You should get some food in you and rest, okay?"

He could practically see her mind racing as she tried to figure out what the best course of action was. But when she looked up to the sky, it seemed to settle her decision. The rain was set to continue for the rest of the night, judging by the thick gray clouds drifting off into the horizon, and it was starting to get dark. She could stand out on the side of the road for the rest of the night in the hopes some passerby would take her another few miles toward her destination.

Or, she could follow him inside the lodge for a warm meal and a warm bed.

Her shoulders slumped as she let out a resigned sigh and followed him into the welcoming warmth of the lodge.

Chapter Two

River Robertson felt herself shrinking as she stepped through the large doors of the lodge, glancing around and taking in her surroundings. This place was nice—really nice. Way nicer than anything she was used to, and she was sure she stuck out like a sore thumb. She looked like a drowned rat that had been running wild in the woods for a while. She didn't belong here.

She hung back next to the door, still clutching her backpack to her like a protective shield, as a pretty woman behind the front desk rushed out to greet Cade. Her heels tapped on the polished wooden floor, echoing around the open space. The whole place looked like it was made of the same material, practically glistening in the dim golden light from the fixtures around the walls. It looked warm and welcoming.

"Cade, there you are!" the woman exclaimed. She pulled him into a hug and then called over her shoulder. "Carter, Cade's here!"

A few moments later, another man stepped out from a room behind the front desk, and paused for a moment as he looked Cade up and down. He was similar in build and looks, so…brothers, maybe.

"Where have you been, man?" he demanded. "You're late."

"I know, I know," Cade replied, waving a hand.

"It's the weather," the woman cut in. "It's probably made the roads really difficult, right, Cade?"

"Something like that," he agreed.

"You know how to handle the weather," Carter remarked, shaking his head. "How's your shoulder? You doing okay?"

"I'm fine," Cade shot back, as though it was the last thing he wanted to talk about. Nobody seemed to notice River standing next to the door, but she was fine with that. This way, she got a chance to scope out the people around her and get a feel for their dynamic, whether or not she would really be safe here.

Cade was right, she wasn't exactly going to have much luck waiting for another ride tonight in the pouring rain, but that didn't mean she had any intention of letting her guard down.

Not here, not anywhere.

The three of them talked a little more about the weather and about the drive up.

River looked around, doing her best to take in every detail she could. She had hoped she could make it a little farther north tonight, but she doubted anyone else would have pulled over for her, especially with her looking like she did. Heck, it was a miracle Cade had stopped. She wasn't sure why he had decided to take pity on her, but she was relieved for a chance to get out of the cold for a while.

Finally, the woman glanced over and did a double take when she saw River almost plastered to the wall by the door. She frowned, concern evident in her expression. River was used to that look by now, even if she never intentionally gave someone a reason to stare at her.

"Oh. I'm sorry. Who are you?" the woman asked, turning toward her, and Cade quickly jumped in.

"This is River," he explained. "I gave her a lift up here. She was out on the road hitchhiking."

"Hitchhiking? In this weather?" Carter asked, concern and confusion crossing his face.

River didn't blame him. The roads had been almost deserted, and she couldn't imagine anyone in their right mind would be hitchhiking in the freezing-cold rain.

"This is my brother Carter and our friend Hannah Davies," Cade continued introductions. "Hannah runs the front desk and Carter's a physical therapist here at the lodge."

Carter glanced over at Cade, and River felt her shoulders tense slightly and her legs lock in anticipation to move. She wasn't sure exactly what they were communicating to each other with that look, but she didn't like it—didn't like not knowing. Her eyes darted between them, and she moved toward the door, ready to make a run for it at any moment.

But before she could, Hannah stepped forward, smiling at her. "Come on, let's see if we can find you a shower and some dry clothes while these two catch up."

River shot a panicked look to Cade, who nodded and gave her a friendly smile. "I'll catch up with you in a bit, okay?"

She nodded in Cade's direction as Hannah took River's arm and steered her toward a door at the far side of the lobby. As she let the woman lead her through the halls of the lodge, her eyes darted around, checking out the exits, her avenues of escape. If she needed to make a break for it, then she was going to be prepared, just like she always was.

After a couple more turns, Hannah stopped outside one of the dozen or so doorways in the long corridor they'd been walking down. River peered around Hannah to the far end, checking to see how far it was to the nearest exit. She didn't see an actual door, but there was a large window at the end of the hall that would work as an escape route in an emergency, if necessary.

"It's so nice to have another female around," Hannah said cheerfully, like she didn't notice River's distraction. "Sometimes it feels like the walls of this place just drip with testosterone, you know? Anyway, this room is free, so let's get you settled."

River turned her attention back to Hannah, and followed her into the room where they'd stopped. Hannah held out the key card she'd used to unlock the door, dropping it into River's hand. "This gets you in and out of your room, so make sure to keep it with you. Everything else is either open or has a flip lock on the door."

Hannah glanced around the room. "So, here you go. I think this should do you for tonight, at least. I know it's not much, but there's a fresh-made bed and you won't have to be out there in the rain, right?"

"Right," River quietly agreed, tucking the key card into the pocket of her long skirt and looking around more.

Even if Hannah didn't seem that impressed with the room, River liked it. Like the rest of the lodge, the room had dark wood floors and walls giving it a wooded, cozy feel. The few pictures decorating the walls looked as though they were of the surrounding forest, all green trees as far as the eye could see, some including wildlife. She approached the window and peered outside. It gave her a view down over the main road she and Cade drove up on, which was a relief. She would be able to keep an eye on anyone coming and going from this place, which would give her an advantage if...

If anything happened.

She tried to push that to the back of her mind as Hannah explained how the different remotes for the TV mounted on the wall worked and how to get the bedside light on. It was the closest thing River had come to a real home for a while, but she still felt like she was holding her breath as she tried to take it all in.

"You okay?" Hannah asked, and River nodded quickly.

"I know it's a lot," she remarked, laughing. "Sorry about dropping all of this on you. Oh, one more thing. If you want a shower, they're at the end of the hall in this section of the lodge. It's a huge, shared, locker-room-style bathroom. There're two different sides—men and women, and the doors lock on each in designated areas. The guys normally don't care about seeing each other naked, but just make sure you push the latch all the way across on the women's side, okay?"

"I will," River agreed.

"Okay, you get yourself settled, and I'll bring up some fresh towels and toiletries for you," she told her. "You need some fresh clothes, too?"

"Yeah, I think so," River replied, glancing down at her wet dress. She wasn't even sure how long she'd been wearing it, but it seemed nothing short of a miracle it had lasted as long as it had. The few other things she had with her she'd grabbed from a donation bin in Tennessee. She didn't even know if they'd fit her, but they really needed to be laundered before she wore them. She just hadn't found a place to do that yet.

"No problem, let me see what I can do," Hannah said with a small wave as she walked out the door, closing it behind her and leaving River in silence once more.

River walked around the room she was going to be staying in, taking in every detail she could. She had no idea who these people really were, no idea what kind of place this was, and she wasn't going to let her guard down just because they seemed friendly enough. She checked all the lights for hidden cameras, pulling open the closet and peering around to make sure there was no way they could be watching her. There was a mirror on the closet door, so no way they could have two-way glass, but she would check in the bathroom when she went down there.

Once she was certain she wasn't being watched, she started to unpack her bag. Not that there was much to unpack. A water filtration kit, a couple of tattered maps, a compass she wasn't even certain actually pointed north anymore, and the handful of donated clothes along with the extra set of shoes she had managed to swipe too, even though they barely fit her.

Buried at the bottom was her sleeping bag, which was basically torn to shreds. She would never have been able to sleep in it outside tonight, not with the rain that poured down beyond the window. She had been using it for weeks now, and she was surprised the cheap thing had held up that long, but it wasn't as though she'd had much of a choice about where she could rest. She'd been out on the road this whole time, sleeping in the elements, and anything that could give her a little cover was a welcome change.

Pulling open the drawers, she continued her search for anything that might indicate she was in trouble and needed to leave. She stuck her hand into them, feeling around for a false bottom, but nothing was there.

She slumped back on to the bed, catching her breath, and a sudden wave of exhaustion hit her so hard she could feel her eyes drooping on the spot. She brushed it off quickly. She couldn't let her guard down, no matter what kind of place this seemed to be. She knew better than that: she had to stay alert and aware if she was going to make it to Haven. She had to keep her head on straight, and not let the comfortable coziness of this room get to her.

A knock sounded at the door, and she jumped to her feet once more.

"Hey!" Hannah called brightly through the door. "Here's your stuff. Help yourself to a shower whenever you want, okay?"

"Okay!" River called back, hoping she would leave her alone sooner rather than later. She was nervous enough being in this new place, and adding new faces and conversations in the mix was just draining. She was used to only having herself for company, not having to talk to others. They seemed friendly enough, though, especially Hannah. But she was ready to have a few minutes alone to adjust and settle in.

She was still hesitant to stay. She was so used to being on the run, River wasn't sure if she'd be able to let that feeling go. But she could take advantage of their kindness for a night, couldn't she? Just one night. She could be out on the road again first thing the next morning, but she needed to wash, to warm up, and to get a decent night's sleep. Maybe even some food if she could find some.

Reaching back into her bag, she felt around for the knife—her father's knife. Feeling the cool blade under her fingers, she pulled it out and stared at the sharp, serrated edge. This would have to keep her safe, at least for now. She hoped she wouldn't have to use it, but there was no way to tell, not yet.

She ran her finger along the blade lightly, comforting herself with the reminder of what she could do with it if she needed to. Pushing the knife into the pocket of her dress, she listened until she was sure that Hannah's footsteps had retreated down the hallway once more before opening the door. She glanced down the corridor both ways, ensuring nobody was watching her, and then grabbed for the towels, toiletries and the clothes Hannah had left outside her door. Shaking them out, she checked to see if there were any devices hidden in the folds, but she couldn't see anything. Then she turned to dig around in the toiletry bag as well, also finding nothing.

With the weight of the knife in her pocket, she hurried down the hallway toward the showers.

One night. This is just for one night.

These people probably didn't mean her any harm. And if they did, they had no idea who they were dealing with—no idea what she was capable of.

Or how far she would go to survive.

Chapter Three

Carter placed his plate on the table opposite to his brother—roast beef, mashed potatoes and a healthy serving of greens on the side—and sank down into his seat.

"Well, now that you're finally here, are you going to tell me how you're really doing?" he said gruffly.

Cade grinned. He knew it was the closest he was ever going to get to a friendly greeting from his brother. That had just always been Carter's way with him, ever since he joined the military, and doubly so since he'd been injured. He knew it was Carter's way of showing he cared, though, and he appreciated it.

"Not too bad," he replied. "Glad to get up here for a while. Felt like the walls were closing in and I was feeling a bit useless, stewing down there at home."

"You're not useless," Carter replied at once. "You're injured. You need plenty of time to get back on your feet after what happened, you know that."

"I know." Cade sighed, picking at the food in front of him—the same dinner as Carter had on his plate, but he didn't feel too hungry right now.

He used to have a heck of an appetite, eating everything that was put in front of him, but that was when he had been in training and in combat. His body had needed all the support and sustenance it could get to keep him going.

But that had been before.

Before the injury, before he'd had to give up the one thing that had driven him forward and given him purpose. He'd taken a heavy beating in combat between his shoulder, scattered shrapnel in his body and his skull nearly being split in half that he'd had to relearn basically everything since then.

How to walk, how to talk, how to move, how to say his own name.

There were still memories from before the injury and of his time in the hospital that were hazy, but he knew he'd come a hell of a long way since the moment he'd woken up with his whole life tipped upside down.

At least when he was in recovery, he'd had something to focus on. He needed something moving him forward, and learning how to get his life back had given him that meaning for a while.

But now?

Now he craved the thrill of active duty, and the camaraderie of his life with the guys in his unit. Being stuck with an injury and far from the action was making him feel a little crazy.

"You're doing good, Cade," Carter told him. "Think about where you were just last year—"

"I try not to," Cade replied, cutting him off before he could go any further. "Anyway, you mind me taking advantage of the family discount?"

"How do you mean?" Carter asked, furrowing his brow.

"For the physical therapy," he replied. "I mean, I need

to get back in shape, right? The VA hardly covers what I need to get back out in the—"

"Why do you even want to get back out there again? How do you even know if you can?" Carter asked, and Cade could sense his irritation. "You had a head injury, for crying out loud. That's something to take seriously. You're lucky to have survived." He furrowed his brow and snapped his mouth shut to keep from saying more.

Cade couldn't blame his brother for his response to his wishful plan. Carter had seen a lot while helping him get back on his feet. He couldn't hold it against him that he didn't want Cade to walk right back into the setting that had landed him in all this trouble in the first place. His recovery hadn't been a pretty situation to be around, and Cade certainly wasn't the best company during the worst of his injuries.

"Hey, it's not for you to know why," he joked back. "You just have to do your job, right?"

Truth be told, he was dodging the question. First off, he didn't even know if he'd be allowed back after the injuries he suffered. Probably not, but he could still hold on to that dream a little longer. Secondly, he didn't want to admit to his brother the truth—that he felt useless, hopeless, in the state he was in now. He couldn't just sit around doing nothing for the rest of his life. He needed that hit of adrenaline, the thrill that came with the life he used to have, and he was never going to get it watching true crime documentaries on repeat in his apartment.

He wasn't the man he used to be, and he hated it. He wasn't sure how much longer he could keep living the way he was, and he hoped his brother, who had been working as a physical therapist for the last few years, would be able to get him back on his feet and ready to get out there again. Deep down Cade knew he wouldn't be able to do what he did before with his unit, but there had to be something in some related capacity that could get him back out there, let him feel that rush again. Feel like he was contributing to something that mattered.

But before the conversation could go any further, they were joined by another diner, Xavier Michaels, former CIA, and also one of the owners of the lodge. He cracked a beer as he slid into an empty chair, grinning at Cade in greeting.

"Hey, there," he said. "Didn't expect you to make it here."

"What, to the lodge?" Cade asked.

"No, to your thirties," he replied.

"Trust me, I made a damn good try not to," Cade chuckled, earning a scowl from his brother. But before he could say anything else, the floor creaked behind them. He glanced over and saw River, peering around the cafeteria, looking as pale as a ghost.

She wore a sweater and a pair of ill-fitting jeans. Her hair was pulled up in a ponytail at the top of her head and hung down her back, and she clutched a tray of food like it was the only thing keeping her pinned to the earth.

"That the hitchhiker?" Xavier asked, lifting his chin in her direction, as she went to find a seat on the far side of the room from the guys.

Carter nodded. "Yeah, the one Cade picked up," he replied. "Any idea who she is, by the way, Cade?"

"None," Cade answered, watching as she sat at one of the tables with her back against the wall so she could keep an eye on the room. "Thanks for giving her a place to stay tonight, Xavier. I appreciate it."

"Hey, it was Hannah's doing, but I'm not one to turn

away a woman in the middle of nowhere who looks like she's been on the road for months already." Xavier shrugged.

"Where do you think she's from?" Carter asked.

"Not from around here, that's for sure," Xavier replied. "But anyone on the side of the road out there at this time of the year isn't doing it for fun. She's trying to get away from something, I'd bet. Or someone."

"We need to quit staring, guys. She's skittish enough without seeing us watching her," Cade commented as he got to his feet, grabbing his tray and heading over to join River. It would give him a chance to deflect his brother's questions about what he was planning to do now that he was out here. He also wanted to find out what was going on with her if he could. Maybe even help.

Those giant blue eyes darted up to look at him as he drew closer, and she clenched the cutlery in her hand a little tighter.

"Mind if I join you?" he asked, gesturing to the spot opposite her.

She shook her head. "Go ahead," she replied, and he planted himself down in the chair across from her.

She picked at her food for a few moments, staring down at the plate in front of her as though it held the mysteries to the universe.

Cade snuck glances at her while he had a few bites of his own meal. Taking in her slim build and tired eyes. He could tell she was struggling to get by and running on exhaustion.

Xavier was right, there was no way she was out here by choice. She had to be running from something. Judging by her jumpy demeanor, she clearly hadn't put as much distance as she'd have liked between herself and whatever was after her.

"Are you in some kind of trouble?" he asked her finally.

She startled, lifting her gaze to meet his. "You ask all the girls that?" she shot back, but a whisper of a smile passed over her lips as she spoke.

He grinned back at her, hoping they could break the ice. It was clear this woman had some serious nerve, and he was eager to find out if there was more of it to come once she got some food in her and proper rest.

"Where you headed?" he asked, deciding to try a different approach.

She shrugged. "Wherever I need to end up," she replied, pushing food around on her plate.

She wasn't going to make this easy for him, that much he could tell for sure. If he couldn't get her to talk about herself, maybe he could, at least, make her feel a little more at ease.

"You're safe here," he said gently. "You know much about the lodge?"

She shook her head, finally taking a real bite of her food.

"It's a place that helps people with military or law enforcement experience get back on their feet after they've had an injury, physical or mental," he told her. "Everyone here, they're on the right side of the law. You're not in danger here, River. It's one of the safest places you could be."

She took another bite of her food, and then stirred the potatoes around on her plate before she responded.

"I don't really know where I'm going after this," she admitted to him finally. Her voice sounded small, almost shaky, and Cade frowned. He saw dark circles under her eyes, and her cheeks looked a little sunken, as though it had been a long time since she'd had a decent meal. How long had she been living like this?

He held himself back from asking that question, not wanting to overwhelm her or give her a reason to stop talking. She was eating now and going to be able to get a good night's sleep—that was what mattered.

Soon enough, she had finished her food. He could tell she was still hungry, though, and he pushed his plate over to her. She glanced up at him, her eyes flashing with embarrassment. It was clear she wasn't used to asking for what she wanted or needed from people, but he intended to change that, if he could.

"You can stay here as long as you need to. These guys won't mind," he told her, tilting his head to the guys at the other table. "And you need to eat and get some rest. Otherwise, whatever you're running from is going to catch up with you, and you're not going to have the strength to defend yourself from it, right?"

She chewed on her lip for a moment, but then reached for his plate. Something seemed to have clicked with her. Cade nodded and got to his feet to leave her to finish up and grab some more food for himself. Once he had a full plate, he returned to the other table where Carter and Xavier had been watching their exchange the whole time.

"Well? Find anything out?" his brother asked.

Cade nodded. "She looks to be in her midtwenties, and she's from Florida. That's what she told me on the ride up here. Didn't give me a city or anything, but it's something."

"Her name's River, right?" Carter asked.

"Or that's her alias," Cade replied. "She didn't volunteer a last name. You think we could get someone to look into missing person reports from Florida for the last few months?"

"You think she's actually in trouble?" Xavier asked, raising his eyebrows. "Not just trying to get away from a boyfriend or her family?"

"I don't know," Cade replied, shaking his head. "She's been out on the road for a while by looking at her, with just the ratty bag she has with her. She looks malnourished and tired. Like she's been surviving out there by herself. I doubt she realized how quiet the road up to this place is, and she seems…anxious. Flighty."

Cade fell silent as he watched Hannah approach River. The woman looked uneasy, ready to bolt, her face taut even as sweet, bubbly Hannah tried to talk to her. It was obvious she wasn't going to let anyone get close to her, at least not yet. That only spurred Cade's interest even more.

"Well, she can stay," Xavier said, looking in River's direction. "And I'll do what I can with the little information we have to see if there's anything we can find out about her. But if there's any trouble from her—or if she brings any trouble to the lodge—she's out, okay? I can't have anyone bringing that kind of chaos here. It would jeopardize everything we do here."

"Thanks, Xavier," Cade replied.

He watched as Hannah and River talked. There was something about her that had captured his attention, some instinct deep inside he couldn't ignore that told him she was in trouble. And he wanted to help.

He was going to get to the bottom of it.

Chapter Four

River hurried back down to her room as soon as she had finished her second plate of food, hoping they didn't think she was being greedy. At first, she was hesitant to accept Cade's plate that he pushed toward her, but she was so hungry and the food tasted so good. It was the first decent meal she'd had in weeks. She wouldn't have any more meals like that once she got back out on the road, so she'd taken his advice and dug in before he changed his mind.

She couldn't help but notice the others in the eating area sneaking glances at her while she ate and especially when Cade joined her. She knew they were curious and wanted to ask questions, and she appreciated that they mostly kept their distance—apart from Cade and Hannah. She didn't want to draw more attention to herself than she already had. She needed to do better. If someone came looking for her specifically or asking questions about a stranger and gave her description, she'd be in trouble.

She kept bouncing the idea around in her head to stay. If she decided to, and she really did want to, she couldn't afford for people to ask her questions, especially since she could not give them any true answers. She'd need to lie, and she didn't want to do that. Out on the road, she had been running for her life, doing everything she could just to make it from one day to the next. Would a few days here really be that bad?

Even though Hannah had offered to get her a coffee so the two of them could talk, River had excused herself and returned to her room, locking the door behind her and sliding the wooden chair from the desk against it to make it a little harder to open. Force of habit—she would always think about protecting herself, no matter what the circumstances she found herself in happened to be.

She perched on the edge of the bed, looking out the window to the parking lot to make sure she didn't miss anyone trying to make their approach. She wasn't going to let anyone get the jump on her, even if Cade had gone out of his way to try and assure her this place was safe. She didn't trust him yet, though—she didn't trust anyone, not when it came to getting where she needed to go.

But this place…it seemed like it made sense for her to arrive here. It was like a rehab, right? A place where people could come to fix themselves up after they'd been through hell. Ironic that she could probably use some of the help they offered, but she wasn't going to stick around long enough to take advantage of it. They would probably get tired of giving her sanctuary soon enough anyway, especially when they realized she wouldn't be able to pay them.

That was not a problem, though. She'd get back out on the road, keep moving, and she could work on whatever she needed to when she had finally arrived at her end goal. She wasn't going to let the fact that she didn't exactly know *where* that was stop her journey.

She pulled the knife from where she had stashed it in the pocket of the jeans Hannah had brought up for her. It felt good to be in clean clothes after so long, even if they didn't really fit. Just being able to shower and eat had been a weight off her shoulders. The roast beef she'd had tonight had been the best thing she'd ever tasted. Even though her stomach was full, her mouth still watered for more.

Her eyes started to get heavy, and she wrapped her fingers tighter around the knife as she began to doze off. She knew she needed to rest, but it was hard to let go of the control she had been hanging on to for so long, even for a single night. She knew that she was relatively safe at the moment, but letting down her guard after months of her body being in fight-or-flight mode was hard to do.

Eventually, though, she nodded off with the knife still grasped in her hand, until she was woken with a start by the sound of engines in the parking lot.

She sprang up, eyes wide and heart racing, and darted to the window to peer into the parking lot. The first light of dawn was already filtering through the trees. A couple of cars had arrived, along with a large van. A handful of what looked to be hikers climbed out, spilling into the parking lot. Her eyes scanned the faces, trying to see if she recognized any of them. She searched for a familiar gait, someone looking up at the window for her, anything, but none of them seemed familiar, or to be paying any attention to her.

She relaxed her stance but continued to look around the lot. It was getting busy; there would be too many people around soon. She needed to leave. She had no way to control who came in and out of this place, and that scared her more than she wanted to admit. How could she ever really feel safe if she was constantly second-guessing every person who stepped through the door?

Sliding her gaze past the crowd approaching the entrance, she spotted a row of bikes at the far end of the parking lot. That would do. She could steal one of them, take off, and she would be gone before anyone even noticed. But one look at the gray skies above told her that wouldn't be a good idea. She wouldn't get far before the weather turned again, and then, where would she be? Soaked through, back out in the middle of nowhere with no idea how long it would be before another driver was kind enough to pick her up and take her a little farther down the road. And she had no idea if the next one would be as kind as Cade seemed to be.

She sighed and sat back down on the bed, running her fingers over the blade of the knife again. She could stay for a few days, right? Just a little longer. Until the weather cleared, at least. She could get some supplies, make sure she had a decent amount of food in her stomach, and then move on. Give herself a better fighting chance to be full and rested.

As though agreeing, her stomach grumbled pointedly. She needed to get something to eat. Would the cafeteria be open this early? She didn't think to check for times. She wanted to take advantage of being here as much as she could, no matter how much her instincts were telling her to stay hidden in her room. Eventually, she knew Hannah or Cade would come looking for her, though, so better not to. She would just do better at keeping a low profile, stay out of the way.

In reality, she knew she had already failed at that. What with Cade bringing her here and Hannah trying to befriend her. If it hadn't been for him, she would have been out there all night, in the pouring rain, freezing and probably ending up sick. Who knew if she would even have survived another night out in the cold like that? Her body was getting frailer with every passing day. With no proper food or sleep and always ready to run, she found her body was slowing down. Though her mind was still focused on her end goal, enough to push her forward, if she didn't get proper rest and nourishment soon, she wouldn't make it anywhere.

She removed the band from her hair and tried to run her hand through the tangles with a sigh. She really needed to take the time to run a brush through it thoroughly soon. With as long as she'd kept it and being on the run, it was impossible for it to not look like a rat's nest all the time. It would actually be best if she cut a good chunk of it off, maybe to her shoulders, so she'd blend in better. Deciding to worry about it later, she did her best to make it look as decent as possible before replacing the band. For the time being, she just wanted to keep her focus on staying safe and making sure she didn't get too comfortable.

If what Cade had told her was really true, she couldn't think of anywhere further removed from her previous life than a place meant to rehabilitate people who'd served in the military or in other law enforcement roles.

She kept her head down as she made her way back to the cafeteria, trying to go unnoticed by any of the new guests who had arrived. A few of them were at the front desk, presumably checking in, their attention on Hannah and her instructions. She quickly rushed by as Hannah's laughter filled the room.

River felt a pang of envy and longing when she heard it, and wondered if she would ever be able to laugh like that again. So carefree, with nothing to worry about, nothing to scare her, no reason to hide or be ready to flee from any danger that came her way.

She took a wrong turn coming out of the reception area and wound up in a corridor she didn't recognize. She stopped dead in her tracks and looked around. Where was she? She was about to turn around and retrace her steps when she heard a voice she recognized.

"Damn it," the voice muttered in frustration, and River glanced over at the door it was coming from. She slowly pushed it open and there, on the other side, was Cade. She felt a flood of relief when she saw him. She wasn't sure what it was about him, but there was something comforting about his presence, especially when she was as lost as she was.

As soon as he heard the door open, he looked up and put down the weights he had been holding. He was in what looked like a small gym area, with a handful of fitness machines lining the opposite wall and some free weights closer to the door. He grinned when he saw her, but when he noticed the look on her face, the smile soon faded to a frown.

"What's up?" he asked her. "Are you okay?"

"I—I'm fine," she replied, her voice giving her away. "I was just looking for the cafeteria, that's all. I guess I got turned around."

He eyed her for a moment, and the way he looked at her, it was as though he could tell there was something more going on inside her head than she wanted to admit. He took a step toward her and she felt her muscles tighten, her mind telling her to get ready to run.

She stood her ground. She didn't need to run. He wasn't going to do anything to her. If he was going to hurt her, he would have done it when he picked her up on the side of the road.

His pale gray eyes, the same color as the sky outside, looked at her with a mixture of wariness and concern like she was a wounded animal that could bite at any moment.

"Are you really all right, River?" he asked her softly.

There was something about the way he asked the question that made her stop dead in her tracks. It had been a long time since anyone had spoken to her with such gentleness and genuine caring, like he really gave a damn what her answer would be. She looked away from him quickly, swallowing down a rush of emotions that threatened to rise up and take over.

She didn't want to admit to him how long it had been since anyone had treated her with kindness, or even basic human decency. It wasn't his problem.

Sure, he seemed like he genuinely wanted to help her but she still wasn't going to tell him everything. He probably wouldn't even believe her if she stood there and told him the truth. It would sound ridiculous.

Feeling the tears sting her eyes, she blinked rapidly to clear them away and looked back up at him, plastering a smile on her face and hoping he couldn't tell how close she was to breaking down.

"Why do you care so much about some random hitchhiker?" she demanded. She knew it was just a deflection tactic, but she didn't want to talk about herself right now, didn't want to admit how far from fine she was—and didn't want him to see how much his simple question had gotten under her skin. She needed to keep herself together.

And keep her eyes on the next part of her journey, instead of the man in front of her.

Chapter Five

Cade could tell River was on the brink of crying, and that just made him even more worried. Why would a simple question about how she was doing make her so emotional? Unless the truth was more horrible than she wanted to admit.

"You know, if you're in trouble, you should tell someone. I'm sure there's probably someone here who could help," he said gently.

Her jaw set tight and she lowered her gaze to the ground, clearly indicating the conversation was over. Cade tried to think of another way to approach the subject, not wanting to push too hard since she still looked like she might bolt at any moment. His mind came up blank, so he decided to change the subject altogether.

"You haven't eaten breakfast yet, right?" he asked her, picking up the weights again and moving them back over to the rack. Maybe it would be easier for her to talk about practical stuff, the physical rather than the emotional. She wouldn't be the first who had spent time here to feel that way.

"Not yet," she replied. "That's where I was heading, before I took a wrong turn."

"Let me clean up and I'll walk you down there," he told her. "And how did you sleep?"

"Okay, sure," she replied with a shrug, leaning up against the door.

She was still reluctant to tell him much more than the bare basics, and he could feel the anxiety coming off her in waves, but at least he could try and pull down some of those barriers she held on to so tightly. He wanted to know what was going on in her head, and why she seemed so nervous around everyone. It was clear she was afraid of something or someone and she wouldn't trust him with the whole truth of why she was on the road in the first place. Even though she was so secretive, he wouldn't have felt right about sending her back out on her own without at least trying to help in some way. Offer whatever assistance he could to make things a little easier for her while she was there.

"So, what exactly happens here?" she asked, tucking her hands behind herself and cocking her head at him. It was obvious she was just trying to get the attention off herself, but if she had questions, he was more than happy to answer.

"At the lodge?" he asked, and she nodded.

He shrugged a shoulder. "They have a variety of physical and mental rehab activities to help military and law enforcement deal with all kinds of injuries. That's why I'm here."

Her eyebrows shot up. "You got injured?"

"Yeah, former military. Got shot in the shoulder and my body banged up pretty good," he replied. "I've been working on getting back on my feet these last couple of years. And since my brother's been bugging me to come up for a while and he's one of the therapists, I thought I'd take him up on his offer and take advantage of the family discount at the same time and schedule some therapy."

He continued filling her in on his injury and his recovery, stopping short of coming clean about his doubts over his future. He didn't want to dump his problems on her. She wasn't asking about that part, and it seemed as though she had plenty to handle in her own right when it came to figuring out the future.

The way she reacted surprised him. Most people, when they heard about what he had been through, were instantly apologetic, trying to say the right thing and give him advice about what to do, but she just listened to him. He appreciated it more than he thought he would.

"…so yeah, that's what I'm doing here," he finished up and glanced over at her across the room. For the briefest moment, their eyes locked and the atmosphere in the room changed. Something about those big, blue eyes staring back at him made him stop in his tracks, and he felt something flicker in his chest—something he hadn't felt for a long time.

He could tell she felt it, too. She seemed to freeze for a moment, her eyes widening slightly, then her cheeks flushed a deep red and she tore her gaze away from his.

"Uh, um…" Her voice cracked. "I should go to breakfast, let you finish up. I'll find my way," she told him, ducking her head down and hurrying out of the gym before he could say anything else. He thought about going after her, but figured she needed her space.

Since River rushed out, he decided to continue what he'd started when she arrived. Once he'd finished his workout, he grabbed his bag and headed to the communal showers to get washed up, and then had breakfast. As he was refilling his coffee thermos to head back down to the cabin where he was staying, Lawson appeared beside him, arms crossed over his chest.

"I heard you were here," he remarked.

Cade nodded at him in greeting. "Hey, Lawson."

"And that you brought someone with you," he continued. "Who's that woman you arrived with?"

Cade screwed the cap back on to his thermos before he replied. He should have known that Lawson was going to have questions about River, and he was probably right to. After all, he co-owned the place with Xavier, and he was Hannah's big brother. He had more reason than almost anyone to care about who came through those doors and what exactly their intentions were. And bringing in a mysterious stranger like River raised a whole lot of questions. As another former CIA agent, Lawson Davies was used to getting all the answers he wanted.

But before he could reply, Hannah bustled past, holding a nervous-looking River by the arm. Both men turned to watch as they passed, then Cade turned back to Lawson.

"I don't know much about her," he admitted. "I've been trying to get information from her, but she isn't giving much up."

"You should come in for a meeting with Xavier and me later today," Lawson told him firmly. "Three o'clock in the office. So we can talk. How long is she going to be staying here?"

"I don't know," Cade admitted.

"Well, one more day, and I'll want to talk to her myself," Lawson replied. "See if there's anything we can do to help her out."

"She doesn't talk much, trust me. I've tried." Cade shrugged as he looked after her down the hall where she and Hannah disappeared.

He wasn't sure what it was going to take to get her talking, or if she would ever be willing to open up at all. Maybe she just wanted to keep herself to herself, and do what he'd suggested—rest and refuel—then leave. Lawson was talking about her staying another day, but as far as Cade could tell, she was already ready to get back out on the road and continue on to wherever she was headed.

"Maybe she's in trouble with the law," Lawson suggested. "That's why she's keeping her mouth shut. Probably safer for her that way, huh?"

"I have no idea," Cade replied, but in his gut, he doubted it. She didn't strike him as the type who could cause any real trouble, but she might be caught up in some unwillingly. "She seems harmless, though."

Lawson clenched his jaw slightly. "Yeah, well, I'll be the judge of that," he replied.

"So, this meeting?" Cade inquired, directing the conversation away from River and her secrets. "Is something going on?"

"We want to run something by you, is all. Talk to you then, all right? I have to meet with a client." Lawson clapped him on the arm and then continued down the hall.

"Sure. I'll see you later," he told Lawson's retreating form, then turned to head out to his cabin.

Since Carter was with a patient that morning, Cade didn't have much more to do than wander around the grounds and get to know the area now that he was finally there. His brother had told him a little about the place when he had been trying to convince him to come. Cade was pretty sure the real reason Carter wanted him there was so he could keep a closer eye on him.

His brother knew better than anyone how hard Cade found it to just sit around and do nothing. When the two of them were growing up, they had always tried to outdo each other. From who could climb up the highest in the big oak tree in their backyard, to who could launch himself the furthest off the tire swing, and countless bicycle races down the driveway in between. Because of that, they frequently found themselves in the ER with their arms in a cast or their heads getting stitched up. It was why Carter had gotten interested in physical therapy in the first place, because he wanted to help people the same way he had been helped when he was a kid. Cade, however, had gone the other way entirely, craving the same kind of thrill they'd sought out when they were kids. That same adrenaline rush that lit a fire in his belly.

Cade found himself on a thin, gravel pathway that wound away from the main building. While most of the guests at the lodge stayed in the main building, there was a small cluster of cabins out in a clearing in the woods where people who were longer-term residents could stay. That was where Carter and some of the others lived and where he'd gotten Cade set up for his time there. He hadn't had much time to do anything other than drop his stuff off before grabbing a bite with the others and then crash on the bed the night before, but now that the rain had stopped, he wanted to get a better look at the place.

The path Cade was walking on cut through the dirt

and a little bit of grass surrounding it, and led the way to the cabins. It was fall, and with the leaves beginning to change colors on the trees, it was really pretty out in the woods. This had always been Cade's favorite season, but it had been a while since he'd had a chance to spend it out somewhere rural like this. He sipped on his warm coffee as he followed the trail down to where he was staying, watching a few rays of sunshine peek through the gray clouds above him. Maybe it was going to be a nice day after all.

He reached the cabins surrounded by the low-lying branches of trees that sagged with red and gold leaves, and headed to his place. It wasn't much, but it was cozy enough, and exactly what he needed as long as he was there.

All the cabins were set back in the surrounding trees, like part of nature, and blended in perfectly with the forest. There were walkways leading up to the door of each unit. Each place had the same outside lighting, but they all had different interiors. The inside of his cabin was just slightly larger than the single units, with an open-floor concept in the front, then two small bedrooms separated by a tiny bathroom in back. The living area and kitchen were contained in the same space, the kitchen big enough to hold a small counter with two stools pushed underneath, a couple of cabinets, a compact sink and little fridge. A great place for a basic meal and cup of coffee if he didn't want to go up to the lodge. He liked the social aspects of the lodge, though, and he didn't want to miss out on it. Then there was the gym. He needed that space to get in his daily workout to keep in shape and help settle his mind in the midst of his recovery.

The living area was the larger of the two sections, and allowed for a couch, a small side table with a lamp, a comfy chair and a fireplace. Then the two bedrooms each with a queen-size bed, side table, dresser and small closet and then the shared bathroom.

Just before he reached his new home, he heard a laugh. Hannah's, if he wasn't mistaken. And then, it was followed by another female laugh he'd never heard before. He stopped in front of a cabin toward the end and peered inside, trying to get a look at what was going on in there.

That was when he saw it—Hannah and River together. But instead of the usual nervous, wide-eyed expression she had on her face, River was smiling. More than smiling, she was laughing. Her head was thrown back and her long hair flowed over her shoulders, her face lit up with joy. Her face was completely unguarded and she was beautiful.

Staring for a moment, Cade felt a smile spread over his own face. After how reserved and jumpy she had been, to see her smiling and laughing lifted a weight from his shoulders.

He found himself wondering what it would take for him to be able to get her to laugh like that.

Chapter Six

She had planned her day out in her mind as soon as she woke, before she had even left her room. She'd intended to scope out the area around the lodge, pick up as many supplies as she could and prepare to continue her journey as soon as she got the chance. But soon enough, she found herself running into Cade when she got lost, and then Hannah caught her before she could slip back off to her room.

"Oh, there you are!" she exclaimed, grabbing River by the arm as soon as she saw her. River had just eaten breakfast, a bagel with some bacon, and had been planning on heading back to her room to get started with her day. But as it turned out, Hannah had something else in mind.

"What are you up to today?" she asked, grinning widely at her. River tried to come up with some excuse, something to get away from her without seeming rude, but she couldn't think of anything.

"I was just going back to my cabin. You want to come check it out?" she suggested, and River found herself nodding before she could stop herself. Maybe she could use this opportunity to see a little more of the area this way, get a better idea of the layout of the property around the lodge. It would give her a reason to be seen wandering around if she was with Hannah, rather than possibly looking suspicious roaming around on her own.

Hannah led River down a gravel path away from the main building and toward the woods. River tensed as she followed her, and couldn't stop her eyes from darting around. It was going to be fine. Hannah wasn't going to hurt her. She had been nothing but kind and helpful since River arrived at the lodge. She took a deep breath to relax and reminded herself that not everyone was out to cause her harm.

Still, she kept her guard up as they reached Hannah's cabin, one seated in a cluster of them out in the woods. It was cute and simple with a couple of chairs out front and a little table in between them. A great place to sit and enjoy the sunrise before starting the day. The inside was basically one huge room with a small kitchen off to the side when you entered and what looked like a tiny bathroom in the back corner. It was also surprisingly colorful. Art hung on the walls, and photographs of Hannah with her friends and family were stuck all over a cork bulletin board next to the door. A huge, fuzzy orange carpet lay in front of the couch and bright pillows were tossed on the bed. The entire space matched her bubbly personality perfectly.

"I was just going to make myself a latte, you want one?" Hannah asked, gesturing to the large coffee machine that took up most of the space on her counter. River furrowed her brow.

"I've, uh, I've never had one," she admitted, blurting it out before she could stop herself.

Hannah stared at her for a moment, her eyes widening. "What do you mean, you've never had one?"

"I've just...not tried one yet," River mumbled, feeling her cheeks getting a little warm. She didn't want to seem weird or make her strange upbringing obvious, but she wasn't sure what else to say. She just hoped that Hannah didn't start asking questions that she didn't want to answer. River didn't want to make herself feel more uncomfortable by refusing to talk about her past. Thankfully, Hannah didn't press her for more.

"Oh, you have to let me make you one!" Hannah replied. "What flavors do you like? I have vanilla, hazelnut, pumpkin spice..."

A few minutes later, River held a steaming cup of what Hannah told her was a vanilla latte. It smelled sweet, the scent of it filling the cabin, as Hannah talked her ear off about her time at the lodge so far.

River used the opportunity to confirm that everything Cade had told her about the lodge was true. Everything he'd said checked out and she was relieved to learn that he hadn't lied to her. Maybe he really was just a nice guy who wanted to help her without any ulterior motives and make sure she was okay. She wouldn't let herself think too hard about why that made her so happy.

Hannah sighed, leaning a hip against the kitchen counter and taking a sip of her coffee. "It's so good to have Cade here. I know Carter has been trying to get him to come for a visit for a while now. It's also nice to have some new eye candy too. He is a mighty fine specimen."

"Oh, um, right," River replied awkwardly, not sure what she was supposed to say to that.

Hannah laughed. "Hey, don't get me wrong, I really

like working with the other guys. They're nice to look at too, with the exception of my brother, of course. I see them every day, though. It's nice to have someone new around."

"Oh, your brother's here too?" River looked to Hannah for confirmation and she nodded before River continued on. "I briefly met Carter with you and I noticed him and Cade sitting with another man in the cafeteria last night, but I'm not sure who he was."

"Yeah, my brother Lawson owns the place with Xavier," Hannah replied softly, an emotion River couldn't quite place flitting through her eyes. It disappeared so quickly that River thought she might have imagined it. "Xavier was sitting at the table with Cade and Carter. I'm sure you'll meet them both while you're here."

Why did that comment suddenly make River nervous?

Before she could think of a response, Hannah's face turned playfully mischievous again and she pretended to fan herself. "But Cade…damn!"

River couldn't help but laugh at her antics. Though it was obvious Hannah was trying to get a response from her, she had such a bright, warm energy it was impossible not to be drawn to her.

Hannah leaned in, waggling her eyebrows. "I don't blame you one bit for getting in the vehicle with him, I totally would have too." River felt the heat in her cheeks burn a little darker, and hoped Hannah didn't notice. She would be lying if she said that she hadn't noticed how handsome Cade was. When she had run into him at the gym, the way his shirt plastered to his firm chest and the sweat glistening off his toned arms had made it hard to think straight. Then that sharp jawline, those gray eyes that seemed to cut right through her, there was no denying he was hot. It had been a long time since she'd actually felt an attraction to someone like that and it was both scary and exhilarating.

"So, I hope it's okay, but there's something I wanted to talk to you about," Hannah told her, cocking her head slightly. River's heart jumped in her chest, her panic returning. Had she figured her out? Was she going to ask her to leave? She swallowed hard and looked at Hannah, waiting for her to go on.

"I hope I'm not overstepping," she remarked, dropping her voice slightly. "But I...it's obvious that something's going on with you, River."

River stiffened, parting her lips, about to protest, but before she could say anything Hannah lifted a hand to stop her from speaking.

"And don't worry, I'm not going to try and make you tell me what it is," she promised her. "We all have a past, I get it. We don't have to get into it if you don't want to."

River breathed a sigh of relief. Even if she was getting a little more comfortable with Hannah, she wasn't going to let her guard down completely. She knew better than that.

"But if I were you, I'd take advantage of how much help we need around the lodge," she continued. "There's always stuff that needs to be done, and if you have any practical skills, there's a good chance you could put them to use here, get lodging and food for a while until you're ready to move on."

River wracked her brain, trying to come up with something useful she might be able to do. It wasn't as though she'd ever had a real job.

"Uh, I guess I... I can cook," she began. "And I can sew. I make clothes, actually."

"Oh, like the dress you were wearing when you arrived?" Hannah asked, and she nodded.

"I bet we could do something with that," she mused, tapping her finger on her chin. "There's always gear in the supply room that needs mending. I think Lawson spends a whole bunch of money on it every year. I could talk to them about it, if you want, see if there's a job here for you."

Hannah sounded so determined to help that River wasn't sure that saying no was an option. And maybe it *was* a good idea. If she was working here, she would be able to gather the supplies she needed to get out on the road again without attracting too much attention. It seemed safe enough, and having somewhere she could rest and recharge and focus on getting herself together again before she got back out on the road would be a good thing, right?

Plus, being around people who had combat history and seemed focused on their own recovery was probably going to make for a safer hiding spot than being out on the road ever would. She didn't like the thought of being in one place for too long. It made her feel itchy. It would also make it even easier for them to find her, but who would even think to look for her out here?

Besides, if she was really being honest with herself, she was so exhausted from all the running she had done. She needed time to clear her head and make sense of everything that had been going on, and come up with a solid plan for moving forward. She didn't have to stay forever, just a few weeks. She could get a little money and recharge, then turn her attention to getting back to her travels and finding her family once and for all.

"I guess it would be worth a shot," she replied.

Hannah clapped her hands together and pulled River into a tight hug. "Oh my God, you have no idea how happy I am to hear you say that."

River froze for a moment, not used to someone showing her affection, and then awkwardly returned the hug.

"It's been mostly guys here for way too long," Hannah went on, "We need another woman around the place. Right now, it's just Sarah, the on-site therapist, and myself. I'll talk to Lawson and Xavier as soon as possible, but I think they'll be glad to have someone else around here to help out."

"Thanks," River mumbled against her shoulder. She wasn't sure why Hannah seemed so intent on helping her, but she didn't appear to have any bad intentions, nor did she expect River to spill her life's story.

"There's a single cabin right next to mine," Hannah told her. "They're pretty small, as you can see, but they do the job, and you'll have your own bathroom so you don't have to share showers with the guys up at the lodge."

"Sounds nice," River replied, and she felt a smile spread over her face. She took a sip of the latte that Hannah had made for her, and its sweet warmth spread out over her tongue. She closed her eyes for a moment, savoring it. "Wow, that's really good," she remarked.

Hannah grinned. "You can have coffee with me every morning if you want to."

"I think I'd like that," River replied. She could feel something in her starting to relax and unwind from the tight coil it had been in since she had arrived here. Well, even longer than that if she was honest. Even if Hannah said it wasn't much, having a cabin to herself, something other than her shredded sleeping bag to rest in all night, would feel like the height of luxury to her.

She and Hannah spent the rest of the day together, with River tagging along as Hannah took care of her regular duties. Even though she didn't officially have a job here yet, Hannah insisted on showing her how things ran, and River was glad to have a look at this place from the inside out. The more she knew about how things worked, the safer she would feel. She appreciated any knowledge she could get on how to fit in at the lodge and not stick out like a sore thumb like she'd been doing since she got there. The first step would be to learn her way around so she didn't get lost again as she had that morning.

Hannah and River chatted as they walked back to Hannah's cabin once she was done with her responsibilities for the day. Well, Hannah did most of the talking, but River was glad for the company. Being on her own for so long, she hadn't exactly had a chance to get to know anyone in many years. It felt good to not be alone and to have someone to talk to about ordinary things.

"I'll see you tomorrow, all right?" Hannah told River, once they had reached her cabin. "I'll talk to the guys like I said, and I bet I can get them to agree to you staying here."

"Thanks, Hannah," River told her, and she really meant it. She didn't know why these people were being so kind to her, but she sure was thankful for it.

She made her way up the gravel path to the main entrance after saying goodbye to Hannah. Since it wasn't fully dark yet, she thought she might take the opportunity to do some more exploring around the outside of the lodge. She'd been inside with Hannah most of the day.

She walked in the direction opposite of the cluster of cabins, taking in the sight of the beautiful tress and enjoying the crisp air. The seasonal colors of fall highlighting the deep greens of the surrounding forest was a sight to behold. Off in the distance she heard a thumping sound and what sounded like animals—horses to be exact—milling around.

Curiosity got the better of her and she turned toward the noises, finding a trail that branched off from the one she was on. The whinnying of horses and a man's voice reached her ears right before the pathway opened up to a shelter-type area with a few horses trotting around a fenced-in area. A man she'd not seen before was hammering boards on the frame of the building. A handyman, maybe? Not wanting to interrupt or be caught somewhere she shouldn't be, she turned back to the main trail, deciding she'd ask Hannah or Cade about it later. She'd never ridden a horse before and wasn't sure she'd want to, but she would love to get a closer look at the beautiful creatures.

She realized she'd walked farther than she intended when she spotted another small building on the opposite side of the trail from where it branched off to the horses. She must have been so lost in thought on the walk out here that she hadn't even noticed it before. She wasn't going to pay attention to it now, but the light inside suddenly turned on and she could see the shadows of people moving around. She immediately felt unsettled and glanced around, making sure nobody was watching her.

She needed to know who was in there, and she wouldn't be able to relax until she did.

As quietly as she could, River slipped over to the building, feeling her heart thrumming in her chest as she went.

She reached the door and pressed her ear to it. She heard muffled voices—men, by the sound of it—coming from the other side. She pushed the door open slightly and peered around. A short distance inside, she could see men talking. River recognized a few of them—Cade, of course, and the couple of men who had been sitting with him in the cafeteria her first night. Xavier and Carter, maybe? Then there was another man she didn't think she recognized, but it was hard to tell because his back was facing her. And beside him, the sight of a man that made her stomach drop.

A cop stood right there, in the cluster of men. The hair on the back of her neck rose, and she felt a shiver run down her spine.

Chapter Seven

"So, what exactly is this about?" Cade asked as he looked around the group that had gathered in one of the small buildings behind the main lodge. Carter had walked out with him telling him that there would be someone else joining their meeting with Xavier and Lawson.

"Cade, this is Sheriff Willis," Lawson introduced the other man in the room.

The man extended his hand to Cade, and Cade took it, looking him up and down. He was a cop, no doubt about it.

"Good to meet you, sheriff." Cade nodded in greeting. "Now, is someone going to tell me what's going on here?"

"I've been hearing some rumors I thought you might be interested in." Willis replied, furrowing his brow. He brushed back a strand of his thinning gray hair, a concerned expression on his face.

"Rumors?" Cade asked, ears perking up. "About what?"

"We had a meeting with some other local law enforcement across state lines," he explained. "And all of us are seeing a marked uptick in gang activity. Not the usual kind, though, and that's what worries me."

"What's been going on?" Lawson asked, crossing his arms over his chest.

"All across the Carolinas, there's one group who's causing us a whole lot of headaches," he continued. "The Shep-ards of Rebellion."

Shepards of Rebellion. Cade repeated the name in his head, seeing if it stuck anywhere, but he couldn't place it at all.

"And what's this got to do with the lodge?" Xavier wondered aloud.

"We've been hearing stories of people getting robbed out on the Appalachian Trail, not far from you," he explained. "Figured you might want to let some of your guys know about it."

"People have been robbed? What for?" Carter asked, frowning.

"Weapons, mostly, but they've been taking other survivalist stuff too," Willis replied. "The Shepards, they don't seem like your normal gang, from everything we've seen. We can handle them making a little noise, starting a few bar fights, but this goes way beyond that."

"So, what have they been up to?" Cade demanded.

"Some dark stuff. Anarchist-type stuff," Willis remarked, shaking his head. "We're not sure how deep it goes, or exactly what they're planning, but they've got their tentacles across several states now, and it looks like they're going to try and keep expanding from there. You'll want to be on your guard. They've been on the Feds' radar for a couple of decades now, ever since they started back in Florida."

Florida? Cade's mind flashed to River at once. No way she had anything to do with that group, right? No, it was just a coincidence. She couldn't be involved in something like a dangerous gang. And besides, these gangs didn't exactly have people running around looking like cult members. They would try and keep their appearances as subtle as possible so they could blend in.

And there was no way River blended in anywhere she was in the world.

"Thanks, Willis," Xavier told the sheriff. "I appreciate you coming out here to let us know. If we hear anything about them, or notice anything suspicious around the lodge, we'll reach out to you, okay?"

"Sure thing," Willis replied. "Just keep your hikers off the trails for a while, make sure they know what they're dealing with. We don't want to cause a panic, but we don't want to give the Shepards any more victims to get their hands on, either."

"Of course," Xavier replied. "I'll walk you out," he gestured for the sheriff to follow him. "I've got to get back to the lodge anyway. Guys," he added with a chin lift before they walked out the door.

Cade watched until he was gone, and then turned back to the others.

"So, anything come up on those missing person reports?" he asked.

Lawson shook his head. "Nothing I could see outright," he replied. "Doesn't look like there's anyone out there looking for River, at least as far as I can tell with the little information we have on her."

Cade nodded, not sure if that was a good thing or not. Surely there had to be someone out there who had noticed she was gone? Someone who was searching for her. Whatever she was running from, it was clear she had reason to think it might catch up with her, and he didn't want to let anything get close to her.

"So, why exactly did you want me here for this meeting?" he asked, a little confused. He didn't work at the lodge. Just because his brother did and Cade was visiting, it surely didn't mean he had to be a part of these serious conversations with the cops.

Carter sighed, and then looked over to Lawson. "Go ahead."

Lawson turned to Cade with a serious expression. "Cade, there's something I'd like you to know about one of the things we do out here," he explained. "We run a tactical operations team out of the lodge. Well, mostly me. Xavier handles more of the day-to-day functions but he helps out when necessary."

Cade glanced between the guys, trying to figure out if this was some kind of joke, but they looked back at him with serious faces. He'd always thought something like this was going on up here in the background. No way could you get together so many people who had been involved in such demanding and all-consuming work and expect them to just forget about it while they focused on their recovery. They'd need to do some kind of physical activity, at least, for the missing adrenaline rush and to keep their skills sharp. So it didn't surprise him at all to find out that Lawson and Xavier, both being former CIA, had found a way to utilize those honed skills to help when necessary.

"And what exactly does that involve?" he asked.

"We work with law enforcement and other agencies in different capacities to help them take down any troublemakers in the area," he explained. "Usually, it's nothing too difficult, nothing too physical. A lot of it involves background research-type work, but it keeps us busy and makes sure the guys are keeping all areas of their skills current for when they want to get back into the field."

Cade cocked an eyebrow. "And you're telling me because…?"

"Because we want you to be part of it."

Cade felt a grin spread across his face. Of course that was what this was about. They knew as well as anyone how good he had been at his job, how seriously he had taken it. And even though his brother might have wanted him to keep his head down and focus on getting better, he was always going to be restless, searching for another way to use his skills.

He looked at each man in the room. "Just a reminder—I nearly got my skull split in two. Another injury, and I'll be out for good."

"We know," Lawson replied.

Carter bristled at Cade's words, and Cade knew his brother probably wasn't happy about this offer. But Carter knew better than to try to stop him; knew he'd go crazy without something to keep him busy.

Lawson continued. "Most of this work is surveillance-based, so you're not going to be in the line of fire. Backup to law enforcement is about as much action as you'll see. You shouldn't have to worry much about a reinjury. So, what do you think?"

Cade tapped his finger on his chin. It was a great offer, and something for him to stay active doing. He wanted to feel useful and to keep himself strong, physically and mentally. But he wasn't sure if he was ready for responsibility like this before he finished all his therapy. The last thing he'd want was to let them down or get himself or someone else hurt because he wasn't up to the job yet. At the same time, he'd never been one to back down from a challenge.

"I'll think about it," he replied to Lawson and held out his hand. "Thanks for the offer. It means a lot you'd consider me."

It was the best he could do right now. He didn't want to commit to anything without thinking it through. Even being asked to join the team was a boost to his ego, but he needed to be in the right headspace to consider the pros and cons of the role. He wanted to be useful again, to have a purpose that meant something and made a difference. This could be the opportunity he was looking for to prove to himself and others that he was capable.

Lawson dipped his chin and gave him a firm handshake. "Thanks for meeting with us."

Cade turned to leave, giving Carter a slap on the shoulder as he passed. He was sure they had some real work stuff to discuss, and he didn't need to stick around for that. He had never been as interested in the practical side of things—the day-to-day stuff—like running a business. Taking out bad guys was more his speed.

Besides, he was starting to get hungry.

He was just about to start down the path to the main lodge again, when he spotted someone hurrying away, like they didn't want to get caught.

He peered after the person's retreating form for a moment, and then he realized who it was—River. All that hair was a dead giveaway.

"Hey, River!" he called after her. Had she been eavesdropping on them? He couldn't imagine they were saying anything that might have interested her, but he didn't know for sure. And why was she trying to get away from him now that he had noticed her? It didn't make sense.

He took off after her and caught her arm just before she vanished back down the path to the woods once more. She spun around at once, and landed a sharp jab on his jaw, sending him reeling back in surprise.

"Damn!" he exclaimed, rubbing his jaw. She stared up at him, her eyes wide, her face pale.

"I'm sorry," she blurted out.

He shook his head in disbelief. "Where did you learn to hit like that?" he asked.

She was so slight, almost fragile, it was hard to believe she could hit that hard.

"Street fighting," she replied, and he couldn't tell if she was joking or not. There was a lot about her that was hard to read, but he got the feeling that was by design. She didn't want anyone getting too close, finding out too much about her. But she could only get away with that for so long before she would have to tell them at least something about her past and what she was running from, especially if she wanted to stay. Lawson wouldn't have it any other way. It was his and Xavier's responsibility to make sure this place was safe for their guests. If either of them thought she was a threat in any way, they'd surely ask her to leave.

She wrapped her arms around herself protectively, her eyes lowering to the ground.

Cade stared at her. He still didn't know what was going on with this woman or how to get by her walls, but he wanted to help her if he could. If she'd just meet him halfway and open up some...

He decided to try again, "River, please tell me what's going on with you."

She shook her head and held herself tighter. "It doesn't matter."

"Yes, it does," he replied gently, trying to keep his voice as patient as he could. "I know you're going through something. It's obvious. I just want to help you…"

He trailed off with a weighted sigh. He could immediately tell this approach was not working, again.

Stubborn woman. She obviously didn't want anyone's help. Or maybe she didn't believe that anyone would want to help her. He wasn't sure if there was anything he could say or do that would convince her to trust him, even a little. Well, he could be stubborn too and he was damn sure going to try to change her mind.

Cade watched her hug herself tighter and she still wouldn't meet his eyes. He decided to try a more direct approach and hope that didn't scare her off for good. "If you're going to stay here, then you're going to need to open up a little. Give us a little background on yourself."

No matter what had happened to her, he was sure there were plenty of people out there who had been through the same. Nobody suffered in a way that was exclusive to them, he had learned that in his recovery.

She paused for a moment, going completely still. Cade could almost see the wheels turning in her brain, clearly trying to decide how much she should tell him. What she could trust him with. Cade tensed and held his breath in anticipation. Then something seemed to shift inside of her. He saw it when her eyes lifted to his. It was like she finally realized that she couldn't keep all of her secrets hidden.

She let out a resigned breath. "I was going to have to

get married to someone I didn't want to marry. It wasn't a good situation," she replied, not making eye contact again. "So, I left."

And just like that, Cade felt some of the barrier she held between them come down and his body somewhat relaxed at her confession. It wasn't much, but it was a start, and right now he would take what little bit he could.

Chapter Eight

She stood there pushing the toe of her shoe around in the gravel and staring up at Cade, wondering if she had just made a huge mistake in giving him even that much information.

Maybe she should have told him it was none of his business, but how long was that going to work before they asked her to leave? How long was she going to be able to keep the truth hidden?

Besides, she knew they were taking a big risk by letting a stranger whom he'd picked up on the side of the road stay at the lodge. They had to protect themselves and their guests from whatever trouble someone like her could bring to their door.

Better to give Cade a little than have him go looking for it himself and dig up the reality of what she had left behind. They all knew something was going on with her, and her appearance when she arrived spoke volumes on its own.

"You were going to marry someone?" he asked. He looked a little confused, and she couldn't blame him. After all she had been through, sometimes she still had a hard time believing any of it was actually real. It seemed like it had come from a different reality, a reality she never wanted to be anywhere near again as long as she lived. But she knew she wasn't going to be able to hold that reality at a distance much longer. She had been through a whole hell of a lot, and at some point, she was going to have to admit it to herself. And deal with it before the past caught up with her.

"Yeah," she replied, kicking at a bit of dirt on the ground to distract herself from the conversation.

"Seems like you've gone to great lengths to get away from this person," he observed. "You said you came from Florida, right?"

"I wanted to make sure there was plenty of distance between us," she replied. "I…he's not the kind of guy who gives up easily. Especially when he thinks he's owed something."

She knew she shouldn't say too much, but there was something about Cade that made her want to trust him.

"Owed something…? Was he violent with you?" Cade asked.

She nodded.

Anger flashed in his eyes but his voice came out controlled. "I'm sorry," he told her sincerely.

She shrugged. "It's fine," she replied. "I… I'm away from him now, that's all that matters."

"Was there any reason you didn't try to take a plane or train to get away from him?" Cade asked.

She sighed. "He didn't exactly leave me with any money of my own," she admitted. "And besides, he's the kind of guy…if he wanted to track me down, he could. If someone saw me on public transport, it would get back to him, and he would find me. I'm sure of it."

She pressed her lips together tightly and shivered at the thought. Even imagining him within ten feet of her made her want to vomit. She tried to remind herself how far she had come, how much distance she had managed to put between them. It wasn't enough, though. Not even close. She wasn't sure if it was ever going to be enough.

Cade nodded grimly. "I see."

She wasn't sure he really did. She could see him processing everything she'd told him as he stood there in front of her, a multitude of emotions flashing through his eyes.

Finally, his eyes met hers. "Then you're staying here," he said in a tone that brooked no argument.

She felt a wave of relief pass through her. Even though Hannah had all but made that decision for her, having the guys on her side—especially Cade—would only make things easier. For a moment, she thought about telling him about her plans to get to her sister, to find her family in New York, but the less anyone knew about her family, the better.

"I think Hannah already decided that," she remarked with a small smile.

He started walking in the direction of the lodge. "Yeah, she likes to have things her way," he replied with a low chuckle.

River caught up with him, falling in line with his pace. She felt more of her tension leaving her body as they walked down the path. Now that she had told him a little bit of her story, it was like a weight had lifted from her shoulders. She didn't have to worry anymore about him finding out what was going on behind the wall she had put up between herself and the rest of the world.

"I think I'm starting to find that out," she replied in a brighter tone. "Has she been working here a long time?"

"She's Lawson's little sister, so I think she's been here since the start," he replied, as he held the door to the main lodge open for her.

She brushed past him, and caught the scent of his aftershave for a split second—something deep and woodsy and masculine that filled her senses and made her head spin. She forced herself to keep walking, even though all she wanted was to press her face into his neck and breathe it in. She could feel her cheeks burning, and she tried to shut down that embarrassing line of thought. She needed to remember why she was in her current situation. She definitely would *not* be jumping into something—relationship or otherwise—with another man anytime soon. Even one who seemed as nice as Cade.

Before she could think on it any longer, Hannah called her name from the other side of the reception desk. She stood there with a familiar-looking man, who had a slightly bemused expression on his face. Cade and River walked over to where they stood.

"So, I was just telling Xavier… You've met, right?" Hannah asked, looking between the two of them.

River turned her attention toward the man, Xavier, who replied, "No, not officially. Nice to meet you, River."

"Hello. You, too," she replied politely, though her stomach was suddenly in knots.

"Anyway," Hannah continued. "I was telling Xavier about your skills with clothes. That you could sew, right?" She eyed River for confirmation.

River suddenly felt the words catch at the back of her throat. Xavier turned to her expectantly. Panic seized her and she swallowed heavily, trying to pull herself together. She knew she needed to make herself useful if she was going to convince them to let her stay, but a small part of her still didn't know if she should trust them.

"Uh, yeah, I can sew," she answered in a small voice, darting her gaze between them, then lowering her eyes to the ground. It was something she'd learned the hard way a long time ago, avoiding eye contact, especially with men, so it didn't look like they were being challenged in some way. Make herself seem smaller, meeker, more submissive.

"Well, we do need someone to mend up the gear and catalog everything we've got," Xavier remarked. "But we can't hire you without ID. Are you willing to provide that?"

She tensed up. She couldn't. She couldn't give them any more information than they already had. What would happen if they found out too much and wanted to hand her over to the cops—or worse, to him? She tried to find the words to tell him she couldn't do that, but under the scrutiny of his gaze, she couldn't seem to muster the courage to tell him no.

All at once, she felt Cade step behind her, the comforting weight of his presence at her back helping to calm her so she could think straight.

"Domestic dispute with an ex, Xavier," he told the other man. "And she's trying not to be found."

Xavier eyed her for a long moment, and River couldn't bear to look up at him. She was glad she had told Cade the little that she had, so he could share what she couldn't. It was nice to finally have someone on her side, or she might have run and never looked back.

To her surprise Xavier nodded decidedly. "Then you can stay," he said simply. "We'll pay you under the table. Nobody has to know you're here."

River breathed a sigh of relief and leaned lightly back into Cade. She opened her mouth to thank him, but he continued before she got any words out.

"On the condition that you take advantage of the facilities we have here," he went on. "Therapy. Anything else you need. And when you're ready to go public with it, we'll be here for you. Okay?"

She was speechless for a moment and she couldn't help the tears of gratitude that gathered in her eyes. It was more than she could ever hope for. They believed her. They were letting her stay. She hadn't felt this safe or comfortable in a long time. And maybe if she had the chance to work and take advantage of the counseling and other resources offered at the lodge, it would help her find her footing and allow her a chance to mentally heal.

She nodded, finally returning her gaze to his. "Okay. Thank you, Xavier."

Hannah clapped her hands together. "This is awesome!" she exclaimed. "I'll help you move your stuff down from your room to your cabin later, if you want."

"Cade, can you show River the supply room?" Xavier asked.

"Sure thing," Cade replied.

She turned to him with a bright smile on her face. She wasn't sure she was ever going to be able to communicate to him just how grateful she was for how he'd helped her. But she was going to do her best to pull her own weight and be as helpful as possible. She might not have a lot of useful skills, but she would do what she could to the best of her ability.

She followed Cade to the supply room, which turned out to be more of a supply basement. It was filled with seasonal clothes, equipment and other stuff that would have made it all too easy for her to swipe stuff and take off again if she wanted. The thought crossed her mind as she looked around the room, but when she glanced back at Cade, she felt a twist of guilt for even considering it. After all the kindness he'd shown her, she couldn't do that to him. She quickly pushed the thought out of her mind and turned her attention back to him.

He gestured to the scattered mess in front of them. "I know it's a lot to sort out, but Hannah'll be able to point you in the right direction on where to start," he said. "I've been here as long as you have and I still have a lot to learn."

"Right," she agreed, and she slipped her hands into her pockets as she looked around the room more. She felt Cade watching her, and she turned around to see him staring at her intently. Judging by the expression on his face, there was something bothering him.

"What is it? Are you okay?" she asked, worried. She took a step toward him, trying to gauge his emotions and what might've disturbed him. She was used to being highly attuned to the emotions of everyone around her. She knew it was a defense mechanism she had learned to protect herself. Even though she had no reason to think Cade was going to treat her the way she'd been treated by others in the past, it still made her nervous.

He gazed down at her for a moment and the air in the room grew taut, those striking gray eyes on hers, and she felt her breath catch. She wasn't sure what was on his mind, but she wished she could figure it out. The longer she was trapped in his gaze, the more unsettled she felt.

"Yes, I'm fine," he replied. "I'll leave you to it." He looked at her for another moment, almost like he was committing her face to memory, and then turned to the door.

River stared after him, her heart in her throat as she tried to figure out what had just happened and what she should do next. What if being here was putting these people in more danger? What if someone got hurt because of her? She was glad she had someplace to stay for a while, but her mind suddenly drifted back to that building and the meeting the men had with that cop. She hadn't been able to make out anything being said, but what if it had been about her? Or worse yet, *him*? Guilt suddenly settled heavily in her stomach.

But she didn't have any other options right now, no choice but to stay put and hope she was safe here. Maybe she would tell them the truth at some point down the line after she was more familiar with everyone. When she knew for sure she could trust them.

Or maybe she would keep the rest of her past to herself in hopes she wouldn't be tracked this far. Not knowing for sure, it would be better not to share more than she had to Cade. Safer for everyone around. It would save them from being aware of the horrors she'd already survived.

Chapter Nine

"You're really thinking about joining Lawson's crew?" Carter asked as he guided Cade's knee back to his chest to test his mobility. Cade sighed. He should have known this physical therapy session was going to turn into an interrogation when Carter had offered it that morning. He had hoped everything that had been going on with River and the news of the Shepards of Rebellion being in the area would keep his brother distracted.

Cade shrugged. "It'll give me something to do."

Carter shook his head. Cade was currently laid out on his brother's therapy table like an offering of some kind, being tortured physically—with different stretches and movement rotations to test his flexibility—while also forced to endure Carter's questions. He'd rather be doing almost anything than this.

Carter narrowed his eyes. "You have plenty to do," he reminded him. "You've got to focus on your recovery, remember? That's what's important right now."

"Yeah, well, I need something to work toward," Cade replied. "This'll do me good. And Lawson knows what my limitations are. He's not going to try and push me into anything I can't handle."

Carter looked doubtful. "Yeah, I'll believe that when I see it."

"Are we done here?" Cade asked a little impatiently. He knew his brother was just trying to help, but he didn't want to deal with his questions and concerns right now. Carter should know better than anyone how much he needed to keep himself busy because he was the exact same way.

Carter nodded. "Let's get in another session this week."

Cade agreed and headed out the door to go grab some coffee in the cafeteria, but he was stopped by Hannah in the lobby.

"Hey, Cade, have you got a minute?" she asked.

"Sure," Cade replied. He could already guess this had something to do with River. It seemed to be all anyone could talk about since they had officially decided to keep her around.

"I was talking to Lawson this morning about getting River moved into one of the empty cabins," she explained. "And he doesn't want her...rooming alone, if he can avoid it."

Cade bristled slightly. What did this have to do with him? And why was Hannah suddenly not looking at him? He'd just opened his mouth to ask but snapped it closed as she continued.

"They've got some guys coming in for a conference in the next week or so, and all the rooms will be full. They're also going to spill over into a couple of the cabins, and he wants to keep the others free for any emergencies that might pop up with the lodge being at capacity," she continued. "So, um, Lawson asked if...she can bunk with you for the time being."

Cade stared at her. "He wants her to stay with me?" he asked. "If he's just trying to cut down on the cabin space being used, wouldn't it make more sense for her to bunk with you? I feel like she might be more comfortable with that. Since you're both women..."

He left the rest of that sentence hanging and continued to watch Hannah squirm under his scrutiny, pursing her lips. He could suddenly tell from the look on her face that this request was about more than saving space.

"Lawson wants me to keep an eye on River. That's what you're not saying, right?"

At the shift in her posture and widening eyes, Cade knew he had guessed right. It wasn't exactly ideal and he didn't really like it, but he understood the reasoning behind it. Since River was going to be with them long-term and he had brought her to the lodge in the first place, Lawson wanted him to be the one to watch her to make sure she wasn't causing trouble or doing anything she shouldn't be.

Hannah ignored his questions. "She only had her backpack and I've already taken that down to your cabin," she quickly continued. "She's getting breakfast now and I mentioned to her that you needed to chat with her and would find her there. So, she should be waiting for you. And I thought you could walk her over after you got through talking so she could get settled."

"You're leaving it up to me to tell her? Hannah, I don't think..."

"You'll do just fine, Cade. The guys do want to help her and I want her to stay. I love the idea of having another woman around to talk to. She seems closest to you, though, and we thought this would be easiest coming from you." Hannah patted his arm and turned away with a smile.

Cade released a heavy sigh. This was not going to go well. She was on the run from an abusive ex, and now she was going to be stuck bunking with a guy she barely knew? He couldn't imagine she would be very happy about it. But they would have to find a way to work it out, no matter how inconvenient it was for both of them.

Cade debated on going straight to the cafeteria, but decided he needed a minute to collect his thoughts. He headed down to his cabin, and sure enough, her backpack was already sitting on the couch when he got there. He stared at it for a moment, fighting the urge to go through it and see what else he could find out about her. Now that they were up close and personal and staying in the same cabin, he guessed he was going to be finding out more about her than he had ever imagined he would. Whether that was a good thing or not remained to be seen.

Before he could do anything with her bag, his phone buzzed—a message from Xavier asking him to come up to the lodge so they could talk.

Was he going to get a break today? He guessed this was what he'd wanted when he had come to the lodge in the first place…a chance to actually keep himself busy instead of sitting around on his ass doing nothing. He redirected his route to meet with Xavier first since his conversation with River would probably be more involved. Cade rapped his knuckles on the open doorframe before stepping farther into Xavier's office, and saw him seated behind his desk working.

"Ah, there you are," Xavier greeted him, closing his laptop. "I've got a job for you."

"Okay, what's up?" Cade asked, sinking down into the chair opposite him. Anything that would keep him out of the cabin and allow him a little space after he spoke to River was a welcome distraction.

"We need someone to head down to Blue Ridge and pick up some supplies," he said, pulling a credit card from the drawer beside him and pushing it and a printed list across the desk to Cade. "Here. Use this. It's the one we use for all the expenses tied to the lodge."

"Sure thing." Cade scanned the list, then pocketed it and the card as he stood.

Xavier lifted a hand to stop him. "One more thing," he added. "Take River with you."

"What?" Cade jolted slightly at the request. "Why? Isn't she working on the clothes?"

"Yeah, but some of the supplies we need are for her, along with the food list I gave you," he replied. "We don't want people going down to the town alone anymore, not after everything Willis told us."

"You think there could be trouble out there?" Cade asked, shoulders tensing slightly.

"We don't know, but we're not sending people out alone for the foreseeable future," Xavier replied. "Groups of two or three until further notice. And River will know what she needs for the mending, so she'll be best suited to go down there with you today. Maybe you can also help her pick up some items for herself while you're down there. And keep an eye out."

"All right, yeah, sounds good," Cade replied. If it was what it took to keep the rest of the team feeling safe, he would do it. And besides, maybe it would give him a chance to get River's thoughts on them sharing a cabin. Spending time together was something they were going to have to get used to, now that they were living under the same roof.

He wandered through the lodge until he spotted her in the cafeteria. She wore the same dress she'd had on the first time he'd seen her on the side of the road, but it had been cleaned, so it looked like new. The skirt nearly brushed the floor, and the sleeves fluttered over her slim arms. Her hair was loose around her shoulders, held away from her face with a couple of clips as she filled up a thermos with tea. For a moment, Cade just stood there and looked at her. She was beautiful.

He didn't want to shout across the room, so he walked toward her and waited until he was next to her to say her name. When he did, she jumped so hard she nearly spilled her tea.

"Oh my gosh!" she exclaimed, spinning around to face him. "Don't sneak up on me like that!"

"I'm sorry," he apologized. "I spent too long in the army. I'm used to making a quiet approach."

She looked up at him, her eyes wide, and he could see her chest rising and falling rapidly with each breath. She was genuinely terrified. He could only imagine what she had been through with her ex. He was determined to show her she had nothing to fear when it came to him.

"How about I start wearing a bell?" he joked. "That way, you'll always hear me coming."

She let out a giggle and brushed a strand of hair back behind her ear. The way her fingers skimmed across her skin was far too distracting, but he did his best to push that out of his mind. He was here for a reason, not just to check her out. Xavier had asked him to do a job and he was going to be as helpful as he could during his stay at the lodge.

"Sounds like a plan to me," she replied with a small smile. "Hannah said you needed to talk to me. Do you want to go sit?"

He grinned back at her and shook his head, then held up the credit card he'd been given.

"Actually, I've been tasked with heading down to the town to pick up some supplies," he explained. "And they want us to start going in groups, so I'm supposed to take you with me. I thought we could talk on the way."

Her face lit up. "Oh, great," she replied as she reached into her pocket. "I actually have a list of stuff I need to get so I can work on mending clothes and stock up on supplies." She held the list out to Cade. "You think we'll be able to get all of this stuff in town?"

"I think so," he replied, taking it from her and looking it over.

It looked pretty easy to him, nothing too extreme—basic fabrics and a few glues and needles to make her work a little easier. He was a little surprised that she seemed so eager to go to town with him, given how nervous she had been about being seen outside this place. Maybe she was beginning to feel more comfortable and had realized that nobody would come looking for her in a place like this.

She screwed the cap onto her thermos and smiled up at him. "Then we should get going before it gets too late."

She had the prettiest smile when she let herself relax and Cade was mesmerized. He was really glad to see she was starting to let her guard down, especially with him. Maybe this was the start of a healing journey for her, just like Blue Ridge had been for so many others. There was still a long way for her to go, but even the small change he'd seen in her since yesterday felt huge.

"Great. I'll bring the truck around," he told her. "Meet me outside the front entrance in five minutes?"

"I will," she replied, and she gazed up at him for a moment like she was trying to puzzle something out.

For a split second, Cade was rooted to the spot, looking back at her.

But then, he remembered they were not alone and he had a job to do. He quickly broke the eye contact and turned to go get the truck. She had just gotten out of an abusive relationship. The last thing she needed was him drooling over her like a hormonal teenage boy.

He was trying to help this woman, that was it.

That was all it could be.

He had his own life to sort out.

Chapter Ten

River rolled down the window as they pulled away from the lodge. It was a cool, clear day, the sky was blue above them, and the air smelled fresh and clean from the recent rain. She stuck her hand out of the opening and swam it in the air as they made their way down the winding road that led to the town at the bottom of the mountain. A smile spread over her face as she tipped it up toward the sun.

Even though her time at the lodge was just beginning, she was starting to actually believe she had something good here. A safe place to stay, new friends, a job of her own where she'd make her own money. It almost felt like a dream.

"You sleep well?" His voice suddenly broke their peaceful ride.

She glanced toward him and nodded. "Actually, I did."

It was the truth. For the first time in a while, she had actually slept through the night instead of jumping up every five minutes to check that nobody was following her or she wasn't being watched. And she had actually slept in the bed instead of sitting on the edge of it, dozing off clutching her knife in her hand. She wasn't sure how much longer this newfound confidence was going to last, but she wanted to enjoy every moment of it while she could.

"Good, that's good," he murmured, and she glanced over at him. He had one arm leaning on the window, and his eyes on the road, but she could tell his attention was on her. "Speaking of that, there's something we need to discuss. I actually just found out this morning."

River couldn't help but tense a little at his odd-sounding tone and clench her fingers in her lap. Did something happen concerning her? She wasn't sure she wanted to know, but the mood in the truck suddenly shifted. Instead of asking, she waited silently for Cade to continue.

"So, apparently, there's going to be some sort of event happening at the lodge and it's booked out to capacity." He cleared his throat and shifted in his seat, suddenly nervous. "I, ah, was told that we're going to be sharing my cabin for a while."

"Oh." River couldn't help the anxious energy that washed over her at his words. She wasn't sure what else to say. She was hoping to have her own space and sharing with Cade certainly wasn't ideal—but she didn't mind too much. She was really curious what he thought of them sharing space but she wasn't sure how to approach the subject.

"Yeah, ah, Hannah brought your backpack over this morning and thought it'd be easier if we discussed it rather than having a go-between." He turned to look at her for a moment before concentrating back on the road. "If it's really uncomfortable for you, I'm sure Xavier can work something else out. She mentioned them holding a couple of other cabins for overfills, but I'm sure they'd consider one for you if it was an issue…"

He sounded about as nervous as she felt. She didn't know if it was because he didn't want to room with her or if it was something else. "So, roommates, then." River darted another glance in his direction before looking down at her lap. So much for her newfound confidence. She was out of her league here. The thought of being alone with this man… No, she wasn't going there. She'd find a way to make do. Stay away from the cabin as much as possible, if she had to. "I'm sorry to inconvenience you like this. I'll try to be as quiet as possible. You won't even know I'm there."

"I don't know about that," she heard him mutter under his breath. Clearing his throat he replied, "Don't worry about it. I just hope it's not too uncomfortable for you, what with me basically being a stranger and all. I promise you're safe with me, though." River felt a rush a warmth spread through her body as Cade's steady gaze shifted again to her before turning back to the road.

"You think we'll be able to find what I need in town?" she asked again, trying to change the subject to a safer topic.

She still wasn't totally sure about showing her face in Blue Ridge, but with Cade there as well, at least she had someone she could hide behind. It was hard to believe anyone would think to look for her here, and she just had to hope the locals weren't interested in who she was or why she had showed up there out of the blue.

"I think so," he replied with a nod. "A lot of people around here take care of their own clothes like you do.

There's a craft store that sells pretty much everything you could need."

"You know this place pretty well, then?" she asked, and he nodded.

"Yeah, I stayed here for a while before I moved up to the lodge," he explained. "I started off in the city when I was recovering, but I came down here to be closer to my brother and his work."

"What's it like?" she asked curiously.

"Well, everyone knows everyone," he said with a smile. "At least, during the off season. In the summer, they get a lot of tourists through here, which is how the town makes most of its money. Mostly hikers looking to hit the trails. But the rest of the time, it's pretty quiet."

He filled her in on the town a little more, and she nodded as she took it in, watching the road outside as it wound down into the town. She hadn't had a good look at it the first time she had been out here, but it was really pretty in the sunlight. The leaves on the trees that lined the road were turning gold and red and brown, and a few floated down on to the road as they drove.

They reached the outskirts of the town, which wasn't much more than a few streets wrapped around a small central square. Cade pulled the truck to a stop next to the square, which was framed by perfectly manicured bushes on each side. He climbed out and rounded the hood, and this time, she allowed him to open the door for her instead of flinging it off its hinges herself. He offered her a hand to jump out, and she slipped her fingers onto his palm for a moment.

There was something about touching him that seemed to make the whole world slow down around her for a split second, something she couldn't quite put into words. He smiled at her, and she just looked at him, the moment freezing and burning itself into her head.

She hopped out of the truck and forced her mind back to reality. It was nothing. It was such a long time since she had actually felt safe with someone. That's why she was reacting this way to him. She wasn't falling for him or anything. She wasn't even sure she would know what that felt like, if she was being honest. She could admit, though, that she did enjoy having him around. If it wasn't for him, she would probably be out on the freezing roads again, trying her luck with whatever driver would pull over and pick her up.

"The craft store's just over there," he said, pointing down the street to a quaint little shop called Thread the Needle with seasonal decorations in the window—pumpkins with carved-out faces, plastic skeletons and fake cobwebs dangling from every corner.

"I have a few errands to run afterward, so maybe we can explore some more?" he suggested.

She nodded. "I'd really like that. I'd like to see about getting a few things for myself, if possible. Xavier gave me a little advance to grab some stuff."

He held the door open when they got to the store. A bell over the door announced their arrival, and an older woman behind the counter looked up and smiled when she saw them come in.

"Oh, hello there, Cade! It's been a while," she greeted them brightly. "And who's this? I don't think we've met, sweetie."

"This is River. We've come down from the lodge to

get some supplies," Cade said, hooking a thumb in her direction.

River lifted her hand in an awkward wave and gave the woman a small smile that she hoped didn't look too nervous.

The woman's eyes darted over her dress, taking it in. "I'm Mary. Mary Cinder." After introducing herself, she stepped around the counter and planted her hands on her hips. "Did you make that dress yourself?" she asked.

River tensed, but nodded.

"It's wonderful," she said, shaking her head as she looked it up and down. "Totally unique. I love the design you've used for the bodice and the sleeves...so rare for a young woman like you to take an interest in sewing like that."

"Thank you," she replied softly, smiling bigger this time.

It had been a long time since anyone had complimented anything she had done, and she would be lying if she said it didn't feel a little strange. But the woman, Mary, seemed totally sincere, so she tried to brush off the doubts in the back of her mind.

"Of course, dear," Mary replied. "It's a lost art, and it's people like you who are going to keep it alive for the next generation. Do you quilt, too?"

"Um, I've done a little in the past, but not much."

"You should join our quilting group," Mary told her firmly, as though she wasn't going to take no for an answer. "We meet bimonthly, it's a lovely group of ladies. I bet you could teach them a thing or two, based on this dress, anyway."

"Oh, I don't know about that."

"Do you mind if I take a closer look at your stitching on the collar?" Mary asked, taking a step toward River. River hesitated for a moment, not sure if this was a good idea, but she forced herself to nod.

"Sure. Go ahead," she replied, and Mary examined the back of her dress, chatting away to her about the skills she'd have needed to make it. River didn't tell her the truth of how she'd learned those skills—their necessity for survival—but she appreciated her kindness.

"Give me your list, River, and I'll start getting the stuff while you ladies chat." Cade made his way around the store, picking up everything on her list, and by the time Mary was done looking at her dress, he was ready to check out.

"Thank you for coming," Mary said on their way out the door. "River, hon, please keep in mind about the quilting. I'd love to see you again."

"I will. Thanks," River gripped the bag of supplies as she and Cade left the shop.

Once outside, he led her to the next shop, which looked like some sort of ladies' store where she could get a few items of clothing and personal things.

"You think you can make me a new winter jacket?" he asked as he took the bag from her hand when they entered. "Sounds like you really know what you're doing, if you've got Mary that impressed."

"I could try," she replied. "But fair warning, my favorite color to work with is pink."

He chuckled. "Hey, I've been told it looks good on me," he teased. "Besides, if you made it, I'd wear it with pride. A River original, right?"

She blushed slightly and grinned at him. She felt

lighter than she had in a long time, even though she knew she should have been nervous, being out in public like this. But with Cade, it was as though nothing bad could happen to her—nothing could even come close.

They made their way around the town, picking up everything Xavier had asked him to get. He even introduced her to a few of the people he knew from his time living here. They all seemed happy to see him. A good sign, right? People liked him. He had clearly made a good impression on them when he had been staying in town, and they all treated her like an old friend because of him.

They grabbed lunch at a little place not far from the square. It was just a tiny hole-in-the-wall café, but after so long on the road having to live on whatever scraps she could find, it all tasted like gourmet food to River. She ate her toasted sandwich and soup like she had never seen food before in her life. She was still getting used to having three meals a day, her body recuperating all the lost calories from her previous lack of meals.

"Good?" Cade asked.

She nodded, holding her hand over her mouth to avoid showing him her mouthful of food. "Really good," she replied once she had swallowed the delicious bite.

"I'm glad." Cade chuckled.

He had a slightly crooked smile, but it lit up his whole face every time, as though he was genuinely glad to be with her. She felt that flutter in her chest again, and did her best to ignore it.

It wasn't until their drive back up to the lodge with the supplies that it hit her—she hadn't thought about leaving today. Not once.

It was all thanks to Cade. He made her feel so comfortable in a way she hadn't in a long time—maybe ever. That was making it more difficult to think about walking away when the time came. But if he knew who she really was and what she was running from, she was sure he would feel differently about her and her being at the lodge.

But she wasn't going to tell him more than she needed to. He made her feel safe, but she was going to keep her mouth shut and focus on taking care of herself. She wasn't going to get too settled into the lodge's atmosphere. It was way too dangerous to do that.

"You okay?" Cade asked.

She nodded and forced herself to smile. "I'm fine," she replied. "Thanks for bringing me with you and helping me get everything today."

"No problem," he replied. "You need any help getting your stuff out to our cabin?"

Our cabin. It was strange for him to say it like that. She supposed it was the right way to talk about it, but it still threw her a little hearing it. Staying with him was going to make it harder to steal supplies if she needed to run again, but she'd figure that out when and if the time came.

"No, I'm fine. I just had my backpack in my room and then what I got today," she replied once the truck had pulled up at the lodge again. She jumped out of her side, not waiting for him this time.

"I need to run these supplies inside and check in with Xavier before heading to the cabin," he volunteered as he turned off the engine and started gathering bags to haul inside the lodge. "You want me to take the sewing stuff with me?"

"That's okay, I'll take it with me and then just bring it up to the lodge tomorrow," she replied as she turned and headed to the cabin they were going to be sharing for the next little while.

"I'll be down in a bit after I get all this settled, then," he replied and she gave him a little wave as he walked away.

She'd have to work on getting used to having him around, in the same space. She'd been on her own for so long now, she wasn't used to other people being so close. Especially someone like Cade.

Luckily his cabin had a second bedroom, so when she got inside, she went straight to it and closed the door behind her. She just needed a few minutes on her own, to decompress and settle her mind. Her head was a mess as she thought about how she was going to handle him, but she didn't want to lose the flutter in her chest when he was around.

No matter how much harder it was going to make things for her.

Chapter Eleven

He stared at the ceiling, listening to the sound of the wind rustling through the trees outside, and wondered how the hell he was supposed to keep River off his mind.

They had spent the better part of the day together, and he couldn't stop thinking about her. No matter how much he tried to push her to the back of his mind, she was right there, insisting on taking up his brain space. If he was honest with himself, he didn't really mind.

She was just… There was something about her that drew him to her in a way he couldn't quite put into words. He liked her—liked the way she made him feel, how at ease and relaxed he felt when he was around her. And seeing her smile and interact with the people they'd seen in town had been a gift. He hadn't realized how much she'd needed that until he saw Mary fussing over her, and River's face lighting up as they talked about making clothes.

Now she slept just a few feet away from him, in the other room of the cabin. If she was sleeping at all. Maybe she was tossing and turning just like him. He hoped so. He didn't want these feelings he had to just go one way, but at the same time, he knew she had been through so much. He wasn't going to try and push her into something she wasn't ready for, even if he couldn't stop thinking about her.

It was getting late, and he knew he needed to get some sleep, but every time he closed his eyes, there she was, gazing back at him with that warm, open expression on her face. He couldn't help but wonder exactly what she had been through to bring her here, beyond the few details she had shared with him so far. He hoped that eventually she would share the rest of her story with him.

For now, he would just try to focus on figuring out his own life and not the growing attraction he felt between them. He had plenty of other things to think about—like his recovery and whether he was going to join Lawson's tactical operations team. Even though he knew his brother had some serious issues with it, Cade couldn't deny how much the idea appealed to him. It was a chance to secure a new direction in his life, and give himself something to focus on that wasn't the grueling reminder of everything he left behind.

He eventually drifted off to sleep and woke early the next day to the light peeking through the window next to him. He opened his eyes and lifted his head from the pillow, feeling a smile spread over his face before he could stop it. Something about waking up so close to River made him happy. Waking up in the same bed would be even better, but he quickly redirected his thoughts. He wasn't going down that road...not yet anyway.

He climbed out of bed before his mind could wander any further, and headed out to the small kitchen. He expected to see River there, but she must have already headed out to work. The door to her bedroom was open, and she was nowhere to be seen. He made himself a cup of coffee and sipped on it as he leaned up against the counter, watching as a few more leaves drifted down from the trees outside the cabin. He loved how peaceful it was this time of year.

He rinsed his mug and headed up to the lodge to grab some breakfast, and spotted River working on something in one of the rooms off the main corridor. Xavier must have gotten her set up with her own little space. He peered around the door to see her with a few needles pressed between her lips, brow furrowed as she fixed up one of the old windbreakers that looked as though it had seen better days. He thought about calling out to her, letting her know he was there, but thought better of it. He didn't want to throw her off her concentration.

He grabbed a quick breakfast and then headed to another physical therapy session with Carter. If he was lucky it would just be physical therapy today and no brotherly concern like yesterday.

"You know," Carter said casually while walking Cade through some mobility exercises. "Your physical recovery is just one aspect of a full recovery. You need to take care of your mental health too. You've been through a lot."

So much for no brotherly concern. "I know that," Cade said a little impatiently. "It's just easier for me to focus on the physical stuff right now." He'd never been great at talking about his feelings.

"You should go see our counselor here, Sarah," Carter told him, raising his eyebrows at his brother. "She could help you talk through the things that have happened and teach you some strategies for moving forward."

That sounded like torture to Cade. He'd rather run into a burning building. "Why would I want to do that?" Cade asked.

Carter rolled his eyes skyward. "It's what this place is for, Cade. Helping people make a full recovery, which means both physically and mentally. You're nearly there when it comes to the physical side of things, but you have to focus on your mental recovery too."

"Yeah, okay, I'll think about it. Maybe I'll see if I can schedule her in," Cade replied to appease Carter.

Thankfully, Carter dropped it, and they spent the rest of the session talking about more neutral topics.

After he left Carter's office, he went to find Xavier to see if he needed Cade's help with anything. He enjoyed helping out around the lodge because it helped him stay busy and earn his keep. He also enjoyed it because it meant that he often ran into River throughout the day.

Like that very moment, as he saw her leaving the cafeteria. He couldn't help the grin that spread across his face.

He fell into step beside her. "Hey, how's your work going today?" he asked as they made their way from the cafeteria down to the room she had been working out of. She seemed happier today and she had a spring in her step that hadn't been there before. It was amazing what good rest and enough food could do for someone.

"Hi, Cade. I think I'm starting to make a dent," she replied with a grimace. "But there's still so much left that needs to be done. I think it'll take me the whole rest of the year to catch up with it."

Cade grinned at the thought. Having her around for at least another few months? It sounded good to him.

"I see Xavier moved you up from the basement. You like your new space?"

"Actually, I do. I've got a window so I can see outside and it's really helpful with the natural light coming in," she replied more animated than he'd seen her yet.

"That sounds nice. Well, keep up the great work and let me know if you ever need any help," he offered. "I'm not good with a needle but I am good company."

Her smile lit up her face. "I'll have to take you up on that sometime."

He really hoped she did.

THE NEXT AFTERNOON, when he was heading back to his cabin to grab a change of clothes after a gym session, he was waylaid by a woman he'd seen around but hadn't spoken to before. She stepped out in front of him, extending her hand and offering a smile.

"Hi. I'm Sarah Peterson," she introduced herself. "I'm the counselor here. Your brother mentioned that you might be interested in having a counseling session with me?"

Cade took her hand and silently cursed his brother for his meddling. He didn't want to seem rude, but he also didn't know if he was ready to talk about his feelings—especially with a stranger.

He shrugged noncommittally. "Yeah, he thought it might be good for me to have a couple of sessions to work through my...the stuff I've been through, I guess."

"I don't have any other sessions planned this afternoon," she remarked. "Are you free right now? We could cover the basics, lay down the groundwork for our future time together."

"Uh, well, I just left the gym and was going to change." He nodded in the direction of the cabins.

"Oh, I don't mind. People come to sessions from the gym all the time. But I can give you directions to my office and you can come down after, if you'd rather."

Cade really didn't want to do this, but if it would get Carter off his back, then so be it.

He nodded. "That sounds great. I'd really like to change, then I can come over," he replied.

Sarah quickly gave him directions to her office and he headed to his cabin with the promise he'd be there soon. He hurried to change and walked back to the lodge before he could second-guess himself, trying to give himself a pep talk on the way.

"Thanks for waiting," he said after knocking on the counselor's open door a short time later.

She smiled, pushing her glasses up her nose, and rose to meet him. She then gestured for him to take a seat while she closed the door. "Let's get started."

As she sat back at her desk, she offered him another warm smile. Cade couldn't relax, though. He didn't like talking about what had happened to him, what had led to his discharge from the military. He hated remembering and he did everything he could not to ponder on it any longer than he needed to.

"So," she began, clasping her hands together on top of her desk. "Let's start from the beginning. Can you tell me about your time in the service?"

He launched into his story—this part, he had no problem discussing with her, the part where everything had been going right. He had been sent to Afghanistan with his unit, and they had worked to free a city from the control of an oppressive terrorist group. It had taken months of hard work, but when they had finally managed to pull it off, he felt like he had found the career he needed. It was exciting and stimulating; he got to help people, and it kept his mind and body busy. It might not have been completely safe all of the time, but when was anything worth doing ever safe?

He had stayed out there for another couple of years, taking brief breaks to come back to America to see his brother. But he had been so focused on helping the people they had liberated, he didn't need anything else.

"And I think it would have stayed that way too," he remarked, with a sigh. "Until…until the ambush."

"The ambush?" she asked, scribbling on the page in front of her.

He nodded, and began to recount the story to her. He could still remember the day as clearly as if it were happening right in front of him. The heat from the midday sun beating down, the chatter in the truck as they transferred from one side of the city to the other. They had to take this little back road, nothing out of the ordinary—a lot of the streets had been damaged in the conflict, and it didn't give them room to move their trucks around with particular ease.

Then, he had heard it. The whistle of a projectile, swiftly followed by the sound of an explosion. One of their trucks had been taken out. Seconds later, chaos erupted.

He had thrown himself from the truck to try and help his comrades, but before he could, gunfire exploded around them, throwing up dust clouds in the sand. He had tried to use the truck for cover, but they were surrounded. A grenade was thrown close by, sending shrapnel flying into him. As he dove away from the blast, he'd caught a bullet in the shoulder.

"And that's the last thing I remember," he finished, shaking his head. "Next thing I knew, I was waking up in a field hospital, and they were telling me they were going to have to fly me back to the US."

She nodded, her face sympathetic. "That must have been so difficult for you, having to step away from the job that had become your identity at that point."

He grimaced. He hated thinking about it. Thinking about who he was before his injury and who he was now. He had purpose then, now he had no idea what his future looked like. He felt like he was floundering most days.

Cade sighed. "Yeah," he replied. "It's been hard."

And that was the most he would admit to. Even if it was the understatement of the century.

Chapter Twelve

Glancing around to make sure her bedroom door was firmly shut, River knelt beside her bed and pulled out the shoebox she'd found in the supply closet. Inside, she had been stashing any small supplies she'd managed to take from the main lodge. It wasn't much, but it was something—something she could focus on, something she could use to plan for the time when she had to move on, even if it made her feel guilty just thinking about it.

She tucked another spool of thread into the box, doing her best to push the guilt aside. She knew she couldn't stay forever; this was a temporary stop to rest and regroup before she moved on to find her family. She was really starting to settle in and enjoying her new day-to-day. It was going to be hard for her to leave when the time came.

Slipping the box back into place, she sighed and sat on the edge of her bed. It was strange to even think about leaving, after everything she had been through to bring her here. Living on the road had come so naturally to her before, but now that she had found this little corner of safety and security, leaving again seemed downright impossible. How was she supposed to just walk away from this place, especially when everyone had been so kind to her? At first she didn't give it much thought, assuming the others had ulterior motives for letting her stay. But the longer she'd been here, she realized differently. They were friendly and helpful to everyone; after all, that was what this place was about, helping and healing.

That was what she had to keep reminding herself. Not everything or everyone was out to harm her or cause her trouble. Just because she had been so used to it in her old life and always had to stay on guard didn't mean anyone here was looking to do the same thing. No matter how easy it would have been to believe it, she had to give them the benefit of the doubt until they gave her reason to think otherwise.

Hannah had been so sweet to her, and Xavier had given her a job. And Cade…well, Cade had been going around and around her head in a way she didn't know if she could deny any longer. Being near him, which she was a lot these days with them living together, made it feel like everything was going to be okay. Instead of the usual chaos in her mind, she felt like she could take a step back and relax.

She knew it was dangerous to let her guard down in any way, especially around him. There seemed to be some invisible force that pulled them together when they were around each other, especially alone. It would be a bad thing for her to get any more involved with him than she was already. He hardly knew anything about her but he seemed to care about her, even without all the specifics about her past and where she'd come from.

Maybe that would all change when he found out the truth, if she ever told him everything. All the more reason to keep it from him, she decided.

Outside her door, she heard Cade arrive, and she quickly checked to make sure the box was hidden out of view under her bed. Even though she had given him no reason to doubt her, she was always paranoid he would catch her doing something out of the normal and ask her questions she didn't want to answer. The last thing she needed was for him to figure out she was stealing supplies from the lodge and turn her in. They would definitely ask her to leave or, worse, notify the cops and have her taken away.

Taking a deep breath to settle her nerves, she stepped out of her room, and Cade raised his eyebrows when he saw her.

"I thought you were up at the lodge still," he remarked.

She shook her head. "Sorry, I'm here."

"No need to apologize," he replied, as he dropped his bag on the floor next to the couch.

"How was your day?" she asked, biting her lip as she watched him pull off his jacket. When he moved, the muscles beneath his shirt bulged slightly, and she felt a little tingle in her stomach.

"It was good," he replied, grinning. "I helped do a little gardening out near the edge of the forest. It's pretty out here this time of year. I also ran into Aaron, the handyman. We chatted a little and checked out the horses."

She returned his smile. "It really is nice. I heard the horses the other day when I was exploring a little. I actually meant to ask you or Hannah about them."

"We could walk over and see them sometime and maybe check out one of the trails while we're at it," he suggested.

"They do seem pretty quiet this time of year. I think I'd like them."

"Have you been hiking?" he asked. "Before you came out here, I mean?"

She shook her head. "Not as much as I'd like."

"So there's still plenty for you to explore," he agreed.

She nodded, her teeth resting on her bottom lip as she watched him. She couldn't help looking at his arms again. They were big, strong. The way they filled out his shirt, she wondered what they'd feel like wrapped around her.

She drew her gaze away from him, cursing herself for making it so obvious. She suddenly felt like a schoolgirl with a crush on a cute boy. She needed to get herself together. She couldn't just keep hanging around him like this, obsessing over every little moment they had together.

"I'm going to take a shower," she suddenly announced. She hurried into her room to grab her stuff, slipped into the bathroom and closed the door behind her.

She leaned back against the door and breathed deeply, trying to pull herself together. What was she doing? She needed to snap out of it. She couldn't let herself get attached to him. Even if he was the first guy to treat her kindly, maybe ever. She knew how much trouble she would be in if she allowed herself to get tied down, when what she needed was to keep her feet moving, keep herself heading toward her end goal.

Undressing, she flicked on the shower to let it warm up. The hot water could be seriously temperamental here, so she never took it for granted. She stepped underneath the rush of water, closing her eyes and tipping her head back, letting all her stress fade away.

See? She could do this. She was fine. She was still planning for what she was going to do next. A few weeks here to get her feet under her again, to get some decent food and rest. Save up some supplies. Then she could set out and look for her family once more. It might not have been easy, doing it like this, but it was easier than being out on the road with no idea where her next meal was coming from or—

"Ahhhhh!" she exclaimed, shrieking at the top of her lungs as the water suddenly turned from comfortably warm to freezing cold in an instant. She tried to jump back from the water, but bumped into the shower curtain behind her, bringing it crashing down around her.

"River?" Cade called out in a worried voice. She was too shocked and cold to speak. She grabbed the towel off the floor to try and warm herself up so she could tell him what had happened. But before she could answer him, the door flew open.

He looked panicked, his eyes darting around the bathroom and searching every corner before landing on her.

"Are you okay? What happened?" he demanded, catching her by the shoulders and looking into her eyes. "I heard you scream."

"I... I'm..." she began, but the sight of him like that made it hard for her to speak. He looked as though he was ready to fight whoever or whatever dared to cause her harm, ready to take on the unseen enemy on her behalf. She'd never in her life had someone step forward to defend her in such a way. She was stunned, grateful, excited...too many emotions to sort through in the short span of time. Now, as they stood opposite each other in that tiny bathroom, with Cade's strong hands gripping her arms, all she could do was stare at him. He was breathing hard, his eyes swirling with emotion as they bore into hers, and she suddenly found herself unable to resist.

Before she could stop herself, she leaned forward and kissed him.

His hands were still on her shoulders, but they dropped to her waist as soon as their lips touched, and he drew her in close. Their bodies pressed together, her arms went around his neck as his tongue slid into her mouth. The moment his tongue touched hers, they both moaned and Cade pulled her tighter into his embrace. It felt like time stopped and the only thing that mattered was the two of them, in that moment. Every worry, every doubt vanished instantly. She suddenly couldn't remember why it was such a bad idea to start something with him. She felt her heart slamming against her ribs, but this time, it wasn't fear that had caused it—no, it was want, desire, a need for him she had been doing her best to deny all this time.

The towel was the only thing between them, and she thought about tossing it aside. He groaned against her mouth as she tangled her fingers in his hair and pulled him impossibly closer. She sank deeper into him, their bodies pressed together from chest to hips and she still wanted to be closer. It was as though this was what they had both been waiting for since the moment they first laid eyes on one another.

And then, all at once, he pulled back. He was breathing hard, his lips slightly parted, his hands still gripping her waist and his eyes fixed on her, dark with desire.

He took a deep breath, closing his eyes and taking a step back. It felt like there was suddenly an ocean of space between them.

"I'm sorry." His voice sounded rough, and he forced his gaze from hers.

She furrowed her brow and shook her head. "No, Cade, I—"

"I shouldn't have come in here like that," he interrupted her, turning toward the door. "I'm sorry. I'll let you finish your shower in peace."

He quickly stepped out of the bathroom and pulled the door shut behind him, leaving her standing there wondering what had just happened. She reached up to skim her fingers across her mouth, trying to hold on to the memory of his lips on hers. She could still taste him, the sweetness of his kiss, his desire for her and hers for him. She now had a longing inside her, a craving she didn't know how to sate.

She sank down on the edge of the toilet and took a deep breath, trying to calm her racing heart. She had no idea what had just happened, but she got the feeling it was going to change everything between them, whether she wanted it to or not.

She looked around the tiny space, at the shower curtain that now lay in a heap in the tub and the rod askew against the wall, and sighed. She'd have to forgo the rest of her shower and ask Cade to reset the curtain.

First, she needed to get herself under control and dressed, then she'd address Cade and hope their kiss didn't make things more awkward than they already were.

Chapter Thirteen

Cade ran a hand through his hair as he stepped out of the cabin, trying to pull himself back together.

He couldn't think straight. The only thing he could think of was his lips on hers, the feeling of her body against his, nothing but a towel to keep them apart. How easy it would have been to just push that towel aside and…

No. He couldn't let his mind go there. No matter how tempting it might have been to finally give in to his desire, River had just left an abusive relationship and he did not need to complicate matters for her. The last thing she needed was for someone like him to come into her life, demand her attention when she was trying to find a safe place and heal.

When he had heard her scream in the shower, he hadn't even thought twice before going in there. How could he? He needed to know she was okay. After everything she'd been through, he couldn't help but wonder if it was all going to catch up with her, and he wanted to make sure he did everything he could to ensure she stayed safe.

But she deserved her privacy. She wasn't here because

she chose to be for fun or just to pass time. She was here because she wanted to stop running, she wanted to feel safe and not have to look over her shoulder for her ex. And no matter how good that kiss had felt to him, he needed to remember that. Her being here was about what she needed, not him.

No matter how deep his attraction to River seemed to run.

He pulled his jacket over his shoulders and started back up to the lodge. He had been hoping to relax for the rest of the afternoon, but after their encounter, he knew he needed to give her plenty of space. He didn't want to make her uncomfortable or feel pressured into something she wasn't ready for.

The image of her wrapped in that towel and the kiss were both already burned into his brain. He knew he wasn't going to be able to forget either anytime soon, but he was going to have to do his best to shove his feelings aside so things weren't awkward between them. They still had to share a cabin, after all.

He wasn't going to push for more. If she wanted something from him, if she felt the same way for him that he did for her, then she would have to come to him. No matter how badly he wanted to turn right around and go back to their cabin and show her just what he had been imagining in those long nights he had spent alone in his bed.

He arrived up at the lodge just in time to see Xavier waving off the sheriff from the door. He frowned as he walked over to him.

"Hey, Xavier. What's that about?" he asked.

Xavier sighed, looking stressed. "There's been a break-in at one of the warehouses we get supplies from, about fifty miles from here," he explained. "The sheriff thinks it might have to do with that group he was telling us about before, the Shepards of Rebellion."

Cade nodded. "Yeah, I remember."

"I've told him we're going to have one of our teams look into it for him," he continued. "You think you could meet with Lawson and his team? Help with some tactical training? I don't think they're going to run into anything too heavy out there, but I'd rather they were prepared, you know?"

"Sure. Not a problem," Cade replied.

In truth, he was glad for the excuse to get away from his cabin for a while. He needed to clear his head, and he knew he wasn't going to be able to do that with River so close to him.

"What do you think's going on with these guys?" he asked, crossing his arms over his chest.

Xavier shook his head. "I have no idea, but this is the most worried I've seen Willis about any kind of trouble in the area," he remarked. "I don't know if he's just over-reacting because all of this is new to him, or if there's actually something to it, but I'd rather be safe than sorry."

"Sure," Cade replied, frowning. He couldn't help but wonder if the Shepards drawing in closer to them had anything to do with River, but he quickly shook off that thought. He couldn't let his brain stray that way, not now. He had no idea what all she was running from, but he wasn't going to push her to come clean. Hopefully, when she was ready, she would trust him with her secrets.

The more time they spent together, though, the more Cade hoped she'd learn to trust him and tell him about her past. No matter how drawn to her he was or how much he wanted to pursue a relationship with her, they wouldn't be able to move forward until things were out in the open between them.

Just then, he saw Hannah approaching. Cade opened his mouth to greet her, but instead of stopping to talk, she narrowed her eyes in Xavier's direction and breezed right past them. He turned his head and watched her walk away at a fast clip.

Cade chuckled in surprise. "Damn, what's got her all angry?" he asked. "Did you do something to piss her off?"

Xavier shook his head as he watched her walk by, but Cade could tell there was more going on there than he wanted to admit to. He grinned. At least he wasn't the only one having woman trouble right now. It was totally unlike Hannah to be anything other than her bubbly self, so there was definitely something more going on under the surface than he knew.

This lodge had its fair share of secrets, more than Cade was sure he would ever know about. But right now, he couldn't worry about other people's secrets or problems.

He had enough of his own.

Chapter Fourteen

As River made her way back up to the lodge to continue her work for the day, she tried to push down the guilt stirring in her stomach.

How could she have kissed Cade like that? It was one thing to have a crush, but to actually do something about it? That was something else entirely. If he hadn't pulled back the way he had, she knew she would have wanted to go further. She would have gone all the way, and that would have tied her to him even more than she already felt now. No matter how much she wanted to be with him, she knew she could not allow that to happen. She had a plan and she needed to stick to it. Even if her heart wished things could be different.

She had to keep moving forward. She had to find Haven in New York and make sure her family was safe, make sure they had been able to leave behind the nightmare they had escaped for good.

And that wasn't going to happen if she found excuses to hang around the lodge and pretend like she didn't have a life outside of this place. Regardless of how tempting it might be, she had to get herself and her feelings under control. No more flirtation, no more making out, no more nothing.

She was going to throw herself into her work for the rest of the day and keep herself as busy as she could. Hopefully, Cade would be asleep by the time she got back to their cabin later and they wouldn't have to talk about what had happened between them. It was going to be over and done with, forgotten. Nothing more than a crazy mistake neither of them would mention again.

At least, she hoped so.

She arrived at the lodge and paused by the water fountain to fill up her bottle. A few people passed by her, but she didn't recognize any of them. She knew a few new guests had recently checked in to work on their recovery, but the new faces no longer bothered her like they did when she first arrived. She would catch herself hesitating slightly when several new people were around, but nothing like before, when she used to freeze in fear or hide until she was alone. She still found it best to stay out of the way, not to get distracted and focus on her work.

She dumped her bag on the floor to get her water bottle out, and it landed with a slight *bang*. Beside her, one of the men passing by froze on the spot, and then crumpled to the ground.

She recognized it at once, the way he reacted—the sound of her water bottle hitting the floor had brought a memory or experience to the surface so terrible that it caused him to physically react. She wasn't a doctor, but she'd seen PTSD before, and this looked like he was having a flashback.

He lifted his arms up to his head, clamping them around his ears as he balled up on the floor beside her.

She felt horrible for causing his reaction. She glanced around, checking to see if anyone was coming to help him. When she didn't see anyone, she took a deep breath. Well, she wasn't going to leave him to deal with this alone. If she had to step in, so be it.

"Hey," she murmured, dropping down beside him. She knew that touching him could make it worse or cause him to unintentionally hurt himself or her, so she kept a small distance between them. The best she could do was to try to bring him back to the present instead of staying in whatever nightmare the sound of her bag clattering on the ground had caused him.

He didn't react to her, but she didn't get up. He needed to know that he was safe and that someone was here to help him, not hurt him.

"I don't know where you think you are right now," she continued, speaking slowly but firmly. "But the reality is that you're at the Warrior Peak Sanctuary, with me. My name is River and I work here. That sound you heard was my water bottle hitting the ground. I'm really sorry about that."

When he didn't react to her words, she decided to switch tactics. "You can feel the floor underneath you, right?"

He didn't reply for a moment, but he lifted his head. His eyes seemed glazed and distant, but he wasn't hiding from her anymore.

"Yeah, there you go," she continued. "You're here, right? Now, take a deep breath, feel the air go into your lungs. Now exhale. You're doing great."

He followed her guidance, and she talked him through his panic as best she could. Slowly, he began to unfurl from the ball he had pulled himself into. She coaxed him upright again, and she guided him to lean up against the wall as he breathed deep. She grabbed a paper cup and filled it with cold water and gave it to him to sip while he continued to calm down. Grabbing her bag, she was about to continue to fill up her bottle when she heard a voice behind her.

"Hey, there."

She turned to see a middle-aged woman with glasses standing behind her, smiling at her warmly.

"Hi," River muttered.

She was sure she was about to get told off for interfering with one of the guests. She had only been trying to help, but she really didn't have any idea what she was doing. She didn't want to cause any harm, but she couldn't leave that man on the floor in the middle of a crisis without at least trying to help. Especially since it was her fault.

The woman walked over next to the man, asking him a few questions to make sure he was okay. He assured her that he was doing better and she told him to come to her office later that afternoon so they could talk. When he nodded his agreement, she turned back to River.

"I'm Sarah," the woman introduced herself to River, extending her hand. "I'm the counselor here."

"River." She shook Sarah's outstretched hand. "I'm sorry about that, I didn't mean to… I mean, I was just trying to help him."

"No, no, you did a really good job," Sarah said. "You clearly knew what you were doing. Where did you train?"

River stared at her for a moment, shocked, and then shook her head.

"I, uh, I didn't train for anything," she muttered, feeling a little embarrassed to admit it. She was sure a woman like Sarah had probably gone through years of training, and here she was, standing in front of her, with hardly a clue of how to handle herself without looking like a total fool.

Sarah shook her head. "Wow," she replied in surprise. "You have incredible instincts, then. Have you ever thought about training as a therapist?"

"Uh, no," River answered. "I just… I've seen people act like that before and I just wanted to help. It was my fault after all. I dropped my bag and the noise startled him."

River tried to turn and walk away, but Sarah stopped her before she could get too far. River tensed up slightly, not sure exactly how this interaction was supposed to go, but deciding to see it through either way. She couldn't keep running from everything.

"You really did an amazing job with him," Sarah remarked, as the man turned in the opposite direction of them and continued on his way. "I've seen plenty of specially trained PTSD therapists who don't have the instincts you do, River."

"Thanks," River replied with a slight blush staining her cheeks. Was that a compliment? It felt like one. The way Sarah was smiling at her, it seemed like she was truly impressed with what River had done.

"If you're ever looking for something else to do around here," Sarah continued, "you come by my office, I could always use some help."

"Your office?" River replied, confused.

"Yes, to help out with some of my clients," she continued. "In a peer-mentoring type setting, since you don't have any formal training. But I think you could do a lot of good with people who are dealing with flashbacks."

River stared at her for a moment, trying to wrap her head around the offer that was being laid out in front of her. There was a part of her that was flattered that someone like Sarah, who clearly knew what she was doing, would see potential in someone like her. But could she really risk creating any more connections to this place and the people here than she already had? The more ties she put down at the lodge, the harder it was going to be for her to leave when the time came.

River offered her a smile. "I'll think about it."

Sarah grinned back. "Wonderful," she replied. "Well, I hope I'll be seeing more of you, River. You did something really important with that man today. I hope you're proud of yourself."

River felt her face heat under the other woman's praise. She wasn't used to being complimented, and having a professional like Sarah tell her she had done something worthwhile made her chest warm in a way she hadn't felt in a long time. This place, it was full of people who seemed to see her differently than she saw herself. They saw more, even, than she knew she was capable of. They looked at her and didn't see a failure or a pathetic loser with no job skills to her name. They saw someone who was actually worth something.

As Sarah turned and walked away, River filled up her water bottle and pondered the offer. Maybe it would do her good, going outside of her comfort zone to help others who needed it. She didn't really know what she was doing, but it had felt good to help that man through his crisis. Heck, maybe she could even pick up some skills to navigate the pain she carried herself.

The offer was something she wanted to give serious consideration, but only if she stayed.

She could not think of making this detour on her journey permanent right now. She had other priorities to see to first—her family and all their safety. But maybe in the future, it would be something for her to consider. For now, she needed to remember her purpose for being here.

She arrived at the room off the lobby, where she'd been working. She appreciated Xavier letting her use this space instead of having to stay in the basement. River loved having a window to look outside. As soon as she stepped through the door, she felt her heart skip several beats in her chest.

Because she wasn't the only one there. No, someone else was in the room, inspecting her work like it was the most fascinating thing in the world.

It was Cade.

Chapter Fifteen

Cade wasn't entirely sure what he had hoped to achieve by coming to see her. He knew it wasn't a wise decision, especially after what happened earlier in the bathroom at their cabin. He should keep his distance, give them both a little space. He just couldn't seem to stay away, though. It was like an invisible force pulling him toward her.

River stopped on the spot when she saw him, and Cade grinned at her.

"Hey," he greeted. The tension in the air was thick between them, which didn't surprise him. How could it not be, after what had happened? Her lips slightly parted in surprise, and it took every bit of restraint he had not to lean forward and kiss her again, remind himself how good her mouth felt against his.

"Hey," she replied, her voice a little higher than usual.

She must have been able to feel the heat between them too. Even though he had stopped himself before things could go any further, he still wanted her so much it made his head spin.

"I was just checking to see if you'd made any progress on that winter jacket for me," he joked. He knew it was a lame excuse but it was all he could think of right then.

She smiled. "Not yet, but I haven't forgotten. I just need to find the right shade of pink for you."

"I trust you to know what looks good on me," he teased back.

She tucked a loose strand of her long hair back behind her ear. The way the light was coming through the window beside her, she looked almost radiant, as though she was exuding her own halo.

She flicked her gaze up to meet his, eyes darting back and forth as she looked at him.

Taking a deep breath, she spoke again. "Cade, I just... I wanted to apologize about what happened between us," she began, shaking her head. "I know I shouldn't have kissed you like that. It was just a spur-of-the-moment thing, and I know it's not appropriate, given that we're living together now."

"It's okay, River," he replied.

She shook her head. "No, no, it's not. And I need you to know it's not going to happen again. It was just...a mistake. You don't have to worry about me making it again."

"I'm not worried about it," Cade retorted quickly, trying to stop her before she went any further.

The last thing he wanted was for her to shut down any chance of that happening again, not when that kiss might have been the best damn kiss he'd ever had in his life. She didn't need to tell him she was sorry. He wanted to kiss her again, right then and there, wanted to pull her into his arms and—

But before he could say anything else, someone burst through the open door, and both of them turned to see what was going on.

"Cade," Xavier panted as he caught his breath in the doorway. "You need to grab your gear."

"What for?" Cade asked, furrowing his brow. This interruption really couldn't have come at a worse time. He didn't want to walk out of this room letting River think he didn't want to kiss her again, but the way Xavier had come barreling in there, it was clear something big was going on.

"Sheriff Willis called. We need to get down to the warehouse, *now*," Xavier told him. "The Feds are going to meet us there. We don't have time to waste. Come on, get moving!"

Cade shot a look at River, a silent apology for having to leave before they'd resolved what they were talking about. He really wanted to finish their conversation but Xavier was waiting and there was an urgency in his tone. He opened his mouth to find out more, but Xavier took off before Cade could ask him. River stepped forward, her eyes wide, her face colored with confusion.

"What's going on?" she asked, her voice shaking slightly.

Cade realized he couldn't walk out of there without calming her down at least a little, or she might assume this had something to do with her. That was the last thing he wanted.

"There's this group who've been causing trouble in the area for a while," he explained as quickly as he could. "They must be stirring up some problems again. The Feds just want us to help out, you know, with our training and all."

"What's the group called?" she asked. Her voice was taut, even as she tried to sound casual. He could tell she needed to know this before he walked away. Maybe it had something to do with what she had been running from.

"The Shepards of Rebellion," he answered, and at the sound of those words, all the color drained from her face. Her eyes widened, and she crossed her arms over her chest like she was trying to protect herself from something.

"Oh," she replied. He saw her trembling as she stood before him, pretending like she was okay. He took a step toward her, but she flinched back.

"River, are you okay?" he asked gently. "Do you…do you know who they are?"

She cleared her throat and tried to act casual. "Never heard of them," she replied, shaking her head.

He paused for a moment, searching her face. He wondered if he should push for more, but he could tell by the look on her face that she wasn't going to tell him anything else right now.

"We can talk later," he promised, and he turned to follow Xavier down the hall. He had run through a few basic protocols with the tactical team earlier, but he had no idea what he was going to be walking out into now. He wished they'd had more time to train as a team and be more prepared, but they would just have to figure it out as they went.

Despite that, he felt a nudge of excitement in his chest. It had been a long time since he'd been called into action of any kind, and though he didn't know if they were even going to be able to help out at all in this situation, he could feel the familiar adrenaline rush starting to pump through his body. He wanted to put all the skills into action that he hadn't been able to use since before his injury. The pain that sometimes throbbed in his shoulder seemed to have vanished, the pressure of it gone for now. Whatever this day threw at him, he knew he could take it.

He went back to the cabin to quickly change into some fatigues and strap on his weapons and gear, then he met up with Xavier at the front of the building. Lawson was nowhere to be seen, but Xavier had his arms crossed and he tapped his foot impatiently, clearly ready to get on the road.

"What do you know about what's happening?" Cade asked. His mind raced as he tried to figure out the best way to handle all this. The last thing he wanted was to make a mistake that might cost them, and it had been such a long time since he was out in the field, he was worried he was going to do just that.

"Not much," Xavier replied, checking his watch as though in a hurry. "We know the Feds are already down there, ready to move in. They're waiting for us as backup."

"They couldn't get anyone else out there?" Cade asked, frowning.

"They couldn't get anyone else down there in time. We're closer," he said, shaking his head. "You ready?"

"As I'll ever be," Cade responded. Cade and Xavier headed out to a truck parked just outside the main building. "Where's Lawson?"

Xavier narrowed his eyes. "He's already out there," he replied. "Didn't want to wait. We'll convene with him there."

"Right," Cade muttered, but in truth, he wasn't thinking about Lawson right now. No, he was thinking about River. He knew he should keep his mind on the mission but he couldn't stop thinking about the way she had reacted when he mentioned the name of the group they were going after.

What did she know about the Shepards of Rebellion? Had she encountered them in her time on the road? Maybe. They had been going after travelers, and she had been on her own long enough that she might have been a target if she wasn't being careful enough.

But the way she had responded, the way the blood had drained from her face, it seemed to Cade like it was more than that. As though the Shepards of Rebellion were tied to something she never wanted to think about again.

She would have just told him if they had mugged her or something, right? She had started opening up to him, a little at least. If something bad had happened, he thought she would have at least mentioned it to him.

But the fact she hadn't said anything about it made him wonder if something darker and more dangerous was going on. Something that might have been tied to the life she had tried to escape before. He could only imagine what she had been through and how bad it had been for her if she had been anywhere near those psychos. From what he'd heard about them, they got their claws into people and never let go.

What if she was one of them? It would explain why she had been so reluctant to talk about her past, if she had been wrapped up in something involving the Shepards.

Or maybe he was jumping to conclusions again.

Maybe he should just focus on what was right in front of him instead of trying to figure out what was going on with River. He had a job to do, and he needed to get his head in the game. He could worry about her and whatever she was keeping from him later. He'd be damned if he would be the cause of their team failing.

As Xavier pulled the truck away from the lodge, he couldn't help but glance back over his shoulder toward the building. That invisible string that drew him to River pulled hard. He wondered if she was watching them right now. Wondered if she was panicking as much as she seemed to be when he mentioned the Shepards.

But mostly, he wondered when she was finally going to tell him the truth about her past, and what had led her to be standing on the side of the road in the rain on that night he'd met her.

Chapter Sixteen

Her mind raced so fast she couldn't even stop to think straight. All she knew was that she had to get the hell out of there as soon as possible. She had to put as much distance between herself and this place as she could, and she needed to do it right now, before the Shepards caught up with her.

As soon as those words had come out of Cade's mouth, she knew there was only one thing for her to do—run. Immediately. No matter how much she wished she could stay, how much she wished she didn't have to do this, she didn't have a choice. If they were that close to her, even within fifty miles, she was in danger. And she was going to put everyone else in this place in the line of fire, too. She couldn't bear the thought of it. These people had been so nice and welcoming to her, she couldn't stand even the idea of causing them so much pain. They didn't deserve it.

But she knew Cade and the others would try to stop her if they were around when she ran, so she had to take the chance while they were away. She waited until after she saw Cade and Xavier drive away to make sure they were really gone then went back to the cabin to gather the supplies she'd managed to put together.

Even though the cold was really starting to set in, she had to get on the road again. Fast. If she had learned one thing from these last few months, it was to trust her instincts, and they were screaming at her to get as far from here as fast as she could. The sooner, the better.

Her hands shook as she ripped open her bag and started stuffing it with all the supplies she had managed to secure so far. There wasn't much, but it was more than she had set out with the first time around. If she had made it this far before, she could do it again.

She was doing her best to convince herself, even though all she wanted was to curl up in a ball and hide. Her heart hammered in her chest, and she was sure she had given away the truth of at least some of her past to Cade when he had mentioned the Shepards to her. If he hadn't been so distracted by the mission he was going on, she had no doubt he would have taken the chance to interrogate her. And when he found out the whole truth, he wouldn't have wanted anything to do with her. How could he? He would want to put as much distance between the two of them as possible, and she wouldn't blame him.

She sealed up her bag, her hands shaking, and tried to steady her breathing. She wished there was a vehicle she could take, or even a bike. But they would notice the absence and someone would come after her before she got far enough way. Either one of them or the cops. That would be even worse. No, she was going to have to leave on foot, like before. She'd walk as long as she could before finding a place to hole up for a bit and make a new plan.

At least this time she'd have the rations she'd stocked

and the clothes she got in town. She'd make a quick detour to the basement in the lodge and grab another sleeping bag, then be on her way. With winter coming in soon, she'd need the extra layers and protection.

She tried to take a deep breath as she swiped away tears that had started to fall from her eyes. It was going to be okay. It had to be. This had only been a stopping point, a short rest. She'd known she'd have to move on soon. That was why the thought of leaving had never been far from her mind. Yet, the thought of leaving the friends she'd made and Cade… His name alone sent a sharp pang through her chest.

She should have known better than to let her feelings get in the way, especially when it came to Cade. Whatever she felt for him, whatever they had stirring between them, it was nothing more than a pipe dream. A fantasy she had concocted based on a truth that was never real. He could never be with someone like her. He was so kind, so caring, so protective—because he thought she was on the run from an abusive ex, not that she had been part of a group like the Shepards of Rebellion. The very group he was out to help stop now.

Stepping out of her room and into the cabin's small living area, she noticed Cade's jacket draped over the back of the couch. He must have forgotten to take it with him when he left. She grabbed it without thinking and lifted it to her face, inhaling his woodsy scent. It would be the only thing of his she could take with her, the only reminder of him she would be able to cling to when she was out on her own again. She hoped he wouldn't mind her taking it. Maybe he would be able to forgive her if he knew what she was saving him from. How bad things would have been if she hadn't left while he was gone and he found out about her connection to the Shepards. The danger she could have brought to their door. It was better this way.

She put the jacket on, almost laughing at how it swallowed her small frame, and hooked her bag over her shoulder, readying herself for what was to come next. Throwing open the door, she sprinted out and ran straight into Hannah, who was hurrying down to her own cabin.

"Oof!" Hannah exclaimed as they crashed into each other. River stopped dead in her tracks, cursing to herself silently. She should have checked that no one was around. She had hoped she would be able to make a clean getaway, but now that Hannah had run into her, it was going to be next to impossible to make it out without drawing more attention to herself.

River looked up, and her heart twisted when she saw that Hannah's eyes were wet with tears.

Her eyes widened in horror. "I didn't hurt you, did I?" she gasped.

Hannah shook her head. "No, no, I'm fine," she replied, but River could tell that wasn't true. In the short time she'd known her, River had never seen her this upset, especially not in tears. She was always bubbly and had a smile for everyone. It was obvious to her that Hannah was definitely *not* fine right now.

"Hannah, what's going on?" she asked, already panicking that this had something to do with her. Hannah sniffed, and River put an arm around her and guided her down to her own cabin.

Once they were inside, River set about trying to make her some coffee. It took her a few minutes to figure out how to use the coffee machine, but eventually she pulled it off, and handed Hannah a steaming mug as she sat down opposite her.

"What's going on?" River asked again, concern dripping from her voice. She would never forgive herself if she had managed to bring some kind of danger to this place or if she had landed Hannah in trouble because of what she had been keeping from them all this time.

"I... I don't even know anymore," she admitted, shaking her head. There were dark rings underneath her eyes, and it looked as though she hadn't slept properly in days.

"You can tell me," River urged her. "It's okay."

Hannah sighed, lifted the coffee to her lips and took a long sip.

"I don't know where to start," she confessed. "It's all been going on for so long, I guess, I just got used to nothing ever happening between us, you know?"

"Happening between who?"

"Between Xavier and me," she replied.

River's eyes widened. "Wait, there's...there's something happening with you guys?"

"That's the problem, I don't even know," Hannah replied. "I... I've had feelings for him for a long time. Ever since I was a kid, pretty much. Him and my brother, Lawson, they've been friends for years—best friends. I knew he was always off-limits, so I never even thought about making a move. But the more time that passed, the harder it became to pretend I didn't feel the way I do about him."

River's eyebrows rose as she listened to Hannah. She had noticed some tension between Xavier and Hannah, but she had no idea this was where it came from. Not knowing either of them well, she'd assumed it was something work related, not personal.

"I know, I know," Hannah added, shaking her head when she saw the look on River's face. "It's such a mess. I don't know what it was, but I just… I decided I had to tell him the truth. So… I did. I told him how I felt."

"And?" River prompted.

"He kissed me," she replied, a smile brushing across her lips at the memory. "I told him I had been in love with him for years, and he…he kissed me. He didn't say anything back, but he didn't have to. I knew what was going on in his head. I knew…" She trailed off again, shaking her head.

"But someone saw, and they told my brother," she continued. "And he's furious. I mean, I always knew he would be upset. I knew he warned Xavier to stay away from me years ago, but I had no idea he would take the news this badly. He's so angry at both of us. Livid. I don't know what kind of damage it's done to their friendship, or our relationship, or…any of it, really. It's such a mess and it's my fault. I should never have said anything."

"You can't keep your mouth shut about something like that," River replied at once. "If the two of you have feelings for each other, you can't let your brother get in the way of that."

Hannah smiled a little sadly. "Yeah, I guess," she murmured, and then she seemed to notice what River was wearing for the first time. She stared at her for a moment, eyes sliding up and down her outfit, taking in the bag on her shoulder and Cade's jacket wrapped around her.

"Why are you dressed like that?" she wondered aloud. "You going somewhere?"

River hesitated before she responded. Could she tell her the truth? She would feel bad keeping her mouth shut when Hannah had just told her something so personal.

She could tell her a piece of the truth, at least. That was something, right? She slipped the bag from her shoulder and set it on the floor next to her.

"I... I was worried about Cade," she confessed. "I thought I would go after him and see if there was some way I could help."

"At this raid thing?" she asked with wide eyes.

River nodded. "Yeah, that's what I was thinking," she replied with a half-hearted laugh. "I know it's crazy."

"It's not crazy," Hannah assured her, smiling sweetly. "You...you have feelings for him, don't you?"

River bit her lip. If she said this next part out loud, there would be no more hiding from the truth, no more pretending like she didn't feel the way she did about this man. But maybe there was something to be said for being honest. Maybe it was time for her to confess how she felt, and share it with someone she knew she could trust. Hannah had just told her about her love life, after all. River might not have had much of one yet, but she needed to talk to someone about it.

"Yeah, I do," she replied. "I can't get him off my mind. I know it sounds crazy because we don't know each other that well yet, but I really like him."

"Hey, I can't blame you," Hannah replied, managing a laugh. "He's really hot. And the two of you have been living together. Has anything...you know...happened between you yet?"

"We kissed," River admitted.

Hannah clapped a hand over her mouth. "Oh my gosh,

really? That's so great," she gushed, and River couldn't help but smile. It felt good to finally talk to someone else about it, to admit her feelings out loud. It felt like a tiny weight had been lifted. Hannah might not have known the whole story, but it had been a long time since she'd had a girlfriend she could talk to about stuff like this.

"Yeah, and I think I'm really falling for him," she continued. "I don't know what's happening between us, and I don't want to push him. I know I should have more self-control around him."

"Girl, have you seen the way he looks at you?" she exclaimed. "He's the one who's been needing the self-control out of the two of you."

"You really think so?" River asked, chewing her lip. It had been so many years since she'd had anything resembling a normal relationship, she could hardly remember what it felt like to have someone show interest in her. How was she supposed to recognize it? But if Hannah seemed to think there was something going on there, maybe she wasn't imagining his attraction to her.

"Yeah, I really do," Hannah replied, reaching over to give her hand a squeeze. "And you deserve it, River. After everything you've been through, you deserve someone like Cade."

River wasn't sure if she entirely believed that yet. But she knew, at least for the time being, that she wasn't going to be able to leave now. She couldn't go back to living on the road, on the run. So maybe she should get used to sticking around here for a little while longer.

Even if the thought of remaining in this place with the Shepards potentially so close by scared the hell out of her.

Chapter Seventeen

As the truck pulled to a stop outside the warehouse, Cade opened the door and jumped out. The adrenaline was pumping and it had taken all the restraint he had not to leap out of this truck half a mile down the road and sprint the rest of the way there.

It was a cold day, clear and bright, and Lawson stepped out of the doorway to the warehouse and waved them over. An FBI agent stood next to him. Cade recognized the regulation haircut and the windbreaker those types always wore.

"Hey," Cade greeted Lawson, as he joined them. "What's happened? What did we miss?"

"They're long gone now." Lawson sighed. "But they did some real damage to this place. And the owner? He was unlucky enough to be here when they arrived, and they beat the hell out of him. Put him in the hospital. He's recovering now, but his jaw's wired shut, so there's not much he can tell us."

"And they think it was the Shepards?"

"They know it was," he replied, shaking his head as Xavier caught up with them. "There were reports from people who saw them passing through a small town not far from here. But law enforcement couldn't intercept them in time to stop this."

"And they raided this place for supplies?" Xavier asked.

Lawson shot him a look, then turned his attention back to Cade, addressing him and not Xavier.

"Looks like it," he said. "Best we can do now is take a look around the place and get an idea of what they took. This place is usually a storage facility for survivalist supplies—canned food, stuff like that—but they have a decent amount of weaponry too, most of it smaller handguns and a variety of ammunitions. If they've taken off with a lot of that, they could be planning an attack somewhere."

"We'll take a look," Xavier volunteered.

Lawson didn't even look at him before he headed over to the truck to fill the other guys in on what had been happening.

"What is going on between the two of you?" Cade asked, as Xavier watched Lawson walk away.

Xavier shook his head. "You don't want to know," he replied. "It won't get in the way of what we're here to do. Come on, let's see what we've got."

Cade raised his eyebrows, but knew better than to push for more information, especially in the middle of a mission. They had a job to do here, and what mattered was getting it done, not figuring out whatever drama was going down between them.

They headed into the warehouse, and Cade grabbed an inventory paper from where it had been dropped next to the front door. He scanned the space—it was all in disarray, and it looked as though they had taken almost everything they could get their hands on.

"Do you think they were looking for something specific?" Cade asked Xavier as they started to make their way in and out of the rows of tall shelving that had been knocked over to figure out what had gone missing.

"I honestly don't know," Xavier replied. "I'm still trying to figure out what they're doing this far north."

"Oh, yeah?"

"Yeah, I've been doing some research into them since Willis said that the Shepards might become our problem soon," he explained. "And they've never really come this far out of their territory before. I can't figure out what it's about, but there has to be a reason."

"You don't think they're just trying to expand their territory?" Cade asked.

He shook his head. "The movements they've been making, it's more than that," he replied. "There's something he's looking for out here. I'm not sure what it is. Hell, I'm not sure if he even knows what it is, but there's a reason behind it, I'm sure of it. They might be crazy, but they don't do things for no reason."

"He?" Cade locked on that one word. "You talking about the guy who runs the Shepards of Rebellion?"

"Ryker," Xavier stated. "That's his name. There's not a whole lot out there about him, but what I do know is that he's some seriously bad news."

"In what way?" Cade inquired. The more he knew about this guy, the better. If there was one thing he had learned during his time in the Special Forces, it was to learn as much about your enemy as you could.

"The way he treats his followers," he replied. "There

aren't many who have managed to get away, but those who have all say the same thing. That he uses them like possessions. He doesn't let anyone else get close to them, totally cuts them off from their friends and family. Shuts off their connections to the outside world so they don't have anything other than him. It's crazy. He really is running a cult out there."

Cade nodded as he thought about what Xavier had said. He'd known men like that before. Men who treated everyone else like they were owed something. They were some of the most dangerous out there, some of the most ruthless. Whatever this Ryker guy was looking for out here, he wasn't going to stop until he got his hands on it, or until someone got in his way and couldn't be pushed around like everyone else.

"You think the Feds will get him?" Cade asked as they started to take the inventory.

Xavier shrugged. "I don't think they're confident about it, and I can't say I blame them. He's been running this gang for years now, and nobody has managed to get close enough to bring them down. But leaving his territory like this, he might open himself up to the possibility of being caught. He's not going to be as strong out of his usual hunting ground in Florida."

"Right," Cade muttered. There was something about even hearing of this Ryker guy that made the hair on the back of his neck stand on end. He was obviously really bad news. And even though Cade was used to handling trouble during his time in the military, he didn't like not knowing what they were dealing with when it came to this guy and the gang he ran.

"Let's start at the back and work our way forward," he suggested to Xavier.

Lawson still hadn't come in to join them. There was clearly something serious going on between the two men, but it was the last thing on Cade's mind right now. They had intel to gather, and the more they could find out, the easier it was going to be to track this Riker guy down and stop his gang before they moved any farther across the country.

Cade handed Xavier the inventory sheet and headed to the back of the warehouse, where some of the shelving was still upright.

"Okay, so bottom shelf is..." he began, but before he could get any further, a man sprang out from behind the shelves.

"What the hell?" Xavier exclaimed.

Cade managed to step to the side before the man could make contact with him.

The man, who appeared to be in his midforties, looked panicked as he followed Cade's movement. Cade saw his chest rising and falling and his eyes darting around as he tried to find a way out. The man took a swing at him, but Cade dodged it easily. His hand flew into the metal shelf behind Cade instead. The clanging noise filled the warehouse, and the man let out a cry of pain, drawing his hand back in shock. Cade moved toward him to try and capture him, but the man surprised him, slamming his forehead into Cade's jaw and sending him reeling back. Cade clutched at his face, the pain not registering yet as he tried to figure out how best to handle this.

"Xavier, cut him off," Cade called to his friend, gesturing to the other end of the row before the man could turn that direction to run. Cade might not have known exactly what this man was doing here, but he was sure they could get something useful out of him.

The man tried to beat Xavier to the other side, but Xavier managed to catch him before he could get away. He almost squirmed loose of Xavier's grip, but Cade grabbed him before he could continue his escape, and pinned him to the ground with his hands behind his back.

"Xavier, get the others so we can make sure there's no one else hiding in this place," Cade said, still holding the man to the ground. His arm twinged with pain, but he hardly felt it. He hadn't expected an attack here, but his instincts had kicked in without a second thought. It felt good to be back in action.

Moments later, the warehouse filled with noise as the rest of the guys came flooding in. The man had given up trying to escape from Cade's grip, as though he knew there was no chance for him now.

Who was he? Had the Shepards left behind one of their own, or was this someone else entirely? He didn't have a clue.

But they had someone here, at least. Someone they could use to shake out a little more information about this gang.

And that was more than they'd had before.

Chapter Eighteen

She paced back and forth in the cabin as she waited for Cade to return, wondering how much longer they were going to be away from the lodge.

It had been nearly a day since she had last seen him, and her mind had been torturing her with questions about where he was and what was happening to him. She didn't know if she could take much more of the waiting.

She was so worried about him, worried about what might have happened out there. What if he had encountered the Shepards? She knew all too well what they were capable of. If he had been hurt as a result of going after them, she would never be able to forgive herself. Because she knew what they were doing here, and that it was her fault they had managed to creep their way across the states and so close to the lodge.

This place should have been safe. It was what they had tried to create here, a space where those dealing with physical or mental trauma could recover. The thought of being the one to ruin that was more than she could take.

And after the talk she'd had with Hannah, River had decided she needed to tell Cade how she felt about him. She couldn't leave this place with it unsaid. Even if it might be more complicated than she was able to wrap her head around, he deserved to know. She needed him to understand that her feelings for him were real. That even though she had not been completely truthful and open about her past, when she looked to her future, she wanted him to be a part of it.

She had fallen asleep on the couch waiting for him to come back to their cabin, and now it was the next morning and there was still no sign of him—no sign of anyone who had gone out on that mission, actually. She had the brief thought about going out to try to find him, or even asking Hannah if she knew where they went and ask her to take River there. She knew that was crazy, though. She needed to keep her head on straight and her emotions under control and wait for him to return.

Finally, she heard it—the sound of an engine, the rumble of a truck heading up the path to the lodge. They were back? They were back! She threw open the door and hurried out toward the lodge, sprinting to catch up with them by the time they reached the entrance. She prayed Cade would be with them.

Sure enough, the truck drew to a halt outside the lodge, and Cade was one of the first ones out. She rushed toward him, but as she got closer she began to slow down. There was a large bruise forming over his jaw. What had happened to him?

"Cade!" she called to him, and he turned toward her voice. When he saw her, a smile spread over his face, followed by a wince as he stretched the painful-looking bruise on his jaw.

"Are you okay?" River demanded, grabbing his hand and squeezing tight. She was just so glad he was there right now, she couldn't think of anything else, even to ask what had taken them so long or how the mission had gone.

But before he could respond, others who had been with him came pouring out of the truck, splitting Cade and River apart once more. Cade locked eyes with her, giving her a nod as though to let her know that everything was okay, but she could tell it wasn't. This was the most action she had seen at the lodge since she had arrived here, and she was worried that it had to do with her. Concerned that she might have brought more danger to their door and left them all unaware by not being up-front when she arrived.

Some of the men hurried back in to the main lodge, talking over each other while a few still hung around outside. There was an excited buzz in the air, which she took as a good sign, but she was still confused as to what had actually happened. Why wasn't anyone attending to Cade? They must have had something more important to focus on right now.

Finally, everyone vanished inside and she and Cade were alone again. She rushed over to Cade and stared up at him, her brows tight with worry.

"Are you okay?" she asked again.

He nodded and smiled down at her. "I'm okay."

"What happened to your face?" she asked, reaching up to touch the bruise on his jaw without thinking. He winced and pulled back.

"I'm sorry, I'm sorry," she blurted out. "Did someone hurt you?"

"I got attacked when we were at the warehouse," he explained, and her stomach clenched with panic.

"Attacked?" she whispered.

"It's okay, though," he replied. "He didn't manage to do much to me. We got him under control."

He? Her mind began to race as she tried to figure out who it might be. Surely it couldn't be Ryker, right? They wouldn't have been able to subdue him so easily. He would need a whole army to take him down. That man was evil. And he probably wouldn't have let Cade walk away with nothing more than a bruise on his face.

"This is my fault," she muttered under her breath, she was sure of it.

"What are you talking about?" he replied with a frown, cupping her face in his hand.

She shook her head and drew her gaze away from him. She didn't want to tell him, but the truth was she had dragged them into this. If she hadn't arrived here, he would never have gotten hurt.

And if she stayed, he was only going to get hurt again, and again, and other people would too. Other people who had come here for safety only to be met with the danger that would follow her wherever she went. Guilt stabbed at her hard. She needed to go. She should have left the night before when she'd had the chance. But after she had spoken to Hannah, she had made herself believe for a moment that she could find a way to make it all work.

But looking at Cade now, she knew she couldn't. Tears brimmed in her eyes and dripped down her cheek, and Cade wiped them away with his thumb. She squeezed her eyes shut and tilted her head into the palm of his hand, wishing she could stay here, in this moment. She wished she could tell him everything and promise that it would all be okay, even though she knew it wasn't the truth.

How could anything ever be okay again after what had happened? She knew what the Shepards were capable of, and it was only going to get worse from here. She didn't want to put more of a target on the lodge or the people living here than she already had.

Before her mind could stray any further back down that path, she heard voices behind her. One voice she recognized. A voice that made her feel as though she was about to throw up on the spot. She spun around, trying to place it.

All at once, she figured it out. Cade turned back to the truck and helped Lawson and Xavier guide out someone she had never seen at the lodge before.

But he wasn't a stranger to her. He lifted his gaze up from the ground as though he could sense her presence, and his face drained of color when he saw her. He froze on the spot, not taking his eyes off her. Staring at her like he had seen a ghost.

"River?" he breathed.

Hearing the man say her name made her knees tremble, the panic starting to set in. After all this time, after as far as she had managed to get from them. Right here in front of her was a remnant of her old life—a part of her past she had prayed she would be able to get away from for good.

"River, what are you doing here?" he demanded.

Chapter Nineteen

Cade looked from the man to River and back again. River looked as though she was about to be sick right there, hardly able to draw in a breath, and the man stood frozen, like he had seen someone he had never expected to lay eyes on again.

"Wait, do you two know each other?" Xavier asked with a frown.

River shook her head and looked at the ground, but the man nodded.

"River, don't you remember me? It's Louis. Dr. Louis."

She wouldn't even look at him. Wouldn't look at any of them. Cade put an arm around her waist and she leaned into him like he was the only thing keeping her upright in that moment. He squeezed her in close, and felt her body trembling helplessly against him as she tried to pull herself together.

"I want the two of them in my office, *now*," Lawson demanded, snapping his fingers and making her flinch. "River and Dr. Louis both have some explaining to do."

River tried to pull away from Cade, but he kept a firm grip on her. She needed to face this, whatever it was, but he wasn't going to let her do it alone. No matter how she knew this guy, no matter what had happened between them in the past, she had to come clean and tell them what she knew. This man had been found at the location of a break-in by the Shepards, after all. Did that mean she knew something about them, too?

Cade guided River into the lodge, where Xavier and Lawson steered the man—the doctor—to Lawson's office. Cade's mind reeled as he took it all in. Maybe it was the hit he'd taken from the doctor still scrambling his head, but he couldn't make sense of it.

Xavier and Lawson went to get coffee before they began their interrogation, leaving Cade, River and the man who called himself Dr. Louis waiting in the office. Louis stared at River but she wouldn't look him in the eyes. Instead, her eyes darted nervously around the room.

"River, you must remember me," he said in a soft voice.

She stood stock-still, eyes pinned to the wall next to him. A tear ran down her cheek, but she hardly seemed to notice it was there.

"You're looking for Haven, aren't you?" he asked her.

She still didn't respond, but she began to shake when he said that name. Who was Haven? Cade was utterly lost as he tried to figure out how River knew this guy. He knew they were going to get to the bottom of it one way or another when the others got back.

Lawson and Xavier returned, taking their seats behind the desk and gesturing for the rest of them to do the same. Although Louis had fought them when they'd first met, he'd been surprisingly cooperative when they'd told him they were working with the Feds. He had allowed himself to be transported up to the lodge without too much more of a fight, even apologizing to Cade for headbutting him.

"So," Lawson began, raising his eyebrows at the doctor. "Are you going to tell us who you are?"

"I'm Louis," the man replied at once, shooting another look at River like he was trying to figure out if she was going to say anything. "I… I'm a doctor. Or, at least, I was. I've been working as an informant for the last few years against the Shepards of Rebellion."

Xavier narrowed his eyes. "How do we know you're working against them and not with them?" he asked, leaning forward.

"I can't prove it to you, but trust me, I wouldn't have come so quietly if I was a bona fide member," he replied. "I've been acting as their doctor for a long time now, but I've been feeding information to the Feds the whole time."

"Can we confirm that with our contact?" Lawson asked, and Xavier nodded, getting to his feet to take care of the request. Once he was out of the room, the doctor continued.

"I'd heard them mentioning you before, the Feds I was working with," he explained. "Ever since the Shepards started moving on a little farther north, things have been…changing. It's been harder to stay on top of everything that's going on. But when I saw what they'd done to that man, the one who owns the warehouse, I… I just couldn't continue. I couldn't keep standing by and pretending anymore. That's why I broke with them. I didn't feel as though I had a choice."

His voice hitched in the back of his throat as he spoke, and Cade wondered just how much he had seen over the years he had been an informant for the Feds on the Shep-ards of Rebellion. How much had he had to keep his mouth shut about?

And how did River tie into all this? That was the part he couldn't make sense of. Was it like he had suspected, and she was part of the Shepards? Was that who she had been on the run from? Was someone in that group the ex she had fled from, or had that just been a cover story?

Xavier returned to the office and nodded at Lawson.

"He's telling the truth," he replied. "He's been working with the Feds for the last few years on this."

"If there's anything you need to know or anything I can help with, please just let me know," the doctor told them, glancing between Xavier and Lawson. "I know you're helping with the case, and trust me when I say you're going to need every advantage you can to bring these guys down. I've seen what they can do, how far they'll go…"

He trailed off. A shiver seemed to run through the room. The enormity of what they were facing wasn't lost on Cade. This man had been ready to fight his way out of the situation he'd found himself in to get away from the gang. Cade could only imagine how bad things had gotten for him. How terrified he must have been that he was going to be exposed at any given moment, and what it might have meant if he had been.

River still stared at the wall, tears falling silently down her cheeks. It was clear being close to this guy had triggered something in her, drawn a memory back to the surface she didn't want to even think about.

Finally, the doctor turned his attention to her again. He dropped his voice slightly, leaning toward her. She recoiled from him at once, like he was toxic.

"They don't know where you are, River," he assured her, his voice gentle. There was clearly a history between the two of them, even if it was a history she wanted to forget.

His mind flashed back to when he had first met her, how fearful and jumpy she had seemed. Was it because she knew she was being chased? Because she knew she couldn't leave behind her old life as easily as she wanted to?

"You're probably in the safest place you can be," he continued, and River let out a sob.

Cade had seen her cycle through plenty of emotions in the time that he'd known her. But this? This was unlike anything he had seen before, and he would have been lying if he said it didn't worry him to see her like this. He wanted to pull her into his arms and tell her it was all going to be okay, but he knew she wouldn't have believed him. Whatever she had been running from, it had well and truly caught up with her now, and there was no way she could pretend otherwise. Whatever she had been heading toward, whoever Haven was, she had halted in her search for her, staying at the lodge and trusting them instead of moving forward.

Trusting him to protect her against her past.

Lawson and Xavier flicked their gazes between the doctor and River. Lawson's face bristled with anger, an anger Cade could only guess came from knowing how much trouble River had brought right to their door. Despite that, though, Cade felt protective of her. He would do anything to make sure that whatever nightmare was following her didn't get any closer than it already had.

The doctor reached for River's shoulder, but she pulled back from him, letting out a whimper. Xavier eyed the two of them skeptically, trying to piece together what was going on. Cade wasn't even sure what was actually going down, but he stayed by River's side, not wanting to break away from her for a second. She seemed to have been doing so much better in these last few days, so to see her so upset and scared like this made him feel... angry. Angry, knowing there were people out there who had given her reason to feel this way. People who had scared her and hurt her enough in the past to turn her into this terrified woman before them now.

"Take our new friend to get some lodging," Lawson told Xavier. "Make sure there are guards on the door at all times."

"I'm not going to try and go anywhere," Louis replied.

Lawson shook his head. "It's not about you getting out," he replied grimly. "It's about others getting in."

Cade nodded in agreement. He couldn't imagine that the Shepards wouldn't notice one of their own had gone missing, and when they did, they might put the pieces together about what he had been doing while he'd been with them. They didn't strike Cade as the type to forgive and forget. Better to keep the doctor safe and get all the information out of him they could, than risk a break-in that would get him hurt—or worse.

Once Xavier had escorted the doctor from the room, Lawson turned his attention to River. His mouth was set in a hard line, his expression unreadable.

"River," he began, his voice low. He was doing his best to control it, not to spook her, but as soon as she heard her name, her whole body tensed.

"I think I need to talk to you. Alone."

Her eyes darted over to the door, and she didn't say a word.

Lawson's eyebrows shot up. "Don't you dare make a run for it—"

But before he could stop her, she dashed out the door and into the corridor beyond.

Lawson sprang to his feet. "Dammit," he muttered, and he went to follow her. But before he could, Cade put out his arm to stop him.

"Leave her," he told him firmly.

Lawson glared at him. "I need her to explain to me exactly what the hell she's doing here. And what her connection is to the Shepards."

"I know," Cade assured him. "You deserve an explanation. I get it. But don't go after her. She's terrified. She's not going to leave, I know that. Let me talk to her, okay?"

Lawson didn't exactly look happy about the suggestion, but he rolled his eyes skyward and let out a sigh. "Fine," he grunted.

Though his anger was evident, he was smart enough to see that Cade was going to get a whole lot more out of River than he would ever be able to. Cade nodded his thanks.

"I'll find out everything we need to know," he promised.

Lawson shook his head. "I hope so," he replied. "And I hope that woman you brought to our door isn't more trouble than she's worth."

Cade turned to leave the office, Lawson's words ringing in his ears. There was no doubt River had brought a whole lot of trouble with her—trouble beyond what Cade could ever have imagined when he had seen her by the side of the road, in that dirty homemade dress, looking like she had been living in the wild.

But no matter what kind of trouble she had chasing her, Cade knew one thing for sure: she was worth it.

Every bit.

Now he just needed to prove that to her.

Chapter Twenty

River felt the tears streaking down her face as she ran back to the cabin, but she let them fall unchecked. It felt as though she had gone back in time to relive everything again the moment she had laid eyes on Louis—the moment she had been reminded of a past she wanted nothing more than to leave behind. Her heart pounded in her chest, her body screaming at her to do one thing—run.

She should not have put off leaving as long as she had. She should not have let running into Hannah stop her yesterday. And now, with them at least suspecting her connection to the Shepards, thanks to Louis and her reaction to him, she was truly left with no choice. It was too dangerous here. Maybe she'd get enough of a head start that Ryker and the others wouldn't find her and they'd leave this place alone. And then there was Cade. Her heart clenched at the thought of him. He already knew more than she wanted him to and would probably be glad to see her go.

She arrived back at the cabin and started restuffing everything back into her bag that she'd removed the night before. This time, she wasn't going to be stopped, she wasn't going to let her emotions get the better of her. No matter how tempting it might be to stick around just a little while longer, she was leaving.

She would figure out which direction to go once she got back on the road. Eventually, she'd forget about her time here and her new friends she was leaving behind. They were definitely better off without her around to cause them unnecessary pain and bring danger to their door. She had no clue what the Shepards would do if they found this place, though she could guess from past experience. She didn't want these people to suffer any ill will trying to help her.

But before she could race out the door, Cade arrived at the cabin. She could barely even look at him. She tried to brush past him but he blocked off her exit, stopping her from fleeing.

"Hey, River, I need you to talk to me," he told her. "Lawson is practically blowing his lid back there. If you're going to stay, you need to tell us what's been—"

"I'm not going to stay," she shot back before he could get out another word. No point in pretending any longer.

"What are you talking about?" he replied, catching her arm before she could make a break for the door again. "Of course you are. You're not going anywhere. They're out there, you can't risk—"

"You don't understand, Cade!" she exclaimed, staring up at him, her eyes desperate. "They're coming after me. If I stay here, they're going to come to this place, and they're going to ruin everything you guys have worked so hard to build. I don't want that for you. I can't stand the thought of it. So will you just...just let me go? Please?"

His eyes were wide as he looked down at her, trying to take in what she had just said.

He shook his head slowly and crossed his arms in defiance. "If you think I'm going to let you walk out that door without explaining what you mean," he replied, "you've got another think coming, River."

Cade wasn't moving out of her way and River wasn't sure what to do next. She took a deep breath, trying to collect her scattered thoughts. She had to think of something to say to make him let her go. Every minute she stood there was costing her time and distance on the road. Bringing danger closer to them all.

But looking at Cade, seeing his confusion and the different emotions crossing his face…she couldn't just leave like this. He had given her so much in these last few weeks, a safety and security she didn't even know was possible for her. And a kindness she had been craving for longer than she could remember. The least she could do in return was tell him some part of the truth. She owed him that much.

"Fine," she muttered. "I'll tell you everything."

She sank down on the couch and dropped her bag at her feet. Maybe it was better this way. She was so tired of running, of being afraid of everything. She pulled her knees up to her chest and wrapped her arms around them like a shield. Her heart skipped a beat when Cade sat down beside her and wrapped one of her hands in his. The warmth of his touch was all she needed to get the words out. Hesitantly, she told him the story of what had brought her out here.

When she and her sister, Haven, were kids, their father had wanted to make a better life for them, the way so many fathers did, and so he'd started working for a shady character called Hector Neimons in the small town they lived in. Before long, Hector had brought him and his family into the Shepards of Rebellion, a biker gang that basically functioned as a cult worshipping at the altar of the Neimons family, especially Hector's son, Ryker. Even when things started getting darker and more dangerous, their hold on River's father was too intense.

River had grown up in a world of paranoia and violence, where every wrong move had been punished harshly. There wasn't a single choice she could make that wasn't scrutinized by the other members of the growing Shepards group. They were cut off from the rest of the world, only allowed to rely on the Neimonses for food and supplies. It was why she had learned to sew, so she could at least mend the tattered old clothes that they had given her to live in for years on end.

And she had been used to it. It had been normal for her, because she had never known anything else. Even when the crime and violence started getting out of control, she reminded herself of how much the group had done for her and her family, how they had supported them when they had been struggling.

Of course, she had to put to the back of her mind the fact that the gang had been the one to cause most of that struggle in the first place. Like when her father had been kept away from work for months because they were suspicious of his intentions. But it was easy to forget that part when everything she'd had—clothes, food, shelter—all came from them.

Eventually, it had become too much for her father, and he had decided he wanted to get his family out of there. It was when River was a teenager, and the thought of something new was tantalizing to her. She had to find out what there was in the rest of the world, what existed beyond the bounds of the life the Neimons family had created for her.

And so, her father started to put together a plan. It wasn't much at first, but it was something. They put away supplies, enough to cover them while they were on the road for a few weeks to find somewhere new. He seemed sure the gang would come looking for them, but he assured his family it wouldn't go much deeper than that. He swore they didn't care enough about the family for them to really try too hard to get them back. As long as River and her family kept their mouths shut about the gang and their criminal activity, they would be able to escape unharmed.

And maybe River had believed that at some point. Maybe she had trusted her father and actually allowed herself to believe that they would be able to get out, make a clean break and never look back. How naive she had been. But now, all this time later, she could see it had been nothing more than a pipe dream, a fantasy they had all been clinging to because the alternative was more than they could bear.

The alternative being that they were trapped, and there was no way out, no matter what they did.

That was how it went. On the night they were due to leave, they had everything packed up and ready to go. Haven and their mother were in the car, and River and her father were packing up the last of their stuff before they hit the road.

Before returning to the house to grab the last of their belongings, her father had given specific instructions to her mother for her to keep watch and if anyone approached, or there were any signs of trouble, then she and Haven should leave immediately. He'd get River and himself out and they'd rendezvous at a location her parents had already agreed upon.

But before they could get anywhere, a shot rang out.

"River, get down!" her father yelled to her, and she ducked back inside their small house for cover. Outside, she heard the roar of the engine and watched as her mother drove off with her sister. As soon as the dust had cleared, she saw her father's body sprawled on the driveway.

She ran to him at once, but it was too late. They had killed him. She cried out, suddenly all alone in the world. Her mother and sister had followed the plan and fled, and she was still trapped here, without even her father to rely on.

"Don't worry, River," Ryker had told her. "We'll take good care of you."

It sounded more like a threat than a promise.

And so, she'd stayed. She had nowhere else to go, nobody else to turn to. She just had to trust in herself, and pray that one day, she found a way out.

The Neimons family took good care of her. She was moved into their home so they could keep a better eye on her there, and she hated every moment of it. Someone was always watching her. Things only grew more and more dangerous as time passed. What had started out as little more than a ragtag group behind their leader soon began to build into something with real focus, something really violent and obsessive.

Even more so when Hector died and left Ryker in charge. Ryker was so much worse than his father. More of a control freak than Hector had ever been, and when it came to recruiting new members, he didn't wait for them to come to him. If he saw someone he liked the look of, he would snatch them up and brainwash them until they didn't have any choice but to go along with the sick, twisted nightmare he dragged them into.

River had no idea what had happened to her mother and sister, but prayed they had made it out. Ryker held their escape against her, and eventually made good on his threat to force her to repent for it.

"You're going to be my wife," he told her. She could still remember that moment, the horror of it. Up until then, she had been almost committed to the Shepards, willing to do whatever it took to make sure they didn't go looking for her mother or sister. But that moment, after he uttered those words to River, it was too much. More than she knew she could ever handle.

She had to get out. She couldn't be his wife. Not in a million years. Even the thought of it was enough to make her feel sick. She swore to herself she would find a way out before she got married to that monster, and she started to plan her escape.

She paid attention to the rotation of people watching her, pocketed and stole stuff to hide for her travels when backs were turned, noted the distances from the different places she was working or sleeping to the nearest exits—hoping to escape into the woods and disappear.

One day, she found her opening. A couple of Ryker's men had started arguing and then a fight broke out and it captured everyone's attention, so she was momentarily forgotten.

She'd made her break for the woods and had been on the run since.

"That was the abusive ex you told me about?" Cade asked, as she filled him in on the story.

She nodded. "He was…rough with me," she replied, lowering her gaze to the ground. "But he was that way with everyone. He was worse than his father. More dangerous. More obsessive. And he's the one looking for me out there right now, I'm sure of it. He's the one hunting me."

"And you were going to your family?"

"Yes," she explained. "I know my mother has a lot of family in a small town in New York called Chittenango. That's where I'm headed. I need to find her and my sister again. I need to know they're okay…but you ruined it."

His eyes widened and he jerked back, dropping her hand. "What are you talking about?"

"You ruined it," she repeated, the lump in her throat making it hard to speak. "Because I… I couldn't risk caring about anyone, Cade. I couldn't risk getting sidetracked along the way. But now I'm here, and I… I really care about you! And I don't want to leave, even though I know I have to. Even though the Shepards are going to come looking for me, even though—"

Before she could say another word, he reached out and pulled her to him, planting his lips firmly against hers. She let out a surprised squeak, but then, closing her eyes, leaned into the kiss.

When he pulled back, he caught her face in his hands and looked deep into her eyes. The way he stared at her, it was like he was trying to see all the way into her soul. Her breath caught in her throat at the intensity of his gaze.

"You're safe here, River," he told her. "I'm going to make sure of that, you hear me?"

"Cade, you can't—"

"I can," he replied with conviction. "You don't know what I'm capable of. But I know I can protect you. Whatever it takes. And then, we'll get you back to your family, okay?"

She gazed at him for a long moment and, to her surprise, she found herself starting to relax. Even though she knew she should be terrified right now of what could happen, when he spoke those words to her, she believed him.

"Okay," she breathed back, and he kissed her again. And this time, she knew it was more than just a kiss. Now that she had laid herself bare to him, she wanted nothing more than to take their relationship to the next level.

To give herself to him utterly and completely.

Chapter Twenty-One

"Are you okay?" he murmured to her, tucking her hair back behind her ear as they lay next to each other in bed.

She nodded, leaning over to put her head on his chest. "Yeah," she whispered back. "I really am."

He smiled and wound his arms around her, pulling her in close. Being this intimate with her was a dream he'd never thought would come true. But the moment he had seen that desperate, helpless look in her eyes, he knew he had to take the chance to show her how much he meant it when he said he was going to protect her. She needed to know he was all in this with her.

Sleeping with her for the first time had been incredible, their bodies matching with each other as though it was the most natural thing in the world. And now, as they lay together in his bed, it was like the enormous weight of everything that had been holding them back was starting to drift away.

She had finally told him the truth, and though he could hardly wrap his head around the vastness of it, he was grateful that she had. It meant she finally trusted him completely. He could only imagine how hard it must've been for her to come clean to him like that. But it made everything about her just fall into place. All the questions that hadn't added up suddenly slotting together in a way he could make sense of. He was so glad he finally knew where she was coming from, even if it had been hard for her to tell him.

She had escaped from a cult. A damn cult. He couldn't imagine how painful it had been to lose her father like that, to be left behind by the rest of her family, and then having to rely on the people who had killed him to survive. And then to be told she was going to be married off to some psycho? From what he had heard about the Shepards, Ryker was a real piece of work, and the thought of him getting anywhere close to River was enough to make him feel sick.

He'd told River he would protect her and he meant it. He was going to do whatever it took to keep that promise. No one was going to lay a hand on her, not on his watch.

He smoothed his hand over her hair, letting his fingers drift down her back and follow the curve of her body. He was sure Lawson was waiting for him to return so he could fill him in on everything he had found out, but right now, he didn't want to break this moment. He didn't want to share her with anyone else. He wanted their time to last a little longer.

"So, now that you're going to be staying a while longer," he remarked. "Do you think you'll keep working on mending clothes, or see about doing something else?"

She smiled, snuggling into his chest. "I don't know," she replied. "I like sewing, it's what I know and I don't mind doing it. But also, I think I'd like to try something else. I was talking to Sarah, that therapist?"

"Yeah, I know her."

"Well, she said I could maybe help out with some of her patients. Peer mentorship-type work," she replied, shaking her head. "It sounds crazy to me, but I...maybe I could help. It did feel nice to help that man the other day."

"Man?" he questioned. "What happened?"

She let out a small sigh that tickled the hair on his chest. "When I put my bag down to refill my water in the lodge, a new group of people were coming in and it made a loud bang noise when it hit the ground. It startled one of the men and he started having an episode. No one else was around, so I tried to talk him down. Bring him out of it. I felt so bad for causing him distress, but it felt really good to help a little." She shrugged and smiled into Cade's chest. "Anyway, Sarah was there and saw us and approached me about helping."

"That sounds amazing," he replied, stroking her hair. "I think you'd be really good at that."

"I don't know..."

"I do," he told her, and she smiled up at him.

It was clear it had been a long time since someone had actually talked to her like she was worth something. To give her praise or even a compliment. It killed him to think of how much she had been through already, knowing she never deserved anything that had happened to her. Cade wished he could take those burdens off her shoulders.

"Thanks," she murmured. "Maybe I'll take her up on it once things have calmed down. I'll think about it. That also will depend on if Lawson and Xavier will even let me stay here after this."

"You should," he urged her. "You would be a great help to her, I'd bet. And don't worry about the guys.

Once they understand what's happened, they won't turn you away."

"I hope you're right. What about you?" she asked, turning the conversation to him once more.

"I'm going to help out with the squad, I think," he replied.

"The squad?"

"The one that Lawson runs," he explained. "It's a way for the guys who come here to get back on their feet and out into the field. They're helping out with the Feds' investigation into the Shepards right now."

"You think that's safe?" she asked, sounding fearful.

He squeezed her a little closer. "I know it is," he replied. "I can handle myself. And if it means taking down the group that has been causing you so much pain, it's not even something I have to think twice about."

She nodded but didn't reply. He knew she was worried and afraid, but it was something that he needed to do. He'd been trying to find his place, his new start since his injury, and this was the right fit for him. A way to keep his mind, body, and skills acquired through the years sharp. He also wanted her to know he meant what he said about her being safe and protected. And if he could use his skills and knowledge to help bring down the Shepards, that would be a bonus for them both.

Lying here with her in bed, he felt content for the first time in a long time. Even when he had been at peace before, he had always felt a hole inside him that never seemed to go away. He had been sure it was just because of his job—because of the life he'd left behind.

But when he was with her, all of that seemed to just fall away. Maybe it wasn't his work that he had needed, but a purpose. Something to drive him forward, even when things seemed impossible. And she was that purpose. Protecting her, making sure she had the life she needed and would never to have to fear for her safety or that of her family ever again.

Everything he had been looking and waiting for, it was lying in his arms at that moment. He couldn't imagine anything better, anything that would make him happier. His whole life had changed when he had suffered that injury, and he had thought it would be an uphill battle trying to get back to the point where he felt like a person again. But now, when he was with her, he had a purpose. He had a reason.

And it was River.

"I guess we should go talk to Lawson, huh?" River sighed.

Cade let out a groan. "No, let's just stay here," he replied. "I need to rest. And so do you. I'll talk to him in the morning."

She grinned and closed her eyes, hooking her leg over his. It was as though she couldn't get close enough to him.

He knew how she felt.

Even with their bodies pressed tightly against each other, he still wished they could be closer.

"I have to go to town with Hannah tomorrow," she murmured, smoothing a hand over his chest. "We have some supplies to pick up."

"I'm not sure that's a good idea. You think that'll be safe?" he asked. He could already feel himself starting to doze off, but he wanted to make sure she wasn't about to walk into the middle of a mess by heading off by herself.

"I hope so," she replied, and he ran his fingers through her hair, pushing it back from her face. "We didn't have any problems and there's been no sighting in the town, right?"

"As far as I know, no, there hasn't. You'll be extra careful?" he asked her, and she nodded.

"I promise I will," she swore to him. "And Hannah too. We only have a few places to go, so it should quick. I don't think they'd try anything with a town full of people. There'll be plenty of people around while we're there."

"Stay close to populated areas, and don't go off on your own for any reason. It's not going to be long until we have Ryker and his gang behind bars," he promised her. "Soon you won't have to worry at all."

"I hope so."

"You don't have to hope," he replied. "I'll make it happen, River. Just watch me."

She smiled as her eyes drifted shut.

He stayed awake until he was sure she had dozed off to sleep, and then let himself drift off as well. When he fell asleep with her in his arms, he was even more sure than ever of what he had to do next.

Whatever it took to keep her safe. And whatever she needed to have the future she deserved.

Chapter Twenty-Two

River glanced around as she and Hannah stepped out of the truck, suddenly feeling like eyes were on her. She knew she was being paranoid after everything that had happened and how close the Shepards seemed to be. She couldn't help it, though. She was second-guessing everything about being here without Cade, or even one of the other men from the lodge. She'd had a large knot in her stomach since she'd gotten up this morning.

Hannah knew what was happening, but didn't seem to let it be diminishing her normal bright and cheerful disposition. Or maybe she was just trying to help River feel more comfortable. Either way, River just wanted to try to enjoy spending time with her friend.

"Thanks for coming into town with me today," she remarked, hooking one of the reusable totes that River had made for them over her shoulder. "It's so much more fun with some company, isn't it?"

"Yeah, exactly," River agreed, but in truth, she was more than a little nervous about being out in the open like this, regardless of what she'd told Cade yesterday. She had promised Hannah she would come to town with her to help her pick up her stuff since Hannah didn't want to ask one of the guys. Apparently, her brother and Xavier were still only barely talking and she didn't like the thought of her friend being stuck between them, so River had volunteered. But there was a part of her that was fearful the Shepards might swoop in as soon as they got the chance.

But she couldn't let the fear of them get in the way of her living her life, she knew that much. Besides, Cade had sworn to her the night before that he wasn't going to let anything happen to her.

And she believed him, she really did. The way that he spoke, it was as though he had never been surer of anything in his entire life. She trusted that—trusted him. He had a long history in the military, and he had taken a serious injury as part of his service. If anyone could take whatever the Shepards and Ryker threw at him, it would be Cade.

"You want to get some breakfast first?" Hannah suggested, gesturing to the small diner sitting just off the square.

River grinned and nodded. "Sure. That sounds great," she agreed.

They headed to grab a spot at one of the booths on the far side of the diner. Hannah insisted that River try the waffles, and the two of them tucked into a steaming plate of syrupy breakfast as the rain began to fall outside.

"Wow, that's good," River murmured.

Hannah grinned. "I told you so," she replied proudly. "So, what's on your mind? You've been a little quiet today. More quiet than normal, I mean."

"I, uh..." she began. She didn't want to tell Hannah the truth about her past. The fewer people that knew, the better it would be for her. Plus, she didn't want to get into all the details in a place so public or take more time than necessary to get the supplies. She just wanted to help Hannah get what was needed and return to the lodge... to Cade. But she had to give her something.

"I'm thinking about what I'm going to do at the lodge when I've finished with all the clothes and supplies," she replied.

"Oh, yeah? You got something in mind?"

"Sarah said I could maybe help her out in some way with the therapy," she replied. "I don't know if I would actually be any good, but..."

"I bet you would be," Hannah replied encouragingly. "You're always a really good listener, River. You would do a great job with that. Have you ever thought about becoming a therapist?"

"I—I guess I could train." River shrugged, raising her eyebrows as the thought of it crossed her mind.

She had never really thought much about what life might look like for her down the road, after the Shepards. But after her conversation with Cade, realizing she wanted to stay there at the lodge, she might need to start. She could actually think about what she wanted to do with her future. And maybe she could help others with the knowledge she had gained from her own suffering.

She and Hannah continued with their meals and chatted about the possibility of her working with Sarah. For the first time in too long, River felt really hopeful. Like there was a future beyond what she had imagined for herself. She wasn't going to be trapped in a marriage with Ryker. She was free—and that freedom was almost dizzying as she tried to wrap her head around it.

"Okay, I guess we should actually get going and get the errands done since we're finished here," Hannah said, once they both cleaned their plates. "Come on, I left the lodge business credit card in the truck. Let's grab it and finish up so we can get back."

River wholeheartedly agreed. They had already wasted enough time stopping to eat, though it was really good and the food had actually helped settle some of her nerves a bit.

She followed Hannah out of the diner, and she had a smile on her face as they walked back to the truck. Her mind kept wandering to her future—to a future she had hardly dared imagine for herself before, but that now seemed within her grasp. And that future was more tempting than anything in the world. A future she got to choose for herself—maybe a future with Cade too.

But before her mind could stray any further down that path, a car screeched to a halt beside them. River spun around, her eyes wide as panic gripped her. A moment later, a man leaped out of the car and slammed a rag over her mouth.

"River!" Hannah screamed, and it was the last thing River heard before the blackness swallowed her up completely.

WHEN RIVER CAME TO, her head was throbbing with pain. In fact, her whole body ached. Her head had sunk down to her chest, and she lifted it and looked around. She couldn't see anything, couldn't even remember how she had gotten here. She went to lift her hand to brush her hair back from her face, but she couldn't move. Something bit into her arms, pinning them in place.

She let out a whimper as the memory of what had happened before she blacked out rose up in her mind. They had gotten her. She didn't know how they had found her, but as soon as she had felt that rough fabric over her mouth and the thick, chemical scent of a sedative filled her nostrils, she had known it. And now she was here—God only knew where this place was—and she didn't know if she was ever going to be able to get out.

"She's awake."

A light flicked on, hurting River's eyes. She looked around the space again as her eyes adjusted to see if she could figure out where she was. She was restrained in an old, rickety wooden chair with zip ties, the plastic digging painfully into her skin. Her mouth was dry and her stomach twisted and turned inside of her. How long had she been here? She wasn't even sure she wanted to know the answer to that question.

"Good to see you again, River."

Everything in her froze when she heard that voice. The voice of her nightmares. Her ears suddenly started ringing so loud she thought she'd go deaf. Her heart pounded painfully in her chest and her muscles seized as if they would snap apart. She turned her head toward the voice, and there he was. The very last person she ever wanted to see again.

Ryker.

His hair had grown out slightly, hanging in a shaggy mess to his shoulders, and his clothes were dirty and ragged. His wolf-like eyes cut through her, and that predatory grin spread over his face. The combination was startling and chilled her to the bone.

"You miss me?" he asked her, reaching out to cup her

chin tightly in his hand. She tried to pull her face away, but his grip was too strong. Being this close to him again after the past few months on the run was enough to turn her stomach.

No. She couldn't do this. Not again. She couldn't have gotten so far from him just to end up back in his grasp. She should never have left the safety of the lodge. She was so stupid to believe she'd actually escaped him when she knew, she *knew*, there was no way. Ryker would never let her go.

She lowered her eyes to the ground. She wasn't going to give him her attention, no matter how much he seemed to think he was entitled to it. No matter how much he wanted it.

"You've been out for six hours, sweetheart," he continued, letting go of her face, though she could still feel the grip of his finger on her jaw.

Six hours? Her heart sank. Cade. What was going through his mind? Would he be looking for her? How would he even find her? She prayed he wouldn't give up on her.

And Hannah! What had happened to Hannah? She had been with her when River was abducted. What if something had happened to her? What if she had been hurt, or worse?

She wanted to ask the questions but she couldn't get her mouth to form the words. Was afraid of the answers she'd get if she did. She couldn't bear it if something happened to one of her friends because of her.

"Don't worry, River," Ryker continued. "We're going to get you back home. Back where you belong, right?"

River tensed but didn't say a word to him. She knew he

would twist up anything she said and use it against her. He would find some way to make it seem like she had agreed to go back with him, even though they both knew she'd never willingly go back. Especially not with him.

Before he could continue, another man stepped into the small room with them. It looked like an old hunting cabin or something, paint peeling off the walls and old cans of food stacked in the cabinets with doors that seemed to be half hanging off their hinges.

"We need to move, boss," the man told him.

River recognized him—one of her father's friends. She wanted to scream at him, ask him if this was what her father would have wanted him to do. What would he have thought if he had been able to see this man, a friend of his, involved in the kidnapping of his daughter? He couldn't even make eye contact with River, and it didn't surprise her. He knew what he was doing was twisted and wrong. Ryker let out a snarl of irritation. "You should never have let that other girl get away," he snapped at the other man.

The other girl? Hannah? She had managed to get away? River felt a flood of relief hit her. *Thank God.*

"And now she's going to bring the pigs to our door," he continued. "Get everyone together, tell them we're ready to move out."

Move out? Move out where? River glanced between the men, trying to pick up on anything she could, but it was no good. They weren't interested in dealing with her right now; they were intent on doing whatever they could to make sure they didn't get caught.

Ryker flipped out a knife and cut the bindings tying her to the chair before yanking her up with a hard jerk that rattled her teeth. Before she could protest, he had her arms gripped in front of her and fastened more ties around her wrists. She felt a cold chill whipping in from outside, and she wished she had Cade's winter coat with her—something to keep her warm, and something to remind her of him.

"Come on. Move," Ryker ordered, and he dragged her toward the door of the cabin. His grip was tight and unyielding. She tried to pull herself away, but he hung on even tighter. He wasn't letting her go anywhere now that he had her where he wanted her.

Outside, it had started to snow just the slightest bit. There was maybe half an inch lying on the well-trodden ground and it was still coming down. That was going to make it harder for them to find her, or even a trail.

But as she stumbled behind Ryker, who was dragging her roughly through the dense woods, she had to trust that Cade meant it when he said he could protect her. No matter how easy it would have been to let her fear and doubt get the better of her, she was going to trust in him until she was given a reason not to.

Because right now, he was her only chance of getting out of here in one piece.

Chapter Twenty-Three

"What the hell do we do now?"

"Cade, I know this is tough for you, but—"

"Tough?" Cade exploded at Carter. He knew it wasn't going to do him any good to be mean to the people around him, but he felt like he was going crazy. He'd felt like this ever since Hannah had rushed back from their trip to town to tell them that some men had snatched up River off the street and she had no idea where they had taken her.

He'd never forget the look of panic and fear on Hannah's face when she'd burst into their meeting in Lawson's office to tell them what happened.

After kissing River goodbye at their cabin, Cade had called Lawson to see if he and Xavier were available to talk about River's past with the Shepards. Lawson was still miffed that Cade had never gotten back to him the night before but agreed that he and Xavier would meet him in Lawson's office to discuss the specifics and make a plan for what came next. Cade had barely finished telling them what River told him before Hannah had exploded into the office.

"She could be anywhere!" Cade continued as Xavier

got to his feet to try and calm him. "It's been hours. Where the hell is she?"

"We're doing everything we can to find out," Lawson reminded him as Cade began to pace once more. "We've got guys out doing another patrol of the woods."

"She's not in the woods," he muttered, shaking his head. "They couldn't have gotten their cars up there, it's too dense."

"Well, they didn't take the roads, either," Carter reminded him. "There are police stationed on every road in and out of this place. They've been there since she was taken. They couldn't have gotten past them. So she can't have gone far. The woods are the best bet."

Cade rubbed a hand over his face, trying to settle his scattered thoughts. He knew he couldn't let himself spin out of control like this, but it felt like it had been an eternity since River had been taken, not just hours. He was terrified at the thought of what the Shepards could be doing to her.

If she was even still alive.

The moment Hannah had finished detailing what had happened in town, they had all launched into action. Calls were made to send out guys to patrol the area, including searching close to town, and alert the local police. Cade hadn't left out any detail of what River had shared with him about her past in hopes that the smallest thing might give them a leg up in tracking her down. But so far, nothing. No sign of her, or any of the Shepards, either. What had they done to her? Where had they taken her?

"So, what's our next move?" he demanded.

Cade couldn't just sit around and do nothing. He had

to get out there and help. He had to hope they were right when they said she couldn't have been taken too far from the lodge. But even the distance between them right now was more than he could take. He had promised to protect her, and now she was out there, trapped in the middle of a nightmare he couldn't pull her out of.

"We have some thermal imaging cameras," Xavier suggested. "We could set up a camp at the edge of the forest and send out a couple of drones to see if we can find any people out there. Should be easier than normal because of the snow."

The snow. Cade had been trying not to think about that part. He hated the thought of her out there in the snow, freezing and lost and wondering if anyone was coming to find her. He prayed she knew that he was coming for her, no matter what. He wouldn't stop searching until he found out where she was.

"What are we waiting for?" he demanded again. "I'm getting the guys together to set it up now."

"I'll come with you," Xavier replied, getting to his feet. They were in the main office, and Cade couldn't sit around any longer. He had to do something. Xavier had seemed just as invested as him, and Cade wondered if it had something to do with how close Hannah had come to getting snatched up too.

"Okay, good," Cade replied. "Let's go."

They grabbed a few more guys and everything they needed and packed into the truck. Cade insisted on driving, even though the cold had his shoulder aching more than usual. He needed to take control of something, needed to drive this thing forward in any way he could.

He was already cursing himself for letting her go without him by her side. They never would have gotten to her if he had been the one with her in town. But it was too late to worry about that now. What mattered was getting her back.

At the east edge of the forest, the guys unpacked the supplies and began to set up the drones. Cade paced back and forth, feet crunching in the snow, wondering if they could go any faster.

"How long is this going to take?" he muttered to Xavier.

"Not long," Xavier assured him. "You just have to wait a little longer. We'll find her."

"We have to," Cade replied. And then, he heard something—the crack of a footstep on the snow in the woods.

His head snapped up. "What was that?" he demanded.

"I didn't hear anything," Xavier replied, but Cade grabbed one of the flashlights and shined it into the woods. It bounced off the shadows, and then he saw it—a man darting back into the trees.

"There! There's someone there!" he yelled, and he took off after him. The man was winding in and out of the trees, trying to vanish back into the darkness, but Cade wasn't going to let him get away. His eyes were pinned on his target as he cut in and out of the branches around him, feet crunching on the compacted snow beneath him, until he was within grabbing distance.

He threw himself at the man, wrapping his arms around his waist and tackling him to the ground with a sharp thud. The man tried to scramble away, but Cade held on tight. Soon enough, Xavier and a couple of the other guys appeared through the trees to help.

"Get him back to base," Cade spat, pulling the man

upright and shoving him toward the other men. They dragged him back through the woods toward the truck, where a couple of the lodge's men were setting up the thermal drones.

"Who the hell are you?" Cade demanded, shoving the man back against the side of the truck, fisting his collar in his hands. The man wore the same ragged clothing River had worn when he first met her, and he knew at once he had to be part of the Shepards.

"Let me go," the man muttered as he struggled in Cade's grasp.

Cade narrowed his eyes at him. "What are you doing out here?"

"It's a free country, I was just hunting—"

"Not without a permit, you weren't," he shot back. "Tell me what you're doing here. Are you with the Shepards?"

The man's eyes widened in surprise, but he did his best to cover it up.

"Who's that?" he asked. "I've never heard of them—"

"Don't you lie to me," Cade snarled. "You're with the Shepards, aren't you?"

"I told you, I don't—"

"You can tell us, or you can tell it to the cops," he added. "How does that sound? I think they're going to have some big questions for you."

Cade slammed his fist into the panel next to the man's head, and the guy jerked in surprise. Cade needed him to know how far he would take this. He would do whatever it took to get River back, and he knew this man had the information he needed.

"We're sending out a drone over that forest, so we're

going to find your psycho little cult one way or another," he told him. "Better for you to tell us where we should look. Or do you want to talk to the cops about this?" He took a step back, waiting. "Talk!"

The man's expression shifted. Cade could tell by the look on his face he was trying to think of what best to say. Cade glared at him with clenched fists, waiting for him to break—and then, at last, he did.

"They were staying in a hunting lodge on the north side of the forest," he grumbled, eyes lowering to the ground as though he couldn't believe he was really admitting it.

"Over to the north of the forest!" Cade yelled to the guys programming the drone. "Get it out there, now!"

He zip-tied the man's hands and shoved him into the truck, locking the doors to make sure he couldn't go anywhere. He was sure he could get some more information out of him when the time was right. Even if he couldn't, the Feds would have plenty to say to him about his involvement with the Shepards. But right now, he had one goal in mind, and he needed to find out where River was before the Shepards could get out of there.

They launched the drones, and Cade paced back and forth, shooting glances at the screen where the thermal imaging cameras were broadcasting.

"There! There's something," Xavier exclaimed, jabbing his finger at the picture. Sure enough, a cluster of heat spots stood out on the screen.

"It looks like a lot of people," the man running the drone remarked. "Could be the whole group making a break for it."

"What's that?" Cade demanded, gesturing to a couple of smaller spots breaking off from the main group.

"Looks like there's a smaller group splitting from them," he replied, frowning. "Two people, from the looks of it."

Two people. Cade's head spun as he tried to come up with a plan. Two people—Ryker and River, he was sure of it. Even if the rest of the gang were on the run, he was out there doing his best to capture her and keep her to himself.

"I'm going after them," Cade announced.

Xavier grabbed his arm. "Cade, no," he warned. "We need to put some backup together. You can't just go off after them like that—"

"Watch me," Cade snapped back, yanking his arm loose. There was no way he was going to let Ryker get any farther with her than he already had. He was going to catch him and bring her back. He was going to take him down, once and for all. And River was going to be safe.

He couldn't wait any longer. He sprinted off into the woods, Xavier's shouts fading behind him, and rushed toward the woman he loved.

Chapter Twenty-Four

She stumbled behind Ryker, doing whatever she could to stay upright as he dragged her through the freezing woods. She heard a commotion through the trees, but she wasn't sure what was going on. The whole forest seemed to be alive with people rushing around, calling to each other, but she couldn't figure out why. Had someone found them? She could only hope they had.

"Hurry up, bitch!" Ryker spat at her, and she did her best to match his pace, but her body was aching from the cold and the bindings. She couldn't keep up.

"Slow down," she protested.

He spun around and lashed out so fast she had no time to react. She started falling back and he reached out and yanked her to his chest, his eyes flashing with anger. "You don't get to tell me what to do," he snapped. "Not after all the crap you've put me through."

River wanted to protest, but she was sure there was no point. He was in a rage and there would be no reasoning with him. He'd already decided it was all her fault, when he was the one responsible for this nightmare. If Ryker had just let her go and not followed her, none of this would be happening. But no, he had decided that he was owed something from her, and he wasn't going to stop until he got it.

He wasn't going to stop until she was tied to him for life.

"I didn't want any of this, Ryker!" she protested, hoping she could get through to him somehow. He reached out again, grabbing her arm, pulling her forward. She mustered up all the strength and confidence she could as she tracked in his footsteps. If she got lost in this forest she likely wouldn't survive.

"You made your vows to the Shepards like everyone else," he reminded her.

"You think I wanted to make those vows?" she demanded. "I was a child. I was forced to! You would have hurt my family. And it didn't protect my father, did it? He's dead!"

"He's dead because he tried to walk away from everything my father gave to him," he snarled back at her, his voice dripping with venom. "He owed us. If he hadn't been a coward—"

"Don't you call him that," she snapped, her voice colder than she had ever heard it. Her ability to speak to him like that surprised her, but she had put up with enough. Her father was a strong man, stronger than so many of the people who had been nothing but cowards. People who were willing to go along with what the Shepards demanded from them. They could see the evil that was being done, the harm they were causing, but they allowed themselves and their families to remain a part of it because they were terrified of the retribution.

Well, not her father. He had tried to get them out. And, in the case of Haven and her mother, he had succeeded.

River just needed to find a way to leave this all behind, and she would have fulfilled his last wish.

He spun around to face her and drew his hand back, landing a sharp slap on her face. She gasped at the pain, her head reeling.

"I'll call him whatever I want," he sneered at her. "Come on. We've got to get to the meeting point. Then we can get out of here."

Get out of here? River slowed, trying to pull him back, but he grabbed the ties still binding her hands and yanked her forward.

"Don't think you're getting out of it that easy. I'll get what I'm owed yet," he told her, and dragged her onward.

"How did you find me?" she suddenly asked, tripping over her own feet trying to keep up with him. Maybe if she could slow Ryker down some, she could try to make an escape.

He stopped suddenly and River almost ran into his back. He turned with a scowl on his face and she was almost sorry she'd asked the question, but she really wanted to know.

"I've been looking for you since you pulled your stunt and took off. I've had the guys branching out in all directions since we left home searching in every hidey-hole along the way. Just so happened a couple of the guys decided to stop by that lodge where you've been staying and thought they recognized you. Since we hit a warehouse not too far from here, I decided to stop in for a look. We've been keeping an eye on you since, looking for an opportunity to get you back without one of those men around you."

River's eyes widened at his reply. They'd been watching her, so she'd never been safe like she'd thought. She couldn't stop the horrible what ifs running through her mind. Thank goodness they'd just waited to take her away from the lodge instead of doing something more violent. If they'd attacked the others to get to her, she would have never forgiven herself.

He quickly turned and jerked her forward again. She did her best to follow him, but she was so cold, the freezing air clinging to her skin and making her shiver hard. Ryker looked at her, shaking his head as though he couldn't believe what he was seeing.

"You're getting soft, River," he scoffed. "But don't worry, we'll get you hardened back up once we get back to base. I can't have a weakling as my wife. How will you raise our children if you can't even stand a little cold?"

River's teeth chattered too hard to reply, but her mind registered the horror of what he'd just said. Their children? She couldn't imagine having kids with this monster. She couldn't even imagine him touching her without feeling ill.

He continued to pull her along behind him and she felt like a yo-yo. She was beyond frozen and her body was becoming so stiff she didn't know how much longer she could go on. Not that Ryker cared about her well-being. He just kept yanking her behind him until all at once, her foot caught on a rock. Unable to brace herself, she toppled forward and crashed down on the ground, bringing him with her.

"Damn it!" he exclaimed. For a split second, he let go of her. River's mind raced—she had to take this chance. She might not get one again. If he got her to the meeting spot and managed to haul her out of here, she would never see anyone from the lodge again.

She forced herself up as quickly as she could manage and willed her body to move, darting off into the woods, her breath tearing from her lungs in huge gasps. She heard Ryker screaming after her, but she didn't dare turn around to see where he was. She had to put as much distance between herself and that man as she—

Suddenly, the earth dropped away in front of her, and she came to a sharp halt. She was next to a drop-off that led down a steep slope to the frozen river below. She was trapped! She had nowhere to go. She could hear Ryker slashing through the trees, his heavy footsteps getting closer. She looked around frantically and spotted a large, jagged rock sticking out from the snow. With her frozen fingers, she tugged it out of its spot, clutching it in her closed hands. It was the closest thing she had to a weapon right now.

"There you are."

Her heart stopped when she heard Ryker's taunting voice. Spinning around, she found him standing a few feet away from her, with a maniacal grin on his face.

"I'll jump!" she threatened him.

He shook his head. "I don't think you have the nerve," he replied calmly, and he reached under his shirt and pulled out a gun. River stared at the black barrel aimed at her and wondered if this was similar to the last moments of her father's life before he was murdered.

"Go on, then, jump," he told her, motioning to the cliff's edge with the gun. Her foot skidded back slightly, and she looked down toward the water. It was frozen solid. The drop alone would break her legs, or worse.

"That's what I thought," he remarked, taking another step toward her, his feet crunching on the snow as he drew closer to her…and closer still. Her heart sank and she realized this was it. She couldn't escape, there was nowhere to run. The only way she could survive was to willingly go with him. But if she did that, she feared she would never see the lodge—or her friends—ever again. And Cade...

She gripped the rock tighter, wondering if she had it in her to fight him off. He was almost on top of her now, and she stepped back on instinct, her heel skidding over the sharp drop to the openness below. She felt the world shrinking around her as Ryker took the final steps to stop in front of her, and she knew this was it. No more running, no more trying to escape. This next moment would determine if she'd live or die.

Would Ryker grab her and force her to their next destination or would he finally decide she's been enough trouble and kill her where she stood?

Either way, it was over.

Then she saw it. A slight movement in the woods behind him. Her lips parted, her eyes widened, and her heart leaped when she realized who it was.

"Cade," she breathed.

"What?" Ryker demanded, and he spun around to see where she was looking.

Everything seemed to move in slow motion for a moment while she debated what to do. The rock was still in her hand, and she was close enough now to take a swing. If she was going to do this, she had to do it now.

She lifted the rock above her head with both tied hands, and used the momentum to bring it down with a sickening crack into the side of Ryker's head.

He fell like a stone to the ground, not even making a sound as he dropped. River's eyes widened and she gasped. The rock slipped out of her fingers. Had she killed him? His eyes were blank and vacant, the same way her father's had been when she had seen him laid out on the ground of their driveway.

Cade rushed toward her and pulled her into his arms.

"Hey, hey, I've got you," he murmured, and quickly removed the bindings from her wrists before he gently took her face into his hands.

River knew she should say something, acknowledge Cade in some way. But she couldn't take her eyes off Ryker's body on the ground, unmoving. *Dead*. Before she could stop herself, she let out a wail of shock, the sound bouncing off the trees as she tried to wrap her head around what she had just done.

"Are you okay?" Concern laced his words as he waited for her to answer. She still couldn't look away from the body. Cade leaned forward and kissed her forehead before wrapping her in his jacket and trying to move her away from the scene.

She felt like she was floating outside her body and had to force her feet to move. She was shaking so hard from the cold, she thought she'd crumble into pieces.

"Let's get you out of here," he told her, and leaned down to check on Ryker's body before he led her away from the clearing. She was crying, her body wracked by enormous sobs that she couldn't control. Cade pulled her closer to his side and continued walking them away.

Once he had gotten her out of the clearing, he paused to let her catch her breath.

"Are you hurt?" he asked, looking her over.

She couldn't say anything. She couldn't even breathe right now. Had she killed him? She'd killed him, right?

She saw him lying on the ground, empty eyes looking up. He was dead. He had to be. Was it...over?

Cade checked her for injuries, and she let him. She couldn't react to anything he was saying. Her body was in lockdown, both shock from the cold and the adrenaline leaving her system. His hands were strong and sure as they moved over her, and she wondered how she could have done that. Had she had that in her all along? Was she really capable of it? Killing someone? Why hadn't she done it before? He really was gone, right? Dead. So many thoughts. Too many questions. It was suddenly too loud in her mind, but silence surrounded them.

Finally, she was able to speak again.

"Is he dead?" she croaked, her voice sounding broken. It had started to snow even harder, the cold closing in around them. She knew they couldn't stay out here much longer, but she needed to know for sure.

Cade nodded. "He is, River. He is," he assured her. "There was no pulse. You killed him, River. It's over. It's really over."

She felt her legs turn to mush and heard Cade's startled "umph" as she collapsed into him. How long had she been waiting to hear those words? She couldn't believe it. Ryker was dead, just like his father. There was nobody to lead the Shepards anymore.

She couldn't believe it was really true. Ryker was gone. His followers had no leader. He was lying dead in the woods while they were all trying to run away. No one knew. She wanted to laugh out loud, or scream, or...something. Her emotions were scattered all over the place.

She kept replaying the moment where she swung the rock at his head, the feel of it thud against his skull, even the sickening cracking sound. Seeing him fall lifeless to the ground. His dead eyes. She'd done that.

"Let's get you out of here," Cade told her. "You need to get warm and we need to get you checked out for real."

She shook her head and her eyes suddenly felt heavy. She felt like she was wading through mud. It must be the adrenaline crash. Cade seemed to realize this and stopped to pick her up.

"No, I need to walk on my own. I can do it," she said more confidently than she felt at the moment.

Cade nodded and wrapped his arm around her again to steady her. He seemed to know where he was going, so she allowed him to guide her through the trees. It was a relief to rely on him because all of these trees looked the same to her. She'd get turned around in a heartbeat, especially in the state she was in now. She trusted him to get her to safety.

She might have been dragged into this forest as a victim, as just another one of the dozens of people the Shepards had hurt over the years, but she wasn't walking out of it as one. She had finally done it. She'd stood up to Ryker and finally ended his reign of terror. She was free.

The elated feeling was almost more than she could take, and she nearly felt drunk on it, knowing she had freed herself and her mother and her sister and many others from the clutches of a man as evil as Ryker. But she also felt guilty, knowing she had taken a life, even if he had been a monster.

She clung on to Cade for dear life, and kept her eyes fixed ahead of her. She didn't know what she was going to do now that she didn't have to run anymore. One thing she was sure of, though—whatever came next, she could handle it.

Chapter Twenty-Five

Cade lifted his hand to try and keep the snow off his face. The blizzard was really starting to set in now, and he wasn't sure how much longer they would be able to make it out here in the cold.

River wasn't saying anything, but that didn't surprise him. God knew what they had done to her since the last time he had seen her. He would get to the bottom of it once they were safe again, but right now, all he wanted was to get her back to the lodge and make sure she was okay.

He couldn't believe he had found her. His instincts had been right—the two people breaking away from the larger group were Ryker and River. Cade didn't know where Ryker had been planning to take her, but he was glad he had managed to get to them in time. She seemed to have broken free from Ryker's grasp, at least for long enough to put some distance between them, but Ryker had trained a gun on her by the time he reached them.

"It's okay, it's okay," he told her over and over again, as he guided her through the forest and back to the freedom waiting for her beyond. He still couldn't believe what he had seen, but he should have known she was capable of something like that—of showing that strength. She had fought so hard to get away from the Shepards, and she had proven herself willing to do anything to make sure she never had to go back.

All at once, he spotted Xavier in the woods, weaving in and out of the trees along with a few of the other guys from the lodge.

"Cade!" he yelled out.

Cade lifted a hand to acknowledge him. "How far are we from the truck?" he called back.

"A few minutes," Xavier replied, and he glanced over at River. "What happened? Is she okay?"

"I'll tell you once we get back," he replied. "I need to get her to the lodge and out of the cold. And she needs to get checked out. I want to see if they've done anything to her."

"Right," Xavier agreed, and he looped an arm around her waist and helped Cade carry her the rest of the way back through the forest. Cade knew from the heavier snowfall and the cutting feel of the wind that it must be below freezing by now, but he could hardly feel it. The only thing he felt was her, and the only thing he could think about was getting her back to safety as fast as possible.

The guys around them spread out to fill the woods, probably planning on catching the rest of the Shepards who had scattered earlier. They wouldn't get far, not in this weather. And when they found out that their leader was dead, they would surely give up once and for all.

Finally, Xavier, Cade and River broke the tree line, and Cade found himself opposite the truck once more. The guys had set up a makeshift tent to hold off the weather, and he noticed a few medical personnel inside. Cade rushed River toward it.

"I need someone to check her over," he told them, not speaking to anyone in particular. He didn't care who helped him with this, he just needed to make certain she was all right.

"Okay, bring her in the tent," one of the medics, Lawrence, instructed him. "I'll take a quick look at her so we've got an idea of what we're dealing with."

A couple of guys with Lawrence approached and Cade turned River over to them and watched as she was guided into the tent. Cade stopped and took a deep breath, pulling the cold air into his lungs, and Xavier finally followed up on his earlier question.

"So," he asked, as Lawson emerged from the truck to join them. "You going to tell us what happened out there?"

"I was right—the two people separated on the heat sensor were Ryker and River," he explained, sighing. "When I got to them, she was standing at the edge of the cliff and he had a gun on her. I thought she was going to jump to get away from him."

"Damn," Lawson muttered, glancing over at the tent where River disappeared.

"But he...when he heard me coming, he took his attention off her for a second, and she hit him with this huge rock she had hidden in her hands," Cade continued. "He's dead. Ryker is dead."

The two fell silent for a moment, clearly stunned by what they heard. Cade couldn't blame them. Looking at River now, it was hard to believe she would have been capable of something like that just a little while ago.

"Is she going to get in any kind of trouble for it?" Cade asked, lowering his voice. If he had to cover for her, hide the truth of what she had done, he would.

Lawson shook his head. "I doubt it," he replied. "After everything she's been through with that guy, I can't imagine anyone is going to bother pressing charges. They'll just be glad to get rid of him."

Cade nodded in relief. He had thought as much, but with River having been part of the Shepards in the past, he wasn't certain that they would be so quick to let her walk away from this without some kind of pushback. He hoped she'd be free and clear of it all.

"Where are the rest of the Shepards?" he asked.

"We've got our guys tracking them down in the forest," Xavier explained. "Once they figure out their leader is done for, I think it's going to be a hell of a lot easier. They'll give up. They won't know what to do with themselves when they find out he's not there to call the shots anymore."

Cade closed his eyes and rubbed a hand over his face. He was exhausted, but it was only really just hitting him that she was safe. She was going to be okay, and he couldn't think of anything else that mattered right now. Even if there were still Shepards out there, he had managed to get her out—no, *she* had managed to get herself out. She had fought and found a way to freedom, despite everything she had been through. He just hoped she hadn't been hurt in the process.

"Go check on your woman, Cade. The rest can wait," Lawson directed. "There's nothing you need to do now but get her home and take care of her."

"And rest," Xavier added.

"You sure?" Cade asked. "I can stick around, help with rounding up the rest of the Shepards—"

"No way," Lawson replied as he shook his head. "You've done enough. You need to get her back home and warmed up."

"Thanks, guys," Cade replied, and turned toward the tent.

He noticed there were more vehicles around, including law enforcement, as he approached the tent where Lawrence was checking her over. This area was going to be active for a while, and tonight's activities were going to be the talk of the town and the lodge come morning.

Cade saw one of the men from the lodge pointing a couple of officers in the direction of the tent and he picked up his pace to get there first. Lawrence noticed his approach and walked out to meet him and fill him in on River's condition.

"She looks as though she's mostly fine," Lawrence confirmed. "She's got a bruise forming on her face from where she said he hit her, her wrists are a bit raw from the bindings, and she's got a few bumps and other bruises from being taken and dragged around. Nothing that won't heal. The big thing is the cold. You got her back here before it turned critical, but she'll need to get warm as soon as possible, and a hot meal wouldn't hurt, either."

Cade glanced over his shoulder to see how close the officers were and watched as Lawson went to intercept them.

Cade breathed a sigh of relief. All he wanted to do now was get her back to their cabin, see for himself that she was okay, get her warmed up, and then sleep for a week. Everything else could wait. After the range of emotions he'd experienced in the last several hours, he was beyond exhausted, and he could only imagine how River was feeling since she'd been through so much more.

"Cade, before you go, these officers need a statement from you and River," Lawson said with a frown, clearly not happy that they were being detained. "I asked them to wait until later so you could both rest, but they said it had to be done now. Sorry, man." He shook his head and stepped to the side as two officers took his place.

"Hello. I'm Officer Baker and this is my partner, Officer Dobbs. We need a few questions answered before you go," one of them said in a polite but firm voice.

"Later, man. Go as soon as you can." Lawson clapped Cade on the shoulder, then walked back in the direction of Xavier and the others. Cade motioned for the officers to follow him into the tent.

River looked so small sitting in one of the chairs where Lawrence had left her. Someone had given her a couple of blankets and she was so wrapped up you could hardly see her beneath them. She saw him approach and stood to meet him, a wariness in her gaze as she noticed the officers behind him.

"We're going home?" River asked in a quiet voice, as she leaned up against him. Her shivering seemed to have abated some, and her skin didn't feel as cold, but she clutched on to him like she was hanging on for dear life.

"Yeah, soon," Cade murmured to her, pressing a kiss on the top of her head. "We have to give our statements, then we can go."

"Am I in trouble?" she whispered into Cade's chest, her eyes slightly wide.

"You're going to be fine," he assured her and pulled

her firmly to his side. "I promise. We'll be out of here soon."

One of the officers stepped closer and River startled. "Sorry, ma'am. We need to ask a few questions, like Mr. Thatcher said, then you'll be free to go." Officer Dobbs offered her a friendly smile and pulled out a notepad. "Shall we sit?" He directed them back to the chairs.

Cade listened as River told the officers everything that had happened. He was so proud of her. Her voice held strength and confidence as she recalled every detail with Ryker, even going back to her father's death and her running and ending up at the lodge.

The few questions had turned into an interview that took an hour and a half, and River was fading. Her words were sounding like mere whispers when Cade finally put a stop to it all. "Guys, I need to get her home. If you have more questions, you can reach us at the lodge in a couple of days. She won't be available until then." Giving the officers no time to respond, Cade whisked her up in his arms and carried her out to the truck.

Carter appeared as he was tucking River into the seat and offered to drive them back to the cabin. Given how tired he was, he wasn't going to turn down the offer. Any chance he had to just be with River without having to worry about anything else, he would take.

He climbed in and River cuddled into him. He draped an arm around her, pulling her in closer to share some of his body heat with her.

"I'm so glad you're okay," he murmured to her.

She looked up at him, biting her lip. "Do you really think everything's okay?"

"You did what you had to do, River. No one will fault

you for that. And if it hadn't been you, it would have been someone else. You just saved the authorities the trouble of having to take him in."

"You think so?"

"I know so," Cade promised her, and she rested her head on his chest, seemingly satisfied by his answer. He ran his fingers through her hair, and watched as she drifted off to sleep against him.

Soon enough, he found himself following her. He felt his body relax for the first time since he found out she was taken. He wasn't sure what was going to happen next with the investigation or the Shepards still on the loose, but at least she was back with him and safe.

She was the only thing that mattered to him, and he was amazed by her at every turn—her bravery, her strength, her willingness to fight for herself. Even faced with one of the most formidable criminals in the country, she hadn't let him get the best of her. No, she had stood up for herself and fought back.

And now she was calling the lodge home. It was home for Cade, had been for a while, and he was so glad she was starting to see it the same way he did. He hoped it would be a while before she decided to start on her way again.

Slowly, sleep crept up on him, and he let himself drift off with the woman he loved in his arms.

Chapter Twenty-Six

River woke with a start, sat up in bed and looked around in a panic.

It took her a moment to realize where she was. For a split second, she was sure she was dreaming. But then, she felt Cade's hand slide over her waist and pull her in close to his side, and she let out a sigh of relief. No, this was real, she was really here—she was safely back at the lodge with Cade. She had nothing to worry about anymore.

She sank back against the pillow and glanced at the clock on the bedside table. It was nearly two in the morning. She could hardly remember getting back to the cabin at all. She must have fallen asleep in the truck. There was a distant memory of feeling his arms scoop her up as he carried her out into the cold again, but that was it. She'd been so exhausted she could probably have slept for a full day and still been a little out of it. The only thing she remembered about getting home was Hannah being so relieved to see her—crying and hugging her over and over.

River should be sleeping now, but she couldn't. She found herself looking at Cade, staring at him as he slept.

She couldn't believe she was really back with him. When Ryker had managed to grab her, she had been so certain there was no way she could get away from him. She had already escaped once, and it seemed impossible she'd be able to do it a second time. She was afraid Cade would be lost to her for good.

And then, she remembered. Ryker was dead. She expected to feel guilty when she thought about what happened, but she didn't. Instead, when she pictured his body lying in the snow, she felt…free. Not like before, when she had first escaped, and she had been certain they were on her trail. She knew he would never come after her again. She was free, and so was the rest of her family.

Her chest tightened when she thought of how much her father would have loved to see this day. She wished he could have, but she knew he would have been proud of her if he were still alive. She had taken out Ryker for good, and there was no way he would be able to come after her again. He was gone. Forever.

She hadn't felt this way in so long, like the weight had been lifted from her shoulders and she could finally just…be. All the fear, all the doubt, all the worry that she was going to bring some kind of chaos to the lodge because of who she was and the life she'd lived before, it was over. She got to look forward to the rest of her life, whatever she wanted that to be.

And right now, all she wanted was to be with Cade. She wanted to lie there in his arms and focus on the joy of knowing she could be totally honest with him. She didn't have to pretend to be anyone she wasn't. She could never have imagined that this was where she would end up, when she'd accepted the ride from him all those weeks ago. She was so glad things had turned out the way they did.

He had come for her. When he had told her he would protect her, he'd meant it. He'd come out into that frigid forest to search for her, even though he knew how dangerous it was and had no idea what he was up against. If it hadn't been for him, God only knew what would have happened with her and Ryker. His sudden appearance was the distraction she'd needed to muster the courage to swing that rock that had saved her life. If it hadn't been for him, she probably still would have been in Ryker's clutches right now.

He'd given her the strength to do what she needed to do to survive, and she was more grateful than she would ever be able to put into words. She supposed she would just have to show him.

She reached out to touch his cheek as he slept, and he stirred, his eyes opening as he looked at her.

"You okay?" he asked, pulling her in closer. Even though the snow was still falling outside, the warmth under these covers, pressed up close to him, was everything she needed.

She nodded. "Yeah, I'm fine," she replied. And she meant it. When she was with him, the enormity of everything that had happened fell away, and she knew she didn't have anything to worry about. She could survive anything this crazy world threw at her, because he was there. He would always be there. No matter how bad things got, she knew he wasn't going anywhere, and she loved him for that.

She loved him.

"I'm just…really happy to be here with you," she continued, running her fingers through his hair. He smiled that gorgeous smile that lit up his whole face, and she felt her stomach twist into a knot. He was so handsome. She had been so fearful before, it had been hard to let go and just focus on how happy he made her. It felt good to be able to focus on him—on *them*.

"Me too," he murmured, and he moved to kiss her on the cheek—just the softest kiss, as though he was still being careful with her. But she didn't want him to be careful with her, not now. She wanted him to treat her like she was his, because she was—she belonged to him, utterly and completely. She wanted to show him that.

She turned her head to kiss him properly, and he didn't need to be told twice. He pulled her closer to him, their bodies pressed together, and he wrapped his arms around her tight. She smiled into the embrace, the covers still tucked around them as he held her. It was like they were in a little bubble, cut off from the rest of the world—as though this was the only thing that mattered right now. And it was. She knew there was a lot of stuff for them to work through—emotions, where they were headed moving forward, plans for the future—a whole lot more for them to talk about and deal with. But in that moment, all she could think about was him.

And how much she wanted this moment to last forever.

Chapter Twenty-Seven

"Morning," Lawson greeted as Cade stepped through the door to his office. Cade had no idea how Lawson was even standing upright at that moment. He had been on his feet for days on end now, catching the last of the Shepards who were still on the run out in the woods. Finally, all of the members of that twisted gang had officially been accounted for.

"Morning," Cade replied, handing Lawson a coffee. He figured he would need it. Lawson took a long, grateful sip, and then slumped into the chair on the other side of the desk.

"How's it going?" Cade asked, carefully. There was so much he wanted to ask about, but he didn't even know where to start. He had spent the last several days taking care of River and shutting out the world, at Lawson's suggestion, though he doubted he would have been able to spend much more than an hour or so away from her side. The thought of how close he'd come to losing her made his stomach turn. He wished they could stay in their little bubble in their cabin forever.

"Well, the Shepards are officially done for," Lawson replied. "With Ryker dead, the rest of them don't have any reason to keep going, and they've turned themselves in. Most of the lower-level ones in the ranks are turning on each other to try and keep out of jail. I have no idea what the courts are going to decide for them, but that's not our problem."

"What about River?" Cade asked. She was always the first thing on his mind these days, and he would have done anything to make sure that she was safe and happy.

Lawson nodded. "I don't think she's going to have to deal with them any longer," he replied. "The worst it will probably come to is testifying against some of the higher-ranking members in court. I've also requested she be kept out of it all, if possible, since there will be plenty of other ex-Shepards to call on. However, since she did witness her father's murder and kill their leader, she might not have a choice. But again, with the others, she won't be testifying alone."

"Good." Cade sighed. He didn't want her to have to go up against those people again, not if he could keep her from it. She had only just gotten out of it all and he hoped it would be a long time before she was called to testify, if she was at all.

"But we're going to have to figure out what we're going to do with her now," Lawson remarked.

Cade stiffened and furrowed his brow. "What do you mean?"

"I mean, she's going to be sticking around here for a while, isn't she?" he asked.

"I don't know about that."

"I've seen the way she looks at you, Cade." Lawson chuckled. "I don't think she has any intentions of being anywhere else if she can help it."

Cade grinned. He loved being with her, and the thought of being able to spend time with her without having to worry about her past or what she was hiding from him sounded seriously good.

"Exactly," Lawson replied, seeing the look on Cade's face. "And if she's going to continue to stay here, she's going to need real work. She'll need to provide identification and do paperwork like all the other employees. No more under-the-table stuff."

Cade nodded. "Got it. What did you have in mind?"

"I've been talking to Sarah, and she seems to think that with some training, River could help with counseling some of the residents here." he suggested. "But first, she's going to have a whole lot to work through herself."

"I know." Cade sighed.

Sometimes when he looked at her, he wondered how she could be carrying the monstrous weight of everything she had been through inside her. How someone who seemed so fragile could endure what she had without breaking. But she had. He was confident that with the help of the resources at the lodge, she would be able to heal from the trauma of her past and use it to help others. And she would be great at it.

"Let her know that we're interested in hiring her," Lawson told him.

"I will, but I don't want her to feel pressured. Whether she decides to stay or not is up to her." Cade stated.

"I get it," he agreed. "She needs to make her own calls from here on out. Guess she's had enough of other people doing that for her."

"Exactly," Cade replied.

"And what about you, Cade?" Lawson asked, leaning forward with interest.

"What about me?"

"Are you going to stay here?"

Cade parted his lips in surprise. "What do you mean?"

"I mean, you've got a full-time place on the team if you want it," he continued. "But I'm not going to try to make you stay. If you've got other things you want to be doing, we'll see you off—"

"You want me to stay and work for the team?" Cade asked in surprise.

"You helped us take down one of the most dangerous groups in the country," Lawson pointed out. "We're not letting you go anywhere if we can help it. You're a huge asset to us. I'm sure your brother would be thrilled to have you on board, as well."

Cade grinned. There was no way he was going anywhere. Being at the lodge had given him purpose he hadn't had in so long. Not just being with River, but seeing his brother and working with the guys too. He might not be up to the same action he had seen before, but he didn't want to miss out on the chance to find his place here. It was different than his past life and job, but no less rewarding.

"I would love to stay," he replied. "I know my brother's going to try and keep me out of anything too tough, but surveillance, recon, anything like that, you know I can handle it."

"I know you can," Lawson confirmed. "And we'd be glad to have you."

"Consider me a permanent resident," Cade told him with a laugh. "You're not getting rid of me now."

Lawson chuckled in return, rising to his feet, and extended his hand to Cade.

"Welcome aboard, Cade. For real this time."

Cade took his hand. "Thanks, Lawson. Happy to be here."

AFTER THE MEETING with Lawson, Cade stopped by the cafeteria to pick up some coffee and a pastry for River before heading back to the cabin. Though she had physically recuperated from the ordeal after several days of rest, she was still struggling with her appetite, and he had to keep an eye on her to make sure she ate properly. He didn't mind, though. Taking care of her gave him a sense of purpose like nothing else did, as though this was what he had been made for.

When he got back to the cabin, he found her sitting on the couch, several pages laid out around her, with tears streaming down her face.

His eyes widened and his stomach clenched at the sight of her upset. He quickly headed over to the couch and sat down next to her. "Hey," he murmured gently. "Is everything okay?"

She blinked, as though she had almost forgotten where she was, but then she nodded.

"Yes. It's fine," she replied, wiping the tears away from her eyes. "Better than fine, actually. I got an email from my sister. Xavier called in a favor with someone he knows and got me her email address. I think I've already read it a dozen times."

"I just can't believe how well she's doing," River smiled. "She's married now and has a baby. I have a niece, Cade. I can't wrap my head around that. And my mom's there with them too. So they're all together."

"That's amazing news," Cade told her, grabbing a box of tissues and handing her one. He sat back down beside her, draped an arm along the back of the couch and brushed his fingers through her hair.

"It is," she replied. "I can't wait to go and see them now that I don't have to worry about anyone following me or tracking me down. I can actually visit and just spend some time with them. We've got so much to catch up on—it's been nearly ten years!"

She leaned back against his hand, gathering the pages of the letter together again. There was a look on her face he couldn't quite read, a mixture of sadness and hope. She took a deep breath before she said anything else.

"What is it?" he asked.

"I'm just…it's so strange," she confessed. "I've spent the last few years thinking about my family every single day. Thinking that when I got to them, everything was going to be okay. Everything was going to be different. I wasn't going to have to run and hide anymore or look over my shoulder. I could leave everything else behind. But now…" She trailed off, shaking her head.

He rubbed her back softly and waited for her to continue.

She smiled gratefully at him. "Now that Ryker's gone, and the Shepards are disbanded, I don't have to get to them to be safe anymore," she explained. "I want to see my family, of course, but I don't feel as though New York is my endgame. I can have any kind of life I want for myself, and I don't have to try and get to this certain place to make it happen."

She smiled, a smile so huge it seemed to light up her entire face. Cade couldn't help but return it. Seeing the weight lift from her shoulders like this was a gift he didn't even know he had needed until now.

"Whatever you want, I'm here for you," he told her, and he meant it.

He would do anything to help her achieve her dreams. She deserved it, even if it meant she couldn't stay here. She deserved to chase down everything she had always wanted, without the fear of some monster on her tail ready to take it all away.

"I… I think I want to stay here," she confessed, biting her lip as she looked over at him. "Do you think I could do that? I could keep mending up all the clothes to pay my way, I wouldn't—"

A wide grin spread over his face. "Actually, I was just talking to Lawson, and he said that Sarah wants you to work with her. You'd need some training, but she can help with that, and then you can help other people who've been through hardships too. I know you would be amazing at it."

Her eyebrows shot up, and her eyes widened. "Really?" she gasped. "Not under-the-table work, you mean?"

"No, real work," he assured her. "If that's something you want to do, of course."

"I would love to," she exclaimed. "Oh my gosh, I would love to! I really want to help people, Cade. I know there are so many people out there who've been through worse than I have, and I want to help them. I know what it feels like to be afraid…and now I know how it feels to finally be free of it too." She clasped her hands to her chest in excitement.

"And it could help you work through your own stuff," he pointed out. "I'm sure there's still plenty you need to figure out."

"I'm sure there is," she admitted. "I just try not to think about it, if I can help it. But I don't want to run from it anymore. I want to face it, and I want to put it behind me for good. And I... I want to make a life for myself. I want to get my GED, I want a real job, and I want to stay here. With you, Cade."

She gazed at him, biting her lip and smiling. Her eyes shone with happy tears.

"I love you, Cade," she breathed to him.

He didn't even have to think before he said it back. "I love you too, River," he replied, and he leaned across to kiss her.

As he pulled her into his arms, he realized that his mind wasn't reeling like he expected it to be the first time he said those words to someone. Loving her was easy. He loved her, she loved him, and she wanted to stay here, with him. It couldn't have made more sense. Or be more perfect.

When he pulled back, she gazed into his eyes for a moment, staring at him like she was trying to figure out if all of this was real. He planted another kiss on her lips, and she smiled, snuggling into him.

"Let's make this place our home, Cade," she whispered to him. "Me and you. Just the two of us."

"Just the two of us," he replied with a chuckle. "Well, and everyone else at the lodge."

She laughed. "I meant in this cabin."

He grinned. "In that case, yeah, just the two of us," he agreed, and he lowered his mouth to hers to kiss her again. He couldn't get enough of her lips on his, the way it made him feel. The way she made him feel as though he was truly whole for the first time. He'd finally found his place and purpose after being sidelined with his injury. He finally felt like he belonged and he was truly happy.

But he would have gone through it all again, and more, if it meant ending up here with her. Where he belonged.

Once and for all.

Epilogue

It was a bright summer's afternoon, the leaves rustling quietly as she followed the familiar path down to the cabin she shared with Cade. Hard to believe it had already been eight months since she'd arrived here, but the turning of the seasons reminded her how much had changed since she had first come to this place in the fall.

And now she might be looking at a whole new start.

With the letter gripped tight in her hand, River hurried, hoping Cade would be there when she arrived. She didn't want to wait any longer than she already had to open this thing, but she had promised she wouldn't check her application until he was back.

She wasn't sure how much longer she could contain herself. She felt as though she was going to explode as she stepped into the cabin and looked around—no sign of Cade yet.

She sank down on the couch with an impatient sigh and pressed the letter into her legs, looking down at it again. The Chapel Hill logo was on the top right corner, and she was sure this was it, the letter that would either confirm or deny she'd made it in to the university of her dreams.

Heading to town earlier in the day to pick up some

supplies, she had stopped in at their post office box and found it waiting for her. She knew Cade was away doing some training with guys from the lodge, so she promised herself that she wouldn't open it until he was there with her to see what the letter said. She was regretting that promise right about now because all she wanted to do was rip the envelope open.

What if she had been rejected? She couldn't help but wonder how she would feel. She had put so much stock into this moment, into getting accepted by the school, that she could hardly believe it was finally here. Today she would find out one way or another what the next phase of her life was going to look like.

Terrifying? Completely. But she had long since learned that she could take a lot more of the scary stuff than she had ever imagined she could.

She had managed to get her GED, and had spent the better part of the spring writing endless essays and filling out applications to every university in the area. She wanted to become a Licensed Professional Counselor, and even though it was going to be a long journey, she had to start somewhere. Chapel Hill had been her first pick from day one, but she had never really let herself believe she would actually get accepted. Staring at this letter that would decide her fate, she found herself wondering how she would feel if, just maybe, she had actually done it.

Finally, she heard Cade arrive. Good. She needed him by her to get through this.

"What's going on?" he asked, as he went to make himself a coffee.

River held up the letter. "It's from Chapel Hill," she explained.

His eyes widened. "Did you get in?"

"I haven't opened it yet," she admitted. "I wanted to wait until you were here."

"Well, what are you waiting for?" he demanded, grinning widely. "Go for it!"

She had been so excited, almost bouncing off the walls, but now she hesitated. She didn't know if she could. Now that she'd had time to think about it, the fear was starting to creep in.

"You open it," she told Cade, handing the letter over to him. He took it from her, and she chewed her lip and watched his face as he slowly opened it.

A smile spread over his face. "You got in!" he exclaimed, and she let out a shriek.

"You're serious?" She snatched the letter from him, skimming through it. Sure enough, he was telling the truth—they had offered her a place to study psychology, starting in the fall. She clapped a hand over her mouth, hardly able to contain herself. It was such an amazing feeling. She wanted to run and tell everyone she'd done it.

"I knew you would," Cade told her, scooping her up into his arms and kissing her firmly on the lips.

She laughed and hugged him back. "I need to call Haven to tell her the good news."

"Absolutely," He replied. "You do that and I'll go rustle up some grub from the cafeteria so we can have a celebratory dinner tonight."

"Sounds like a plan," she said, planting a quick kiss on his mouth. "Thank you."

She talked to Haven for the next half hour via video chat, sharing her good news and just catching up. Even though River had yet to make it to New York because of school, getting her GED, working on college applications, and everything going on around the lodge, she and her sister spoke every day. Sometimes her mom joined in too.

Their first conversations were so emotional it had taken several calls to just get through the basics of what had happened over the years and not cry every other word. But how wonderful it had been to see her mother and sister and to meet her niece! Now they spoke regularly and made plans to visit each other soon. Just knowing that her family was safe and they had a wonderful life meant the world to River.

The next day Cade had planned a hike with their friends from the lodge. They packed a picnic and hit the trail that ran into the woods and up to a viewpoint over the town below. It was a beautiful day as they set out together.

Hannah walked with her and Cade nearly the whole way. "You've done so well, River. You should be so proud of yourself. I'm so glad you'll be staying here and doing classes remotely—double win!"

"Me too," River replied, grinning widely as Cade gave her hand a squeeze. They'd both agreed that doing her university coursework while living at Warrior Peak Sanctuary would be the best of all possible worlds.

"Sad that you won't get in your wild partying years?" Hannah asked playfully.

River laughed and shook her head. "Not when my other option is staying here with Cade. I'll take that over partying any day. He's all I want."

He looked over at her fondly and winked, and then glanced over his shoulder, seeing the guys fall behind.

"Hey, keep up, guys!" he called to them, and he

dropped back to match their pace, leaving Hannah and River alone.

"You want to wait for them?" River asked.

"No, let's keep walking," she replied, looking downward.

River lowered her voice. "Is everything okay?"

"I don't even know," she sighed. "I'm not even sure where to start. I feel like I'm going crazy. It's been months, and I don't know what I'm supposed to do with all of it."

"With all of what?"

"With the way I feel about Xavier," she admitted. "It's just...it all feels like such a mess, that's all. With Xavier kissing me and Lawson finding out, then the two of them arguing... Everything seems so strained now between us all." She trailed off, and then shook her head.

"I'm sorry, this day is supposed to be about celebrating you," she added. "Let's not talk about my stuff. It's all so jumbled right now."

"I don't mind talking about your stuff, but I understand," River replied. "Just know you can always come to me if you need someone to talk to."

"Hey, you're already acting like a therapist." Hannah joked. "You're going to be at the top of your class in no time, I can feel it!"

River giggled. She was still trying to wrap her head around the fact she had actually made it into the school of her dreams. It all felt so surreal, when she thought about where she had been this time last year. Out on the road, alone and scared, fighting to get to her family, constantly looking over her shoulder because she was terrified that Ryker would find her.

She never would have imagined she would feel this free

and be this happy. She felt ready to take on the world. She didn't have to stay on the run or worry for her life or the lives of anyone she cared about. Discovering who she really was underneath the programming of the Shepards and the fear and pain they had inflicted on her had been a joy.

Cade caught up with them again and slipped his hand into hers. He always held her hand when they were out and she loved it. It was like he wanted to make sure she was always next to him. She didn't want to be anywhere else. She smiled over at him, the warmth of the sunshine bathing her face for a moment as he gazed back at her.

Hannah fell back with the guys for a while, and River looked over her shoulder to see how it was going. Carter was chatting with Hannah, while Lawson and Xavier were off to the side and seemed uncomfortable. River hoped they'd be able to work it all out.

But before she could mention it to Cade, he pointed over to the side. "Look, we're at the viewpoint."

He was right. They had already reached the spot that looked down over the town below. The sun shone through the trees around them, a soft breeze stirring the leaves, and the sky so blue above them it seemed to go on forever.

"It's so beautiful up here," she breathed, leaning her head against his shoulder for a moment. They had come up here a lot since the weather had started to warm up. It had become one of her favorite spots, and it was a perfect place to celebrate getting accepted into college.

"It is," he murmured, turning toward her. The look on his face shifted to something more serious.

He took a deep breath. "River, there's something I wanted to ask you," he said, sliding his hand into his pocket.

"What? Is everything okay?"

"More than okay," he assured her, smiling. "I... These last few months, they've been some of the happiest of my life. Being with you, it's given me a purpose like nothing else. And I want to spend the rest of my life fulfilling that purpose—being here for you, supporting you and loving you while you achieve everything you were meant to achieve."

Her lips parted in surprise. She wasn't sure where this had come from, but when he pulled a small blue box from his pocket, it clicked. She felt a wave of dizziness rush over her and she pressed hand against her stomach to stop the butterflies. He dropped to one knee right there on the grass before her and opened up the box. The diamond sparkled in the sunshine.

He looked up at her, his eyes shining with love. "River, will you marry me?"

"Oh my gosh! Of course I will!" she shrieked, and she pulled him to his feet and leaped into his arms.

He laughed, pulling back just long enough to slip the ring over her finger, and then squeezed her against him once more.

"I love you, River," he told her. "And I'm going to spend the rest of my life making sure you know how much I mean that."

"I love you too," she breathed back, and she kissed him again.

As their friends congratulated them and she showed Hannah her ring, she felt content and so excited for a future she never could have dreamed for herself. A life she couldn't wait to experience with the man she adored right by her side.

* * * * *

COMING SOON!

We really hope you enjoyed reading this book. If you're looking for more romance be sure to head to the shops when new books are available on

Thursday 25th September

To see which titles are coming soon, please visit
millsandboon.co.uk/nextmonth

MILLS & BOON

MILLS & BOON TRUE LOVE IS HAVING A MAKEOVER!

Introducing

Love Always

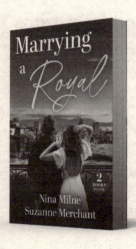

Swoon-worthy romances, where love takes center stage. Same heartwarming stories, stylish new look!

Look out for our brand new look
COMING SEPTEMBER 2025
MILLS & BOON

LET'S TALK
Romance

For exclusive extracts, competitions and special offers, find us online:

- **f** MillsandBoon
- **X** @MillsandBoon
- **O** @MillsandBoonUK
- **d** @MillsandBoonUK

Get in touch on 01413 063 232

For all the latest titles coming soon, visit
millsandboon.co.uk/nextmonth